Peter Watt has spent time as a soldier, articled clerk, prawn trawler deckhand, builder's labourer, pipe layer, real estate salesman, private investigator, police sergeant and adviser to the Royal Papua New Guinea Constabulary. He speaks, reads and writes Vietnamese and Pidgin. He now lives at Maclean, on the Clarence River in northern New South Wales. He is a volunteer firefighter with the Rural Fire service, and fishing and the vast open spaces of outback Queensland are his main interests in life.

Peter Watt can be contacted at www.peterwatt.com

Also by Peter Watt

Excerpts from emails sent to Peter Watt since his first novel was published:

'Your books are so interesting that once we start reading them we can't put them down until we finish. Without question, you are the Wilbur Smith of Australia, and we want you to keep those great books coming this way . . . on behalf of this organisation's members, thank you for all the reading enjoyment that you continue to bring to us!' – Randall A. Brown, Commander, American Legion Post 87

'When I finished *Touch the Clouds* I felt lost because I wanted more. Then I read *To Ride the Wind* and felt worse. Then I just finished *The Pacific* in two days because I couldn't put it down and I feel lost because I want the next book of yours already in the bookcase to read . . . I love every book you have written . . . Thank you for being born and sharing such brilliant writings with the world!'

'Thank you for writing great stories and providing me with ample entertainment while sat in my camper van in the middle of nowhere!'

'I'm a big fan and absolutely love your books . . . Keep up the great work and can't wait until the next book is released.'

'I am an avid reader of your books . . . I am not exaggerating when I say that I have you on a pedestal, even over Wilbur Smith who was my very favourite author. Your stories have opened up a world of Aussie history to me and the way you weave characters into the history makes it all so real. . . . Each time I find another of your books I really get carried away and can't put them down . . . You are a wonderful storyteller and I just wanted to say congratulations and thank you for entertaining me with your stories.'

'*Cry of the Curlew* got me hooked when I first discovered your wonderful books . . . You are my favourite writer and I have lent my copies to my friends as they too have become just as obsessed with reading them.'

'Congratulations on your books. You are a great writer who is thoroughly enjoyed by many, many readers.'

'When I read your books I don't feel like I am reading a work of fiction, it feels like reading a biography of real people's lives. The characters seem so real and like someone you have met in your own life. You work is so well researched that the storyline and characters seem to have existed and the events have happened. That's why your work is such a pure joy to read and why thousands of people worldwide read your work.'

'I just wanted to tell you that over the past ten years or so I have read all of your books . . . I have always found your books to be gripping from start to finish and I have learnt so much about our Australian history . . . I eagerly look forward to reading your next book. You are the consummate story teller!'

'You are such a brilliant writer. Don't ever stop, keep them coming. Thank you for so much reading pleasure.'

'Thank you so much for producing what has given me so many hours of enjoyable reading!'

'I finished *To Ride the Wind* late last week and just wanted to let you know I enjoyed it heaps . . . I loved the way you showed Sydney in 14-18, especially the subculture of pubs and razor wielding toughs. Most of all, I have to say, I loved the scenes of Sean, Patrick, Tom and Alex at war in France. The point you make about the men fighting only for each other and their little patch of dirt really hit home for me . . . Cheers and thanks again for the book.' – Greg Barron, author of *Rotten Gods*.

'Thank you for giving me so many hours of sheer pleasure for there is truly nothing better than sipping a delightful wine while reading a good book. Don't stop writing!'

'I am just writing to tell you how much I have enjoyed reading your books, especially the Macintosh and Duffy family sagas. I first read *Cry of the Curlew*, *Shadow of the Osprey* and *Flight of the Eagle* a few years ago on the recommendation of my sister. I loved the books. I loved the characters (except for the ones we are supposed to hate) and I loved the pictures you painted with your words not just of the Australian landscape but the characters in the books as well . . . may your life as an author be a long, happy and prosperous one. (That way we will get many more of your books to enjoy!)'

'I have been a life-long fan of Wilbur Smith and never thought another author could compare in his genre until a reviewer on his last book recommended you. Having now read *Cry of the Curlew* and *Shadow of the Osprey*, I just wanted to say that I consider you to be, at the very least, his equal . . . I hope you keep us gripped with your writing for many years to come.'

PETER WATT

BEYOND *the* HORIZON

MACMILLAN
Pan Macmillan Australia

First published 2012 in Macmillan by Pan Macmillan Australia Pty Limited
1 Market Street, Sydney

National Library of Australia
Cataloguing-in-Publication data:

Watt, Peter, 1949-

Beyond the horizon / Peter Watt.

9781742611365 (pbk.)

Series: Watt, Peter, 1949- Duffy/Macintosh series; 7.

A823.3

Typeset in 13/16 pt Bembo by Post Pre-press Group
Printed in Australia by McPherson's Printing Group

Dedicated to a great publisher and friend,
Cate Paterson,
Who has been there from the beginning.

It is well that the water which tumbles and fills,
Goes moaning and moaning along;
For an echo rolls out from the sides of the hills,
And he starts at a wonderful song —
At the sound of a wonderful song.

Henry Kendall, *The Last of His Tribe*

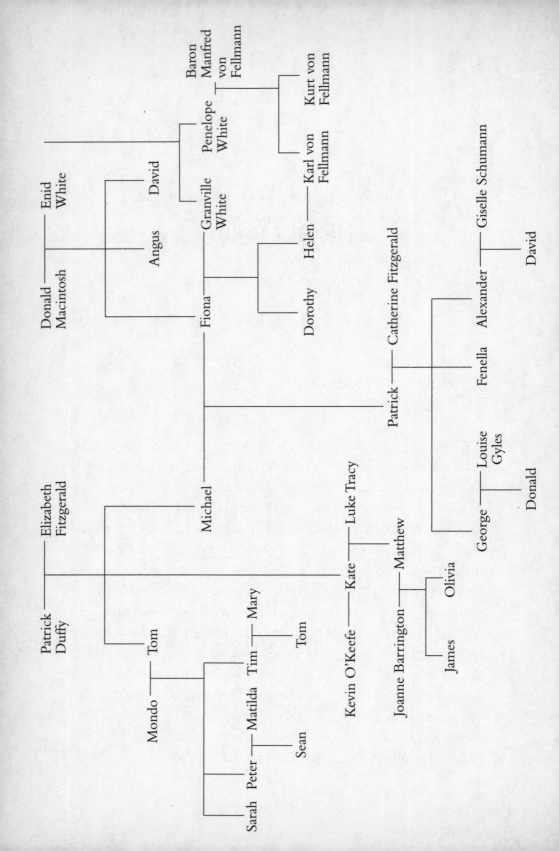

PROLOGUE

Central West Queensland
Early April 1918

The devils danced in the shimmering haze above the stunted brigalow scrub. Wallarie was transfixed with horror, watching the shifting shapes rippling like water.

The old Aboriginal warrior raised his long, hardwood spear, although he knew full well that a spear was no defence against these demon spirits and their macabre corroboree. Wallarie must not approach these devils, whose twisted mouths spoke to him of approaching death. This death was so terrible that it would strike even the young and fit of all peoples, black and white, drowning them from inside, choking off the very air they breathed and carrying them off to a painful but quick death. It would come to the land that Sir Donald Macintosh had given the name of Glen View all those years before, when Wallarie's clan had lived in harmony with the gentle spirits of the bush. Before his people had been slaughtered by the Native Mounted Police and Sir Donald's shepherds.

'Go now,' the ghostly voices told him. 'Go now and do not return until death has swept these lands.'

The demons melted into the haze of the afternoon and Wallarie lowered his spear. It was time to heed the warning and travel beyond the horizon, far from his traditional lands. One day he would return to sit under the bumbil tree in front of the Glen View station house, to smoke his battered clay pipe and wait patiently for Tom Duffy, the last of his blood, to return to him from the other side of the world. Young Tom was the grandson of the infamous bushranger of the same name who once roamed the wild places beyond the colonial frontier of Queensland. The bushranger, who had been felled by a Native Mounted Policeman's rifle, had married a Darambal woman, Mondo, and their children carried Darambal blood into the next generation.

Wallarie was not so sure that Tom Duffy would return, because the ancestor spirits sometimes liked to joke with those still living, and nothing was certain except that he would one day join the ancestor spirits in the night sky.

First, though, he would make a short journey to Glen View homestead to visit the woman and child there, exiled from their home far to the south. There he would gaze on the face of the boy who was inextricably linked to the future of his blood.

Afterwards, Wallarie would leave his place to wander the desolate lands, meeting others of different clans who had also been dispossessed by the white man's cattle and guns. They would sit around the fire and talk of the times past. Wallarie, a warrior of many skirmishes against the white man, would be feared and respected by those strangers for his prowess and magical powers. They would be polite, but he knew they would be pleased to see him pass from their camp. His path was a lonely one, but that was the way of the warrior.

Wallarie scratched his scarred chest and set out for Glen View homestead.

The Western Front
March 1918

With his back to the newly dug trench, Sergeant Tom Duffy slid the oiled metal bolt of his Lee Enfield back into place and locked it down. The young man was in his early twenties, but years of fighting in the trenches of France and Belgium had taken their toll. His dark hair was streaked with grey and his deep brown eyes aged by the horrors he had seen. His dark skin was covered in red rashes from lice bites and he stank, just like his comrades.

'Sarge,' said one of the new reinforcements to his platoon. The reinforcements had come just as the Germans had launched a massive attack across the Western Front, causing both the French and British armies to reel back in confusion. It seemed possible that the Germans might win the war after all, as the German army had changed its tactics, using small groups of highly trained shock troops to rush sections of the front line with submachine-guns, flame-throwers and a good supply of grenades. Tom knew that the aim of the shock troops was to break into the Allied rear echelon where they could disrupt logistics and artillery support. In his desperation General Haig had deployed Aussie and Kiwi troops south to take up defensive positions against the seemingly unstoppable onslaught. The Germans had advanced so deep into the Allied rear that they had been able to bring up artillery to shell Paris itself, and it was only a matter of time before the Imperial German Army would be in France's capital city, beating the newly arrived

American army still being deployed alongside their war-weary Allies.

'What is it . . . Private Dean?' Tom asked, eyeing the new man and pleased that he had been able to remember his name.

'Where are we?' the soldier asked.

Tom had already scanned the red-brown rolling fields from the gentle rise on which they had dug their trenches and he could see the tower of a church and several elegant chateaux. He had also seen a textile factory and cross-referenced these landmarks with the map in his possession.

'The town over there is Villers-Bretonneux,' he told Private Dean. 'But you don't have to worry about where we are – just make sure your rifle is in good working order and your bayonet hasn't rusted.'

Tom watched the young soldier amble back to his section and take a cigarette from Corporal Smithers. Tom knew that the corporal hated him because he had been promoted to platoon sergeant ahead of him. But Smithers had never demonstrated any leadership ability; his promotions thus far had come through attrition in the units he'd served with.

Tom turned away. There would always be bad apples in the army, and he would always cop criticism from some people for being a blackfella. That was the way of the world, war or no war.

'Bloody blackfella,' Corporal Smithers grumbled to no one in particular. 'Wouldn't know his way around a white man's world. Not bloody right that the CO should promote him over a whitefella.' Smithers was a burly, powerfully built man who stood over six feet tall. He had a flat face with small piggish eyes that never smiled. He was a well-known bully who had grown up in the slums of Sydney, where it was rumoured he had been a hard man in the criminal world. It was also rumoured that the only reason he had enlisted was to get away from the law closing in on him for the murder of a prostitute in Sydney's Rocks area. Those in his section feared him with good reason.

'Shut yer bloody trap,' Corporal Dan Frogan snapped. 'Tom Duffy has sent more Huns to hell than the whole bloody battalion put together.'

Corporal Dan Frogan glared at the new recruits strung along the trench. 'Sergeant Duffy was once recommended for a Victoria Cross but the system stuffed it up. If you want to get out of this war alive you'd be well advised to follow Sergeant Duffy without question. He might be a blackfella, but around here the colour of a man's skin don't mean a thing – all that matters is he knows what he is doing when the whiz–bangs are overhead and the enemy is staring down your throat.'

Corporal Dan Frogan fell into silence then and the men looked away uncomfortably. Dan glanced up the trench to where Tom sat alone. He could see his old friend gazing down at the battered photograph he always carried in his breast pocket. Dan loved Tom Duffy like a brother; they had relied on each other to stay alive through many bloody battles.

Dan knew that the photograph was of a young French girl Tom had met a year earlier. Dan had met her when he had been on leave with Tom and had been struck by the girl's beautiful face and soul. Her name was Juliet Joubert and she had short dark hair, big brown eyes and a cherubic face that reminded Dan of the pictures he had seen of pretty young girls on chocolate boxes. Tom had told Dan that when the war was over he would marry Juliet, who was a schoolteacher in her village far behind the front lines.

Tom looked up and noticed Dan staring at him. He gave Dan the briefest of smiles, then tucked the photograph back into his pocket. Dan nodded and returned his attention to his section. Sergeant Tom Duffy was one of the best soldiers in the Australian army and it was just lousy luck that he was considered a half-caste, otherwise he would have been made an officer by now. Dan knew how proud Tom was of his Darambal heritage. There was only one full-blooded member of this central-west clan – an old man by the name of Wallarie – and he and Tom shared a special empathy which Dan could never quite understand. Tom had been spawned by two cultures and was spurned by both, yet he had a deep spiritual connection with the Darambal that was difficult to explain to a whitefella.

Dan hoped to God that he and Tom survived this war and that his friend could marry the girl he loved; perhaps then he would find an acceptance he hadn't found anywhere else in his young life.

The sound drifted in the early morning mist. It was a sound Tom Duffy knew so well, yet it still made his stomach churn.

'What's that?' he heard Private Dean ask in a frightened voice.

'Where's Mr Sullivan?' Tom asked Dan Frogan, who had made his way up the trench to him.

'He should be back by now,' Dan answered, reaching for his bayonet in its scabbard. 'He was at an orders group with the CO.'

'Then it's you and me, Dan,' Tom said.

'What's that noise?' Private Dean asked again, and Tom felt annoyed. It was obvious what the sound was. It was death coming for them in the crackle of small-arms fire and the crump of hand grenades.

'Fix bayonets!' Tom bellowed and his order was followed by the scraping sound of long, sharp knives being dragged from scabbards, followed by the click of bayonets being fixed to the end of rifle barrels.

The spear point of the whole German army was coming, and all that stood between their victory was a handful of Australian and New Zealand soldiers. Should the Germans break through, the war would be over.

'Here they come!' someone yelled, and Tom stood to take his place on the parapet. Through the mist he could see the German shock troopers in their grey uniforms, dashing in small groups from cover to cover. Tom aimed at a soldier carrying a flamethrower on his back.

'Fire!' he roared as he pulled the trigger. He watched as the German with the flamethrower collapsed. He heard a Lewis gun to his right open up on the advancing enemy. All Tom could do now was pray that Wallarie's magic was still with him; pray, and kill as many Germans as possible. The next few minutes could decide the outcome of the war on the Western Front.

Part One

1918

Death and Destruction

I

The elegant sandstone building bedecked with climbing ivy was one of the finest houses overlooking the beautiful harbour of Sydney. Time and technology had changed it only slightly. Where horse stables once stood, there were now garages for cars; but the sweeping gravel driveway still saw the arrival and departure of the city's most notable residents, all come to visit George Macintosh, heir to the vast financial empire of his forefathers.

George Macintosh was well known as a philanthropist, and it was rumoured that he would eventually be knighted by the king for his services to Australia's war effort. Such was his public persona; those close to him saw beyond the veneer of respectability and knew him to be a man with ruthless ambition and little empathy for the suffering of others. Those who knew him even more intimately dared not openly speak of their suspicion that George had had a hand in the murder of his own sister in his efforts to gain sole ownership of the many and varied lucrative Macintosh companies.

It was midmorning and George sat in his library perusing the daily paper and reading the grim war news. Not so grim for him, of course. If Germany won the war he had much to celebrate, as his secret investment in their chemical industries would prove very profitable and he would be viewed by the Kaiser's Germany as a good friend. He could at least thank the war for taking the lives of his stupidly patriotic father, Patrick, and his brother, Alexander, thus eliminating them from any control of the Macintosh empire.

George flipped through the paper to an article about how the infamous fighter pilot, Manfred von Richthofen, aka the Red Baron, had been shot from the skies over Australian lines. A Canadian fighter pilot claimed the victory but so too did Australian machine-gunners firing from the ground. Who really cared? George sneered, flipping the paper closed and reaching for a cigar.

He snipped the end and lit the cigar in a cloud of blue smoke. There had been a time when George had looked down on smoking and drinking, but that had changed in the last couple of years. Perhaps he indulged in both vices because his wife, Louise, did not approve of such practices, and he took pleasure in spiting her. Their relationship might appear sound from the outside, but within the confines of their home it was a different matter. Louise had had an affair with Sean Duffy, the former war hero and Sydney solicitor, and while George would never forgive her this, he certainly wasn't going to allow her to undermine the respectability their marriage brought him. He had threatened to keep their toddler son, Donald, from her, and Louise had very sensibly decided to end the affair and remain by George's side.

There was a timid knock on the door of the library.

'Come in,' George called and the door opened to frame his young housemaid. 'Mr Dwyer is here, Mr Macintosh,' she announced and slipped quickly away.

'Come in, old chap,' George said, not bothering to rise from his comfortable leather chair to welcome his solicitor. After all, the man worked for him and was paid well. George had arranged the meeting at home so as to ensure absolute privacy.

Mr Dwyer entered the library, clutching a leather briefcase with apparent nervousness.

'Take a seat,' George said. 'Would you like a drink?'

'No thank you, Mr Macintosh,' Dwyer answered carefully.

George got up and poured himself a tot of Scotch, then sat down behind his desk. 'What news of my father's will?'

Dwyer flipped open his briefcase and spread legal papers out in front of George. 'The will has been authenticated,' Dwyer sighed. 'It seems he must have had a portent of his own death and rewritten his will before his untimely demise. It appears that the first will has been superseded by the one that Major Sean Duffy produced, naming him as sole executor.'

George swallowed the tot in one gulp, placed the empty tumbler on the desk and stared intently at his solicitor. 'So where do I stand?' he asked in a cold voice. The fact that the probate matters were in the hands of Louise's former lover made the alcohol sour in his guts.

'You are to share the control of the companies with your brother Alexander's son,' Dwyer answered after clearing his throat. 'It appears that Brigadier Duffy stipulated that your sister-in-law, David's mother, is to manage his interests until he turns twenty-one and assumes shared control himself. In the event that she is unable to manage her son's affairs, the brigadier has nominated his solicitor, Sean Duffy, to do so.'

George could not sit still: he rose from his chair and walked over to the large window overlooking the driveway and gardens. He stared out onto one of the flowerbeds, where an old man was hunched over pulling out weeds. His brother's son was like a weed in his perfect garden, George mused angrily. If only he could dispose of him as easily as the old man was disposing of the garden weeds. And what was to stop him? After all, he had reached halfway across the world to have his sister, Fenella, murdered.

'Where does that leave my son?' George asked without turning around.

'Er, um, Donald assumes his control of an equal third when he turns twenty-one,' Dwyer answered and shifted uncomfortably in his chair. 'On your demise, the family companies come under the dual control of your son and that of your late brother. However, you are a man of good health, Mr Macintosh, and I am sure you will be at the helm, guiding your son and nephew, for a long, long time to come.'

George turned, his hands clasped behind his back. 'Thank you for your briefing, Mr Dwyer,' he said in a flat voice.

'If that is all, Mr Macintosh, I will pay my respects and return to the office,' Dwyer said, placing the papers back in his briefcase and rising from his chair. 'Before I depart, I should alert you to a matter that will arise at the next directors' meeting.'

'What matter is that?' George asked sharply.

'It appears the auditors are puzzled by a large amount of money that was transferred to a Swedish bank account last year without authorisation from the board. They are nervous as the bank has a reputation for dealing with the Germans and fear that if such a transfer were to leak to the newspapers it would raise embarrassing questions. I'm sure there is a simple explanation but I thought I should warn you that the matter has been added to the agenda.'

For a brief moment George experienced a chill of fear. The money had been used to purchase shares in Germany's chemical industry, which in turn had produced some of the horrific gas weapons being used against the Allies. Many Australian soldiers had died or been crippled by those gases on the Western Front. It would look bad, George knew that, but he was a businessman and such morality had no place in the making of money. After all, were not some of America's biggest industries doing the same thing?

'Thank you for the warning, Mr Dwyer,' George said calmly. 'Your information confirms you in my eyes as the best legal representative in this town.'

Dwyer nodded once and then left.

George slumped into his leather chair and stared at the wall. In the hallway the old grandfather clock chimed eleven. That damned will and testament had turned up in the mail weeks earlier, after a tortuous voyage from the battlefields of France. It had arrived long after news of his father's death. His gaze fell on a barbed spear adorning the wall and for some reason he recalled that there was a story in the family of an ancient curse brought down on the Mac-intosh name after a horrific slaughter of Aboriginals living on land now known as Glen View Station. But that had been over fifty years ago and George knew it was nothing but a silly story handed down by his superstitious great-grandmother, Lady Enid Macintosh.

George poured himself another Scotch. After lunch he had a meeting in town with the police inspector, Jack Firth. Firth was well known and feared by the city's criminal underworld for his ruthless disregard for the rules of evidence; he preferred to manufacture his own evidence to ensure successful prosecution. But he was a popular figure in the press for his apparent clean-up of the streets of petty criminals. He was a colourful character, built like a brick wall, and even in his early forties he was a man who could handle his fists in any street brawl.

George was slightly concerned that his key ally in the military intelligence world had been abruptly returned to his previous duties in criminal policing. This was a move that had pleased Detective Inspector Firth as he had never considered gathering intelligence about the German and Austrian residents of New South Wales as anything but a pointless diversion. Jack Firth was happiest hunting real criminals in the seedy back streets of Sydney, but his unexpected transfer niggled at George as it seemed to smack of distrust. Had the intelligence agencies smelled a conspiracy between him and the police officer?

There was one advantage to having the policeman back on his old beat and that was George was once again able to collect useful information about his business competitors – which of them kept mistresses, which visited prostitutes on Saturday night and then attended church services on Sunday as respectable members of the community. George wanted to know all the seamy details – after all, you never knew when that kind of information would come in very handy indeed. Today George would ask Firth to investigate Major Sean Duffy; the man must have a few secrets in his past worth knowing about.

★

Sean Duffy had never liked being referred to as 'Major'. He was a solicitor, and the choice of profession had been opportune for a man who had lost both legs fighting on the Western Front. But the people he worked with were proud that they had a genuine war hero in their ranks and wouldn't let him be plain Mr Duffy. He tried to take it in the spirit which it was meant – and he was grateful they were prepared to overlook his occasional bout with the bottle. Several times he had faced up in court bleary-eyed and hungover, leaning on his walking stick even more than usual. He still managed to deliver sharp and incisive defence rebukes to the prosecution arguments.

Sean was still a young man with a lot of life ahead of him, but when sleep came to him at nights he would relive the hell of trench warfare, crying out, his body covered in sweat and jerking as if he had been electrocuted. It was perhaps fortunate that Sean slept alone in his flat in the city. The last person to share his bed had been the wife of another man – George Macintosh – but Louise had broken off their affair for the sake of her seeing her son and Sean had retreated to his work and the relative peace that came with too much alcohol.

It was early afternoon now and many workers were returning from lunch to open shops for the day's trading. It was a pleasant autumn day and smoke lay as a haze over the city from the tanneries and other factories along the harbour shore.

Sitting in a chair beside the window in Sean's office was Harry Griffiths. Harry had lost an eye in the trenches. He had been a Sydney policeman before the war and the stipend he received from Sean for gathering information kept his small family off the streets. Harry was a big, tough man in his mid-thirties and he was fiercely loyal to Sean, who had saved him from a life of petty crime and destitution.

'Well, Harry, what have we got on the Morgan case?' Sean asked and Harry took a small, crumpled notebook from his jacket pocket.

'The shopkeeper couldn't have seen Morgan in the street that night,' he said. 'The streetlights were out.'

Sean smiled. 'Good, there goes the positive identification of Morgan as the one who broke into his shop.'

'Morgan is a good bloke, boss,' Harry said. 'He was one of us at Fromelles.'

Sean had developed a reputation for defending former servicemen who had returned to a world indifferent to their suffering. Many carried the unseen wounds of war in their heads and turned to alcohol for relief. Some had slipped into petty crime to pay for the drink that kept them sane. These were shadow people, disregarded by those who had done well out of the war.

'Any decorations?' Sean asked.

'He got an MID for Fromelles,' Harry said, referring to his notes. 'He was a battalion runner.'

Sean knew from personal experience how dangerous it was to be a runner in the trenches; they were often exposed to rifle and shell fire getting vital messages between headquarters and the front lines. A Mentioned in Dispatches was not a high award but it would show the magistrate that Sean's client had proved himself serving his country.

'Good. We can use that,' Sean said.

'There is one other thing, boss,' Harry said with a frown. 'Word on the streets is that Firth has returned.'

'Is that going to be a worry for us?' Sean asked.

Harry's frown deepened. 'We both know that he works for George Macintosh. There's history between you and Macintosh and I reckon he's out to get you.'

Harry was too polite to mention Sean's brief affair with Macintosh's wife, although they both knew that was the 'history' he referred to.

'I think you need to be very careful,' Harry said, leaning forward slightly to push home his point. 'I can get you a pistol.'

'That won't be necessary, Harry,' Sean said with a smile. 'I have my cane.' It doubled as a weapon, with a deadly spring-loaded blade inside the stick.

Harry didn't look reassured. 'I still think you should carry a pistol. I can get one of those small .38s from an old mate who imports them from the Yanks.'

'I'm right, thanks, Harry,' Sean said. 'Besides, I have you around to watch my back.'

Harry's frown turned into a beaming smile at this acknowledgement. 'If there's nothing more, I'll see what else I can get in the Morgan case.'

'I'll inform Mr Morgan that he owes you a beer for all your effort in his defence.'

'I swore to the missus that alcohol would never pass my lips again,' Harry responded sheepishly. 'It has improved the situation with the family.'

Sean rose awkwardly, grasping the cane tightly, and held out his hand to Harry. 'Good to hear. I'll tell him he owes you a bonus, then.'

'Thanks, boss,' Harry said, matching the steely grip. 'I'll get back to you before the case is heard if I get anything else.'

'Good man,' Sean said, and watched as Harry Griffiths left his office. He had only been gone for a moment when young Michael Hopkins put his head around the door.

'Mail for you, Major Duffy,' he said, walking into the office and placing an envelope on Sean's desk. Sean could see that the young man was bursting to tell him something.

'You look like the cat that got the cream, young Hopkins,' Sean said.

'I've been accepted, Major Duffy,' the young man burst out excitedly. 'I start my training next week.'

'The solicitors' admission board?' Sean replied in a puzzled tone. 'I thought you had a year left to go on your articles.'

'No, Major Duffy, I've been accepted for the army. I'm going to get a chance to do my bit like you did.'

'How old are you?' Sean asked sternly.

'Eighteen, sir,' Hopkins replied, and he looked as though he was starting to regret sharing his wonderful news of enlistment.

'If I remember rightly, Master Hopkins,' Sean said, 'you are only seventeen.'

'Sir,' he pleaded. 'I need to do my bit for the country. I know I lied about my age but I think you would have done the same thing in my place.'

Sean stared at the young clerk; he was little more than a boy, really. He knew him as a bright, hard-working young man with an assured future in law. But what he saw standing before him was a bloody, bleeding soldier screaming for his mother as the red-hot shrapnel tore away his flesh. Sean swayed unsteadily in his chair, gripping the edge of his desk.

'Are you ill, sir?' Hopkins asked but Sean shook his head. He had the power to derail the enlistment, but he could see the age-old eagerness in him to prove himself on the battlefield. Sean knew that would disappear pretty quickly when the first shells and bullets tore into those around him, and possibly into the clerk himself. Young Hopkins would see the futility of it all then. He would realise there was no glory – just the ever-present fear of being maimed or dying.

'I should report you to the recruiters,' Sean said in a tired voice. 'But knowing your eagerness to get yourself shot, you would probably run off to enlist elsewhere.'

Sean glanced down at the letter on his desk. It was from Captain Matthew Duffy, his distant cousin, serving with the Australian Flying Corp in Palestine. Hadn't Matthew enlisted well underage for the Boer conflict, and been baptised in war at the bloody and vicious siege of Elands River almost twenty years earlier?

'Master Hopkins, when you get to the front, make sure that you listen to your platoon sergeant and do everything he says if you want to come home in one piece,' Sean said eventually. 'I will raise a toast to your safe return.'

The young man slumped with relief. 'Major Duffy, I don't know how to thank you.'

'Just keep your bloody head down and come home in one piece,' Sean said.

'Thank you, sir,' Hopkins said. 'I'll make you all proud of me.'

Sean was not a religious man but he prayed to any god who would listen to keep young Hopkins from being killed.

2

Sergeant Tom Duffy felt a hand on his back and turned to see that his platoon commander, Second Lieutenant Mike Sullivan, had returned. There was little opportunity for discussion with the crash of rifle and machine-gun fire interspersed by the blast of hand grenades, but Tom knew that Sullivan's return meant he could relinquish command to his senior office. Tom nodded and returned to scanning the grey shapes appearing and disappearing before their lines.

The situation was desperate. The deadly attack did not appear to be faltering, despite the determined resistance by the Australian diggers. Many of the German stormtroopers had already closed the distance, enabling them to rain hand grenades down on the defenders in the trenches.

From the corner of his eye Tom saw one of the German grenades cartwheel into the trench and land a short distance from where he stood on the firing parapet. Instinctively he flung himself to the bottom of the trench to avoid present-ing a large target for the shrapnel. The grenade exploded and Tom could hear muffled screams and groans from some of the men of his platoon who had taken the brunt of the explosion.

Corporal Smithers's section had taken the blast, Tom realised, assessing the damage to the defences. Among the wounded was Second Lieutenant Sullivan, whom Tom liked and respected, despite the fact that he had only taken command of the platoon two weeks earlier.

Tom scrambled to his feet and moved towards the wounded officer, who sat holding one hand to his face. Tom could see blood running between his fingers. Already Sul-livan was groping for his field dressing. Tom knelt to assist Sullivan with the bandage. Without a word, Mike Sullivan removed his hand to reveal that his jaw had been shattered and his forehead peppered with debris picked up by the blast. Tom tried not to look into the man's pain-racked eyes as he expertly wrapped the jaw; as he did so he could hear the officer attempting to tell him that he was now in command.

'Got it, boss,' Tom replied, guessing what the officer was attempting to say.

When he had finished, he moved on to examine two other soldiers who had taken shrapnel. Their wounds were not severe and one of the wounded was Corporal Smith-ers, who had a small wound to his chest. It was only a flesh wound as the heavy material of his uniform had absorbed the impact of the metal fragment.

'You're all right,' Tom said. 'Get back on the firing ledges and take command of your section.'

Smithers was lying at the bottom of the trench and he glared up at Tom. 'I'm wounded,' he said. 'I need to be evacuated.'

Tom could hardly believe what the man was saying. They were fighting a desperate battle for survival and Smithers was whining about a very minor wound. 'Get up, you gutless bastard, and take control of your men,' Tom snarled. 'Worry about your scratch when this is over.' He grabbed Smithers's collar and forced him into a sitting position.

The hate in the NCO's eyes was evident as he struggled to his feet, shaking off Tom's grip. Both men suddenly became aware that the crescendo of small arms and exploding grenades had faded.

'They're running,' a voice whooped from nearby, and Tom stepped up to the parapet to see that the killing field before them was deserted, only the dead and wounded left behind. 'Hop the bags and advance!' Tom roared.

There was an awkward hesitation until Tom, followed closely by Corporal Frogan, scrambled over the lip of the trench to expose themselves to any counter-fire. The men followed their platoon sergeant with fixed bayonets in a skirmish line, towards the woods where the German storm-troopers had disappeared.

Tom was acutely aware that he had placed the platoon in a dangerous situation, but he had gambled that the Germans were demoralised and on the run. No gunfire challenged their cautious advance and after a short journey across the field they entered the gloom of a thick wood. Here they found wounded German soldiers who quickly surrendered. They had been left by their comrades in their haste to re-establish a defensive line further back.

Tom ensured that the prisoners were stripped of their weapons and given first aid where possible. Those who could walk were ordered to carry their own wounded on improvised stretchers. In all they had captured fourteen enemy soldiers who could prove to be valuable to Allied interrogators behind the lines.

As they were returning to their lines Tom noticed that Smithers was not among those who had followed him over the top. It seemed he had already been evacuated. Tom felt a surge of anger. Bloody coward!

He glanced around at the men who had returned to the trench and noticed that, as usual, the violent action had taken a toll on their bodies and souls. Some attempted to light cigarettes with trembling hands, while others just leaned against the wall of the trenches staring at nothing. Private Dean was vomiting and when Tom approached he looked up and mumbled that his breakfast must have been off.

Tom placed a hand on his back. 'It gets easier,' he said, but his words rang hollow. He dared not light his pipe as he knew that his hands would shake just as badly as those of the men he now commanded.

In the distance the war continued with the crash of artillery shells and the chatter of machine-guns. Tom's war had been restricted to a tiny section of the front line; both sides fought as though every inch counted; was that what this war was all about – a few inches gained here, a few lost there? He noticed that some of the prisoners were showing signs of intoxication and smelled strongly of wine. When searched they'd had mostly captured food stock in their possession. It seemed that the enemy were starving and the greatest prize they could capture was food, not territory.

'The OC wants to see you,' Dan Frogan called out to Tom. 'Just got the message from the company runner.'

'Thanks, Dan,' Tom replied, shouldering his rifle. 'You look after the boys while I'm gone.'

Dan nodded and Tom set off to find the communications trench that would lead back to company headquarters.

He found the company commander, Major Cooper, in a hollow stretch of ground behind their lines. He was deep in conversation with one of his platoon commanders, but as Tom approached he dismissed the young lieutenant.

'Sergeant Duffy,' Major Cooper greeted in a warm tone. 'I want to congratulate you on your leadership. I had a report from one of the other platoon commanders about how you took over after Mr Sullivan was wounded and used your initiative to mount a counterattack to clear the field. Well done.'

'Thank you, sir,' Tom said, pleased that he had received recognition from the company commander.

'I will be mentioning your action in dispatches when I file my report.'

'Thank you sir, that is very kind.'

'Kind nothing,' the major dismissed. 'You should have been commissioned a long time ago. Captain Jack Kelly put your name forward for officer training in England, but . . .' The company commander's voice tapered away.

Tom finished his sentence. 'But I'm a blackfella and it would not be right.'

'Bloody army system decides at levels well above mere company commanders and battalion CO's,' Cooper said with an edge of bitterness. 'At least you know the feelings of the battalion's officers. When a spot comes up for company sergeant major your name will be at the top of the list.'

Tom nodded and turned to leave.

'Sergeant,' said Major Cooper, 'Before you return to the platoon I would like to ask you about Corporal Smithers.'

Tom was immediately on the defensive. The rule was that you did not speak ill of any other NCO in front of commissioned officers, despite how much you might loathe them.

'Was Smithers in control of his section during the action?'

'As far as I could see,' Tom lied.

'And you consider that his wound was serious enough for him to be evacuated?'

'Maybe in his mind,' Tom replied lamely.

'That's what I thought,' Cooper said. 'That's all, Sergeant Duffy, and once again, good show.'

Tom turned without saluting as such a practice in the field could bring an officer to the attention of any lurking sniper. Once outside he almost tripped over Corporal Smithers lying on a stretcher awaiting transport back to a hospital. No doubt he would have seen Tom talking to Major Cooper and guessed what they were talking about.

'What did you say to the boss?' Smithers asked angrily.

'Nothing that concerns you,' Tom replied.

'You told him I shirked my duties, didn't you, you black bastard.'

Tom felt his blood start to boil. He wanted to smash the brass butt of his rifle into the man's face.

'*Sergeant* black bastard to you, Corporal Smithers,' Tom snarled. 'Remember your rank.'

'I'll settle with you one day.'

The corporal's words followed Tom back to the trenches, and for some reason he knew that the threat was not an idle one.

Captain Matthew Duffy of the Australian Flying Corps knew that his chances of surviving were next to nil. He was putting his Nieuport single-seat biplane through all its paces to shake off the six German fighter planes manoeuvring to shoot him down. The air fight was taking place

27

over the fields north of the ancient Palestinian town of Jaffa. Matthew quickly recognised the enemy aircraft as being the German Albatros biplanes not unlike to his own Nieuport in design. The Albatros, however, had two 7.92mm machine-guns fixed forward, to his single .303 Vickers mounted on the nose of his little fighter plane.

It had all started so casually with a call at breakfast in the camp mess that a German reconnaissance aircraft had been spotted over his squadron's airfield. Matthew had scrambled to intercept the enemy plane but it had turned and fled north, with Matthew hot in pursuit and anticipating his first kill in aerial combat for the war. For a long time he had been flying photographic missions in inferior aircraft, but at last he was in the cockpit of a much revered fighter plane. He had not been able to tell whether the enemy aircraft was being flown by a Turkish or German pilot, but it did not really matter; all that mattered was that he bring down the Albatros.

Matthew had kept up his pursuit and had hardly registered that he was flying deep in enemy territory until he had spotted the enemy airfield. His dreams of glory had soon turned to horror as he'd watched the six Albatros rising up from the airfield to meet him.

All his instincts told him to retreat, but a voice in his head told him to stand and fight. Maybe going on the offensive would catch the enemy aircraft by surprise and give him a tactical advantage. He pulled on the stick to rise higher into the cloudless blue sky and rolled over to put the sun behind him as he wheeled around to attack the first enemy aircraft. His tactic worked. He could see his adversary turning his head frantically to locate the Nieuport that had suddenly disappeared from his view. Too late, the enemy pilot realised that the Nieuport was behind him. Matthew armed his

Vickers and fired a burst into the tail of the aircraft only fifty yards ahead of him. He could see from his tracer that his short burst had been successful; the pilot slumped forward and his aircraft rolled over and began to nosedive for the ground below.

Matthew had barely seconds to realise that his first kill might be his last as he had exposed his own six o'clock to the next plane that had risen from the airfield. Tracer rounds flicked through his right wing, punching holes in the treated canvas. The plane shuddered. Instinctively, Matthew rolled away from the line of fire to see a third enemy aircraft flash past his wing, barely avoiding a collision. Matthew knew that his own aircraft did not perform well in a fast dive, so he rolled over and, on levelling out, used every ounce of the tough little aircraft's strength to rise even higher in the sky. Looking over his shoulder he could see that the five remaining aircraft were below him but jockeying to get on his tail. He knew it was madness but he pushed the nose of his aircraft over to dive at one of the enemy planes separated from his wing of attackers. Gun blazing, Matthew could see his tracer raking the aircraft below from tail to nose and he swept past it just as its fuel tank exploded, engulfing the pilot.

Turning his head to locate the remaining four enemy planes, Matthew could see the fireball of a pilot clambering out of his cockpit to throw himself over the side, plummeting to his death. Matthew felt a twinge of sympathy for the man. He himself always ensured that he had a pistol close at hand to shoot himself should his plane catch fire with no hope of landing safely. Better to die quickly from a bullet than burn in agony as your plane went down.

Two aircraft confirmed, Matthew thought as he levelled off to climb once more. But the enemy planes had anticipated his move and dropped down below his own air-craft to angle up, firing from below, where he could not bring his fixed gun to bear. All Matthew could do now was outfly his opponents. Handling these fragile war birds was a skill he had honed over many years and now he needed all of that skill. He quickly checked his fuel and pressure gauges and then he heard a disconcerting sound coming from his engine. It would alternatively cut out and then roar into life.

'God, not now!' Matthew groaned. A bullet must have done some damage to his engine. According to his compass he was heading in the direction of his own airfield, and when he swivelled his head to see what was happening behind him, he noticed that of the four remaining aircraft only one had peeled off to pursue him, while the others were returning to their airfield. Both aircraft were fairly evenly matched in speed and all Matthew had to do was keep at least the half-mile gap between them to stay alive.

Suddenly the engine choked then spluttered into silence. The whistle of the wind through his wire struts and the distant drone of the enemy aircraft was all Matthew could hear. As he went into a shallow glide he desperately fought to make the engine come alive. He succeeded for a second or two, then it died once again. Matthew knew he had no other choice, besides crashing, other than to glide to the enemy airfield and land there. By doing so he would avoid death but would be taken as a prisoner of war of the Otto-man Empire.

Cursing, Matthew used the intermittent starting and stopping of his engine to limp towards the enemy airfield. His pursuer sensed that his plane was in trouble and when Matthew flew abreast of the Albatros he could clearly see the leather-helmeted and goggled enemy pilot. German,

Matthew thought, signalling with his free hand that he intended to land and surrender. The enemy pilot waggled his wings to indicate that he understood and took up a position behind Matthew as he nosed down for a landing.

A curious crowd of pilots and ground crew were rushing from tents and pits as Matthew, his engine spluttering and coughing, brought the Nieuport to flop down with small bounces along the airstrip. He passed Turkish soldiers sporting big moustaches and almost friendly smiles – it was not every day they captured a intact enemy aircraft that could be repaired and put back in service for their own air force. Behind him the pursuing aircraft landed and taxied. Matthew could see the enemy running towards him and it was only a matter of seconds before he would be forced from his cockpit to surrender.

For a moment he reflected on what he would take into captivity with him. He looked down at the photo tacked up next to his knee. A pixie-faced young woman smiled back at him. It was the photo of the woman he had fallen in love with while serving further south in the Sinai. The beautiful and mysterious Joanne Barrington had used her role as a neutral American archaeologist to gather intelligence for the British government against the German–Turkish forces in Palestine. Joanne and Matthew had briefly been lovers, but Joanne had disappeared from Matthew's life after being captured by the Turks and ransomed to her extremely wealthy family in the United States. Matthew had also learned that she had returned home pregnant with his child. He had written to her but his letters had been returned unopened.

Angrily, he flicked over the ignition switch and was stunned to hear his engine roar into life without any sound of the spluttering interference. The first enemy soldier had reached his aircraft and was yelling to him in Turkish.

31

Matthew could see that he was a huge man and was already gripping the edge of the bottom wing. Without hesitation Matthew gunned the engine; his aircraft picked up speed, leaving the startled enemy behind. They had seen how his plane was in trouble when it landed and now, as if by a miracle, it was hurtling down the strip with its tail already in the air. The Turkish soldiers often referred to the Nieuport fighter plane as the instrument of Allah, and the stunned Turkish soldier Matthew had left in his wake must have thought that was true after the engine's miraculous burst of life. The German pilot who had followed Matthew down the runway had turned off his engine and was now desperately attempting to get it started again for the pursuit.

Matthew's aircraft rose gracefully into the air and he pulled his stick to gain altitude, avoiding a burst of anti-aircraft fire. He held his breath, hardly daring to believe that he had escaped. God knew how, but the engine was performing magnificently and he was soon up to his maximum speed of one hundred miles per hour.

He flew low for the first few miles in the hope that he would not be seen from above by any enemy planes. At one stage he was so close to the ground that when he crested a hill he found himself in the midst of a Turkish cavalry encampment. Startled men and horses scattered everywhere. Matthew's heart almost stopped beating when he saw that he was level with the men on horseback flashing past him. The plane shuddered as its tail skid collected a clothes line hung out at the end of the campsite. Trailing washing he clawed for altitude and the clothing eventually spun away to the arid lands below.

Suddenly bullets tore into his fuselage. He craned his neck around to see who was firing at him. It was the Turkish fighter plane flown by the German pilot. The German had closed the gap when Matthew's plane had collected the washing. Matthew groaned – there was not much he could do now; he'd run out of manoeuvres. As a last resort, he wondered whether he could find a cleared, level area to land his plane. He had done that once before during this campaign and survived. He turned his head and that's when he saw them.

'Bloody beauty!' he shouted. Three AFC Nieuports had appeared at his twelve o'clock high and were racing after the Turkish aircraft, which had now wisely broken off the attack on Matthew to defend itself against the new threat. When Matthew stared out across the nose of his plane he could see his airfield through the blur of the propeller. He had survived, and with his first two kills for the war. Three more would make him an ace.

When Matthew brought his Nieuport to a halt at the end of the strip he could see his ground crew running towards him. That was all Matthew remembered until he awoke hours later in the hospital tent. He had collapsed under the mental strain of flying, fighting and trying to stay alive.

'Are you feeling better, old chap?' asked the squadron medical officer.

Matthew eased himself onto his elbows and felt the dull throb of a headache. He was thirsty.

'Got any water?' he croaked.

The medical officer, who had once had a country practice in a South Australian village, passed Matthew a tumbler of heavily treated brackish water to drink. Gratefully, Matthew gulped it down. 'Intercepted Turk radio signals confirmed that you shot down two of their Taubes,' the doctor said. All enemy aircraft were referred to as Taubes by the Australian flyers, regardless of their actual manufacture. 'Well done.'

'I just got lucky,' Matthew said. 'Not my day to go west.'

'Well, the CO wants you to debrief him and it will be your shout in the mess tonight,' the doctor said with a smile. 'I'm discharging you.'

'Thanks, doc,' Matthew said, easing himself from the bed. His limbs felt heavy but his head was clearing. 'I'll get over to HQ now and give my report.'

As he made his way slowly to the HQ Matthew halted for a moment to gaze across at the horizon now sheltering under the blaze of a setting sun. There was a strange peace in this troubled land which he was coming to love. He knew that if he survived the war, this country would always call him back.

3

The sun was setting over the scrub-covered plains of Glen View; already the first chill of the coming winter was in the air.

Giselle Macintosh loved this time of year; at last the sweltering heat of summer had passed, and sleeping at nights was comfortable again. She sat in her chair on the verandah of the sprawling station house, shelling peas for tonight's roast. The peas had been grown in her own vegetable patch, watered by the towering windmill that pumped up from the creek. Her toddler son, David, was covered in dirt. He was outside, playing with the local Aboriginal boys, sons of the property's stockmen and their families. David would need a bath before he went to bed, Giselle thought idly, dropping the shelled peas into a colander.

Since she and David had been exiled to the remote family property by her hated brother-in-law, George Macintosh,

Giselle had actually found a peace beyond any Sydney could offer with all its hustle and bustle. She still missed her beloved Alexander, killed in action on the Western Front barely a year ago, but somehow the grief was more bearable out here. She'd lost her much admired father-in-law, Patrick Duffy, too, but she was grateful that her mother had been able to move out here with her. Karolina Schumann was living on the mission station adjoining Glen View. Giselle was puzzled by the fact that her mother had chosen to live in sin with the Lutheran pastor, Karl von Fellmann, although her mother never spoke about the relationship and Giselle did not ask. It was a strange affair, especially because she and her mother were Jewish.

In the distance Giselle could hear the Aboriginal stockmen calling to each other as they brought in their horses to be unsaddled. It was a soft and pleasant banter in a language she was attempting to learn. The stockmen and their families lived a mile from the homestead in their own camp, and Giselle sometimes attended to their medical needs there. They were paid in the basics of flour, sugar, beef and tobacco, and Giselle thought they seemed satisfied with that. Still, she knew the intrusion of the whitefellas, first with their sheep and then with their cattle, had disrupted their nomadic way of life forever, and very few in the district remained outside the station's influence. The only exception was old Wallarie. His home on the sacred hill was shunned by even the European stockmen, most of whom respected the beliefs of their indigenous colleagues. The years had brought Wallarie a reputation as a mystical man not to be crossed lest he become vengeful.

Giselle smiled when she heard her son chattering in the simple words of a child in the local Aboriginal language. He was a very bright boy and already had a rudimentary grasp of German, which was the language his doting grandmother talked to him in at night. He spoke some English too, but with a Scottish brogue picked up from the station manager, Hector MacManus, and Giselle's family servant, the tough Scottish former soldier, Angus MacDonald. Both Scots vied for the little boy's attention and played a role as de facto fathers in his life. Although very young, David could already sit astride a horse and occasionally use some of the bad words of the stockmen, picked up when he was allowed to join them around the yards. Needless to say, his grandmother and mother chastised him severely for the use of such profane and blasphemous language.

'Come inside, Davy,' Giselle called.

The little boy reluctantly broke away from the game of throwing miniature spears at an empty bully beef tin. He was covered in dust and Giselle wondered if Karolina would bathe him tonight. Giselle had to oversee the portion of prime beef roasting in the oven with vegetables, to be served to the hungry men invited to the dining table tonight. There would be the two Scots and a couple of the station hands, and business would be discussed as the gravy jug was passed down the table; later the whisky bottle would come out, along with mugs of hot, sweet tea.

Later that night, after dinner had finished and the men had gone back to their quarters, Giselle took out the two letters the postman had brought today in his horse and sulky. The man drove the long stretches between the isolated cattle stations of central Queensland, delivering the precious cargo of letters and parcels.

These letters were about Giselle's only contact with news beyond station life. Newspapers that arrived were often a couple of weeks old, and Giselle had little interest in reading the latest war news – the pain of losing Alex was still too great. There were nights that she would hug herself in the privacy of her room and sob for the loss of her beloved husband. Oh, how she missed the feel of his strong arms around her and the smell of his skin lingering between them after they had made love. That she was not the only young wife missing her husband was a fact of war, though, and she guessed that there were nights when the tears of women – wives, mothers, sisters and lovers – could have filled an ocean.

Giselle savoured the moment when she could sit alone on the verandah after all the day's work had been done and read the letters under the yellow light of a kerosene lantern. She looked forward to the tidbits of gossip from Louise Macintosh, her sister-in-law in Sydney. It was rare to receive a letter from her solicitor, Major Sean Duffy, but the embossment on the envelope that had come today indicated that the second letter was from his office.

Giselle sat down and opened it. When she'd read it she stared out across the moonlit yard to the shadowy trees beyond. She could hear the curlew's mournful song far away in the direction of the creek, where, it was said, a clan of Aboriginal people had been massacred many years earlier.

'He's asleep,' Karolina Schumann said, joining her daughter on the verandah. 'He didn't put up much of a resistance this evening – he was absolutely exhausted . . . Is that a letter from Louise?'

'No, it is a letter from Mr Duffy. It appears that Patrick left a will superseding the one that exiled us to Glen View. It seems that David is a major shareholder of the family company, although of course he is unable to assume direct control until he is twenty-one.'

'My God,' Karolina said. 'You're not as poor as a church mouse after all.'

'I'm afraid the change of circumstances will not return Alexander's house to us, or even return us to Sydney,' Giselle said. 'Until my son turns twenty-one we will remain at George's mercy.'

'You do not wish to return to Sydney?' her mother asked.

'This is my home now,' Giselle replied softly. 'This place makes me feel closer to Alex, it's where he grew up. David will grow strong here. And he'll be safe from George. I'm afraid that my brother-in-law will try to harm David in some way. He is a very dangerous man.'

The two women sat in silence for a while. Eventually Giselle sighed and looked over at her mother. 'What do you plan to do when the war is over?'

'If the Australian government grants me permission to leave, I wish to return to New Guinea and take back our plantation,' Karolina said. 'It is all I have – other than you and David.'

'But what of the pastor?' Giselle asked in surprise.

'Karl is a very good man,' Karolina replied, 'and a part of me will always be grateful for the love and understanding he has shown, but we are too different.'

'Are you intending to leave him?' Giselle wondered why she should feel so concerned when she had always frowned on their relationship, living as man and wife when they were not so.

Karolina looked at her daughter with a sad expression. 'There have been letters from his ministry admonishing him for living in sin – and with a Jewess too. God knows how they found out about our circumstances from the other side of the world, but they have, and even though Karl says that he's not concerned about the accusations, I know they could ruin his career in the church. No, it is best if we separate.'

'I'm so sorry it has come to this,' Giselle said with genuine concern. 'But I also understand.'

Karolina reached over and touched her daughter on the cheek. 'You and David are all I have left in this world. For years I carried hate in my heart, blaming your husband for the death of your father. But when I look at David I can't help but see Alexander. A child so beautiful and so much a part of his father makes up for the years of pain.' Karolina shook her head. 'But enough of this gloomy talk. I see that you have a letter from Louise and I expect her news will make us smile. She is a good friend to you.'

Giselle opened her sister-in-law's letter and began reading aloud about parties, balls and afternoon teas. Outside, the curlews continued their cry under the crystal-clear night sky.

The room stank of decomposition, and rising damp had added to the stench. Inspector Jack Firth stood at the feet of the woman's bloated body. She was lying on her back in the middle of the tiny living room. On the walls were faded prints of the Sacred Heart and a couple of popular landscapes. Clothing hung on string from one wall to another and it was already smelling musty. Jack had seen many such scenes in his long career; they were not uncommon in the slums of inner Sydney. Those who could afford the real estate were already moving to the leafy suburbs ringing the city; only the poor and desperate remained in the overcrowded, unsanitary shacks bordered by narrow, rubbish-strewn laneways.

The victim was in her late forties and had probably been stabbed to death, Jack mused as he stood staring at the murder scene.

'You know who she is?' he asked, turning to a young constable in his dark blue uniform and white pith helmet. The constable was staring at the decomposing body with an expression of morbid interest. The dead woman's floral dress was up around her hips and she was naked from the waist down.

'Er, not sure, sir,' he replied.

'You bloody well should know everyone on your beat if you want to be a good copper,' Jack growled.

'Think I know her,' the police photographer said, squinting through the camera's aperture to frame his subject. 'She was one of the girls who worked for a bloke called Lenny Johnson. She mostly worked around Railway Square. I was on a job over there about a month back and noticed her with Lenny. I don't know her name, though.'

'Thanks, Sid. When you've finished, let the fingerprint crew in. Constable, arrange to have the body moved to the morgue.'

'Yes, sir,' the constable replied. 'What do you think happened, sir?'

'Pretty bloody obvious,' Firth answered. 'She was raped and stabbed to death. A client probably left his wallet at home and she said that she didn't put jobs on a chit.'

Jack Firth stepped out of the room onto the narrow landing, but the smell of rotting flesh followed him. From experience he guessed that she had been dead for at least a week and in this part of town no one talked. This was Frog Hollow, an area of Surry Hills into which even police were reluctant to venture. Jack reckoned that his only chance of nailing someone for this murder was to lean on his informants. He patted his suit pockets to locate his packet of cigarettes. He removed one and struck a match. It helped with the smell a little.

There were heavy footsteps on the wooden stairway leading to the landing.

A constable appeared and said, 'Got a message from Phillip Street that you are wanted by the inspector general, sir.'

Jack frowned. It was very rare for the head of the New South Wales police force to request to see one of his subordinates unless something was awry.

He stubbed out his cigarette and made his way to the street. He hopped onto a tram and got off at the corner of Phillip and Hunter. The Star Hotel had once stood on the site but it had been razed and in its place was the multistoreyed police headquarters.

Jack went directly to the office of Inspector General James Mitchell. He knocked and was bid enter. Jack stepped inside the office and looked across to a desk where a man with spectacles and intelligent eyes stared up at him.

'I got a message that you wanted to see me, sir,' Jack said.

'Have a seat, Inspector Firth,' Mitchell said politely. 'There is a serious matter I wish to discuss with you before anything gets committed to paper.'

Jack eased himself onto a leather chair. He felt distinctly uncomfortable – he had a lot in his past that might come back to bite him. But he also reassured himself that he was the best in the business of snatching criminals and his reputation outstripped his rank. 'Well, sir, I have nothing to hide.'

'That's good,' Mitchell said. 'It has come to my attention that while you were seconded to the intelligence departments some impropriety may have occurred on your shifts. What do you have to say to that?'

Jack squirmed but attempted to keep his composure. His focus was drawn to a thick folder on Mitchell's desk; it was marked with his name. He recognised it immediately and felt a cold chill of apprehension.

'Sir, with respect, you have to be more specific.'

Mitchell glanced down at the thick folder. 'I have before me information in regards to certain irregularities concerning an alien prisoner, Karolina Schumann. Possibly you could explain.'

'I am not aware of any irregularities, sir,' Jack protested.

'The matter of having her released last year from Holsworthy internment camp – without authorisation from either our department or that of the military,' Mitchell said. 'That constitutes a serious breach of police regulations.'

'I am not sure what you mean, sir,' Jack lied. 'I may have been negligent in some of my reporting but I have not contravened any regulations. Any investigation into what I did when I was detached will clear me.'

'You sound very sure of yourself, Inspector Firth,' Mitchell said. 'I hope not only for your sake but also for the department's that you are right. You are one of my most senior police and a damned good detective. It will look bad for us all if it turns out there was some wrongdoing in relation to this case.' Mitchell closed the file and pushed it to one side of his desk. 'That will be all, Inspector Firth.'

Jack made a hasty retreat from the office. It wasn't until he had left the building that he could breathe properly again. That file could be the end of his police career if anyone with half a brain read between the lines. But how had the inspector general got hold of it? Jack had made sure it had been buried in the bureaucracy of police paperwork. He was shaking and he reached for a cigarette to steady his nerves.

'Duffy and Griffiths,' he snarled under his breath. Those two had to be behind the file finding its way upstairs to

Mitchell's office. The bastards. It was time to discuss this matter with the man whose payroll financed his weakness for the horses – George Macintosh. Duffy and Griffiths were still a threat to both of them and it was time to eradicate the threat.

Firth knew that this would not be easy. Duffy and Griffiths were tough men who had long ago lost any fear of physical threat, having returned from the hell of the trenches. But they were in his territory now and he knew that he had the edge.

Harry Griffiths sat on a stool in the bar of one of Sydney's less salubrious hotels. He was chatting with another former serviceman, Lenny Johnson, who had decided to use his skills to rob innocent victims out on the mean streets at night, and to pimp out a couple of girls on those same streets. Lenny had been discharged from the army as suffering severe shellshock, although Harry knew different. Lenny had studied the symptoms of shellshock and feigned them in front of doctors in a hospital in England. Harry didn't judge him for that. There had been times when he might have done the same thing to get out of hell. Harry often came to Lenny for information; there wasn't much that happened in the inner city that Lenny didn't know about.

The two men were chatting when Harry suddenly felt the hairs on the back of his neck stand up; this eerie sense of danger had saved his life several times during active service.

'Well, well, well,' a familiar voice behind him said, and Harry turned to face Inspector Jack Firth. Firth was in the company of four uniformed officers who were watching the patrons of the pub warily. 'So you consort with Lenny here, do you?' Firth said with a sneer.

'It's a free country,' Harry said. 'I drink with whoever I want.'

Lenny had not turned to face the police inspector, but slouched over the glass of beer on the counter before him.

'Your lucky day, Griffiths,' Firth said. 'I have come to ask Lenny here to accompany me down to Phillip Street. I might just be coming back for you too, and then your chum Duffy won't be able to protect you.'

'What you want me for?' Lenny asked in a sullen tone.

Firth reached out and grabbed Lenny by the hair, dragging him from his stool. The man hit the hard floor with a sickening thud.

'Resisting arrest for a start,' Jack said, pulling Lenny to his feet. 'Then a few questions about the stinking corpse of one of your ladies.'

The constables looked uncomfortable but obviously knew better than to protest Firth's rough method of arrest. Lenny was frogmarched out onto the street with Jack Firth following.

When the police left, the talk in the public bar started up again, although it was subdued now, as though no one wanted to draw attention to themselves.

The barman idled over to Harry. 'I'd keep my head down, Harry, if I were you,' he said quietly. 'I heard tell that bastard is gunning for you. I'd take his threat seriously and make yourself scarce.'

'Yeah, I might do that,' Harry said, swallowing the last of his lemon squash. 'But Firth will have to be up early if he thinks he is going to take me down. I might just get him first.'

Harry left the pub and made his way home. He was worried now. He had seen the look in Firth's eyes. The same cold look men had after the terrible stress of hand–to–hand combat. It was the look of death.

4

Captain Matthew Duffy sat at the tiny table in his tent, finishing a letter to his mother, Kate Tracy. He did so with some guilt as he was not a very good letter writer, and he preferred that she did not know what life was really like for him flying the dangerous skies of Palestine. He could not tell her how sometimes the strain got so bad that he would be physically sick before he flew missions deep into enemy territory, or that he sometimes had trouble controlling his shaking hands. Publicly, he and the other pilots in the fighter squadron played the game of not feeling any fear, but in private their bodies shook and their nightmares made them shout out their fears into the desert nights.

Matthew finished the letter and placed it in an envelope. Censorship was not applied to officers but he had nothing to censor anyway. It was an only partially true monologue of good times and bad food. He gazed out the flap of his

46

tent at the flat, treeless horizon. The afternoon's briefing to the aircrews of his squadron had not raised morale. They had strafed the railway station of Amman and destroyed a bridge in the north, but the Turkish engineers had repaired the line so their supply trains were running once again. It also seemed the enemy airfield over at Jenin had been expanded to seventeen hangars, and fourteen aircraft had been counted on the airstrip.

Everyone at the briefing was aware what it all meant; that they would have to return to the dangerous, low-level bombing missions where there was a good chance of being shot down by an enemy plane or ground fire.

Matthew stood up from the table, ready to head to the officers' mess, when he realised someone was standing at the tent's entrance. The strongly built, bearded man was wearing the traditional garb of an Arab irregular.

'Saul, you old bastard,' Matthew cried, stepped over to embrace the man he could have called brother. 'What's it been . . . a year?'

Saul Rosenblum was not actually an Arab irregular serving in the cause of Colonel Lawrence, he was just dressed that way to pass in these lands. He was a former Australian cattleman with Jewish ancestry who had enlisted to fight in South Africa eighteen years earlier; he had deserted the army in the name of love, and eventually found himself on a *moshava* in Palestine where he had rapidly risen to be one of the leaders. His military expertise had saved his community on more than one occasion, and his two sons were also learning to protect their small community against their hostile Arab neighbours. Both Matthew and Saul had served together at the battle for Elands River in South Africa and had become firm friends. They had met up again when Matthew had been posted to flying missions in this part of the world and it was through Saul that Matthew had met Joanne Barrington. Saul was older than Matthew by around ten years and time had added a few pounds to his girth.

'Ah, Matthew, how are you, old son?' Saul said, staring into Matthew's face and smiling broadly. 'I hear that you've now shot down four enemy aircraft. One more will make you an ace.'

'How in hell did you know that?' Matthew asked.

Saul tapped the side of his nose. 'That you should ask me such a question,' he said with an all-knowing arch of his eyebrows.

'Come, have a seat,' Matthew said, dragging across a camp stool and unfolding it. 'Tell me, how is your family?'

'They're all well. And we are all still grateful to you for saving our village.'

'I didn't do much,' Matthew said, waving away his involvement in the British-sanctioned operation to destroy a radical Arab leader and his followers. 'You and Joanne took all the risks.'

'Ah, it is interesting that you should mention Miss Barrington's name. I am not sure if you are aware, but she has returned to this part of the world.'

Saul's news gave Matthew a jolt like an electric shock. For a moment he was at a loss for words.

'I see from your reaction that you were not aware of this,' Saul continued gently. 'She is in Cairo working with the British. I saw her when I was there on a matter for the British army.'

'How is she?' Matthew said finally. 'Is she well?'

'She is, although I think she feels torn between her work and her role as a mother,' Saul answered. 'She has twins, a boy and a girl.'

'Tell me, old friend, do you know their names?' Matthew asked eagerly. 'Did she bring them with her?'

'Your son is named James and your daughter is Olivia,' Saul replied with a gentle smile. 'As far as I know they are doing well in the care of their grandfather in New Hampshire. He is a man of great wealth and influence.'

'I know,' Matthew answered glumly; he suspected that Joanne's father had forbidden her to communicate with him. Matthew was not the sort of man he would approve of – a Catholic of Irish descent, and from Australia to boot. That didn't quite fit with the upper-class Protestant world of the Barringtons.

'I spoke with Joanne when I attended a meeting with a British Foreign Office agent in Cairo,' Saul continued. 'I think she was as surprised to see me as I was to see her. She asked after you, whether you were still alive. I told her that as far as I knew then, you were still alive and flying our skies.'

'When the war's over,' Matthew said quietly, 'I'm going to see my children.'

'You have to survive first,' Saul sighed. 'You can't afford to let your heart rule your head until this is all over, my friend.'

Matthew knew Saul was right. He couldn't afford to be distracted while he was flying; a momentary slip of focus could get him killed. But that wouldn't stop him thinking of ways to find Joanne when he wasn't flying. He was due for leave soon and he'd take it in Egypt. With any luck, Joanne would still be there.

'So what are you doing here, Saul?' Matthew asked, changing the subject.

'I'm going north with a small detachment of my men to carry out an independent recon of the Ottoman positions,'

Saul replied. 'The desert wind told me you were here and I thought I would pay you a visit on the way.'

'I'm glad you did, old friend. Now, how about a drink?' Matthew was about to break into his precious stock of whisky when one of his ground crew put his head around the tent entrance.

'Er, ah, sir,' the lance corporal said, eyeing Saul nervously. 'The boss is calling all pilots for a briefing on a mission you have to fly before sunset.'

Matthew thanked the man and rose from his chair. 'Looks like we'll have to have that drink another time,' he said, gripping Saul's hand in his own. 'It's been so good to see you again, old cobber. Take care.'

'You, too,' Saul said. 'My Arab friends have a saying I like – *Inshallah*, if it is God's will. I pray that it's His will to keep you safe.'

Matthew nodded, then strode over to the operations briefing tent. He could see the other pilots making their way towards the briefing and he wondered if they were feeling the same dread as he was. It seemed even worse to know that if he died James and Olivia would never know their father. He had so much to live for and yet he knew the odds were not good that he would get out of this war alive.

As his fighter plane rose into the shimmering afternoon sky Matthew looked over to his right. A younger, new pilot was flying on his right flank; off to his left was an experienced pilot who had been transferred from another squadron. He was glad to have two other aircraft under his command on this mission. They were all flying Nieuports and had been briefed to reconnoitre an area where Turkish troops were mustering. The area they were flying over was an endless sea of craggy hills and deep sandy ravines devoid of any sign of human habitation. It was not a good region to be shot down over and Matthew had to work to keep down the bile that wanted to rise into his throat.

With any luck they would not encounter enemy aircraft and the patrol would prove to be uneventful. The experienced pilot had been tasked with taking photographs of anything of interest while Matthew and the new pilot were flying protection.

Matthew tried not to think about Joanne, but his thoughts kept returning to her. What was she doing in Cairo? In whose care had she left James and Olivia? What did they look like? The rapid tap tap of something hitting his right wing snapped Matthew from his thoughts when he realised that his aircraft was being hit by bullets fired from behind. He jerked his head as far around as he could, only to be blinded by the fiery ball of the sun. He caught a fleeting glimpse of an Albatros fighter on his tail. Yanking on his controls Matthew flung his little fighter plane into a dive to get out of the gun sights of his enemy. As he did so he was horrified to see that the new pilot had taken a full blast of machine-gun bullets through the fuselage of his plane, which was already trailing smoke and going into a spin. Jesus, the pilot wasn't much more than a kid.

Matthew cursed himself for allowing the flight he was leading to fall into an ambush. There was no time for regrets, though; the pursuing enemy fighter was even now coming back at him. Matthew levelled off and started climbing to five thousand feet. When he glanced around he could see that there only seemed to be two enemy aircraft attacking them and the experienced pilot had already engaged one of them in a snarling dogfight. Below, a black pillar of smoke rose from the side of one of

51

the desert hills where the new pilot had crashed in a ball of fire.

The pilot's fate distracted Matthew for only a moment, but already the enemy pilot had manoeuvred into a position on his six o'clock rear and its twin machine-guns were blazing, tearing away at the wings of the fragile Nieuport. Matthew immediately noticed that his controls were sluggish and he knew it was over. The other man was bloody good, he thought bitterly, desperately seeking out a ravine flat and wide enough to bring down his near crippled aircraft.

With great effort he was able to turn and bring his plane down low between two set of hills in a promising wide, flat ravine. The Albatros overshot him when he pulled away and then went into a tight turn to swoop down and finish him off. This was not the first time Matthew had been shot down and he prayed that the luck of the Irish was still with him. The sandy bottom of the ravine was coming up fast and he pulled back on the stick to lift the nose. Already the engine had cut out, and his aircraft touched the ravine, bumped and flipped over as the wheels bit into the soft earth.

He felt the sharp jerk on his harness and his head snapped back as the aircraft tipped forward. The last time he had been shot down his adversary had spared him, but this pilot had no such sympathy for his defeated enemy. Instead, a long string of bullets ripped through the crippled aircraft. Matthew knew he had to get out quickly. He unbuckled his harness and snatched up the water bottle and packet of sandwiches his ground crew had given him before he took off.

There was an ominous silence broken only by the drone of aircraft overhead and the crackle of flames. *Fire!* Matthew thought. His plane was on fire, he had to get out right now. He hauled himself out of the cockpit and over the side, and fell about ten feet to the sand below just as more bullets stitched his downed Nieuport. His adversary was ensuring that the aircraft was well and truly destroyed so he could count it as a certain kill. As Matthew lay winded on the ground he realised that he had been wounded; his arm as was bleeding profusely. He could barely catch his breath but he knew he had to move, to get away from his aircraft. He began crawling as fast as he could, and just then the crackling turned into a whoosh of flames.

He crawled on, ignoring the pain in his arm and the constriction in his chest. When he was far enough away to be safe, he rolled over onto his back to see that there were only two aircraft left in the blue sky. Their rolling dogfight took them westwards and soon the sound of the aircraft faded and was also gone, leaving Matthew alone in the wilderness.

He knew that he was a long way from help and probably in territory patrolled by the Turks; all he had with him was his revolver with six rounds, a crumpled packet of cheese and cucumber sandwiches and a battered metal water bottle. His bleeding was controllable and Matthew realised that the round must have ripped down his arm, opening the flesh. An inch or two to one side would have shattered his arm, so he gave thanks for small mercies, despite the fact his back ached and his neck felt stiff.

As his downed aircraft continued to burn and send a black pillar of oily smoke into the cloudless sky Matthew took stock of his situation. He did not know whether his surviving pilot had made it back to the squadron's airstrip to raise the alarm. His colleague's plane had disappeared behind hills and what happened after that was in the hands of the desert gods.

He realised that his photograph of Joanne would have been destroyed in the fire, and for some reason he regretted the loss of her image more than his being shot down.

The sun was already setting low over the hills and the long shadows of night crept across the ravine. Matthew was grateful for his heavy fleece-lined leather jacket as the night would be bitterly cold.

'Well, old boy,' Matthew said aloud. 'Time to walk home.'

In his pocket he kept a prismatic compass and now he used it to locate the cardinal points of north and south. He knew that he must walk west to find the more fertile lands nearer the Jordan River, where Arab shepherds grazed their goats and ploughed the fields. He made a quick mental calculation from his last known coordinates and reckoned that he was about forty miles east of the ancient river. Between himself and possible salvation lay a long stretch of rugged hills and ravines. There was always the possibility of Turkish patrols and treacherous bandits who were known to kill and rob Allied servicemen.

Matthew began to trek west, climbing the crumbling face of a steep hill only to reach the top and find another, more narrow ravine ahead of him. The sun was now on the horizon and Matthew decided to make camp where he had a good view of the region around him. He had no material for a fire, so, using his bowie knife, he dug out a shallow ditch, big enough to allow him a relatively comfortable bed for the night.

As darkness enveloped the arid land, Matthew could hear the yip of a jackal in the distance. The cold was bitter and he barely slept. At some time in the night he rose to urinate and saw a distinct glow just beyond the next line of ridges. Maybe a camp of Bedouins, he thought; he would head in that direction when the sun rose.

In the morning Matthew's back and neck were still stiff and sore but the bleeding on his arm had congealed. He removed the wax paper from the two sandwiches and took his time eating one of the soggy cheese and cucumber sandwiches before carefully rewrapping the second. He drank two small mouthfuls of water, then removed his flying jacket, placed it over his head as shelter from the sun and began walking.

By midmorning Matthew had reached the top of the next ridge and he paused to get his breath, swig a mouthful of water and gaze down into the flat, wide ravine below.

'Bloody hell!' he exclaimed. There was an Albatros fighter plane down there. Matthew suspected it was the one that had shot down his own aircraft which, in turn, must have been shot down by the other pilot on Matthew's mission. It must have been the burning plane he'd seen last night, not a Bedouin camp. Matthew scanned the area around the burnt-out German aircraft but could see no signs of the pilot. Satisfied, he made his way down the steep ravine to the wrecked aircraft and walked cautiously towards it.

'Do not move, Englisher, or I will shoot you,' said a voice from Matthew's left. He froze, then slowly turned to see a German pilot propped up against a rock, obviously badly wounded. Matthew stared at the man; both his hands were empty. Matthew had to admire his bravado. He could see that both the man's legs were badly smashed and his face was covered in blood. Matthew crouched down beside him and realised that he was barely in his twenties.

'You speak English?' he asked and the German grimaced. '*Ja*. A little,' he gasped.

'I speak a little German,' Matthew replied in that language, surprising the wounded German flyer. German had always been spoken in Matthew's family, they had family in Germany. 'Can I offer you some water?' The German pilot nodded once, his face twisted in pain.

Matthew took out his water canteen and poured a capful into the German's mouth.

'Thank you, my friend,' the pilot said. 'I am Oberleutnant Christian Lang. '

'Captain Matthew Duffy, Australian Flying Corps,' Matthew said. 'Who shot you down?'

'Your comrade. There was only two of us left in the air when I was hit,' Lang answered. 'Who shot you down?'

'You did.'

Lang stared into Matthew's face with a look of sympathy. 'It is the way of war that enemies must kill each other. I know that my injuries will kill me and I hope that you will deliver the coup de grâce to release me from this terrible pain.'

'I suppose, considering I have the only weapon between us, you are officially my prisoner and therefore, under the terms of the Geneva Convention, I cannot execute you unless you attempt to escape.'

Lang tried to laugh at the ridiculous notion of him attempting to escape but he coughed and bent over in pain. It was then that Matthew noticed something else. He gently opened Lang's leather jacket to see his entrails protruding from a tear to his lower abdomen.

'God almighty,' Matthew groaned, carefully securing the front of the jacket to retain the bulging mound.

'I know, my friend,' Lang said through gritted teeth. 'It would be merciful for you shoot me now.'

'We might get found by one of our flights,' Matthew said. 'Either yours or mine.'

'Do you believe that?' Lang said. 'I think that we have

both been posted as missing in action. The front moves on, and if you remain here with me, nothing but our bones will be found.'

Matthew sat back. Lang was right. He did not have enough water to keep them both alive, and remaining with the badly wounded man could cost him his own life. 'How about I stick around until tomorrow morning?' Matthew compromised. 'See if any of our brothers in arms come looking for us.'

'You are a fool, Captain Duffy,' Lang said. 'But I thank you. I do not wish to die alone in this godforsaken place.'

Matthew knew that Lang's life was measured in hours rather than days. His skin was pale and damp with sweat, and his eyes had a feverish look. Even if they were rescued very soon, there was no chance of Lang recovering from such massive injuries.

The sun was fierce now and Matthew went about constructing a makeshift overhang with his jacket to protect the wounded man against the sun. Neither man spoke as the day passed; doing so was too painful for the wounded German. Eventually the sun set and Matthew took a swig of his water before pouring the remainder into the wounded man's mouth.

Lang took Matthew's hand. 'You have used your precious water on a man you should have killed,' he gasped. 'You are a good man.'

'We'll get more,' Matthew said, although he didn't believe it. 'Just close your eyes and get some sleep.'

Lang closed his eyes and when the sun was gone from the sky he slipped into a delirium, groaning and calling out for his mother. Matthew had wrapped the heavy leather jacket around Lang's body but he still shivered uncontrollably. Above, the night sky was a blaze of stars. Lang continued to cry out, but eventually his cries faded then stopped altogether, and Matthew was left alone beside the body of the man who had shot him down.

When the sun rose the next day Matthew laid out the body of the German flyer, crossing his arms across his chest. There was no sense in burying him as that would use up all Matthew's strength; he had to continue trekking west today. He went through the flyer's clothing and found a photograph of a pretty young blonde-haired woman nursing a serious-faced little boy on her lap. Matthew was lucky to find a map and fob watch in Lang's jacket and also papers identifying him. Should he survive, Matthew was determined to have the few personal possessions forwarded through the Red Cross to the mother Lang had cried out for in his final hours. He could at least give her consolation that he had not died alone.

The Australian flyer ate the last sandwich, now little more than smelly mush, and left the body of the German pilot not far from his downed aircraft. Then he gathered up his few possessions and walked on.

By late morning the sun was a searing ball of flame and even the hardy desert reptiles sought shade from it. Matthew trudged on, glad to have a bullet in his revolver to finish himself off if things became hopeless. Dying of thirst was a terrible, agonising death and by evening of that day he was seriously considering using the revolver to end his suffering.

5

Joanne Barrington's father's vast banking fortune could buy just about anything, and it had secured her one of the best suites in the luxurious Cairo Shepheard's Hotel, where she had access to the magnificent Ezbekiyya Gardens and the Royal Opera House, both within a short walk. Cairo had been called Paris on the Nile and its landscape was dominated by elegant minaret spires, noisy street stalls, and tiny shops selling replicas of ancient Egyptian artefacts. Camels, donkeys and automobiles jostled side by side along the streets and narrow lanes.

Joanne was dressed in a long white cotton dress nipped at the waist. She wore a broad but elegant hat to ward off the sun, and as she entered the spacious marbled foyer of the hotel she undid the ribbons and took it off. It had been a long day of poring over maps of the crumbling Ottoman Empire in the company of other archaeologists, British military officers and tropical-suited men from the British Foreign Office.

The request for her services as a consultant on the drawing-up of postwar borders had come directly from the American president's office. Woodrow Wilson was concerned that the French and British intended to colonise the lands taken from the Ottomans in order to dominate the rich oilfields producing much of the world's crude. Not that the USA had much to fear for lack of oil, as discoveries in places like Texas had ensured that the rapidly expanding industrial base of the country had an adequate supply of the black gold. But it was rumoured that the ancient lands of Mesopotamia had even more reserves, to fuel a world requiring the precious energy source for the new oil-driven era. American intelligence concerning the British and French intentions appeared to indicate that those two countries wanted to corner the market, and the USA was not going to be left out of any such scheme.

Joanne's reputation as an archaeologist specialising in Mesopotamian history and culture had earned her a place on the team exploring where borders would be drawn so that the British and French could share the wealth of the conquered. Her inclusion on the team had caused some raised eyebrows among the British. A selected handful knew her dark reputation as a double agent for both Mr Churchill and Mr Wilson.

'I have booked us for a six o'clock dinner at my hotel,' said a man at Joanne's elbow. He had been waiting for her in the lobby, reading a copy of the *London Times*. Joanne had spotted him as soon as she'd walked in.

Jonathan Myles was a handsome man in his thirties, with a touch of grey at his temples. His American accent bore traces of his time studying at Oxford.

'Do you think the Brits have you under surveillance?' Jonathan asked.

'I don't think so,' Joanne replied with a smile. 'My relationship with Winnie ensures that the British military intelligence respect my privacy. The English like to think they're gentlemen, and it wouldn't be cricket to spy on an ally.'

Jonathan had been briefed by his department in Washington on Miss Joanne Barrington. She was an exceptional woman. He had been impressed that she had killed a German officer and two Turkish soldiers while working under the cover of her archaeological profession in the Sinai desert. He also knew that her father controlled a banking empire and was personal friends with Woodrow Wilson. When Joanne had become pregnant while working as an intelligence gatherer in Palestine, giving birth to twins and refusing to name the father, the scandal had been cleverly hidden by her father with a cover story of her British fiancé having been shot down over France. This was partly true, as she had once been engaged to a British aristocrat, killed in action while flying in French skies.

Jonathan Myles had to admit that it would not be hard to fall for this remarkable woman. And they would make a fine couple. He was of the right pedigree, Protestant, from a good family with a background in manufacturing. His family was doing very well out of military contracts, and it was expected that after his stint in the government's foreign affairs department he would return to take over the reins of the family's many companies. A union with the Barringtons, with their banking empire, could be highly profitable for both families.

'I have reserved us a table overlooking the Nile,' Jonathan said quietly, aware that the foyer was filled with high-ranking British officers and British government officials. 'The food is excellent and the breeze from the river makes the heat almost tolerable.'

Joanne nodded, deciding that it would be a good opportunity to debrief him on the British plans for a postwar Mesopotamia. However, she was astute enough to know that the American diplomat was attracted to her.

'Did your enquiries regarding the Australian flyer's whereabouts bear any fruit?' she asked and she could see the shadow of annoyance cross Jonathan's patrician face.

'Yes, Captain Duffy,' he frowned. 'Apparently his plane was shot down a few days ago. He is presumed killed in action. It seems that another flyer with him did not see him escape from his burning aircraft after it crashed.'

Joanne tried to conceal her shock. Surely it couldn't be true? Matthew, missing presumed dead? She could hardly take it in.

She'd known it was foolish to make enquiries about Matthew, especially as she had promised her father that she would not try to contact the Australian airman again. She and her father had had a blazing row and he'd threatened to cut her off without a penny. She'd thought perhaps she could earn enough money to support herself, but she knew she wouldn't be able to support two children as well. She wanted James and Olivia to grow up with all the advantages wealth brought, and so she'd given in to her controlling father. She was glad in a way; Matthew had not replied to any of her letters and she'd started to feel a niggling, painful suspicion that his silence was an indication of his indifference.

James Barrington had arranged for a staff of nurses and servants to take care of the twins in Joanne's absence. She had been surprised to see how much her stern, unaffectionate father had taken to his grandchildren, despite their parentage. He'd been a doting grandfather from the moment he'd held the twins in his arms. She'd convinced herself she had made the right choice; but now, hearing about Matthew's death, she realised she'd been a coward. She should have stood up to her father and demanded that Matthew have contact with his children. Now it was too late.

'Has his death been confirmed?' Joanne asked, trying to sound calm.

'He went down in some godforsaken stretch of land. If he survived the crash, there's no chance he'd make it back safely. I'm sorry, but that's war.'

War, Joanne thought bitterly, staring at Jonathan. *What would you know of war?* Jonathan had spent his war in the world's best hotels; he had no idea what it was like to fight, to risk your life for your country every single hour.

'Will you excuse me,' she said. 'I wish to retire to my rooms and rest. It has been a rather warm day and I have a headache.'

In her room Joanne flung herself on the bed and stared up at the ceiling fan. Outside she could hear the Moslem call to prayer, and the clip-clop of hooves on the cobblestones below. She couldn't hold back the tears any longer and she began to sob. Why had she given in to her father when Matthew was the only man she had truly loved; he had never left her heart or her thoughts.

The pregnancy had come as a shock to her as they had only shared one beautiful and passionate night together. At first she had kept the news to herself – lest she miscarry under the prison conditions – but her father's international influence, contacts and money had secured her freedom. When Joanne had arrived home her condition could not be hidden. Her father had concocted some story about her dead aristocratic fiancé and she had gone along with it. In war, such lapses of morality could be glossed over as unfortunate mistakes deserving of forgiveness. James Barrington knew of a score of eligible men who would gladly take her hand in wedlock and not question his cover story.

Joanne had thought she could forget Matthew, but when the twins were born she had realised that she would never be able to dismiss their father from her heart. She and Matthew had shared dangerous times and he had proved to be strong, funny and brave. She'd felt immensely sad that he would not reply to her letters, but she supposed that he may have forgotten her, maybe even have met someone else.

Then Woodrow Wilson had personally requested Joanne as the American agent for this mission. He knew of her work in Mesopotamia and thought her gender made her less obvious as a spy; she was also a darling of the British politician of some influence, Winston Churchill. Joanne had agonised over whether to accept the position; she felt heartbroken over leaving her little son and daughter, but she also knew that this was daily occurrence among the men being posted to the front. Her gender was no bar to her duty to her country. In the back of her mind she had also hoped that by getting to Egypt she would be that bit closer to Matthew, although she tried to tell herself that she would obey her father's orders and not make contact with him.

How could he be dead? She wondered whether he'd known about his son and daughter. She'd bumped into Matthew's close friend, Saul Rosenblum, one day and told him about the twins in the hope that he would see Matthew again and relay the news.

Joanne sat up, wiped the tears from her eyes with the back of her hand and swore at herself. It was not possible for the enemy to kill the man she loved. Captain Matthew

Duffy, AFC. Until his body was produced she would not accept that he had been killed in action. Somehow she had to use every resource at her disposal to find him and express how much she had missed his slow smile and warm laughter.

It was the fourth day since Matthew's Nieuport had been shot down and he struggled to climb the next ridge. He'd seen desert birds swarm near sunset yesterday and had followed them to the remains of a slimy smear of water trickling from a natural spring. Now he was paying for quenching his thirst with bouts of vomiting and loose bowels. The cramping pain forced him to stop constantly and the dehydrating effects of the illness were starting to make him very weak. Matthew inched his way up the slope and eventually reached the top, only to look out on a scene identical to the one behind him: ravines and arid hills as far as the eye could see.

He lay down on the ground and gazed up into the sky, even now taking on the hues of evening. Then he saw it, and the sight of the great desert eagle circling overhead gave him a glimmer of hope. Surely it must be Wallarie, he thought. Wallarie had come to guide him to safety.

With great effort, Matthew pulled on his leather flying jacket to ward off the chill of the coming night and checked his revolver to ensure it had not clogged with sand. He held the pistol in his hands and considered ending his life again. Thirst was making him delirious and his sun-cracked lips and blistered skin told him how dry his body had become.

Goats! Matthew could smell goats on the gentle zephyr drifting from the west. He crawled to the edge of the ridge to gaze down into the ravine below, and saw a tiny flock of goats grazing on a patch of sparse grasses whitened by the dry air. A young boy was tending the flock, sitting on a rocky ledge. Maybe his camp was nearby, or maybe he even came from a village. Either way, they would have food and water.

Not wanting to frighten the shepherd boy, who he guessed was around ten years of age, Matthew stood and called softly, 'Hey!'

The boy's head jerked around and he stared up in terror. Without hesitation he took flight, scattering the goats who bleated in protest at the disturbance.

'Damn!' Matthew cursed. Maybe the boy thought he was one of the evil desert Jinns prevalent in Arabic folklore. At least the boy would tell those in his camp or village what he'd seen, and someone would have to return to gather the flock.

Matthew slumped to the earth and curled up. He hardly had the strength to pull the trigger of his pistol and he prayed that if he was found by the Bedouin that they would be on the side of the Allies against their Ottoman masters.

Matthew was woken by a sharp pain in his ribs. He blinked up at the fearsome sight of a great bearded man standing over him, prodding him with an ancient musket. The man was dressed in the flowing robes of a desert nomad, and Matthew could see that the man was not dressed as a leader, more as a wandering tribesman. The man held out a water-skin and Matthew took a few small sips, then nodded his thanks.

The man was not armed with a British–issue Lee Enfield, which made Matthew think that he was not associated with the Arab rebellion. He shouted something at Matthew and struck him sharply in the ribs again with the point of the barrel.

Matthew rose slowly – he was so weak he wasn't sure he could support his own weight. He raised his hands in a gesture of surrender. Behind the man, Matthew could see around seven others dressed in a similar manner, and also the boy he had hailed yesterday evening.

'Australian pilot,' Matthew said, using one hand to point at himself, but his gesture did not seem to raise any interest from the fierce-eyed men watching him. 'Need food, water.'

The Arab with the musket pointed down the slope and prodded him in the back. Matthew guessed that he was being directed to some camp or village and was not reluctant to follow orders. Maybe he might find someone who could speak English and explain his position. He could promise financial reward for his care and release to his own forces.

It took only about an hour to march to an area in the ravine dotted with a few scraggly palm trees and a scattering of Bedouin tents, camels and horses. Matthew's entry into the camp was met with curious glances from behind heavy veils, and looks of interest from raggedly dressed children. He was taken to a stone well and more water was drawn for him. It had a brackish taste but seemed relatively clean and Matthew drank gratefully, careful not to take too much and make himself sick again. One of the men noticed his pistol and took it from him. Matthew did not resist – he did not have the strength – but he was aware he was virtually defenceless without his side arm. He was relieved of all other items he was carrying and even his leather jacket was taken. The man who had prodded him awake appeared to be the leader and Matthew saw him push forward a tired and ragged-looking man in his middle years.

'My master wishes to know who you are,' he said, surprising Matthew with his fluency in English. 'I am a slave who once lived in Jerusalem as a free man, praise Allah, but I fell on bad times and was sold by my creditors to this tribe.'

'I am Captain Matthew Duffy of the Australian Flying Corps, and I was shot down east of here a few days ago. I need to return to my squadron.'

The man looked at him with a sad expression. 'Your fate is in the hands of Allah,' he said. 'The people who have captured you have no allegiance to either the Ottomans or your people. They are bandits and your life will only be spared if you are worth something as a ransom. They know that the Turkish will pay to have you handed over. If they find it difficult to get you to the Ottomans and your own people do not wish to barter for you, they will amuse themselves with your slow death. They are cruel beyond imagining.'

The last statement chilled Matthew to the core. He did not know if the Allies would consider a ransom deal with the Arab bandits. 'You can tell your master that I am worth a lot of money to my people,' Matthew said, hoping to at least buy himself some time.

The interpreter nodded and turned to his master; it was clear that the interpreter was the only one who understood English. Afterwards two of the men tied Matthew's hands behind his back. He did not struggle; escape was an impossible option for now. They frogmarched him to a date palm and forced him down with his back to the trunk. At least for now he was alive, had quenched his thirst and had the shade of the date palm. One of the Arab men squatted a few feet away; he was armed with a deadly-looking curved dagger and an ancient musket.

The interpreter was right: Matthew's life was now in the hands of Allah.

★

Joanne had finished the consultation on the possible future borders of new nations to be formed after the war. She had reported back to the State Department in the USA via Jonathan Myles that it appeared the Franco–British alliance intended to go ahead and divide the former Ottoman Empire among themselves, leaving out the USA. Joanne had made it plain to Jonathan that she had no romantic interest in him and he had refrained from pursuing her. Now she was free to make contact with her British Secret Service contacts in Cairo.

'You want to do what, dear lady?' Major Christopher Wilkins spluttered when she walked into his office, marked with the gold sign *Army Intelligence*. It was an elegant, spacious room, with slowly whirring fans and open balustrades overlooking the Nile.

He was standing with his hands behind his back, looking at her with raised eyebrows. He was wearing the khaki dress uniform of a Royal Engineer. Across his right breast he sported the campaign ribands of many colonial wars.

'I want your permission to return to Palestine to continue with my work as an intelligence officer,' Joanne replied calmly. She had reported to Major Wilkins in the past and he had become a friend. She hoped she would be able to count on his support again this time.

'Miss Barrington,' he said, clearing his throat. 'You must know that I have never truly approved of using a woman as delicate as you for our intelligence-gathering missions.'

'Oh, poppycock,' Joanne said. 'You know I can take care of myself. Didn't I prove that when I was swanning around in the Sinai for your department?'

Major Wilkins looked at her carefully. 'Your request to be reassigned to our operations department would have nothing to do with a downed colonial flyer, would it?'

Joanne was only slightly taken aback. Major Wilkins had always been an astute operator, despite looking like a character from the *Boy's Own Annual*. Clearly Jonathan Myles had been talking out of turn. 'Nothing whatsoever,' she replied smoothly. 'I just feel that I can do more good by being back on active service.'

'And what about your children?' Major Wilkins asked.

Joanne winced. She missed James and Olivia more than she had thought possible, but they were safe and being well cared for; she had something very important to do for them before she went home again. 'With all due respect, Major Wilkins, that is not a question you would ask my male counterparts. My children are in their grandfather's very capable hands; had I not been absolutely certain about that, I would never have agreed to leave them in the first place.'

Wilkins sighed, then began to pace the marble floors of his luxurious office, deep in thought. Finally he paused and turned to her. 'What do you need?' he asked and Joanne broke into a winning smile, rising from the settee to go to him.

'Christopher, you are such a darling,' she said, kissing him on both cheeks. 'I will need supplies for at least a month in the field. I intend to use my role as an archaeologist as a cover. Ostensibly, I will be attempting to locate and protect significant historical sites. Needless to say, I will be in contact with the Bedouin, who are always a good source of intelligence regarding the Turks. I will require the services of a trustworthy guide . . . someone who works indirectly for you. Mr Saul Rosenblum will do very nicely, and I believe he can also act as my bodyguard.'

The British officer returned to his desk and removed a folder from the top drawer. 'I will issue orders to our quartermaster, along with instructions for your briefing tomorrow. Just remember, you work for me.'

'Of course,' Joanne replied, eyeing the papers he was filling in, which approved her mission to collect intelligence for the British Army. 'And if I happen to bump into General Allenby I will relate how helpful you have been.'

Major Wilkins snorted. 'Don't think I don't see through your conniving, Miss Barrington.'

Joanne smiled at him sweetly. 'Christopher darling, you are one of the most wonderful men I know.'

'Next to your colonial flyer,' Wilkins said with a grin. 'I pray that you find him hale and hearty. Now, leave my office.'

Joanne left the office with a spring in her step. Major Wilkins knew very well what she was up to, but, like most men, she could twist him around her little finger. Not Matthew, though; he was one man who wasn't swayed by her charms. That was one of the reasons why she was in love with him.

6

Villers-Bretonneux had been taken by the Australians after bloody fighting.

Sergeant Tom Duffy was pleased at the news but it didn't change anything for him and his men. It seemed that the war would go on forever. Under cover of darkness he and five other men of his patrol had the mission of reconnoitring beyond their trenches for enemy activity. They were looking specifically for enemy listening posts, and already they had spotted the dim outline of earthworks and could hear the thump of stakes being driven into the ground.

Corporal Dan Frogan crawled to Tom's side. 'The stone quarry seems to be a bit off to our left,' he whispered. 'Pretty bloody obvious the Hun are digging in.'

Just as the corporal made his observations two enemy machine-guns opened fire, sending fiery tracers over their heads. Tom's fingers dug into the earth as he pressed his face deep into the wet grass. The machine-guns ceased firing and Tom guessed that they were simply sending a message to keep away, rather than actually identifying his patrol's location. The message worked.

Tom glanced at the luminous dial of his fob watch. It was near 2 am, time to return to their lines to report what they had seen out in no-man's-land. He quietly sent word to his men that they were returning to their lines.

Back in the trench they were met by the battalion intelligence officer, a captain keen to hear what they had located in the night. Tom briefed the IO.

'Good show, Sergeant Duffy,' he said. 'Give the lads a good hot cup of tea and stand them down for the night.'

Tom knew that his men were exhausted; they badly needed a good night's sleep, but that was hard to find in the trenches. Hopefully the German artillery 4.2's would leave them alone and not send over the deadly shells that exploded shrapnel and poisonous gas among the men huddled in the trenches.

Tom had hardly furnished himself with a mug of hot tea when the company sergeant major found him. 'Tom, you lucky bastard,' he said in the dark. 'You and your platoon are being relieved for some leave. Effective as from 0600 today.'

'Thanks, sir,' Tom responded, hardly daring to believe the news. At last a break from the front line, away from the terror that they all lived with every moment out here. 'Where are we having the leave?' he asked, taking a sip from his tea and the CSM mentioned the name of the rest area. Suddenly, all Tom's weariness evaporated. He was getting leave in the village near Juliet. Tom's spirits soared. The one true reason for living would be in his arms before the sun set tomorrow.

★

Where the warm winds of spring prevailed in Europe, the cooler autumn breezes blew down Market Street in Sydney. George Macintosh had received a note to meet with Inspector Jack Firth in front of the Dymock's bookstore.

'I am a busy man,' George growled when Jack Firth arrived five minutes late.

'So am I,' the policeman snapped back. 'I have a murder to investigate, not to mention the matter of a certain file getting into the wrong hands. How about we go for a stroll.'

They began walking down the street. Horse-drawn wagons and automobiles clattered by; a sudden wind whipped up a newspaper that had been used to wrap fish and chips, slapping it against George's leg. He shook it off irritably.

'The inspector general has the file on that bloody Schumann woman,' Jack said. 'It raises questions I think we both don't want asked or, worse, answered.'

'It was you who deviated from your regulations,' George answered. 'The matter does not concern me.'

Firth stopped in his tracks. 'It has everything to do with you and your attempt to control all your bloody family's companies. Remember, I was working on your orders.'

'I paid you well,' George replied coldly. 'It is up to you to settle any matters that might prove embarrassing – to either of us.'

'Yes, well, not so easily done,' Jack said, staring at a ragged boy peddling newspapers on a corner. 'You know very well that if we don't stop this right now, it could lead to a treason charge for you. We still hang traitors, you know.'

'What do you want from me?' George asked, acknowledging that if the police detective were to be found out for his illegal activities, they might be traced back to him. They were both in a jam.

'I'll need more money – a lot more money.' Jack frowned. 'Getting rid of troublesome questions requires friends in the right places.'

'Talking of which,' George said, 'I have a troublesome problem of my own to get rid of.'

Firth drew out a packet of cigarettes and lit one, blowing smoke into the air. 'You're a successful businessman. I'm sure you can find your own means of dealing with it.'

'Not so easy,' George said, lowering his voice. 'My dead brother's wife went and had a child, and my damned father stupidly named that child as a partner in the family companies when he turns twenty-one.'

Firth glanced sharply at George. 'What are you saying?' he asked suspiciously.

'A house in the best suburb and a contract to work for the Macintosh companies on a generous salary for the rest of your life,' George said.

'Seems to me you'd be expecting something pretty big for all that,' Jack replied, puffing on his cigarette. 'If I remember rightly, your brother's son would be around two or three years old by now. Sounds to me like you're talking murder.'

George watched the police detective very closely for any signs of a betrayal. 'With your contacts on the streets you must know someone who could do the job very discreetly.'

Jack did not answer straightaway but stared at the newspaper boy selling the next list of war dead and wounded. 'Like the man I set you up with last year who coincidently sails to America just when your sister gets killed.'

'I really don't think you want to know about that,' George said.

Jack took a long puff on his cigarette and dropped the butt on the footpath, grounding it with the heel of his boot.

'I might be a bent copper, Mr Macintosh,' he said, 'but murdering kids is something that even I will not do.'

'I'm not asking you to commit the act itself,' George said. 'Children have accidents all the time. If you can organise that for me, I promise to do my best to make that file disappear forever.'

The detective stared hard at George. 'You make the file go away, and keep your promise to set me up in a fancy house with a cushy job, and I'll consider your offer. But all I'll do is find the right person; then it's up to you. And don't forget that bloody Sean Duffy will be watching you – that kid meets a sudden end and he's going to be immediately suspicious.'

'I have thought of that,' George answered. 'It's time Duffy had an accident of his own.'

'Not so easy when you consider that Griffiths watches his back day and night,' Firth countered. He seemed to think for a moment. 'Isn't the kid way up in Queensland in the sticks? It'll be hard to get to him out there; they're a close mob in the bush, and a stranger will stick out like the proverbial.'

'Giselle could be lured to Sydney with her son,' George said quietly. 'I am sure my wife would be very happy to have her best friend come down for a visit.'

'Right, you do your bit, Macintosh, and I'll do mine. My missus will appreciate a new house. It might get her off my back for all the hours I work. Just remember, we'll both swing if anything goes wrong.'

George felt a flood of relief. He had ways to ensure that the file concerning Karolina Schumann was lost permanently. Certain politicians could make it go away; they had a lot to hide from the newspapers themselves. Consorting with underage prostitutes was never good for a politician's career. George had gone to great lengths to entrap key figures in the government, inviting them to special parties at his private venues. It was easy to procure the underage boys and girls from the slums of Sydney, where destitute mothers and drunken fathers accepted the money without asking questions about the fate of their children. George's hidden photographer was able to collect plenty of evidence as to the twisted pleasures of certain politicians and government officials.

The detective walked away, leaving George to contemplate how he could convince Louise to invite Giselle to Sydney for a visit. Louise knew there was no love lost between him and Giselle; in fact they hated each other. If he were to suggest a visit for no particular reason, Louise would be immediately suspicious. Maybe George's own son's birthday could be used as an excuse. Donald was about the same age as David, and George knew that Louise and Giselle would jump at the change for the two boys to spend some time together. Naturally George would pay all expenses for Giselle and her son to travel south; maybe they could stay for a holiday.

Smiling, George made his way back to his office in the city.

The village was straight out of the pages of a book about medieval Europe, Tom thought as he jumped from the back of the truck that had brought his platoon from the railway station a few miles away. Spring flowers added dashes of brilliant colour to the little gardens and window boxes, while the sun shone in the sky and water sparkled from the old water fountain in the village centre. Tom's heart beat unsteadily when he saw the fountain; this was where he had first met Juliet carrying a basket of fresh eggs for sale to the villagers and cafés.

The men of his platoon tumbled from the truck with kitbags and rifles over their shoulders, milling about like excited schoolchildren on an outing. Their slouch hats immediately identified them as Australians and Tom could see the expressions of pleasure on the faces of local shopkeepers. The Aussies were paid better than their Tommy comrades, and Tom could also see the uniforms of their Canadian cousins already in town on leave. There was a special bond between the colonial troops. Still, Tom breathed a sigh of relief when he spotted the stern-faced, red-capped British military police eyeing the newcomers to the village. The troops might be friendly, but that didn't mean there wouldn't be brawls. The men were wound up tight as springs; add alcohol to that and there was sure to be a fight or two at some time during their leave.

In his bad French, Tom asked an old man sitting on the edge of the fountain where he could find Mademoiselle Joubert. The old man removed his pipe and looked disapprovingly at the handsome Australian soldier. He pointed it down the street and replied, 'At the schoolhouse where she is the teacher.'

Tom thanked him, slung his kitbag over his shoulder and set out for the schoolhouse, which he found at the end of the street. He paused outside and listened to the sweet note of children reciting their times tables, smiling when he heard Juliet correct them.

Very carefully, Tom edged open the main door to look inside. Juliet was standing in front of about fifteen children ranging in age from six to ten. For a moment he stood drinking her in, the love swelling in his chest. Suddenly a little girl at the back of the class began giggling, causing Juliet to glance at the door. The expression of pure delight on her face lit up Tom's world beyond anything he had ever experienced before. Juliet said something to the children and they began tumbling past Tom, eyeing him with some curiosity.

'Oh, Tom, I have missed you with all my heart and soul,' Juliet said, rushing into his outstretched arms. Her short dark hair had grown some since he'd seen her last, but her dimpled, cherubic face was still the same. The tears flowed on Tom's chest as she tried to laugh and cry at the same time.

'Hello, old girl,' Tom said softly, embracing her as if she might suddenly disappear like in all the forlorn dreams he'd had lying in the bottom of a freezing wet trench, snatching what little sleep he could. 'I have missed you more than you could know,' he replied.

Juliet finally broke the embrace to gaze up into his face. 'How long will you be able to stay?' she asked, wiping away the tears. 'Forever?'

'Two days' leave only,' Tom replied glumly.

Juliet's face fell, but then she rallied. 'My parents are visiting the next village while you are here. You will have to take your billet at our farm. I can cook you a real meal, and we can sit together in the garden and admire the flowers.'

'Is there anything else we can do?' Tom asked with a gentle laugh. 'As much as I love your French flowers.'

'Oh, I am the village schoolteacher and that would cause a scandal, but billeting a brave ally of France is acceptable. I will be finished my classes in an hour and I will give the children an early break, which I know they will not object to. We will walk to the farm together on such a beautiful day.'

'I could wait here and just watch you,' Tom suggested, but Juliet shook her head.

'That might cause people to talk,' she said. 'Better you be with your friends until then.'

Reluctantly, Tom took her advice and after another crushing embrace and long kiss left her to gather together the children.

Tom walked away as if his feet were not actually touching the ground.

Corporal Smithers watched Duffy with open curiosity. What was the black bastard up to?

Smithers had been granted wound leave before his return to the battalion and had already spent a day in the village. The men had greeted him cordially enough and two of his closer comrades had invited him to share a drink at a café.

Smithers went to the old stone building on the main street where the café was situated. He entered the cramped, smoke-filled room and spotted his mates. The three men were fortunate to find a table vacated by some Canadian soldiers, and bottles of wine – which the Aussie called plonk – were served.

'Bloody rather have a beer,' said the first soldier, Mick.

'Stop your whining,' Smithers said. 'This stuff will get you pissed faster than beer.'

The second soldier, called Bluey because of his red hair, nodded his agreement and swilled back the wine, which he had to admit was a step up from any wine he'd drunk in the past.

'Has that bloody blackfella been spreading rumours that I was not badly wounded?' Smithers asked.

'Not that I know, Corp,' Mick said, and looked to his comrade. 'You heard anything, Bluey?'

'I've heard nothing from Sergeant Duffy,' Bluey shrugged, topping up his glass tumbler with more wine. 'He keeps to himself.'

'I seen him going to the schoolhouse a while ago,' Smithers said. 'As far as I know there's a pretty young sheila teaching there. Why would that black bastard go to the schoolhouse as soon as he gets off the truck?'

Bluey was intent on getting very drunk, but something Corporal Dan Frogan had said to Tom whilst they were driving from the station came to mind. He had overheard them discussing how fortunate it was for the leave to be in the village where Sergeant Duffy's girl resided. 'I think the schoolteacher might be his sheila,' he said.

'That so?' Smithers said. 'From what I hear, you boys have to return to the battalion late tomorrow, while lucky me has another twenty-fours. I might just acquaint myself with the village schoolteacher – she might be able to teach me about the birds and bees.'

Bluey and Mick glanced at their section leader, who was smiling in a frightening way, but they said nothing – they were just here to get so drunk that they forgot the war even existed.

Tom sat on a bench outside Juliet's family home and gazed at the cows grazing in a green, flower-adorned paddock. In this piece of heaven it was easy to think the war was over. No sound of guns in the air, no constant fear, no cries of the wounded and dying, and he was clean and dry after a hot bath prepared by Juliet in the kitchen. He sipped a glass of red wine while Juliet sat beside him darning a pair of well-worn socks she had retrieved from Tom's kit bag.

'If only the war was over,' Tom sighed, 'I could take you home to Queensland and you would be the queen of all you surveyed.' She would be too. He hadn't told her yet but he had a fortune stashed away in an Australian bank account, thanks to an earlier opportunity to seize a fortune in diamonds. All he had to do was survive the war.

Juliet continued to darn the sock. 'You could leave the war,' she said quietly.

'Desert, you mean,' Tom replied. 'I have heard that a few of our blokes have hopped the bags and are living out in no-man's-land with Huns who have also had enough of the war. It's tempting but the platoon needs me.'

'I need you,' Juliet said, glancing up from her work. 'Oh, Tom, so many young men will never return to those they love.'

'The way some in my army treat me, I wonder why in hell I do stick it out,' Tom growled, remembering the snide remarks behind his back about being a blackfella. But he consoled himself with the thought that not all those he led felt that way. Most of his men would die for him, as he would for them. 'No, I'll stick it out and do my best to stay alive. And when it's over I'll come to your father and ask for your hand in marriage.'

'You have not asked me for my hand, Tom Duffy. I think that you presume too much,' Juliet said sternly.

'I'm sorry,' Tom said, feeling a little alarmed. 'I guess that I kind of thought –'

'It is traditional in my country that a man first raise the idea of marriage with the woman,' Juliet continued. 'It may be different in your uncivilised country.' Then she burst out laughing. 'I am only teasing you, my love.'

Tom looked sheepish. 'Juliet, I know we haven't had much time together, but I also know that I love you more than any other person alive.' He felt Juliet's arm link with his and he could smell the fresh scent of her body as she snuggled close to him. 'I apologise for my presumption. I think I've been living for too long in a world where life is short and brutal. I love you and would hope you might consider being my wife when this war is over.'

Tom held his breath. He hardly dared believe this beautiful, intelligent young woman would even consider marrying a rough and hardened soldier like him.

Juliet broke into a warm and loving smile. 'I have loved you, Tom Duffy, from the day we met. I will allow you to go to my father and ask permission as soon as you can,' she said, a tear welling at the corner of her eye.

'I don't have a ring for you,' Tom mumbled, still hardly believing that his whole future had changed in this moment. 'I will have the finest ring in France when I next have my leave,' he added with some optimism. 'I know a man who can help me.'

'I don't need a ring,' Juliet said gently. 'I just need your promise that you will not do anything foolish when you return to the front. My greatest wish is to spend the rest of my life beside you, surrounded by our children and grandchildren. And now that I know your intentions are honourable, I think . . . we should share the same bed tonight.'

Tom's heart stuttered, barely able to take in Juliet's response. He started to reply but Juliet smoothed her fingertips over his lips. '*Mon amour*,' she whispered, and Tom was lost. He rose, taking Juliet by the hand and leading her into the ancient house that had been built long before Captain Cook sailed to Australia.

That night they made love and in the early morning light they lay in each other's arms. They did not speak of the horrors that lay beyond the house and village; they did not acknowledge that death lay between them. Their love was a shield that would protect them from every evil thrown at them by a cruel world.

★

When it was time for Tom to return to his platoon the next afternoon, he and Juliet walked arm in arm to the village. The trucks were already waiting to take them to the railway station. Most of the men looked bleary-eyed from too much alcohol and silently loaded their kitbags and rifles into the back of the open-tray vehicles. Dan Frogan did not appear to be as hungover as the rest of the men.

'Mostly behaved themselves last night,' he said to Tom. 'Lost a bit of money gambling with those bloody Canadians, though.'

'We have them all?' Tom asked.

'All present and accounted for,' Dan said. He glanced over Tom's shoulder to see Juliet standing at the edge of the men milling to board the trucks. She recognised Dan and smiled at him.

'You old dog,' Dan chuckled. 'I wondered where you had disappeared to last night.'

'Juliet has agreed to marry me,' Tom responded in a guarded tone. 'I'll speak to her father when I'm next on leave.'

'Congratulations, Tom. I reckon you couldn't have picked a better sheila than Juliet.' He thrust out his hand and shook Tom's. Then he turned and yelled to the men, 'Sergeant Duffy is engaged to be married to that beautiful young lady standing over there.'

An instant shout arose from the men, with 'You lucky bastard', from the single men and 'You'll be sorry', from those who were married. Tom could hear in their banter a true warmth, and he knew why he could never desert the men who were just as much his family as any he might have been born with.

When the men were aboard the trucks, Tom walked over to Juliet and took her in his arms, crushing her to him and kissing her on the lips. A howl of hoots went up from the men. 'The buggers will be sorry when I get them back to the battalion,' Tom grinned.

Tears streamed from Juliet's eyes as they broke the embrace. She reached up to touch him on the cheek. 'Remember your promise last night and come back to me,' she whispered.

Tom could hear Dan's shouted warning for him to join the last truck, which was already moving out. Tom ran over to the moving vehicle and hands reached down to haul him aboard. When he was on the tray he looked back at Juliet standing in the village square waving to him. Tom felt his whole being flood with tender emotions, but they were gone in a flash when he noticed a familiar figure standing a few feet behind Juliet.

'Smithers!' he gasped.

'Yeah, the bastard swung sick leave for another day,' Dan said. 'Thought you knew.'

Tom stared in his shock at the burly man and he could have sworn the evil smile was directed at him.

7

The grit stung Matthew's eyes, and the dust whipped up by the sudden storm covered the Bedouin camp like a smokescreen. The ropes securing Matthew had been replaced with chains. At least the date palm under which he was secured provided shade from the hot sun, and his captors had fed him sufficiently that his health had improved enough that he was thinking of ways of escape.

Matthew calculated that he had been a prisoner for at least two weeks, and in that time he'd been mostly ignored except for the occasional random beatings by the women, who used thin canes to inflict the punishment. Matthew had learned the interpreter's name was Aban and he'd asked him why the women beat him for no apparent reason.

'You are an infidel,' Aban had answered. 'They do it to humiliate you. You cannot expect any better treatment.'

'I thought that your people treated a guest with honour,' Matthew had said.

'You are not only an infidel,' Aban had replied, 'but also now a slave, to be bartered or beaten by my master, Abdul-Hamid, as he wishes.'

'What does he intend to do with me?'

'He has sent two of his men to speak with the Ottomans to see what you are worth to them.'

'He would have been better sending his men to General Allenby's army – they would have paid more for me.'

'My master does not like the Europeans,' Aban had said with a shrug. 'The Ottomans will also give him Mauser rifles.'

Matthew crouched on the ground, covering his face with a rag torn from his shirt to avoid ingesting the fine dust. Thankfully the storm passed over quickly, and soon the Bedouin emerged from their tents to inspect their goods and livestock.

The next day the tribe packed up and Matthew found himself being dragged behind a camel as the Bedouin moved their livestock to better pastures. He tried not to lose hope. Escape was a possibility, however remote. Matthew was a resourceful man who had been in many tight spots in his life. He would watch and wait and be prepared to escape at the first hint of an opportunity.

Joanne had finally been able to leave Cairo and travel with an army supply column to Palestine. There she met Saul Rosenblum, who had received a signals order to meet with her in the sacred city of Jerusalem.

Joanne was never so pleased to see his bronzed and bearded face as now. Saul, dressed in the garb of an Arab

Bedouin, strode across the foyer of the hotel with a broad smile on his face.

'He is not dead,' were his first words of greeting. 'My intelligence reports that he survived the crash and is now a prisoner of a treacherous jackal by the name of Abdul-Hamid.'

Joanne felt her knees go weak under her. 'Oh, Saul, thank you. Your words confirm all that I have prayed for.' She shook his hand, wishing she could hug the big, burly man in her joy at hearing his words of hope. 'I knew that a mere aeroplane crash could not kill Matthew. How do we get him back?'

Saul took Joanne's elbow and guided her to a quiet corner of the foyer. 'It will not be easy finding him out there,' he said. 'Abdul-Hamid and his people are nomads whose lives have not changed much since Moses crossed the Sinai. They move around a lot and keep to themselves. Thus far he has managed to keep his people out of the war. A desert traveller paid by my people for information said that he saw Abdul-Hamid's clan travelling east from a well-known waterhole around four days ago. They had a European with them; apparently he was in chains. I am sure it is Matthew; this waterhole is not so far from the area where his plane went down. This is difficult terrain and you had better be prepared to travel on horseback. We may also have to cope with pockets of Turkish resistance.'

'You know from personal experience that I can handle myself, Saul,' Joanne said quietly. 'What do we need to mount our expedition? I have access to supplies, arms and ammunition.'

Saul began to list the supplies necessary to equip a patrol of seven men plus themselves. He intended to take his eldest son, Benjamin, with him; he needed the experience as one day he would become a leader like Saul.

'It will take me twenty-four hours to get everything together. We should be able to depart the city first light the day after tomorrow,' she said when Saul had finished.

After approval from her American superiors, Joanne was able to use a letter of authority from Major Wilkins to procure all they needed for at least four weeks in the arid lands west of Jerusalem, and she was even able to get hold of a valuable Maxim and belts of .303 ammunition for the heavy machine-gun. Everything they needed was carefully packed into crates and when they left the next morning they were a small column of fierce-eyed desert fighters trailing a caravan of packhorses with their supplies of food, water and ammunition.

As they departed Jerusalem's walls Joanne gazed around her and thought about times long ago when others had ridden out to war from this city. She was travelling in the land of King David and her trained archaeologist's eye did not miss the significance of the landmarks they passed. Occasionally she would comment to Saul about biblical points of interest, but she realised that he was not a truly religious man but more of a committed nationalist with a dream of establishing a Jewish nation. She remembered that Saul had been born in Australia and clearly much of the land of his birth still remained in his soul, despite his Jewish identity.

Benjamin seemed to be more of a true Jewish child of the land. His English was not very good and he knew very little about Australia. The boy was the image of his father and showed no fear, although Joanne thought he must be a little afraid of what was to come. She had come to know Benjamin last year when she had accompanied him to Jerusalem for medical treatment. He had received a serious bullet wound fighting a neighbouring Arab village intent on destroying his family's fragile community. 'This will always be the way,' Benjamin had shrugged when Joanne had said that boys his age in Australia would be safely at school instead of bearing arms. 'We will always have to fight to survive.'

Thanks to Wilkins's letter of authority they were able to pass the numerous British patrols, and eventually they found themselves away from the well-ordered country of irrigated orchards and on the edge of the craggy hills and ravines. That night Joanne lay down under a panorama of stars, thinking about her children and Matthew. She found herself uttering a prayer for his safety and wondered which of the three faces of God was listening in this land of three great religions: Yahweh, Christ or Allah.

Juliet walked down the cobbled street between the village's little shops. Ever since Tom had left yesterday she hadn't been able to think straight; she didn't know how she was going to teach the children tomorrow. What if Tom did not return? What if he was injured so badly that he was an invalid for the rest of his life? What if the torment she saw in his eyes never faded? She was realistic enough to know that this war did not spare men just because they were in love. At least her parents would be home from the neighbouring village tomorrow and tonight would be her last night alone.

The sun was still high when Juliet reached the farmhouse. She stepped inside and closed the door behind her. She was preoccupied by her sadness and did not hear the movement behind her until it was too late. Someone had appeared from the bedroom and the next thing she knew a brawny arm was reaching over her shoulder to put her in a headlock. She attempted to scream and struggle but found that her assailant held her as if she were nothing but a rag doll.

'Don't go thinking that you should scream or resist me,' a voice said over her shoulder and she could smell the reek of cheap wine on the man's breath. 'Me and you are goin' to the bedroom for a little afternoon fun.'

But Juliet did scream and for her defiance felt the arm bite into her throat in a way that cut off her air. Sobbing, she was dragged backwards into the room where she and Tom had made passionate love.

It was only when her attacker flung her on the bed that she saw his face and she knew real terror. It was an ugly face worsened by the intent in the dead eyes. 'Please,' she begged. 'Please do not hurt me.'

But Smithers simply began undoing his trousers. Juliet flung herself from the bed but he was quick and a smashing back-handed blow across her face brought blood to her mouth. She fell back in a daze of red stars, tasting the coppery blood in her mouth.

Somehow she was able to disconnect from the horror of the rape; it was as if it was happening to someone else, except the physical pain was real. When he was spent he rolled over on his back and laughed, filling the room with his odour. Juliet stared with unseeing eyes at the ceiling.

'Don't matter if you know who I am,' Smithers said. ''Cos when I get back to the battalion I will be tellin' everyone what a good time you gave me when your blackfella left you. I'll be tellin' the boys what a good romp we had together.'

Juliet barely heard him. She was too aware of her body, of the stain this monster had left on her. It was as if she had been made dirty and nothing could ever make her clean again.

Smithers rose from the bed and pulled on his pants. Juliet lay still, praying God would rain destruction down on the room, killing them both.

'Well, girlie, when I get back to the boys I'll tell them to drop by for a bit of crumpet when they're next on leave,' he sneered. 'Best crumpet in town. I'd stay, but the army needs me back, and I can hardly wait to thank Sergeant Duffy for breaking you in for me.'

After he had left Juliet lay on the bed, not moving until night had fallen. She rose from the bed and picked up her torn dress. Smithers had left dark bruises on her arms and thighs. She stumbled to the kitchen, where the big tub used for bathing was located. She did not bother to warm the water but simply poured in enough for her to wash herself.

She scrubbed and scrubbed; she didn't seem to be able to get clean. When she could remain in the cold water no longer, she stepped out of the tub and dressed herself. She could not bear to think about Tom knowing what had happened; he would not want to marry a woman who had been defiled in this way. She broke down into a fit of sobbing. She wanted just to die, but suicide was a mortal sin. Which left her facing a life sentence without love.

It was pitch dark this late at night and there was something about the Aboriginal weapons mounted on the wall of his library that disturbed George Macintosh deeply. They had been displayed there for many years and they reminded George of the curse that was said to hang over his family. Supposedly an old warrior called Wallarie had cursed the Macintoshes for the violence they had perpetrated against his people. Over the years premature death had stalked the family, but George was not superstitious and did not believe in Aboriginal curses. Bad luck was all it was.

'Damned poppycock,' he muttered and went back to considering how, with the assistance of an accomplice, he might be able to arrange an accident for his nephew; he figured he'd do away with his sister-in-law at the same time; kill two birds with one stone, as it were. He had already worked on his unwitting wife to write a letter to Giselle inviting her to Sydney for the Christmas break and Giselle had accepted. That was more than six months away, which gave him plenty of time to come up with a suitable scenario to kill both mother and son. Maybe a boating accident on the harbour, George thought. That was one option.

George rose from behind his desk and went to the liquor cabinet to pour himself a Scotch. Tumbler in hand, he walked to the great window and pulled aside the drapes to stare down on the darkened driveway. He had barely pulled them aside when he felt a sudden change in the room that caused his hair to stand on end. It was as if someone had entered the room and was now standing behind him, watching him curiously.

For a moment George was frozen with fear. Then he cursed himself for an overactive imagination – it was impossible for anyone to have entered the room without him hearing or seeing them. Slowly, he turned his head; from the corner of his eye he thought he saw a faint shadow shaped like a naked black man. He screamed and the tumbler of Scotch slipped from his hand and crashed onto the floor.

The shadow was still standing in the corner of the room, and George struggled against fainting. The shadow held a long wooden spear and George sensed he was an

Aboriginal warrior. He slumped to his knees as if to beg for mercy.

Long seconds later, the door burst open and Louise came rushing into the room in her nightdress.

'George, what is the matter?' she asked, kneeling beside her terrified husband.

George was shaking uncontrollably. 'Over there,' he whispered, pointing behind her. 'An apparition.'

Louise turned to see what her husband was pointing at. 'It's just a shadow on the wall from the tree outside. I have asked the gardener to trim it, but he hasn't yet had a chance to,' she chided. 'You exposed the shadow when you opened the drapes.'

George stared at the wall and eventually saw that his wife was right. It was nothing more than a shadow, enhanced by the library's dim lighting. With help from Louise he rose to his feet but he could still feel his hands shaking. Despite the shadow, George was sure something had entered the room. He could not tell his wife this, though; it would make him look weak and foolish.

'I think you can retire now,' George said coldly, not bothering to thank his wife for her concern. He would follow her upstairs; there was no way he was going to stay in the library a moment longer tonight.

A tiny speck of a campfire burned on the vast inland plain of brigalow scrub under a spectacular sky of sparkling stars. A dingo howled in the distance, calling to its pack as Wallarie sat cross-legged before the fire, staring into the gently flickering flames. He glanced up at a cluster of stars and identified the one he knew to be his white brother, Tom Duffy, grandfather of his namesake now across the sea in a foreign land. Tom looked down and told Wallarie that his grandson was still alive, but Wallarie knew there was danger coming to the Duffy family.

Wallarie began his chant. He sang the ancient song taught to him by the elders after his initiation as a warrior into the clan. As he chanted he saw visions rise from the flames and form into pictures in his head. The song continued. It was not his song but the song of the ancients in the Dreaming.

Wallarie's spirit was flying high above the earth at a speed beyond even his understanding. In his fear he closed his eyes and when he opened them he was once again in a familiar place. It was a room in one of those whitefella houses. He had once visited Lady Macintosh there many years earlier, and now he was standing staring at the back of a man whose evil permeated the very air he breathed.

Then the vision was gone and Wallarie snapped open his eyes to find himself once again by his fire. He had seen the evil and knew that it threatened his world and that of his friends at Glen View.

For a long time Wallarie reflected on what his dream meant. He had visited a *debil debil*; one of those evil spirits that lived in the night – and which were to be avoided at all costs. He did not know who the *debil* was and thought it must be one of the Christian *debils* Pastor von Fellmann had tried to teach him about. Maybe he should talk to the pastor and ask him what it meant. But the Pastor von Fellmann was a man who said *debils* were in another world, and so he could not have visited one while he was still alive. So it would not be any good talking with his old friend about the dream.

Wallarie sighed, rose with some effort to his feet and went in search of some more dry timber to throw on his fire.

He was careful not to stray far from the light of his camp-fire as the curlews began their sad wailing song. It was well known that the evil spirits of the dead were out there in the dark and even Wallarie was not immune to their magic. Maybe the meaning behind his vision would come when the sun rose once again across the dry scrub plains and the heat rose to warm his old, scarred body.

8

They came staggering back, across the colourful flower-spattered field, arm on the shoulder of the man in front of them, rags wrapped around their eyes, led by a soldier who could see. Sergeant Tom Duffy paused. He was ensuring the platoon had their allotment of supplies from the company quartermaster, which was his primary role now that the platoon commander, Lieutenant Mike Sullivan, had returned.

'Poor bastards,' the CQM muttered. 'Bloody gas attack on our work party down in the valley.'

Tom did not comment. He had seen it all before, and he just thanked God that it had not been him. Many of the men in the column would be temporarily blinded, but some would be blinded permanently, depending on how much gas they had copped.

'Any of your lot with the work party?' the CQM asked.

'No, thank God,' Tom replied. 'They're back here a bit, waiting to go up as soon as I sort out the requisition for their kit.'

'Like to cut off the balls of the Hun who invented the bloody gas shells,' the CQM grumbled as he counted out ammunition boxes for dispatch to Tom's platoon. 'Bad enough that we have to put up with their arty hammering us with shrapnel.'

Tom gestured to a couple of his platoon soldiers to come over and fetch the wooden cases of .303 rounds, and when he checked his list he saw that the platoon allocation of other supplies was complete. He thanked the CQM, then joined the two privates lugging not only the ammunition cases but also sandbags full of bully beef tins and the rock-hard biscuits the soldiers called dog biscuits.

Tom reached the thirty or so men of the platoon, lying about in the picturesque field covered in the wild flowers of late spring. It was the end of May and summer would be upon them with its long days of sweltering heat.

Lieutenant Sullivan was away at battalion HQ receiving his orders for the day and Tom had completed his duties for the moment. It was time to sit down and enjoy the warmth of the afternoon sun before they were inevitably sent up to the front under cover of darkness.

He found Dan Frogan smoking his pipe and cleaning his rifle. Tom joined him, sitting down on the grass beside his friend. Dan glanced up. 'I see you got all our supplies.'

'Yeah,' Tom answered. 'Only wish I had shares in the bully beef company. That's all we seem to get at the front. That, and those bloody biscuits harder than shrapnel.'

Tom retrieved his own battered pipe and took his time packing the bowl and lighting up. The first puff felt good as the nicotine was absorbed in his blood.

'Hey, Sarge!' a voice called out. Tom turned his head to see Corporal Smithers sitting with his section. 'Hear you got engaged on your last leave.'

'Thought that bastard was still on sick leave,' Tom muttered to Dan, ignoring the burly corporal.

'Got back a few days ago, but was posted to BHQ on light duties. They sent him back to the platoon today,' Dan said.

'Hey, Sarge,' Smithers persisted. 'She's a nice sheila, from what I know of her personally.'

The hair on the back of Tom's neck rose at this last comment and he made to rise to his feet, but Dan gently restrained him. 'Ignore the bastard,' he said. 'You know he's got it in for you.'

Tom stared at Smithers and saw him turn to the men around him and snigger. 'You're right,' Tom said, knowing full well that the last thing Lieutenant Sullivan would want would be for his superior NCO to start a fight. Such an event would lead to charges levelled and Tom would probably be stripped of his rank and given field punishment. Although Smithers was a coward and a troublemaker, as platoon sergeant, Tom had a duty to keep all his men from harm, despite his personal feelings towards them.

That evening Lieutenant Sullivan briefed the men: they were going up to the front in the early hours of the morning to relieve another company. Tom was soon occupied ensuring that the soldiers all had their equipment. They napped in the field until 0200 hours when Tom roused them from fitful sleep to assemble. He went down the ranks of the three sections to check that none of the men's gear rattled on the march to the front. When he reached Smithers he heard him mutter, 'Nice sheila, Juliet, if you know what I mean.'

Tom stood eye to eye with the corporal. 'No, I don't, Corporal Smithers. If you have something to say, spit it out.'

'Nothin' to say,' Smithers replied and Tom moved on. He was starting to worry about Juliet; he hoped she was safe, that Smithers hadn't been hassling her. He would have to wait until his next leave to find out what Smithers was alluding to. Before then, they were going up to the gates of hell and maybe Smithers might not make it back.

The company found themselves on the left forward flank of the defence, and after a briefing from the outgoing men, they began to settle into the routine of trench life once again. A few grumbled that the previous company had left the trench in a shambles, but soldiers needed to complain, Tom thought, so he listened patiently to their gripes.

Tom noticed that Corporal Smithers seemed to allocate the rewiring of sections along the front edge of the trench to his section, and remained safely down in the trench to avoid any possible sniper fire.

'Get out there and join your section, Corporal Smithers,' Tom barked. 'Set an example to your men.'

Smithers stubbed out his cigarette and rose slowly to his feet. 'I run my section as I see fit,' he growled.

'Sergeant,' Tom said, reminding the NCO of military protocol.

'Sergeant,' Smithers spat. 'Hope nothing happens to you in the dark, Sergeant Duffy. But as a blackfella, who would see you in the dark anyway?'

For a moment Tom was tempted to swing at Smithers, but he restrained himself. 'Just do your job,' he said with menace, and Smithers reluctantly climbed over the parapet to join his men rolling out barbed wire and driving in steel pickets.

In the early hours of the next morning Tom dozed in a niche that had been dug out of the trench walls to provide a sleeping space. The night was cold despite the fact summer was just around the corner.

'Stand to!'

The alarm was shouted down the trench just as the first crash of incoming rifle and machine-gun fire threw up spouts of dirt along the edge of the trench.

Tom tumbled from his resting place, rifle in hand and shaking the little sleep he'd had from his body. It was obvious they were under attack and he stumbled in the dark to the section of the trench where Lieutenant Sullivan was located. A German grenade exploded behind him and he knew the enemy must be close.

Lieutenant Sullivan was already pushing his way down the trench, revolver in hand, ensuring all his men were on the parapet. Tom could see that his officer was doing his job and stepped up beside Private Dean, who was rapidly working the bolt of his rifle, firing blindly into the dark until a flare exploded in the night sky, illuminating the scene before their defences.

Tom calculated that they were under attack from a couple of company-sized units. The helmeted men advancing in their grey uniforms were hunched forward, firing and moving in a disciplined manner.

'Aim, Private Dean,' Tom snapped when he noticed that the soldier had his eyes closed. In Tom's experience this was not uncommon as not all soldiers could face the reality of taking a man's life. 'Where is your section commander?'

Terrified, Corporal Dean waved over his shoulder. Tom glanced back to see a shadowy figure crouched in the trench a few feet away. He leapt across to confront the NCO cowering with his hands over his head.

'Get up, you yellow dingo,' Tom shouted in Smithers's ear. He grabbed the man by his collar and hauled him to his feet. Even in the dark Tom could see the glazed look in the NCO's eyes. 'Your bloody section needs you.'

Tom shook Smithers and that seemed to snap him out of the state he was in. He blinked and focused on Tom.

'Leave me alone, you black bastard!' Smithers screamed.

Tom released his grip and Smithers reached down to scoop up his rifle. He chambered a round and pointed the gun directly at Tom, who realised that he was trailing his own rifle and would not be able to bring it up to defend himself in time. Smithers thrust his rifle into Tom's chest, his finger on the trigger.

So this is how it ends, Tom thought slowly. But his finely honed instincts were working without his conscious thought, and he realised that his hand was gripping the barrel of Smithers's rifle, thrusting it up and away from him as the shot was fired.

Tom brought up the barrel of his own rifle to slam Smithers under the chin, knocking back his head and forcing him to drop his weapon. Before Tom could continue with the hand-to-hand fight he heard a desperate cry from Private Dean.

'Sarge! Sarge!'

Tom turned his attention to the parapet. He could see that a cluster of German soldiers were concentrating their attack through the barbed wire, which they had cut through, and were laying down a withering fire, forcing Dean to duck his head and discontinue fighting.

Tom took in the desperate situation. He calculated five enemy already emerging through the wire; within seconds they would be at the trench with hand grenades. Tom reached for the bayonet in the belt scabbard; he slid it out and clipped it onto the end of his rifle before hauling himself over the lip of the trench. Then, with a roar, he charged the five enemy men preparing to overrun this section of the trench.

Tom was hardly aware that he had placed himself in mortal danger; all he could feel was the red rage of combat. The world had narrowed down so that there was nothing else except killing. The looming figures seemed to hesitate at the sight of him charging at them and he claimed his first victim before the man had time to react.

The Germanstorm trooper screamed as the long knife caught him under the sternum and was twisted up into his chest cavity. He fell to his knees, desperately gripping the barrel of the rifle as Tom used all his strength to rip the bayonet free again. Tom hardly felt the German bayonet glance off the back of his ribs and through the rear of his jacket, entangling as it did. He swung, leaving his rifle still half-sticking out of the dying German soldier.

Tom jerked around, forcing the rifle from the soldier behind him. Using his tin helmet, Tom smashed at the face of his adversary. The aim was true, bringing a grunt of pain from the German soldier, who reeled back in stunned confusion. The other three German soldiers who were part of the breaching team had disappeared in the dark towards the trench, armed with grenades.

Tom did not allow his opponent to regain his senses but launched himself at him. As he did so he lost the grip on the helmet he had used as a weapon. Both men were now down to using their bare hands to kill each other and the German was a big man. Tom knocked him from his feet and was able to drop him on the ground, straddling him at the same time. He rained punches down on the soldier's face, smashing his nose and jaw. The German was pleading something but Tom ignored him, wrapping his hands around the man's throat and squeezing until the words were strangled and the breathing stopped. Bullets were cracking dangerously close to Tom's head, so he rolled off the dead man and groped for his rifle still sticking out of the body of the German he had bayoneted. Tom gave one more yank, dislodging the long knife with an awful sucking sound, and scrambled back to the trench where he could see three dead German soldiers lying on the forward edge. None had made it through the breach, thank God.

Tom fell over the trench and bounced off the parapet, winding himself as he hit the wooden slats below. As Tom lay on his back he stared up at the night sky slowly fading to daylight. The sound of gunfire was ringing in his ears. When he turned his head he could see his platoon standing to along the parapet.

'Sergeant Duffy, are you wounded?' a voice said as if from down a long tunnel. Tom's could see that it was Lieutenant Sullivan bending over him. It was then that Tom became aware of the terrible stinging pain along his side where the German bayonet had grazed him.

Wincing, Tom sat up and reached around to feel the tear in his jacket and the wetness of the blood. 'Got a bit of a cut on my back, boss,' Tom answered through teeth gritted in pain. 'Probably not much to write home about.'

'Stretcher-bearers, over here,' Sullivan called, gesturing to a couple of men wearing Red Cross bands on their arms and carrying a fold-up canvas stretcher. 'We'll get you back to be looked at,' Sullivan said. 'I saw what you did. Either bloody stupid or bloody brave, but your action slowed the Hun enough for us to bring rifles to bear before they got among us, Sergeant Duffy.'

It was now that Tom started to think about what he had done. He cursed himself for what appeared an act of bravery when all he was doing was reacting instinctively, as a warrior would. Hadn't he sworn to Juliet not to place his life in danger unnecessarily? He was an idiot.

'Got to do the roll call,' Tom said as one of the stretcher-bearers quickly and expertly examined the wound along Tom's ribs. Turning to Sullivan, the bearer said, 'The sarge isn't hurt too bad, but he'll need a few stitches and bandaging back at the aid post.'

'In that case, sir, I can take the roll call,' Tom said, tucking in his shirt and adjusting his jacket.

'If you think you are up to it, Tom,' Sullivan said quietly. 'Your parade.'

Tom pulled out the battered platoon roll book and a pencil. He called off the names of the platoon and was relieved to hear each one reply, 'Present, sir.' All except one – Corporal Smithers.

'Smithers,' Tom called again and heard Private Dean reply, 'I think Corporal Smithers was wounded, Sarge.'

'Anyone see Corporal Smithers cop it?' Tom asked and the silence answered his question.

The sun was now above the horizon and in the shadows of the trench the men stared at each other. They could hardly believe they had beaten off a ferocious night attack by at least a company-strength plus unit of the elite German stormtroopers of the Kaiser's army. Men sat with their rifles between their knees, staring blankly; others took out cigarettes and lit them with shaking hands.

'Two men per section back on the parapet,' Sullivan called loudly. 'They might be back.'

Reluctantly, men climbed back on the parapet on sentry duty, careful not to expose themselves to possible snipers left behind by the retreating Germans.

'Your job is done for now, Tom,' Sullivan said. 'Frogan

can hold the fort while you go to the aid post for treatment. I hope you're back with us before sunset.'

Tom was able to walk and he followed the stretcher-bearers down the communication trenches to the safer, rear area in a shallow valley. Here the spring flowers had been trampled into the mud by the horses and carts bringing up supplies and moving the big artillery guns around into their gun parks.

Inside the large tent marked with a red cross, Tom was met by the regimental surgeon, who examined his wound and stitched it with great care and skill.

'You will have to remain here until sunset,' he said, washing his hands in a bowl of bloody water.

Tom was pleased to see that there were only two other wounded men, and they were being treated for minor injuries. He was surprised that there was no sign of Corporal Smithers, who had been reported as wounded and having been evacuated. Only now did Tom remember that Smithers had tried to kill him.

He walked out into the morning sunshine and sat on a bench outside the tent. He was pondering on what he should do about Smithers when he saw the regimental sergeant major, Warrant Officer First Class Bob Pink, striding towards him. He had a grim expression on his face.

'Hello, sir,' Tom greeted as the regimental sergeant major came to a stop in front of him.

'On your feet, Sergeant Duffy,' the RSM commanded and Tom knew immediately that something was very wrong.

Tom came to his feet smartly, despite feeling exhausted now the adrenaline had finally flowed from his body.

'Sergeant Duffy, I have a serious allegation laid against you by Corporal Smithers,' the RSM said. 'He has made a formal complaint that you attempted to kill him during the attack by the Hun early this morning. What do you have to say to that?'

Tom shook his head in disbelief. 'That is a lie, sir. He was the one who attempted to kill me. Just get the gutless bastard here and ask him in my presence.'

'I am afraid that we cannot do that, Sergeant,' the RSM said. 'He has been evacuated further back to a hospital to be treated for a gunshot wound to his foot, which he claims you were responsible for.'

'Sir, this is a bloody joke,' Tom said, his anger rising.

'No joke, Sergeant Duffy,' the RSM replied. 'An investigation will have to be carried out, and until then, I want you to remain at BHQ under my watchful eye.'

'Do you think I tried to kill Corporal Smithers, sir?' Tom asked. He had always respected Pink for his professionalism and competence as the right-hand of the battalion commander.

'Not up to me to make that decision, Sergeant Duffy,' the RSM answered almost sadly. 'I do not have the privilege of voicing my opinion, that is up to the officers – but I personally cannot think why in hell you would shoot the bastard in the foot.'

'What happens now?' Tom asked.

'You report to the adjutant and he will allocate your tasks until the matter is cleared up,' the RSM said. 'In the meantime, keep your head down. A board will be convened in the field to decide whether you should be charged with attempted murder and court-martialled.'

'Sir,' Tom said and the RSM strode away, leaving Tom bewildered by the allegation, and regretful that Smithers was still alive.

★

It did not take long for the rumour to circulate in the battalion that Sergeant Duffy had been cited for attempted murder. Those outside Tom's company who did not know him well speculated that this kind of thing could be expected of a man who had spent months out in no-man's-land as a sniper. He was the best known killer in the battalion and they reckoned he must have snapped.

To those in Tom's company and platoon the idea was preposterous, and that night in the rear area a brawl broke out between the men who supported Tom and those who thought he was guilty. The regimental police broke up the brawl and the matter was reported to the commanding officer the next day.

'Get the bloody matter settled,' he growled to his battalion adjutant. 'I want either a charge laid by the end of the day's proceedings or Sergeant Duffy cleared. Call in his platoon and company commanders.'

The adjutant immediately sent for the two men, who made their feelings well and truly known that Smithers was a shirker and a soldier of dubious qualities. How he had been given positions of leadership in the past was a total mystery to them both. Lieutenant Sullivan then passed over a report he had made recommending Sergeant Duffy for a medal for courage displayed leaving the trench to thwart an attempt by the Germans to storm the trench on the battalion's flank.

'All very impressive, Mr Sullivan,' the adjutant said, skimming through the platoon commander's account of the fight. 'But I also have a statement on my desk from Private Dean, who I believe is one of your men, stating that he saw Duffy and Smithers brawling in the trench just before Duffy hopped the bags. Sadly, as commendable as his action was, it does not in any way ameliorate the attempted murder charge.'

'Adj,' the company commander broke in, leaning forward across the desk. Although he outranked the captain filling the adjutant's position, he was also acutely aware of the role of the adjutant in the battalion as an executive officer for the battalion commander. 'I was on the verge of transferring Smithers,' he said. 'The man has been reported before for shirking his duties during action. He is a liar.'

'Unfortunately, he also has a bullet in the foot,' the adjutant replied. 'Very hard to lie about that evidence.'

'The man could have shot himself in the foot to get out of the trenches. He's not the first and he won't be the last, as we all know,' said the company commander. 'I am sure that if Sergeant Duffy had intended to kill Smithers he would have done so. He's too bloody good a soldier not to have succeeded. In my opinion, the matter should be dropped.'

'I wish I could drop it,' the adjutant sighed. 'But there is also a matter of motive, and some of the men in Smithers's section have stated there was bad blood between the two over a woman they met on leave. It sounds like she was seeing them both.'

The company commander glanced at his junior officer. 'Do you know anything about that, Sullivan?'

'I heard from Corporal Frogan that Sergeant Duffy had got himself engaged to a French girl on the platoon's last leave. I am not aware of anything else at this moment.'

'Do we have the eternal triangle here?' the adjutant asked. 'A feud over a woman that has led to the incident?'

'With all respect, sir,' Lieutenant Sullivan said, 'I cannot imagine any woman that Sergeant Duffy might be interested in being interested in Corporal Smithers. To put it politely, Smithers is a pig of a man known for being the platoon bully.'

109

'Well, there's not much else we can do until Corporal Smithers provides his official statement,' the adjutant said. 'Thank you for your time.'

The company commander and Lieutenant Sullivan rose from their chairs and made their way out of BHQ.

It did not look good for Sergeant Duffy, the adjutant mused, not with the rumours he had heard about Duffy being a blackfella. It was well known that blackfellas were excitable chaps and impulsive, although he'd never actually met any Aboriginals himself, growing up in wealthy Sydney suburbia as he had.

No, it didn't look good at all. If it was the word of a white man against that of a blackfella, the white man would be believed every time.

9

For a week Joanne and her small expedition trekked west, ever vigilant for Turkish military units; even dressed as Bedouin they could be a target for the Ottoman army, as the Arabs had risen up against their former overlords from Istanbul.

The journey had been uneventful so far, and only twice had Saul's men stumbled across nomadic goat herders, who had no useful information for them. On the eighth day, however, they came across a goat boy in a gully, shepherding his small flock.

At the sight of the fierce-eyed mounted men the Arab boy fled. Benjamin easily caught up to him and jumped off his horse, calling out in Arabic that they would not harm him. Clearly realising that he couldn't outrun a party on horseback, the boy slowed to a halt. Benjamin promised him a reward of silver coins and food if he provided information.

The boy was around ten years old and, despite Benjamin's assurances, clearly terrified. He sat in silence as Benjamin opened a tin of bully beef and took out a half-loaf of unleavened bread. The boy sniffed the meat when it was offered to him and watched Benjamin take a bite, then he followed his example. The fear began to leave his eyes, and when he was given a cup of tea to wash down the bread and meat, he relaxed, sensing that he was not going to be killed by these men.

When asked, the boy said that he belonged to the tribe of Abdul-Hamid camped nearby, about a half-day to the west.

'Ask the boy if Abdul-Hamid has a European prisoner,' Joanne said eagerly.

Benjamin spoke again as the goat boy stuffed more bread in his mouth with his fingers. He answered before swallowing.

'He says that his master captured an infidel pilot some weeks ago and has sent a couple of his men to speak with the Ottomans about a reward for handing him over to them.'

Joanne glanced at Saul, who had been listening with great interest and broke in, 'Son, ask the boy how long ago the men were sent to speak with the Turks.'

Benjamin did so. 'He said about seven nights ago.'

Both Joanne and Saul looked at each other as they made their own calculations. 'That could mean the Turks might already be on their way here – if Abdul-Hamid's men made contact with the Turks up north. We don't have much time. Maybe not even hours,' Saul said.

'What are you planning?' Joanne asked. She was trying to keep her excitement in check; of course the infidel pilot might not be Matthew, but surely it was too much of a coincidence for it not to be him.

Saul thought for a moment. 'I should conduct a recce of the campsite, to confirm that Matthew is the prisoner. That done, we would have the element of surprise and the fire-power to carry out an assault to free Matthew at first light tomorrow.'

'Won't the boy go back to his people and report our meeting?' Joanne asked.

Saul slid a finely honed knife from his belt. 'I think you should go for a walk just now,' he said.

Joanne looked at him in confusion, and then suddenly realised what he was planning to do. 'You can't kill the boy!' she exclaimed. 'You can't trade Matthew's life for his.' It was morally wrong; besides, she would never be able to live with her guilt, knowing she had traded the boy's life for the life of the man she loved.

Saul looked dismissive. 'How else are we going to get Matthew back?'

Joanne strode across to her horse, hobbled with the others and eating fodder out of a nosebag. She slipped the straps on one of her saddlebags and withdrew a small leather pouch. She walked back over to Saul and opened the leather bag, upturning it to spill shiny gold coins she had obtained from a bank in Jerusalem into her hand. The sight of the coins made everyone hold their breath.

'I am sure that Abdul-Hamid will be persuaded to trade his prisoner for gold,' Joanne said. 'All we need to do is set up a meeting with him and haggle over a price.'

Saul grinned, stroking his beard. 'I have not met a man in Palestine who would not sell his whole family for what you hold in your hand. Maybe your plan will avoid blood-shed. Any attack would no doubt catch up women and children in the crossfire.'

'Good,' Joanne said, replacing the gold coins in the bag.

'I'll send the boy back to his people with a message that we are prepared to pay good money for the prisoner,' said Saul. 'I think if you give the boy one of those coins it will induce Abdul-Hamid to meet with us, but I will warn you, he has a reputation for double-crossing and is something of an outcast among the tribes around here.'

'What do you suggest?' Joanne asked.

'That I get one of my men to volunteer – for a few of your coins – to go with the boy and pass on the message,' Saul said. He turned to his men; those 'few' coins would be a substantial amount of money to them. He spoke and one of his men stepped forward. He was young and due to be married in a month's time; the money would help set up a future for his wife and himself.

'Pesach says he will go with the boy to the camp,' Saul said, placing his hand on the young man's shoulder. 'He is one of my best, and he speaks Arabic.'

Joanne extended her hand to the young man, who took it gingerly. 'This is a down payment for you,' she said, slipping five golden coins into his fingers. 'You get another five when you are safely returned.'

Pesach thanked Joanne and turned to Saul for his instructions. Saul had worked out a site where he could position his men and the precious Maxim gun should the Bedouin attempt to take what they had by force.

'Tell Hamid that there are many of us . . . around a hundred . . . and tell him to come to this place over there. The meeting is to take place when the sun is rising. No sooner, no later, and ensure that you guide him on a path that takes you toward the rising sun. It is essential that he bring the European prisoner with him for the exchange. Do you have any questions?'

Pesach shook his head.

'Get the boy to guide you to the camp, and for his efforts he will be rewarded with one of the coins when we make the exchange.' Saul clapped Pesach on the shoulders. 'Good luck, lad. See you at sunrise.'

Pesach and the goat boy set off towards the Bedouin camp and Saul gathered in his men and briefed them on the positions they were to take up the next morning. The Maxim machine-gun was unloaded and assembled. Saul sited it where it would have the best spread of bullets, and he also planned to have the rising sun at their backs at first light. Now it was only a matter of waiting and praying that Abdul-Hamid's greed would induce him to the meeting.

In the early hours of the morning, while the stars sparkled above, Saul roused Joanne and his men. They ate a cold breakfast of tinned bully beef and dispersed to their locations in the surrounding hilly country. Joanne and Saul remained together to meet with Abdul-Hamid and his party – if they came.

'At least you and I can afford to have a hot cup of tea,' Saul said when his men were gone into the night to their positions. 'A fire might help guide Abdul-Hamid to us, and we may as well be comfortable.'

Soon a small fire blazed into life and Saul placed the blackened tea urn over it.

Joanne's nerves were at breaking point. The waiting was terrible and the tea would help steady her. She and Saul sat beside the fire, sipping the hot, sweet tea in silence, both deep in their own thoughts. Eventually Saul rose from beside the fire to gaze down into the small valley they had chosen for the meeting. If he were the Arab leader travelling to this meeting he would have outriders to clear the flanks,

Saul worried, even though he had concealed his men to avoid detection by outriders.

Saul stood very still, just watching, with the sun warming his back.

'What is it?' Joanne asked, rising to her feet to join him.

'Over there,' he said, pointing at a distant ridge. 'Dust.'

Joanne strained to observe the dust and finally made out the slight shimmer. She had to admire Saul's eyesight; in this country finely honed senses kept a man alive.

After a few long minutes they could see around twenty men on horseback travelling slowly towards them.

'Abdul-Hamid,' Saul grunted. 'Leave the talking to me.'

Joanne did not question his command; she knew that in the Arab culture it was an affront for women to address men to whom they were not related. It rankled to remain out of the negotiations, but she knew Saul was right. Joanne raised the scarf around her face so that only her eyes were showing and ensured that she had a firm grip on the revolver hidden in a fold of her long flowing dress.

As the column approached across the shallow valley Joanne scanned the men for Matthew, but she could see no sign of him.

Saul took a step forward, his rifle cradled in his arm and his finger on the trigger.

'I am Aban, and I will translate for my master, Abdul-Hamid,' one of the men said in English.

'Where is the man I sent with your goat boy and the prisoner you hold?' Saul asked bluntly in the same language.

'My master is not a trusting man, although beloved of Allah. He demands that you show him the money that you have promised for the infidel pilot we have at our camp.'

Saul removed the leather pouch, which Joanne had given to him for just this purpose, and opened it so the coins were visible. He could see one man at the head of the column lean forward to stare at the glittering gold and guessed he that must be Abdul-Hamid. If anything went wrong, Saul knew who to kill first.

'You will get this money when you return my man to me, along with the infidel prisoner,' he said.

The man Saul had identified as Abdul-Hamid said something to his translator, who turned to Saul. 'He says that if you go with us to the camp he will give you both men for the money you carry, and he also asks where are the hundreds of men you are supposed to have with you.'

'Watching us as we speak. They are heavily armed should your master foolishly attempt to seize the money,' Saul replied.

Abdul-Hamid sat back on his horse and smiled. Just then Saul and Joanne heard the outbreak of gunfire from the distant ridges, but none of it was directed down to where they stood. Saul quickly guessed what had happened: somehow the Bedouin had turned the tables on them and had sent out men to attack his positions on the ridge. Both he and Joanne were helpless against the party of armed men surrounding them.

The Arab chief continued to smile and his eyes flicked to Joanne. A cold shiver of fear ran through her body. She gripped the pistol and curled her finger around the trigger. Better to die by her own hand than at the hands of these men watching her with a terrible expectation.

'My master thinks you should give him both the money and the woman now, and he will promise you a quick death, unlike the death your man received at his hands last night. The gunfire you hear is from our Ottoman friends, who have your Englishman. They arrived late yesterday and my master made the trade for him. They kindly decided to stay with us and ride out to attack your vast force of . . . it must be six men, given that you lost one last night.'

Just as Aban finished speaking, the sound of the Maxim shattered the early morning air and Saul was stunned to see men falling from their horses before his eyes. He had instructed his son the previous evening to man the heavy machine-gun and he was now pouring a deadly stream of .303 bullets into the close ranks of the Bedouin leader's party. Men screamed in fear and horses whinnied in pain as the bullets tore into them.

Abdul-Hamid wheeled his horse around and fled with the handful of his surviving men. One man who had not been wounded but felled from his horse drew a wicked-looking scimitar and charged Saul, screaming in Arabic. Saul calmly levelled his rifle and waited until the man was almost upon him before firing. The high-velocity bullet ripped into the man's stomach, knocking him to the ground, and Saul stepped forward to chamber another round, shooting him in the head.

He turned and shouted to Joanne, who had her pistol out and even now fired at a wounded Arab attempting to regain his feet. She saw him look at her in surprise before collapsing from the bullet that had hit him in the heart.

Both dashed for their horses hobbled a short distance behind them, quickly releasing the ropes. They flung themselves on the mounts and galloped towards the ridge where the Maxim was now firing long bursts at an unseen target.

Both dismounted and led their horses up the steep incline, until they reached the top of the ridge, where they saw Benjamin and his offsider serving the machine-gun with belts of ammunition. Now they could see the khaki uniforms of Turkish soldiers some three hundred yards away and Saul calculated at least twenty men belonging to a mounted Turkish camel unit. He also counted at least ten enemy bodies strewn across the gentler slope on the other side of the ridge.

The Turkish soldiers were obviously retreating and they fell out of sight behind a slope. The Maxim fell silent. Saul led his horse over to where his son sat behind the machine-gun. The boy looked stunned.

'Well done, Benjamin,' Saul said, patting his son on the head. 'You saved our lives.'

Pale under his olive skin, Benjamin said, 'They surprised us. Had it not been for Adar here spotting the Turkish assault from our flank, we would not be alive. We were mostly watching you in the valley, but fortunately I had zeroed the Maxim onto the position you had marked out and was able to divert fire away from the Ottomans for a moment.'

'It worked,' Saul said. 'Where are the others?' he asked, scanning the positions he had allocated further down the ridge.

'They were overrun, we're all that's left,' Benjamin replied with a tremor in his voice. 'I'm sorry that I couldn't save them, but they fought hard and took some of the Otto-mans with them when they died.'

'Then we four are all who are left,' Saul said quietly. 'At least we still have enough horses and supplies to fight our way out, if necessary, and return to Jerusalem.'

'No!' Joanne said fiercely. 'If the Turks have Matthew, then we go after them.'

The three men stared at her.

'From what I could determine, we are outnumbered by at least ten to one,' Saul said. 'And these are trained sol-diers, unlike Abdul-Hamid's rabble, who I suspect will also come after us for the gold we carry. I guess that puts the odds around fifteen to one. We have to return to Jerusalem.

I'm afraid we will have to leave Matthew in Turkish captivity.' Saul looked genuinely sorry at this decision.

'He is your dear friend and he did not hesitate to help you last year,' Joanne said, feeling her body start to shake, as much from anger as from what she had just been through. 'Haven't you yourself fought against your enemy when the odds were stacked against you, and yet still prevailed?'

Saul frowned and tried to balance the foolishness of love against the reality of their situation. He was bitter that he had lost men who had trusted his command and he felt a great urge to take revenge against the Bedouin who had contravened all the rules of the desert concerning respect and hospitality. It was no wonder that Abdul-Hamid was an outcast among his own kind. 'He who dares will prevail' had always been Saul's motto, and the last thing the Turks would expect was such a tiny party coming after them.

'I will only ask my son and Adar to come with us if they wish to volunteer,' Saul said, turning to his son.

'The rest of the gold I have will be theirs,' Joanne said. 'To be shared with the families of the men killed on this expedition. I promise you that.'

'We will do it not for the money but to save my friend and to have revenge on those who killed my men,' Saul replied. Benjamin and Adar nodded in agreement.

Joanne experienced a moment of joy. No matter what the odds, she knew she would win back Matthew's freedom and together they would return home to their children.

The rough and bumpy ride on the camel was far better than remaining in the Bedouin camp, Matthew thought. What he had witnessed last night had been the worst example of man's cruelty towards his fellow man. Matthew had seen the stranger enter the camp with the goat boy and he'd watched with interest as he conversed with Abdul-Hamid outside his tent.

Then suddenly the stranger had been pounced upon by Abdul-Hamid's men, stripped naked and bound. Before his eyes, the stranger was beaten with a whip. Matthew felt great pity for his treatment but was horrified to see the man dragged naked onto a smouldering fire to scream in agony as the hot coals cooked his flesh. Matthew felt himself gag at the pungent smell. His own sense of impotence made the man's cries even harder to bear. Eventually there was silence and Matthew knew the man's suffering was over.

'Who was that?' Matthew asked Aban as he was passing by.

Aban slinked over to Matthew and said quietly, 'He was a Jew, the true enemy of my people, and my master has sent him to the fires of hell.'

'Why was he here?' Matthew pushed, but before Aban could answer there was a stir in the camp as a contingent of camel-mounted Turkish troops rode in. They looked down from their saddles with expressions of disgust and anger at the blackened body still manacled in the campfire, but they spoke civilly with Abdul-Hamid, who pointed at Matthew under the palm tree.

'I must go,' Aban said nervously and slipped away.

Abdul-Hamid and a Turkish soldier approached Matthew; he could see that the Ottoman was an officer of equivalent rank to himself. The man wore a sword and pistol at his side and was dressed in battle uniform.

'How are you, old chap?' The Turkish officer asked by way of greeting, and Matthew was stunned to hear the Turk speaking with an Oxford accent.

'I could be better,' Matthew replied. 'But after what I witnessed here last night, I have to say I am hoping that the bastard beside you is about to hand me over as a prisoner of war. The longer I remain here, the greater the chance I'll enjoy the same fate as that unfortunate man in the fire.'

'What has happened here is barbaric,' the officer said. He was a man with clear olive skin and jet-black hair slicked back with oil, and Matthew guessed he was in his late thirties. He had a bushy moustache and was over six feet tall. All in all he made a rather dashing figure.

'I am Captain Yuzbasi Barak,' the Turk said without offering his hand. 'I have come to exchange you for a couple of cases of rifles and ammunition. That must be the going price for Australian pilots. I had planned to leave with you tonight, but my Bedouin friend has brought to my attention a plot to free you.'

Matthew gaped at the Turkish officer in disbelief.

'From what Abdul-Hamid was able to extract from the Jew before he died, the expedition to save you is planned by an American woman, Miss Joanne Barrington, and that Jewish scourge, Saul Rosenblum. But I am afraid your friends are in for a nasty surprise in the morning. However, that won't concern you as we will be leaving at first light and taking you with us. In the meantime, I will appeal to Abdul-Hamid to leave you in my care overnight in case they decide to continue their macabre amusements.'

Matthew was at least thankful that he was now a prisoner of war, rather than an infidel worth only what could be fetched in ransom. He prayed that his old friend Saul had anticipated that things might not go to plan. All their lives depended on it. The mention of Joanne in the rescue party had at first stunned Matthew but now all he could do was worry about her safety. At the same time, he counted the seconds until he could once again look into her eyes and tell her how much he loved her.

Still shackled, Matthew was given shelter under a small tent but still closely guarded by the Turks. All he could think of during the long night was that Joanne and Saul were somewhere out there planning to free him. Worse was the knowledge that a 'nasty surprise' was coming their way in the morning. Matthew felt utterly helpless.

The next morning Matthew, bleary-eyed with lack of sleep, was shoved towards a camel. He was helped aboard the great beast and when he glanced around he could see that the Bedouin camp was alive with men mounting horses and riding out. Some time during the night many of the Turkish soldiers, including Barak, seemed to have disappeared and he guessed that they had left on a mission. This made him feel uneasy. Only a handful of Turkish soldiers remained.

The order was given and Matthew's small caravan of camels plodded north into the rising heat of the day. It was then that he heard the distant sound of gunfire and the rapid tearing sound of a heavy machine-gun. Matthew hoped that the machine-gun did not belong to the Turks. He did not think so as he had made it a point yesterday evening to try to evaluate the weapons and kit of the Turkish patrol. He had not seen a Maxim and could only conclude the deadly fire was from Saul's forces.

They rode on for half an hour to the base of a hill, where the order to halt was given. Matthew was helped from his camel and he had to stretch to ease his wasted limbs grown weak from lack of exercise. They waited in the shade of the camels, and after another half-hour Matthew could see a rising column of dust. Within minutes exhausted and shocked Turkish troops straggled in. Without understanding what they were saying to each other, Matthew could tell that they were falling back in a retreat as one or two had lost their rifles, and a few were wounded. Barak was among them and he had blood on the sleeve of his khaki uniform.

The Turkish officer assembled his men and gave them orders. It sounded as though Barak was berating his men, who stared at the ground in silence.

Saul has beaten them, Matthew thought in exhilaration. *You beauty, you old bastard!* At the same time, the thought crept in that Saul's own men may have taken casualties; Saul himself might be hurt or, worse, dead. What if Joanne had been hurt, or worse? He didn't want to think of all the terrible possibilities.

It wasn't until that night, when the military patrol stopped to make camp, that Matthew found out from Barak what had happened.

'Your rescue party was very good,' Barak said, squatting beside Matthew. 'They turned the tables on my men.'

'Did your men inflict casualties on the rescuers?' Matthew asked, not really expecting the Turk to answer.

'If you are wondering about the American woman, I can reassure you that she was not among those we killed in our attack,' Barak said. 'You look surprised – yes, I know of Miss Barrington. She is a remarkable woman. Now, no more questions. I can tell you nothing else.'

Barak rose and walked back to his men gathered around a small campfire. Matthew watched him as he strolled away. He couldn't quite put his finger on it, but something about the Turkish officer intrigued him.

IO

Inspector Jack Firth feared no man – with the exception of the inspector general of the police force. Jack had been summoned to the man's office and he stood nervously before him, knowing that his summons had to do with the damned Schumann file.

'Inspector Firth,' the inspector general said in a cold voice, 'I have been directed by the government to suspend any further enquiries into the matter I raised with you. The Schumann file has been sent to a parliamentary body and what they do with it is up to them. From what I understand, you have been very lucky. I have no doubt that had the investigation continued, you would have found yourself in the dock answering charges of perverting the course of justice – or worse. Someone up there must like you. Count yourself lucky this time, and from now on I don't want to have to see you in my office unless it is to brief me on a solved case. You can consider yourself reprimanded, and it will be noted in your service record.'

George Macintosh had promised to make the problem go away and it appeared that he had done just that. But Jack also knew that this assistance came at a high price. 'Sir, I can assure you that if you had had the opportunity to examine the file in more detail you would have discovered that I was innocent of any indiscretion –'

'Don't give me that baloney,' the inspector general cut in. 'You and I both know that you've cut corners for someone, and if I hear that you are taking any backhanders, I will personally come after you, do I make myself clear?'

'Yes, sir,' Jack answered dutifully, realising that he should have kept his mouth shut.

'I will give you credit as having a good record on the force,' the inspector general continued in a more conciliatory tone. 'Nevertheless, I expect you to have a suspect in the dock over the Mary Jackson murder before the week is out. The newspapers are bleating that we have little concern for dead prostitutes and I expect you to silence their protests.'

'I have someone in mind for the murder,' Jack answered, feeling more at ease. 'I hope to have it tied up by tomorrow.'

'Good.' The inspector general looked down at the scattered papers on his desk. 'See that you do.' He waved his hand dismissively and Jack left his office as quickly and as quietly as he could.

In the hallway he let out a great sigh of relief. Bloody Macintosh could do just about anything he wanted, Jack reckoned. Even get away with murder.

Jack already suspected that the murdered prostitute's pimp had killed her and he had dragged the man in off the streets to extract a confession. But Lenny Johnson had proved tougher than the average criminal and had resisted

the beating delivered by Jack in his office, away from pry-
ing eyes. So Jack had dictated a statement to Lenny, which
Lenny had then signed, albeit reluctantly. He didn't have
any choice really; otherwise he'd find himself swinging at
the Darlinghurst gallows. Lenny knew from the trenches
that to survive you had to put your own life ahead of others'.

Jack smiled when Lenny was released. He walked down
the hall to his office to fetch two of his detectives and line
up a couple of uniformed police. It was time to snatch the
man who would most definitely hang for the brutal murder
of Mary Jackson.

Harry Griffiths had no time to react when the front door
of his terrace house was smashed open and a team of uniformed and plain-clothes police tumbled in. At their head
was Detective Inspector Jack Firth, his pistol levelled at
Harry.

Harry's wife screamed and Harry was glad that his children were at school so as not to be witness to what was
happening.

'Harold Griffiths,' Jack said in a formal voice, 'we are
here to arrest you for the murder of Mary Jackson.'

Harry stood with the newspaper he had been reading in
one hand and glared at his old nemesis. 'You bloody well
know that I had nothing to do with that woman's death,' he
spat. 'What is it? Settling old scores? You don't have a leg to
stand on, Firth.'

Jack slipped the small pistol into the pocket of his suit,
took off his hat and rubbed his brow with the back of his
hand.

Harry turned to his wife. 'Leave us, luv,' he said gently.
'I'll only be gone a short while.'

His wife hesitated, then left the room, and Harry turned his attention back to Jack. 'What bloody evidence do you have?'

'A statement from your old cobber, Lenny, saying that you were seen by him entering the house of Mary Jackson on the day she was last seen alive, and when he saw you come out a short time later you were covered in blood and in a distressed state mumbling that she deserved to die.'

Harry shook his head in disbelief. 'You made a deal with Lenny, didn't you?' he said. 'That rubbish won't stand up in court.'

'I don't know what you're talking about,' Jack replied with a smirk. 'I can only believe what a witness says to me in his statement. Why would your cobber make up a story about you? Clearly he felt it was his duty to put aside his feelings for you and tell us the truth.'

'That's almost laughable,' Harry said as two uniformed police stepped forward to grip his elbows, formalising the arrest.

'Take him away,' Jack said, replacing his hat.

Harry swung around and yelled over his shoulder to his wife in the next room. 'Get on to Major Duffy straightaway and tell him that I am being taken unlawfully by Jack Firth.'

'Duffy won't be able to save you from going down,' Firth said cheerfully. 'His day is coming soon enough, but let's get you hung first.'

Harry felt a chill run through him. Not just for his fate, but for the fate of his friend and employer, Sean Duffy. It was a set-up, and Firth was planning on getting rid of them both.

Mrs Griffiths was almost hysterical as she sat in Sean Duffy's office blurting out the events of the past couple of hours.

Sean had sent his clerk to fetch a hot cup of tea for the woman, hoping that it might calm her down.

'Inspector Firth said that he was arresting Harry for the Mary Jackson murder?' Sean confirmed between the woman's sobs.

'Yes, Major Duffy,' Harry's wife answered, accepting the cup of tea offered to her by the sympathetic clerk. 'I heard everything from the next room and I heard Inspector Firth say that my Harry would hang.'

'I can reassure you, Mrs Griffiths, that your husband will not be hanged. We all know he did not kill the unfortunate woman. I will do everything in heaven and hell to have Harry back with you before too long.'

Mrs Griffiths's crying eased and she took a sip of her tea. She looked up at Sean with a grateful, weak smile. 'If anyone can save my Harry it's you, Major Duffy,' she said. 'He worships the ground you walk on.'

Sean shifted uncomfortably in his chair. 'Leave it with me and go home to the kids.'

Mrs Griffiths rose, shaking Sean's hand with both of her own.

When she was gone, Sean reached for his walking cane and hat. He excused himself from the office and began walking. By the time he had reached police HQ he was sweating, despite the cold day. He didn't think he would ever get used to walking on wooden legs; it was painful and exhausting and only his force of will kept him from giving up and retreating to a wheelchair.

Inside the police building he was forced to wait before he could see his client. Sean had expected this; Firth was not going to make it easy for him. Eventually Sean was shown to the cells, where he found Harry sporting a face blackened and swollen with bruises. Clearly Firth had already carried out an interrogation, Sean thought as Harry came to the bars to greet him.

'How are you, Harry?' Sean asked and immediately felt stupid for doing so, given the man's physical injuries.

'That bastard Firth did a number on me, but I signed nothing,' Harry spat, bringing up a glob of blood. The custody officer hovering nearby cautioned Harry about manners but both men ignored him.

'You have any idea why Firth would pick you up?' Sean asked, gripping the bars for support to ease the pain where his legs connected with the artificial limbs.

'I suppose we both know that the bastard has it in for us,' Harry replied, wiping the blood from his mouth with his shirtsleeve. 'He made a threat against you when he picked me up, so I would be watching your back closely, Major Duffy. That bastard Firth has realised that by locking me up he isolates you. He says he has a sworn statement by Lenny Johnson that he saw me coming out of the Mary Jackson house the day she was murdered covered in blood, and saying that she deserved to die.'

'Don't worry, Harry,' Sean said. 'If I remember rightly, the day Mary Jackson was killed you were on a job for me on the other side of the harbour. Even Firth must know that Lenny's statement will not stand up in a trial. I don't know why he would attempt such a stupid thing as to frame you for the woman's death.'

'Maybe, with me inside, he could arrange for you to have an accident,' Harry suggested and Sean took him seriously.

'I think you could be right,' he said quietly. 'He must have worked out by now that we had the Schumann file placed in the inspector general's hands, and that would make us very unpopular with him.'

'Will the police go after him over that?' Harry asked.

Sean shook his head. 'Sadly, the last thing I heard was that the file had been sent over to Parliament House. I can only guess that George Macintosh pulled a few strings and has had the matter filed away for good. Firth has more lives than a bloody cat.'

'You have got to make sure that you take every precaution you can, Major Duffy,' Harry said. 'Lay low until I can get a hearing for bail.'

'I'll do that,' Sean replied. 'In the meantime, sign nothing. We will have you free before you can say Jack Robinson.'

'From anyone else I might have my doubts, but not from you, boss,' Harry said with a feeble smile. 'Keep your head down and I'll see you soon.'

Sean gripped Harry's hand through the bars and then left the gloomy place to return to the street. He did so with a deeply uneasy feeling; there was more to the matter than Firth settling a personal score. Why was it that the name of George Macintosh kept cropping up at the edges of everything? Why would it be in Macintosh's interests to frame Harry? To get him out of the way – if Firth or Macintosh were really planning to have him killed. But why would Macintosh want him killed? He thought of Giselle and her son and the new terms of Patrick Macintosh's will. George Macintosh was capable of anything, even having a child murdered. And he would benefit by his nephew's death. If this was what he was plotting, Macintosh would know that Sean would be a threat to any such heinous crime. Sean had also had an affair with Louise, and he didn't think Macintosh would take that kindly. Put all these reasons in a pot and stir it and you had a strong motive to have him killed.

Sean paused in his painful walk back to his office. 'God almighty,' he swore softly. Could Macintosh really be so evil that he would scheme to have his nephew murdered?

The elite Australian Club in Sydney's Macquarie Street had been founded in 1838 by the leading members of colonial society. That George Macintosh had been accepted for membership demonstrated to society that he was a man of worth. Here he rubbed shoulders with the most influential men in finance, politics, law and the public service. It was within these hallowed rooms, with their rich carpets, leather chairs, glass-fronted bookcases, chandeliers and prized art, that George conducted a great deal of his business.

He lounged back in his great leather chair, newspaper on his lap, armed with a Scotch. The gentle clack of billiard balls wafted in from a room nearby, and the smell of expensive cigars filled the air.

'Another Scotch, sir?' asked a well-dressed waiter.

'No,' George replied, picking up the paper, and the waiter discreetly disappeared into the background. George opened the paper and his eye was caught by the headline of the morning *Gazette*. A man had been arrested for the murder of Mary Jackson. The article went on to name the legendary Detective Inspector Jack Firth as the man who had arrested Harry Griffiths. Sydneysiders could breathe a sigh of relief that a callous murderer was behind bars.

'Good show, Firth,' George muttered. With Griffiths off the streets it would be easier to get to the damned lawyer who had had the audacity to sleep with Louise. More importantly, Duffy had to be removed from the picture so that George could dispose of his sister-in-law and nephew. A boating accident was definitely the best way to go with her.

It would look like an unfortunate event that was not all that uncommon around Sydney's waterways.

Smiling, George closed the paper and laid it on a small table by his chair. Maybe he would have another drink before returning to the office.

Wallarie was confused. The current dreams of black water did not seem to have any meaning and the ancestor spirits were of no help interpreting them. He sat cross-legged in the shade of the temporary bark shelter he had constructed and poked at the earth with a stick. The sun was low on the horizon as it went to drink at a billabong beyond the plains before it returned in the morning, giving life and heat to this vast country.

Never mind that the ancestor spirits had told him not to go near any whitefellas, Wallarie decided that it was time to visit his old friend, the Lutheran pastor at the Glen View mission. He and Karl von Fellmann would sit under the bumbil tree in the front yard of the station house and ruminate on what the dreams meant. It had been almost a year since he had visited Glen View, and he could argue with the spirits of the ancestors at a later time, Wallarie thought, standing and stretching his limbs to relieve the ache that had lately come to his joints.

Karolina Schumann and Pastor Karl von Fellmann had been guests for dinner at the station house and were leaving in the horse-drawn sulky for the mission station a short distance away. Karolina had been able to catch up with her daughter and grandson, while Karl had talked with the station manager and Angus MacDonald about ordering

133

medicines he needed to treat the Aboriginal people who came to him for help.

Karl took the reins and urged the horse into motion. The horse knew its way in the dark and walked on easily. They had not been travelling long when Karolina gasped.

'Over there!' she said, pointing in the direction of the bumbil tree silhouetted against the stars. 'I saw someone.'

Karl turned to stare into the dark and now he too could see the outline of a man standing and holding a long spear.

'Wallarie,' Karl murmured and brought the sulky to a stop, clambering over the side and striding towards the solitary figure.

'Hello, Pastor, you got any baccy?' Wallarie greeted.

Karl came to a stop before his old friend. 'We have been worried about you,' he said, restraining himself from grasping the old warrior and giving him a hug.

'I bin all right,' Wallarie replied with a smile that exposed his nicotine-stained teeth.

'You need to come with Mrs Schumann and myself to the mission house and have a good meal – and some tobacco.'

'Can't do that,' Wallarie replied. 'Dunno why, but ancestor spirits telling me no.'

Karl ignored his superstitious talk of spirits. 'Why did you come?' Karl asked. 'I know that it takes a lot to get you to venture out in the night.'

'Bad dreams about black water and *debil debils*,' Wallarie replied. 'Dunno what they mean. Making me worried something bad goin' to happen.'

Karl could see that the old man was worried, but he didn't know how he could help him. He could hardly start talking to him about Sigmund Freud's interpretation of dreams. 'Everything is worse in the dark, old friend. I wish you'd come home with me and eat. We can talk there, in front of the fire.'

Wallarie frowned. 'Maybe I go and dream some more,' he said. Then he turned and walked away, leaving Karl wondering whether he had been a figment of his imagination. There was always something eerie about the old warrior.

'It was him, wasn't it?' said Karolina as Karl resumed his seat and took the reins.

'It was Wallarie,' Karl confirmed. 'It has been a long time since I saw him last.'

'What did he want?'

'He wanted to talk to me about a strange dream he was having,' Karl said, flicking the reins. 'He said that he was dreaming about dark water.'

Karl heard Karolina's sharp intake of breath and glanced in her direction. She had her hands up to her face and even in the dim light of the sulky lantern he could see fear etched in her features. 'What is it?' he asked in alarm.

'The dream of dark water,' Karolina said, staring ahead into the darkness. 'I was speaking with Giselle tonight, and we both said how recently we had both been plagued by a disturbing dream of water. And now you say that the Aboriginal is having the same dream.' She turned to Karl. 'This could not be coincidence. What does it mean? I feel it has a terrible link with death – yet I cannot say why.'

Karl shook his head. 'It is just a coincidence,' he said softly. 'Wallarie is always babbling about strange things. Dreams do not predict our future. Only God can do that.'

'But the dreams?' Karolina said. 'It cannot be a coincidence.'

She fell into a deep silence and did not say another word all the way home.

★

In the sacred cave Wallarie sat before his small fire as the flames brought alive the ochre paintings on the walls depicting the life of his now dead people. Wallarie knew that he had annoyed the ancestor spirits by disobeying the command to stay away from the Europeans, and he accepted their punishment. He was going blind, his vision slowly blurring until eventually his world would be filled only with darkness.

Possums rustled in the treetops outside and the musty smell of ages permeated all corners of the cavern. This was a place where only men should enter. Wallarie began chanting his song, staring at the flames dancing small corroborees for him. After the constellations had wheeled across the southern skies he saw the dark water mixing with the flames. As he continued to stare beyond pictures of flames and water he saw a distorted face flowing with the water. Wallarie did not know the man's name but he had seen him before when he had flown on the night sky to a place far to the south. He had known then that the man was evil and now the meaning of the water became apparent.

A dingo howled from far away and its call brought the old warrior back to where he was in the world of living men.

'Bloody ancestor spirits,' he mumbled softly lest they hear him. 'Bugger a man around. Could have told me before.'

He knew that he had a duty to go to the pastor and warn him about a man who would bring death. But would he believe old Wallarie? He hadn't seemed too concerned when he'd tried to talk to him about the dream. Besides, the old warrior would have to find a way of delivering his warning without causing the dreaming spirits to become angry again; if they took his eyesight away after last time, who knew what they'd take away next time. Those ancestor spirits, they were such an easily annoyed mob.

II

The weeks of being confined to battalion HQ had been frustrating for Tom. The battalion had been pulled back behind the front line to conduct training, so at least they weren't in the thick of things without him. The regiment had had reinforcements sent up and for the platoon it had generally been a quiet time away from the horrors of the fighting.

But the lull fooled no one as the soldiers watched their officers hurrying backwards and forwards to brigade HQ for orders. This was simply a preparation to return renewed to the fighting. The German army had spent itself in its spring offensive and had fallen back on old defensive lines. There was even an optimism among the Allies that the Kaiser might be feeling the strain of the newly arrived American army entering the fray with fresh troops and an enthusiasm not yet blunted by the realities of trench warfare.

It was the height of summer and Tom sorted through a pile of newly issued gas masks while his platoon sat around a short distance during a break in their lessons on the use of the Lewis gun. The field was now dotted with drying flowers and browning grass as the sun beat down on the rolling fields. Birds could be heard above the distant thump of artillery shells, which reminded the men at rest that the war was always ready to welcome them back to hell.

Tom picked up a mask, searching quickly but thoroughly for any faults. He was diligent in his work as he knew the user's life might depend on its efficiency. He was being assisted by Private Dean, who had been detached from his section to carry out battalion duties for the day.

The young soldier passed Tom a mask. 'At least this got us out of a route march, Sarge,' he said, gazing over at the rest of the platoon. They had all been on a long training march and were now having a lesson from a young second lieutenant who had recently joined the battalion. It was obvious that Tom's platoon were humouring the young officer, whose keenness had not yet been dampened by the harsh realities of combat. The Lewis machine-gun had been the company's constant companion, and all knew it as well as any tool they had ever used.

'Who's your section commander now?' Tom asked, rejecting a mask that he found to have a hole in it.

'We got Lance Corporal Paddy Bourke,' Dean answered. 'I'm sure he'll get his second stripe when he takes over from Corporal Smithers.'

'You got a good man there,' Tom said. 'He'll look after your lot.'

'When you coming back to the platoon?' Dean asked.

Tom took out a pipe, stuffed the bowl with a plug of tobacco. 'How about we take a smoko break?' he said to

Dean, who was pleased to have a time away from the tedious but essential task of checking gas masks, even though he didn't smoke. Both men sat down on the drying grass and gazed across a paddock where fat cows grazed behind a low stone wall.

'You did well back a few weeks ago when the Hun almost overran us,' Tom said and he could see Dean grow warm with his praise.

'Thanks, Sarge,' he mumbled, ducking his head. 'I know it's not my place but I don't think you tried to kill Corporal Smithers,' he blurted out. 'I told the investigating officer that I saw Corporal Smithers cowering in the trench during the attack, but the adjutant didn't put that in my statement. I wouldn't have held it against you if you had done away with him anyway. He's a real bastard, that one. The things he was saying about you had to be lies.'

Tom puffed on his pipe, watching the smoke curl away on the hot air of the midday sun. 'What was he saying about me?'

'Well,' Dean squirmed, realising that he had started something now.

'C'mon, Private Dean, what was Corporal Smithers saying about me?'

'Well, that when we last had leave in the village, your fiancée was sleeping with him behind your back,' Dean replied awkwardly.

'A bloody lie,' Tom scoffed, but he could not forget the sight of Juliet waving to him tearfully as the truck drove away, and Smithers standing behind her, grinning with malice. The letters he had written to Juliet had not been answered, and that worried him. Something was wrong, and he only hoped it was the French mail system.

Both men were still sitting when Tom spotted the regimental sergeant major marching towards them. They jumped to their feet and stood to attention. 'Are you satisfied that all the masks here are ready for use, Sergeant Duffy?' he asked by way of greeting.

'Yes, sir,' Tom replied. 'Those over there failed the test.' He pointed to a much smaller pile of discarded masks.

'Good,' RSM Pink said. 'Private Dean, you are relieved of your duties here and are to report back to your platoon commander. As for you, Sergeant Duffy,' the RSM said, 'you are to report immediately to BHQ. Ensure that you are spick and span as you are to report to the commanding officer. So make sure your boots and brass are polished. I will be parading you within the hour.'

Tom did not need to ask why he was being paraded before the CO. At last it was time for his case to be heard.

The adjutant sat in a foldaway field chair in the corner of the CO's office while the battalion's commanding officer pored over his final report, flipping through statements. The adjutant sat very still as he watched his CO ruminating on what he had written in his summary.

'You are satisfied that your findings are correct?' the CO finally asked.

'Yes, sir,' the adjutant replied. 'I feel that Sergeant Duffy should be considered for a court-martial on the charge of attempted murder.'

'Hmm,' the CO sighed, looking up at his adjutant. 'We're going back into the lines in a few days. All I have to add to your report is my concurrence on your findings, and the Sergeant Duffy matter will be handed over to the provost marshal.'

'That is where the matter belongs, sir,' the adjutant said. 'I feel sorry for the man. It is not his fault that he was born with a stroke of the tarbrush in him. From what I have heard, the black blood makes them unreliable and shiftless. Besides . . .'

'Besides, how do you explain that Sergeant Duffy was awarded a DCM when he was actually recommended for the VC?' the CO finished for him. 'But then again, how do you explain that his platoon commander's report is on my desk recommending Sergeant Duffy for a Military Medal for his actions in the last bash by the Huns?'

The adjutant squirmed at the obvious rebuke from his CO. 'I am sorry, sir, but I can only base my findings on the evidence placed before me and what is known of the Aboriginal people.'

'I understand that, adj,' the CO said. 'As you are aware, I trust your judgement. Send Sergeant Duffy in.'

Tom was waiting at attention outside the office door of the CO in the company of the RSM, who stood stiffly to attention with his swagger stick tucked under his arm. Tom noted that there were no soldiers to escort him away if he was to be charged. Not that their absence necessarily meant he wasn't facing a lengthy time in a prison.

The door opened and the adjutant poked his head out. 'March Sergeant Duffy in, RSM,' he commanded.

Barking his orders, the RSM led Tom into the CO's office, where Tom snapped a smart salute on the orders of the RSM and remained stiffly at attention before the CO's desk. Tom was aware that he was sweating and his heart was beating too quickly.

'Stand Sergeant Duffy at ease, RSM,' the CO said quietly and the RSM barked out the order. Tom relaxed only slightly, and hoped that his trembling knees would not give way under him. From the corner of his eye he could see the adjutant standing to his left just behind him, his hands behind his back.

'Sergeant Duffy,' the CO said, 'a thorough enquiry into the matter occurring a few weeks ago between yourself and Corporal Smithers has been conducted. The adjutant, as the investigating officer, has given me his report, which is now on my desk.' He tapped a close file. 'He has concluded that there is enough evidence to have you charged with attempted murder and it is up to me to sign the report and concur with his findings.'

Tom legs shook and his palms began to sweat. His whole future hung in the balance. The CO had paused and Tom could see that he was deep in thought, clearly struggling with some sort of problem. Finally, he spoke.

'Sergeant Duffy, based on my personal knowledge of your contribution to the battalion, and that of Corporal Smithers's reputation as well . . . Also based on the purely circumstantial and inconclusive statements of witnesses, and the rather strong support from your own officers and RSM Pink, I am not going to concur with the adjutant. Instead, I am going to recommend that you return to your role as platoon sergeant under Mr Sullivan. I am going to initiate an investigation into the possibility that Corporal Smithers's wound was self-inflicted. I am sure that the adjutant will nominate a suitable investigating officer in that matter. That is all, RSM. You can march Sergeant Duffy out and return him to his platoon duties.'

Tom felt as though his legs really would give way under him now.

'Yes, sir,' the RSM barked, snapping a smart salute and delivering new commands at the top of his voice to Tom to salute, turn about and quick march from the office.

As he left, Tom caught a glimpse of the adjutant. He looked stunned.

The door was immediately closed behind him and Tom felt the heavy weight of the investigation fall from his shoulders.

'Well done, Tom,' the RSM said quietly and accompanied the goodwill with one of his rare smiles. 'The CO knew what he was doing, and when I get my hands on that maggot, Smithers, he will wish he were dead.'

'You know I never shot him,' Tom said.

'I knew that,' the RSM replied. 'Wouldn't have put in a good word to the CO if I didn't think you were innocent, would I?'

'Thanks, sir,' Tom said. 'It'll be good to be back with Mr Sullivan and the boys. I've missed them.'

'Well, Sergeant Duffy,' the RSM said, returning to his gruff demeanour, 'if I find any of the gas masks you passed as fit today are faulty, I will have your guts for garters.'

Tom grinned. 'Thanks again, sir,' he said and turned to march away.

He was welcomed back into the platoon with broad smiles and slaps on the back.

'The boys are glad to have you back,' Dan Frogan said.

'Despite the fact I'm a blackfella,' Tom replied with wry smile.

'They don't see you as anything but a bloody good NCO. The men trust your judgement and courage, and don't you forget that,' Dan said fiercely.

'Sorry, Dan,' Tom replied contritely. 'It really is good to be back.'

'We go up tomorrow morning,' Dan said, changing the subject. 'Mr Sullivan wants to have a briefing with you in half an hour at platoon HQ.'

Tom nodded and stared off across the fields. They were pitted here and there by craters caused by German long-range artillery attempting to disrupt the rear-echelon areas. The firing had been random and the battalion was lucky enough to escape its effects. Not so a small herd of cows that had scored a direct hit and now lay swelling black under the summer sun.

Tom was seriously worried about Juliet's silence. He wished he could seek emergency leave to visit her but he knew that it would not be granted because the battalion was about to move up into the front lines. Even if he were to be granted leave, he didn't want to let down his cobbers. Tom reflected on the fact that he thought of the men as cobbers. Back in Queensland he would have not gained the same respect from the Europeans he came into contact with, but in hell, race had little meaning, and men only judged you on your ability to keep them alive. Heaven was returning to Australia with Juliet as his bride, but he was concerned that he would always be labelled as a blackfella and looked down on by the whites. If only they knew he was wealthier than half of Queensland put together, Tom thought with a savage satisfaction. Maybe wealth would wipe the smirks from their faces.

With a sigh, Tom rose and made his way to the platoon HQ for the briefing. He found Lieutenant Sullivan squatting over a map.

'Sergeant Duffy reporting, sir,' Tom said.

Sullivan glanced up and broke into a broad smile. 'Welcome back, Sergeant Duffy,' he said and rose to extend his hand. 'We have missed your company.'

Tom accepted the outstretched hand. 'Good to be back, boss.'

'Pull up some grass,' Sullivan said, resuming his position

hovering over the map marked with many lines in red, black and blue indicating trench systems and terrain.

Tom squatted over the map and both men stared at the picture it presented. 'At 0100 we move out to our positions here,' Sullivan said, using the mouthpiece of his pipe to point to the position on the map. 'We take this route,' he indicated it with his pipe, 'and we have to be in position before first light.'

Tom nodded. As the senior NCO his secondary role was to assume command if the platoon commander was in some way put out of action. He therefore had to be aware of the tactical situation as if he were in command himself.

Sullivan glanced at him. 'Thought you might like to know that Corporal Smithers has been listed as AWOL from the hospital. He up and left when he was informed that there was going to be an investigation concerning his possible self-inflicted gunshot wound.'

Tom was not surprised that the man had deserted. Despite his intimidating size and vicious nature, the man was a coward.

'At least it's a chance to promote Lance Corporal Paddy Bourke to command his section. What do you think of that idea?'

'Bloody good decision,' Tom replied. 'Paddy has proved his worth many times.'

'Good,' Sullivan said, returning his attention to the map. 'I'll call him up and present him with his stripes after dinner tonight, when the platoon is assembled. I just wanted to hear what you thought, before making the decision.'

Three days later the men of the battalion knew they had walked once again through the gates of hell. This time they were joined by an American infantry regiment receiving its blooding among the Australian veterans.

They were welcomed to the front with shelling by the dreaded German 4.2 and 5.9 artillery guns firing high explosives. The shelling commenced around midnight and Tom's platoon bunkered down in their newly dug trench as the heavy artillery rounds slammed into the earth, exploding with a force that made the ground tremble like a wounded animal. With clods of dirt showering down, Tom wondered if Wallarie was correct in saying the earth was alive, because the wounding by the German shells seemed to be proving him right.

Tom wondered how the young and inexperienced Americans were coping with their first exposure to the most feared aspect of trench warfare. Just waiting, praying that a shell did not explode close enough to do serious damage, stretched nerves beyond breaking. Not all artillery explosions resulted in mutilated bodies; Tom had seen bodies of soldiers without a mark on them – they had been killed by the concussive effect of the artillery blast. The massive force of compressed air produced by a shell going off could cause irreparable internal damage, although the main cause of death was mostly from the red-hot jagged fragments of metal cast off by the artillery round breaking up. Or the lead balls sprayed out from shells exploding overhead for maximum damage.

Tom had his eyes closed and could feel the terrible fear rise up in him. Each exploding round caused his whole body to twitch in expectation of agonising death. He forced himself to remain crouched and not to give in to the urge to jump up screaming and run away from an enemy he could not fight back against. Tom knew the terror he was experiencing was being felt right along the line of trenches.

For a moment he opened his eyes and could see Lieutenant Sullivan curled up with his arms around his head, trembling with each crash and thump of the earth. Time lost all meaning and Tom closed his eyes again in an attempt to bring Juliet's face and smile into his world of terror. But this did not work: all he could think of was not being killed or maimed by the explosions.

Suddenly he felt his whole body lifted a few inches off the bottom of the trench as a huge round impacted at the edge of the trench only yards away. Tom knew it was a German 5.9 centimetre shell because he recognised its incoming sound.

Men screamed and shouted, and when Tom opened his eyes he could see that the section of trench beside him had collapsed inwards, burying alive anyone who had been beneath the lip of the trenches. Without hesitation, Tom snatched an entrenching shovel and scrambled on his hands and knees to the freshly cut earth of the trench. He was joined by Lieutenant Sullivan and two other soldiers who used tin helmets and their hands to dig furiously into the pile of earth. The shelling continued but Tom no longer had time to reflect on his own fear. None of them said a word as they grunted and gasped, digging through dirt until a leg appeared.

'Grab it and pull like buggery,' Tom yelled above the crashing noise. Mike Sullivan grabbed the booted ankle and he and Tom yanked with all their strength. The leg came out easily and Mike Sullivan fell back, gripping a man's leg cut off by shrapnel above the knee. For a brief moment he sat on his rear holding the leg and staring at it with glazed eyes.

'Keep digging!' Tom screamed and the men went back to their desperate task. One of the great fears of all soldiers on both sides was being buried alive by cave-ins like this.

They dug until they found the rest of the body and dragged Private Dean from the earth. He was barely alive and rolled on his back to stare up at the summer stars. Then he started retching, bringing up his last meal along with dirt and bile.

'Private Dean,' Tom yelled down at the badly wounded soldier. 'Who was beside you?'

Private Dean blinked and mumbled something.

Tom leaned over and put his ear to Dean's mouth. 'Who?'

'Bluey,' Dean whispered and Tom turned away. 'Stretcher-bearers,' he bellowed, hoping that his call would not be drowned out by the tremendous noise of the exploding shells.

They were now joined by men from the other side of the destroyed earthworks and the frantic digging continued until they found Bluey. They were too late. He had suffocated under the heavy pressure of the earth. Tom looked away, not feeling anything, and he noticed that the shelling had tapered away and the sun was casting its first pink light on the horizon.

The stretcher-bearers arrived to find that Private Dean's leg stump had been tied off with a tourniquet and he was still alive. Tom had completed his roll call of the platoon: they had suffered one KIA and one WIA. He reported to Sullivan, who had also moved up and down the platoon sections to check on the welfare of the men. He was a good officer and, despite his own terror of the bombardment, had been able to retain an outward appearance of calm, talking quietly to the men, all of whom had been badly shaken by the experience.

Tom had ensured that the men's minds were on maintaining equipment and preparing for any assault that might follow the bombardment, although he doubted this would happen. He had come to sense the difference between German harassment shelling meant to unnerve them, and preparatory shelling intended to soften a position before an attack. The early morning bombardment had been a routine harassment shelling.

When Tom reached Private Dean lying on a stretcher alone, he squatted to speak reassuringly with the man.

'You got a Blighty there, son,' Tom said referring to a wound that would ensure the soldier was sent to England for treatment – and out of the trenches for good.

'Sarge, there's something I have to tell you,' Dean said, reaching up and gripping Tom's sleeve. The morphine had kicked in and Dean had the dreamy look of a man not quite in the real world.

'What's that?' Tom said.

'Bluey, before he got it,' Dean said in a voice that seemed to come from a long way away. 'He told me that Smithers told him that after we were on leave he went to your lady's cottage and had his way with her. I didn't want to say anything but now Bluey is gone I suppose you should know the truth. Smithers said she had a strawberry birthmark on her arse.'

Tom felt the blood drain from his whole body. Only someone with intimate knowledge of Juliet could have known of her small birthmark on the cheek of her well-rounded buttock. Raped! Tom now felt an overwhelming urge to leap from the trench and run as fast as he could until he reached Juliet's farm. Then he would hunt down Smithers and kill him.

'I'm sorry, Sarge,' Dean said as the stretcher-bearers returned to take him on the first leg of his long journey back to England.

Tom barely noticed him go; all his thoughts were of murder and grief. Maybe Juliet had been badly hurt and could not write, Tom thought. There would be a reckoning, he vowed. But first he must go to Juliet, no matter what.

The cobbled street was crowded with troops mostly in the uniform of the French army. The pretty young girl stood hesitantly before the doors of the stone building. She gripped a small suitcase containing the few articles she had put together before fleeing her village in shame.

Juliet Joubert caught the attention of one or two soldiers ambling past the houses and the offers were blatant. Money for sex was the norm in this section of Paris known for its brothels catering to soldiers on leave. The French army had suffered terribly in the big battles and the year before had actually mutinied for better conditions. Fortunately the mutiny had not been known about by the German intelligence or they might have launched another attack and won the war.

Juliet had travelled a long way and her meagre savings were almost gone. She felt such shame that she had not been able to write to Tom, nor had she been able to tell her parents what had happened, although they had known there was something wrong with her. For over a month she had continued teaching in an almost trancelike state; then she had found herself suffering nausea and vomiting. She had understood that she was pregnant, and the terrible realisation came to her that she could not know whose child she was carrying.

It had been an agony for her, so one night she'd packed her small suitcase and left her parents' cottage without

150

leaving a note. All that had been in her mind was that the man she loved would shun her, and without Tom life had no meaning. In her despair she thought she was not fit to be Tom's wife if the child she carried was not his.

Knowing that she had very little money to keep her going, Juliet had decided to take a cleaner's job in a relatively respectable brothel for gentlemen and officers. The thought of working in such a place sickened her but it was all she could find. She walked up the steps to the brothel's large double front and rang the bell. In a couple of minutes the door swung open to reveal the outline of a large man wearing a stylish suit and hat. Juliet and the man stared at each other and the young woman blinked in horror, while the man also appeared to be taken aback at the sight of her standing forlornly on the step.

'Well, I'll be buggered,' Smithers said, a broad smile crossing his face. 'So you couldn't keep away from me, eh? Of all the places you had to come to in Paris it had to be Madame Leclerc's. Come in, and I suppose you are wondering how I got here,' Smithers continued, opening the door wide. 'Me and the army decided to have a parting and it just happened that when I got to town Madame Leclerc was looking for someone who spoke English and could handle rowdy customers. So here I am – and here you are.'

Juliet was frozen with fear and disbelief. She was in the presence of evil and the devil had come to fetch her soul.

12

The sun was at its blazing zenith as Saul Rosenblum and Joanne Barrington lay on their stomachs side by side, observing the Turkish patrol halting for a rest. From their viewpoint on the hill they calculated that the Turks were about a half-mile away. Joanne scanned the campsite with her binoculars in an attempt to locate Matthew. As her small rescue team had tracked the patrol over the last three weeks their supplies had dwindled, and she knew that if an attempt was not made in the next twenty-four hours they would be forced to withdraw.

'I can see him!' Joanne exclaimed. 'There, standing to the rear of the camel train.'

Saul swung his binoculars to the rear of the convoy and caught sight of his friend swigging from a leather water bottle. For days and weeks they had kept a course parallel with the patrol, always out of sight but close enough to carefully observe the military routine of the patrol. Saul had calculated that they had the task of reconnoitring for British units on the Ottoman flank. Had this not been the case, the patrol would most probably be back in its fortified base by now and any attempt to rescue Matthew would have been impossible.

The time observing the enemy unit had given Saul a good idea of numbers, weapons and tactics. He had noted that the patrol had grown slack in the last few days – maybe because they were comfortable in territory nominally held by them – and the sentries posted on the flanks were now being pulled in closer.

'Twenty-three men armed with carbines and no sign of any machine-guns,' Saul had briefed that morning. 'I think they are suffering a shortage of supplies like us, so that means they will be expecting to reach a depot very soon. If we are to make our move it will have to be tonight – or at first light tomorrow. I notice that they seem to be preoccupied with breakfast lately and not keeping a good lookout. I would prefer first light when we have a clear view of Matthew, so he does not get caught in any crossfire. Our Maxim will even the odds considerably.'

All four of them had agreed with the plan as they had the high ground and surprise on their side. Now they just needed a lot of luck.

As they lay on the bare hill top observing the patrol, Benjamin hissed at his father. 'Do you hear that?'

Saul lowered the glasses and strained to hear any strange sound that stood out from the usual noises of the arid lands. And then he heard it. A low droning noise approaching from the south.

'Aircraft!' he said and turned to locate the source of the droning that was growing louder by the second. They all spotted the little biplane flying low at around a thousand feet, and Saul brought up his binoculars to identify it.

'British,' he said. 'Bloody hell! It must be going after the Turks!'

Joanne glanced at Saul and they both registered their horror as the British aircraft was already lining up the Turks, now wisely scattering in all directions, leaving their camels to mill about in panic.

The chatter of the aircraft's twin machine-guns reached them across the plain, and they could see tiny puffs of dust as the bullets walked their way into the camp, felling a couple of the camels and three Turkish soldiers unable to get away in time.

'Matthew could be killed,' Joanne said, rising to her feet. 'We have to do something now.'

Saul took in the situation with the practised mind of a tactician. He could see that Matthew had sprinted away from the rear of the encampment and flung himself on the ground in a very shallow depression. The fighter biplane had made one strafing pass over the encampment and was climbing for a second run. Already some of the Turkish soldiers were standing their ground and firing their rifles at the aircraft.

'Get the Maxim into action now!' Saul bellowed at his son. 'Concentrate on placing your fire into the Turks towards the front of the caravan.'

Benjamin and Adar were already setting up the heavy water-cooled machine-gun on its stand and feeding a belt of ammunition into the breech. Benjamin jumped down behind the gun, pulled back the cocking lever, chambering the first round, and swivelled it to bring its fire to bear on the Turkish troops.

Saul ran to his horse and threw himself astride it. With

a savage kick he spurred it into action and forced it over the edge of the hill onto the rocky slope that tapered away to the plain below. The horse was sure-footed and kept its balance as it went down the side of the hill, while Saul prayed that the British pilot would not concentrate his attack on him, mistaking him for an enemy soldier.

He glanced over his shoulder and swore in Hebrew. Joanne was following him down on her own mount. He had not had time to warn her off. There was not time for Saul to stop and order her back to the hilltop. He forced his mount into a gallop, and when he reached the bottom of the hill he calculated that he had around four hundred yards before he reached Matthew. Beside the noise of the horse's hooves hitting the ground, Saul was sure that he could also hear his own heart beat.

Initially, the Turks had not noticed him galloping in a line past the rear of their encampment, but now a couple of soldiers close by turned to see him heading for the depression. The Turkish soldiers snapped off shots at him and Saul who could hear the crack of bullets passing close by. He pressed himself against his horse's neck to make himself a smaller target. Three hundred yards, he thought, and when he turned to see where Joanne was he saw that she was only about twenty yards behind him, with her pistol in one hand and the reins in the other. Saul had to admire her skill in the saddle.

The fighter plane threw up spouts of dirt in front of Saul and he realised with chilling fear that he was the target now. The aircraft flew so low that Saul could actually see clearly the goggled face of the pilot looking back at him.

Two hundred yards, Saul calculated; Matthew was still wisely out of sight in the depression. Just then the Maxim opened up from atop the hill, catching the Turkish soldiers in a crossfire. Confused, they milled about, attempting to identify the second deadly threat as three or four were cut down. A Turkish officer was yelling and waving his pistol at his men.

Saul did not envy the Turkish officer's position: he was being attacked from the air, and now a machine-gun on the hill was pouring fire down into his ranks and some madman dressed as a Bedouin was galloping towards his prisoner.

One hundred yards, and overhead the British fighter plane was preparing to make a third low-level strafing run against what was left of the Ottoman patrol. By now Joanne had caught up to Saul and was galloping by his side.

Fifty yards and Matthew suddenly rose to his feet and began waving.

Saul and Joanne were off their horses in a flash, and Matthew flung his arms around Joanne.

'Oh, God, is this a dream?' he gasped, hugging her to him. There were tears in his eyes, and hers too.

'Let's go,' Saul growled, gripping the reins of his horse as it skittered nervously at the sound of the aircraft returning, and the chatter of its machine-gun.

'Get on my horse,' Joanne said. 'We'll ride back up the hill together.'

'Bloody hell!' Saul swore. 'The bloody pommy bastard is coming for us!'

Both Matthew and Joanne glanced up; the pilot had finished his strafing run and had turned his attention on them out in the open. It seemed impossible that he would miss them; death was only seconds away.

Suddenly Joanne scrambled from the safety of the low depression and, to the utter astonishment of Matthew and Saul, ripped open her blouse to reveal her breasts to the oncoming pilot, who was now flying at almost ground level. Both men gaped in shock, making easy targets of themselves.

'Joanne! No!' Matthew screamed.

It was obvious that the pilot was not going to squander his remaining ammunition until he was close enough to ensure a kill, but the aircraft suddenly nosed up, and when both men swung to see the face of the pilot as he passed them by, they could have sworn that he was grinning. He waggled his wings and droned away, leaving the desert almost silent except for the pitiful grunting of wounded beasts and the cries of badly wounded men.

Joanne had closed her blouse and turned to the gawking men. 'That seemed to work,' she said with a smile.

Neither man commented, and the almost comical situation was rudely interrupted by the sound of scattered rifle shots. The Maxim gun had fallen silent, and Saul guessed that something had gone wrong with it. The Turkish officer had also guessed the same thing and now rallied around seven survivors to concentrate their fire on the single remaining threat – the trio in the depression.

'We have to get out of here now,' Saul said unnecessarily, and Matthew followed Joanne onto her mount, clinging to her waist with all the strength he had. The initial shooting proved to be well off as the traumatised men regained their composure, but as the two horses galloped across the plain towards the hill the shooting became more accurate.

A bullet clipped the back of Matthew's shirt and he felt the searing pain as it scored a burn across his back; still he managed to maintain his grip as Joanne leaned forward, encouraging her mount to even greater speed. Saul was off to their left and keeping pace with them.

The slope came closer and the welcome chatter of the Maxim gun once again opened up to spray death down on the Turkish patrol. Over his shoulder Saul could see that the Turks had scattered, taking cover behind felled camels, and were returning fire.

When Saul, Joanne and Matthew reached the bottom of the hill they dismounted and placed their horses between themselves and the Turks now trapped on the plain, leading the exhausted horses up the slope slippery with shards of loose rock. It was then that Matthew noticed Joanne half-doubled over, her face ashen with pain. A great red blot spread on her white blouse and before Matthew could react, she stumbled and collapsed, releasing the reins of her horse.

'Joanne! No!' Matthew shouted.

Joanne lay on her side, clutching her stomach.

'God, no!' Saul groaned.

Matthew knelt down beside Joanne and placed her head in his lap. He couldn't believe this was happening. Tears streamed down his dirty, unshaven face. 'You'll be all right, my darling,' he choked. 'Just got to get you up the hill and off to a hospital.'

Joanne had her eyes closed in agony but she opened them to stare up at Matthew. She reached up and touched his face. 'I have found you, my darling Matthew,' she said weakly. 'I will never let you go again.'

The pain and loss of blood brought merciful release to her and she slipped into unconsciousness. Matthew held her to him gently, lest he cause her any more grief. He felt Saul's hand on his shoulder.

'We have to get her up to the others,' he said quietly.

Matthew turned to him with desperation written all over his face. 'We can help her,' he pleaded. 'We just need to get her to medical help.'

Saul felt a lump in his throat. With a wound like that, death was almost a certainty — even with the best hospital facilities. 'Yes, old cobber, and first we have to get her out of the line of fire of the Ottomans over there.'

Saul turned his attention to the summit where he could see Adar, armed with a rifle, descending the slope. Within minutes Adar was beside them.

'We have to get Miss Barrington up the hill,' Saul said in Hebrew and Adar knelt to take her legs, while Matthew gripped her under the arms. It was tortuous going, carrying Joanne's limp body up the slippery hillside, while all the time being careful not to cause her more distress. Still, Joanne groaned at the movement, slipping in and out of consciousness. Saul led the two horses and eventually they reached the top to see Benjamin manning the heavy machine-gun. A shimmer of heat lay over the hot barrel and a pile of shiny brass cartridges lay in scattered heaps where they had been ejected by the weapon.

Benjamin left the gun to go to Joanne as she was laid gently on the dry earth. The bloodstain now completely covered the front of her blouse. He glanced at his father's grim face, and Saul shook his head.

Matthew fell to his knees beside Joanne and used his torn and dirty scarf to scatter away the flies that settled on her face.

'Get some cover over here,' Saul said to his son.

Benjamin retrieved a section of canvas wrapping from his horse's saddlebags and pitched it with two rifles to form a crude shelter from the blistering sun.

Matthew held Joanne's limp hand, crooning soothing words of forlorn hope.

'We'll leave them alone,' Saul said quietly to his son. 'The Turks down in the valley are still a threat, so we must prepare to ride out of here within an hour.'

'What will happen to Miss Barrington?' Benjamin asked

anxiously as he walked away with his father. He saw tears in the corners of Saul's eyes and knew not to ask any more questions.

Joanne gazed up at Matthew with pain-racked eyes. 'I . . .' she winced, and could not go on. She gripped his hand.

'We're going to get you to a hospital, my love. Everything's going to be all right,' Matthew said.

'No hospital,' Joanne replied through gritted teeth. 'Pain too bad.'

'Saul will organise transport for you. Before you know it you will be on your feet again,' Matthew said with conviction. He would not let her die.

A crippled smile crept across her beautiful but ashen face. 'Not going to live,' she said with great effort. 'You must kill me . . . Right thing to do . . . No hope.'

The shock of her words hit Matthew like a bullet. 'I will get you to a hospital,' he reiterated.

With effort Joanne shook her head. 'So much to say,' she said as her body rippled with a spasm that choked off her words. She cried out and the sound of her pain tore through Matthew. He didn't want to confront the fact that she was dying, but he had no choice – she was in agony. He could let her linger in her suffering – or give her the peace she asked for.

Matthew heard Saul's footsteps behind him and turned to see the big bearded man looking down on them both with an expression of gentle sympathy and grief. He stretched out his hand to Matthew. 'Here,' he said. 'I have morphine for Joanne's pain.'

Matthew took the handful of glass capsules and the needle. The medical rule was that victims suffering stomach or head wounds were not to be given morphine. Surely Saul must have known that, Matthew thought, and was about to reject the offer when the realisation hit him. He exchanged a pitiful look with Saul, who now turned and slowly walked away.

Joanne had her eyes closed as Matthew prepared the syringe. His hands shook so badly that he dropped the needle, but he picked it up and wiped away the sand.

'Matthew my love,' Joanne muttered and Matthew leaned over to kiss her lips, dry and chaffed from the sun. As he did so he slid the needle into her arm and gently pushed down on the pump. Joanne opened her eyes at the prick of the needle and smiled at Matthew. 'I love you with all my body and soul,' she said. 'Thank you, my love. Love our children . . .' Her voice trailed away as the powerful drug took hold.

Matthew cradled her head in his lap and stroked her hair until her breathing stopped and her eyes glazed over in death. Then he was racked with a pain and a sobbing that seemed as though it would never end. Saul stood close, his hand on his shoulder.

'She's at peace,' he said softly. 'She is with the angels.'

Benjamin and Adar removed their head gear out of respect for the remarkable young woman. It appeared that the Turks had fled and the small party was not in any immediate danger, so they remained on the hilltop until late afternoon. Matthew stayed by Joanne's body, talking to her as if she were still alive.

Saul was satisfied that the Turkish patrol had cleared the area but still remained cautious as there was a chance that they were rallying to pursue them. He was anxious to get away, but did not want to disturb Matthew in his last moments with Joanne.

When the sun was low on the horizon, in that time before the arid lands took on the coolness of the star-filled night, Saul and Benjamin buried Joanne in the hard earth, finding rocks to mark her gravesite. There was nothing more that Saul could do for her, so he turned his attention to Matthew, who sat on a rock holding Joanne's revolver in his hand, staring blankly into the distance.

Saul walked over to him. 'We will leave under cover of darkness,' he said. 'I am certain that Joanne will expect you to look after your son and daughter, so don't go and get yourself killed.'

Matthew did not look up or reply. Eventually, though, he rose and tucked the pistol into the waistband of his trousers. Saul felt a great sense of relief as he had feared his friend might choose to join Joanne in death.

Matthew rode in silence on Joanne's tough little mare. The four men picked their way westward towards Jerusalem under a sky of spectacular stars. They stopped in the early hours of the morning to tend to one of the horses that had gone lame, and Matthew joined Saul examining the horse's hoof by kerosene lantern light.

'I killed her,' Matthew choked. 'I killed her.'

Saul was bent over the horse's foot. 'No, Matthew,' he said, looking up, 'the war killed her. You ended her suffering, you gave her peace, but you were not responsible for her death.'

Matthew stood silently for a moment. 'If it hadn't been for me, she would have been safely back in Cairo.'

Saul eased down the horse's leg and stretched wearily. 'She loved you, Matthew. She would have done anything to make sure you were safe. You would have done the same for her. There's nothing more important in this world than love, and Joanne died knowing that. She would want you to carry her love with you into your life, into the lives of your children. Don't waste the gift she has given you, old cobber.' Saul embraced his friend; he could feel Matthew's body shaking with grief.

'Thanks, my friend,' Matthew said eventually and broke from the embrace to walk back to his horse.

He knew now that he must ensure the futures of his children – it was all that mattered now. One day he would be buried in these ancient, biblical lands beside Joanne – when his own time came to him for that endless peace. Matthew had often heard Saul use both the Hebrew and Arabic words for peace. After love, peace was the next most beautiful word in the universe.

13

Sean Duffy hated the winter charity ball season. He was never comfortable in the company of Sydney's elite, who knew nothing of the hell of war. Civilians would prattle on about shortages, about no longer being able to buy the luxuries they had once taken for granted. It infuriated Sean, who knew that just being safe and well was a luxury soldiers fighting in the war had long since foregone. He had only accepted the invitation to tonight's ball because it was raising funds for wounded servicemen.

Sean was standing in the glittering ballroom of one of Sydney's best hotels, surrounded by elaborately dressed men and women, a handful in uniform. He propped himself on his walking cane, glancing around at the throng of laughing guests. He had attended unescorted – his work and, to an extent, his drinking, left little time to socialise with the eligible ladies of Sydney. He wore a black suit and bow tie and wore his medals in miniature, as required by protocol.

A solicitor he knew from a rival firm greeted him, extending his hand. Sean racked his brain for the man's name. Clarence Hurley, that was it. He was the same age as Sean, but heavy, with a red flush to his face that indicated a taste for good ports.

'Major Duffy, old chap,' he said, shaking Sean's hand with a limp, sweaty grip. 'No need for you to avail yourself of charity, not from the way your firm is fairing. But it's grand that you bring some colour to the place and, with your gammy legs, a reminder of why we have spent our hard-earned money to be here.'

'The men we are gathered here to support have given a lot more than money,' Sean said quietly, fixing the pomp-ous man directly in the eyes and causing him to look away sheepishly. Sean had never liked his learned colleague much; he had resigned his military commission with a militia reg-iment at the outbreak of war to pursue a career in politics. He had gained a seat in the state parliament but maintained his legal firm. Sean had heard rumours that Hurley was George Macintosh's fix-it man in the government.

Hurley looked over Sean's shoulder. 'Excuse me, old chap,' he said. 'Someone I really must talk to,' and he hurried away.

Sean leaned on his cane, hoping a waiter might pass by with a tray loaded with drinks. The band struck up a waltz and the crowd gave way to dancers, who swirled across the highly polished floor.

'Hello, Sean,' said a voice behind him. Sean fought the feeling that he might topple over. 'I think you should find a seat.'

Sean turned to see Louise standing an arm's length away. The sight of her beautiful face caught him offguard and he couldn't speak. The old feelings welled up and memories of their lovemaking flashed through his mind.

'Hello, Louise,' he finally answered. 'It's good to see you. It's been a long time. What? A year or more?'

Louise's smile flickered with uncertainty at the mention of their last encounter. They had been lovers until George had threatened to take their son from her, although Sean was not aware of the reason she had broken off the affair.

'Where is your husband?' Sean asked, leaning hard on his walking stick.

'Oh, I daresay he is off plotting another scheme to enrich the Macintosh coffers,' she answered, glancing around the room.

'Is it wise for you to be seen speaking with me?' Sean asked.

'I cannot think why anyone who knows me would see any scandal in that tonight,' Louise said softly. 'After all, when I look around I do not see many other men wearing decorations for bravery. This event is a kind of recognition for those who have sacrificed so much, too much.' Sean knew that Louise was making reference to his legs, which had been blown off in the trenches by a German artillery round; he was not offended, and it had never worried her in the depths of passion.

'It's good to see you looking so well,' he said as a waiter appeared and Louise took two small flutes of champagne from his tray.

'Why don't we sit down for a moment,' she said, and led him to a table with several free chairs.

Sean was astute enough to notice two matrons putting their heads together behind the fans they waved, to tut-tut about him being seen in the company of Mrs George

Macintosh. Sean ignored their snooty looks and sat down beside Louise. For a moment they watched the dancers swirl past in a foxtrot.

Sean took a swig of his champagne. 'Giselle tells me that she receives a steady stream of news from you in your letters,' Sean said by way of polite conversation, trying to ignore the desire that was flooding through his body.

'She and David are coming down for Christmas. I am so looking forward to seeing them. It was George's idea, oddly enough. I am hoping that this is my husband's way of mending broken bridges.'

'It was George's idea?' Sean frowned.

Louise did not miss his dark expression. 'I know that George can be ruthless in his business dealings, but I also think he may be capable of some charity.'

Sean snorted, but before he could say anything the man he hated most in the world appeared at the table, his face full of fury.

'Louise, you will accompany me back to our guests,' he said, ignoring Sean.

'Your wife was just discussing how the proceeds of tonight's ball should be administered,' Sean lied. 'Perhaps she and I might discuss the matter a little longer.'

'Keep out of this, Duffy,' George snapped. 'I will not allow you, a damned cripple, to question my right to command my wife.'

Sean could feel his anger boiling over into rage but this ballroom was no place to start a scene. 'Commanding is something I know a little about,' Sean replied icily. 'But have I never applied the word to women.'

George Macintosh looked Sean up and down, as though weighing him up and then dismissing him as being beneath his attention. 'I do what I like,' Duffy,' he said. 'You are not playing soldier boy with your men any more. You are in my world now, and I would remind you of that.'

'Is that a threat?' Sean countered. 'If so, I doubt you would be man enough to carry it out yourself. Who will you hire – Detective Inspector Firth? Or will the threat come from some hoodlum you have on your payroll? No matter, Macintosh – I will be ready.'

A silence had fallen around the men as people strained to hear what they were saying.

'George, I will accompany you back to our table,' Louise said wearily, rising from her chair. 'This is no place for grown men to fight.'

Sean did not stop her but continued to fix George's eyes with his own. 'I am sorry we did not have the opportunity to finish our conversation,' he said to Louise, still keeping George's glare. 'Another time.'

George took his wife by the wrist and pulled her after him. Sean watched them go, picked up his flute of champagne and turned to those still watching avidly. 'Cheers,' he said, raising his glass in a mock toast. They looked away with embarrassment. No doubt the heated exchange would be all the talk in Sydney's upper-class parlours tomorrow, but Sean did not care.

All he could think about was Louise. How beautiful she was; how much he missed her. Then he remembered that George had suggested she invite Giselle and her son down for Christmas. *A leopard does not change its spots*, Sean thought. There was something wrong, and George's words – 'You are in my world now' – brought that fear into focus. If Giselle and her son were to come to Sydney they would be in George's world, and Sean knew how murderous that could be.

Not bothering to excuse himself from the table, he made his way to the exit. He had put in an appearance and given everyone something to talk about, and now it was time to be alone to think. He knew his own life was in danger – because of his connection to Giselle and David. Sean had sworn an oath to Patrick Duffy before he was killed in action that he would protect Alexander's family. But with Harry still locked up awaiting a bail application, and him with his crippled legs, Sean didn't think he stood much chance if Macintosh set his hired thugs on him.

Before he left the room he looked back to see Louise watching him with an enigmatic expression. He smiled and nodded his head, and carried the memory of her out into the night.

George refused to speak to Louise on the journey home in the chauffeured limousine, but as soon as they were inside the house he turned on her savagely.

'How dare you speak with that man?' he snarled. 'Do you wish to make me the laughing stock of Sydney?'

Louise brushed past him into the spacious foyer of their palatial home. 'The servants will hear you, George,' she hushed.

'I don't give a damn if they do,' George shouted, and Louise could see that he was in a dangerous rage. 'I explicitly told you that you were to have no contact with him.'

'I was merely engaging in harmless chitchat,' Louise replied mildly, trying not to show how frightened she was. 'It was, after all, an event to raise money for Major Duffy's comrades who have been wounded as he has.'

George gripped her arm and brought his face close to hers. 'Do you still hold feelings for him?'

Louise attempted to step away, smelling the alcohol on

his breath. 'No, he is nothing to me now, merely someone I once knew.'

The back-handed blow to her face sent Louise reeling back and smashing against the wall. She could feel that her lip was split and her thoughts spun in a shower of stars. She sank to the floor, tears welling as much from indignation as pain. She struggled to sit up, aware that her husband was now towering over her. Inflicting pain had changed his expression to that of sadistic pleasure.

'I would not strike me again if I were you,' Louise said, looking up at him defiantly.

'I will do what I damn well like to my property,' George sneered.

'I can inform you that I am with child again and you might damage your *unborn* property,' Louise said, and George's expression changed. He occasionally forced entry to her bed, to prove his virility more than anything else.

'How long have you known?' he asked.

'A week or two,' Louise said. 'But do not think that my pregnancy has made me joyous. I shudder every time I think that I am simply bearing you heirs to this empire built on innocent blood.'

George glared at his wife, then turned around and walked out the door, slamming it shut behind him. No doubt he was off to visit one of his many mistresses, she thought bitterly. Her life was nothing but a sham; from the outside they looked like the model couple. George could be so charming, but Louise knew that beneath the veneer of good manners lurked a man without a soul. She thought of Sean and his tender love for her, and the tears of pain turned to tears of sorrow. Oh, how she had missed him, but this pregnancy sealed her fate with her husband. She would grow old raising her children and in her latter days remember the strong, courageous and intelligent man who had once loved her so passionately. So often she had considered divorce, but she knew that divorce would bring the full weight of George's wrath down on her head and she would lose her children to him. She could not approach her father for help – he would only remind her of the duties of a wife. She had nowhere to turn, and the only friend she could confide in was a thousand miles north in Queensland.

Louise raised herself from the floor and stumbled to her bedroom. The servants had had the good sense to remain in their quarters. It did not pay to come between a man and his wife – especially if that man was their employer.

That night Louise lay staring up at the dark ceiling of her room. It was cold and she pulled up the thick eiderdown to stave off the chill. At least she would be seeing Giselle and David in a few months; maybe she would be able to talk her best friend into staying in Sydney for a while. Sleep did not come easily but as she slipped into the small death of the night she thought of the baby that she carried in her womb and tried to be glad.

George felt his rage turning to desire as his weary chauffeur drove him to one of the many tenements he owned in the inner city. It was not the worst of areas but it was still squalid and rough.

George made his way to the front door of the double-storeyed house and rapped on the big brass doorknocker. After a few minutes the door was opened to reveal a young woman. She had a shawl wrapped around her shoulders and wore a long, filmy nightdress. Her face was pale but pretty, and her long raven hair flowed over her shoulders.

'It is you, Mr Macintosh,' she said, blinking away the sleep from her eyes. 'It's the middle of the night.'

George pushed past her and immediately reached down to grasp her buttock and squeeze it. She did not attempt to shake him off. 'It is late and I need to sleep,' she said.

'I pay for you and you do what I want,' George said savagely, taking her by the hand and leading her to the narrow stairs. 'You know what I want.'

Maude Urqhart let him take her upstairs. Maude had left the slums and her abusive father when she was eleven. She had become an urchin on the hard backstreets of Sydney, where she turned to prostitution to survive. Maude was a streetwise and ambitious young woman who had decided that she wanted more from her life. She'd met the eminent George Macintosh at the brothel and discovered that she could manipulate him by pandering to his perverse needs. It was not long before he proposed to free her from her constant stream of clients and moved her into one of his tenements for his exclusive use. Maude had happily accepted the position of his mistress, and the money he gave her provided freedom from the streets.

Out of curiosity Maude had once travelled across the city to the Macintosh mansion on the harbour. She had stood outside the gates of the big sprawling house with its manicured gardens and had seen a woman exit with a toddler. Maude guessed that the lady with the boy was George's wife and she felt a surge of jealous anger towards her, not because she was married to George but because she lived in such luxury and had the air of one born to money. Why should this woman have so much and she have so little? Maude wanted those privileges for herself.

After George had sated his lust he rolled over to reach for his suit jacket and take out a cigar.

'I really enjoyed that,' Maude lied. 'I wish we could just lock ourselves in a room and see what else we could get up to.' George did not answer but sat up in the bed to light his cigar. 'We could – if I lived with you,' she continued.

George stiffened. 'That cannot happen,' he warned. 'This arrangement suits us both.'

Maude reached over to touch his face and George pulled back. 'I love you,' she said as convincingly as she could. 'What if you did not have a wife but just me in your life?'

'But I do have a wife,' he snorted. 'And will for a long time.'

'You and I could live together, and every night would be the best in your life,' Maude crooned. 'Don't I please you and help take away your worries?'

George turned his attention to the girl, and in the dim light he could see that she was in the prime of her life; a beautiful young woman with a depraved mind equal to his own. The idea was tempting, but it could never happen, not with his position in Sydney's society as a stalwart of family ideals. Maybe he could employ her as a housemaid, he mused. He had done that before, until Louise had insisted that he fire the last one, whom he had made pregnant. She had been a simple country girl with little imagination, and George was secretly pleased to have an excuse to let her go. He did not wonder about the child she was carrying; she could not prove the child was his, and there was no way he would recognise a bastard as his own. Maude, however, was something very different, and he did not want to lose her too soon.

'If I did not have a wife, you and I could live together,' he said to placate her, and saw the sudden shining in her eyes. She wrapped her arms around him and kissed him on the lips, drawing him down to her.

14

Sean Duffy was appalled but not surprised to see what poor physical condition Harry was in when he appeared for a committal hearing in the courthouse. Shackled, he stood with his head bowed, but Sean could see that he had been beaten again. Harry's wife was crying openly, tears streaming down her face at the sight of her battered husband. Sean turned to her and said quietly, 'I'll get him out of here, I promise you.'

She glanced up at Sean and he could see the pain in her eyes.

'He suffered enough in France,' she said and Sean knew what she meant.

The magistrate entered the courtroom and all stood respectfully.

Sean had armed himself with every piece of evidence and now presented it with every ounce of his professionalism.

The prosecution then rose and called on Detective Inspector Jack Firth to give his evidence.

Sean grilled him savagely, and once or twice was reminded by the magistrate that he should not make insinuations against the police officer. The prosecution's main witness, Lenny Johnson, failed to appear when called, so in the end the magistrate gave in Harry's favour, deciding that the prosecution had not established a case to put him on trial before a judge and jury.

Sean walked out onto the steps of the courthouse. Harry's wife had gone to the petty sessions office to wait for Harry's release. She'd thanked him over and over, but he knew he would have gone to any lengths to get Harry off; he was a good man and he had been a good soldier. He didn't deserve to be treated like a criminal.

'Think you're smart, eh, Mr Duffy,' Firth's voice said from behind him. 'Smartarses usually come unstuck around me.'

Sean turned to see the police officer glowering at him. 'You and I know that your star witness did the killing and I just wonder why he failed to appear today.'

'Lenny Johnson,' Jack Firth reflected. 'He and I will sort that out later, but in the meantime I would watch yourself. Never know about a bad accident happening to a man as disabled as yourself, do we.'

Sean controlled his anger, remembering the time when the policeman had deliberately pushed him under a steam train at Central Station, fleeing before any action could be taken to apprehend him. Sean had only survived thanks to Harry but had known that it would be a waste of time bringing the matter to other police as the detective inspector was feared by those of his colleagues who weren't bent, and admired by those who were. 'I heard that a certain file found its way into the hands of the inspector general recently,' Sean retorted. 'It must have caused you a few sleepless nights.'

Firth blinked. 'And the same file has now disappeared,' he replied with a smirk. 'Any sleep lost has been compensated for by a friend.'

'If you are depending on George Macintosh's support in the future, I would think twice about that,' Sean said. 'The second you are of no use to him he will throw you to the wolves.'

'Did I say anything about Mr Macintosh?' Firth responded. 'I think you have things confused. Must have been all that shellshock you blokes sob about like little girls when you come back from a bit of fighting.'

At the slur Sean felt his rage rising in a way that brought murder to mind. But he also sensed that Firth was deliberately goading him to do something rash. Sean was trembling violently now and he could not control it; he knew it was linked to shellshock but he did not know how or why.

'Look at you,' Firth sneered. 'You're trembling like a scared little girl already.'

Sean gripped the walking stick hard and wished he could sit down and bring his shaking under control, but to do so would only satisfy Firth's sense of victory over him. This fight was with words and so far Firth was winning.

'You never had the guts to enlist, did you, Firth?' Harry appeared on the courthouse steps, his wife beside him. 'I heard what you said to Major Duffy. I would have loved to have you with us in the trenches to see you soil your pants when the shelling started.'

'You two'll keep,' Firth said with a shrug, and sauntered away.

Harry's wife stepped forward and placed a gentle hand on Sean's trembling shoulder. 'It will be all right, Major

Duffy,' she said quietly. 'You saved my Harry from the hangman today.'

Sean gave a weak smile.

'Luv, you go home and prepare dinner,' Harry said, stepping in. 'Me and the major are going to have a beer or two to celebrate.'

Harry's wife glanced at her husband and this time she did not remonstrate with him. There were times when a man needed to drink, and she obviously reckoned today was one of those days.

'C'mon, boss,' said Harry, helping Sean down the street. 'Let's go get rolling drunk.'

Lenny held the curtains apart and stared out onto the narrow street below. He knew that the court hearing was probably over, and that Firth would be looking for him.

He let the curtains fall back and reached for the bottle of whisky he had brought with him. It had been fortunate that Lenny had remembered his half-sister's address, finding her place without much difficulty. He hadn't seen Maude Urqhart for years, and hadn't she grown into a lovely thing. He took another swig from the bottle.

The door to the bedroom opened behind him and Lenny turned nervously to see who it was. He breathed a sigh of relief — it was only Maude.

'You want a swig?' he asked her as she sat down on a chair in the corner of the room.

'No, but you can't stay here tonight,' she replied, crossing her legs under the filmy material of her nightdress. 'I may be expecting a guest.'

'You call them guests in your business?' Lenny said with a twisted smile. 'I thought they had another name.'

'I am now a woman of means,' Maude replied haughtily. 'I am the mistress of a very powerful man and he looks after me.'

'Mr George Macintosh, I heard on the streets,' Lenny said, sitting himself on the edge of the unmade bed.

'How come you never went to court?' Maude asked, changing the subject. 'I thought everyone was scared of Mr Firth.'

Lenny took another swig from the whisky bottle and wiped his mouth with the sleeve of his shirt. 'He might be a bad bastard, but I knew he would never get a case against Griffiths,' he replied. 'Besides, I'd rather face Jack Firth on the street than an angry Harry Griffiths, any day. Old Harry had a reputation for killing Huns with his bare hands. He can be a dangerous bastard. All I got to do is keep my head down until Firth cools off. Maybe make a deal with him about Mary Jackson.'

'Did you kill her?' Maude asked bluntly.

'Don't ask me questions like that,' Lenny snapped. 'Not if you want to keep your pretty looks and make your next birthday.'

Maude rose from the chair and walked over to the bed to sit beside Lenny. 'I'll make a deal with you,' she said, touching him on the arm. 'If you help me out, I'll get you enough money so that you can leave Sydney, maybe go down to Melbourne, get away from Firth.'

'You? With a lot of money, don't make me laugh,' Lenny chuckled. 'Where would you get money enough to help me?'

Maude stood up and walked to the window. 'I have a way of getting enough money to pay you to top someone,' she said without looking at him.

'Do what!' Lenny exclaimed. 'For a moment I thought you said you wanted someone dead.'

Maude turned from the window. 'That is exactly what I want you to do, and I will pay you well for it.'

'Jesus, you're a cold one,' Lenny said, surprised at how calm she was. It must be in the blood, he thought.

'Who do you want topped?' he asked.

'A woman,' Maude replied. 'You seem good at that. Her husband will pay a lot of money to rid himself of her,' Maude continued, lying. She had yet to convince George to give her a large enough sum of money to pay for the death of his wife – unwittingly, of course.

'Who's the husband?' Lenny asked, curious now.

'I can't tell you that until you agree to do the job, can I,' Maude said.

Lenny shrugged, took another swig of whisky and burped. 'It'll cost you a heap,' he replied. 'But I'll do it.'

Maude sat down next to him on the bed once again. 'You must swear on your life that you will never tell anyone of our deal,' she said, running her hand up the inside of his trouser leg, causing Lenny to stiffen in surprise.

'I swear,' he said. 'Who do you want me to do in?'

'George Macintosh's missus,' Maude said and Lenny looked at her in shock.

'What on earth do you plan to get out of this?' he asked.

'Everything she has,' Maude answered with an enigmatic smile. 'And more.'

'Bloody hell, Maude,' Lenny said. 'This will cost you an arm and a leg.'

'I can give you more than that, Lenny. I can give you my whole body if you promise to do the job,' Maude purred.

Lenny could feel her hand tightening on the inside of his thigh. Her invitation had the thrill of the forbidden, and the Sydney criminal had never really lived by conventional morality. He reached for Maude and pulled her down onto the bed, forgetting the rest of the whisky. At least here he was safe from Jack Firth for the moment. Killing a toff's wife was a little different to killing a working girl, but he reckoned he was up for it.

In a hotel not far from the courthouse two men sat in a corner of the bar drinking quietly.

'Who did the beating you got?' Sean asked as Harry brought over another couple of frothy ales to their table.

'The screws,' Harry said. 'They had orders from Firth to do me over.'

'The bastard.' Sean took a swig of his beer. 'One day he'll get his.'

'Not much more the screws could do to mess up my handsome looks,' Harry said lightly. 'Being inside, though, you get to hear things.'

'You shouldn't have been there in the first place,' Sean replied, gazing around at the almost empty bar. The lunch-time rush was over and most of the pub's clients had returned to work.

'Well, put it down to experience,' Harry said, drinking his ale with obvious relish. 'Besides, my missus felt so sorry for you she gave me a leave pass to get pissed and fall over on the front doorstep this evening.'

Sean smiled. He knew that Harry's wife had once been an active member of the Woman's Christian Temperance Union, and the pressure they brought to bear with politicians had seen the introduction of six o'clock closing of hotel bars. He knew that around five o'clock this bar would be packed and towards 6 o'clock closing time the swill would start as men drank as much as they could before the doors closed and they were forced out onto the street. In some ways the decision had given Sean's law firm extra business as sly grog shops opened up to cater to desperate men seeking alcohol and police nabbed the owners to bring them before the courts.

'I heard on the prison grapevine that Lenny wouldn't be turning up to give evidence,' Harry said. 'Word is he's more scared of me than of Firth.'

'I don't blame him,' Sean grinned, raising his glass in a salute. 'Did you hear anything else of worth?'

Harry thought for a moment before speaking. 'A bloke inside I did a favour for said that Lenny was going to hide out at his half-sister's place in the city. The funny part about that is Lenny's half-sister is none other than Maude Urqhart, George Macintosh's mistress. He keeps her in one of his houses in the inner city. I knew her when she was working on the streets. She must be about sixteen now, so it seems Mr Macintosh likes his women young.'

At the mention of George Macintosh's young mistress Sean experienced a strange feeling of satisfaction. It confirmed to him that Louise was being neglected by the man who had married her. Louise had been much in his thoughts since the meeting at the ball.

The two men continued drinking until the first of the workers spilled into the bar and they left to avoid the crush. Harry and Sean had to help each other along the street as they were both worse the wear for beer.

Harry could not help but think that it had been like this on the battlefields of France and Belgium – the more able-bodied helping the wounded back from the trenches. And it did not escape Harry's thoughts that they were far from out of danger even now they were back in civvie street. It started to rain, but at least there was no artillery shelling to follow the two men back to their homes.

★

George Macintosh was a worried man as he sat in his office, gazing out at the buildings adjacent to the company's headquarters. His bookkeeper had just left after discussing irregular entries in the company books. These concerned a bank draft for a considerable amount of money transferred from a Swedish bank account to the Sydney account. The transfer was not supposed to have happened yet, and besides being worried, George was angry. Maybe there had been a misreading of the codes he used in dealing with his German industrial partners who were producing the chlorine and sulphuric acid for the deadly mustard gas used on the Western Front against the Allies. But the stupid bookkeeper had taken it upon himself to query the transfer of funds with telegrams to Sweden, before raising the matter with George, and the bank had responded with a clear message that the profit was his share in German chemicals.

A shocked bookkeeper had produced the telegram to George and it now lay on his desk. At least the bookkeeper had not mentioned the matter to anyone else yet. George had explained that there must have been some kind of mix-up in communications and that he would sort it out immediately; then, without much subtlety, he'd mentioned that he would increase his bookkeeper's salary to thank him for his discretion as such a telegram could easily be misconstrued. What he'd seen in the man's eyes did not reassure George that the bookkeeper would keep his mouth shut. George was beginning to regret investing in the German chemical company. Originally he had done so because he had faith in German scientists to develop profitable pharmaceuticals for the future. That his hefty investment was producing the deadly gases used in the war was not an outcome he had foreseen, and although it did not concern him from an ethical or moral point of view, he certainly did not want anyone to know about it.

With the matter weighing on his mind, George made his way to his club to meet with a knighted member of the civil service. Sir Hubert had long filtered money into his favourite political party from George in return for government contracts, and he had taken a commission on those contracts. Ironically, Sir Hubert had promised George a knighthood for his charitable causes in support of the war effort. George did not like the man and knew the feeling was mutual, but the club gave them an opportunity to discuss business at what from the outside looked like a casual meeting.

George found Sir Hubert, a greying, nondescript man in his fifties, sitting back in a comfortable leather chair, reading the newspaper while armed with a gin and tonic.

George took a chair adjacent and ordered a Scotch from the waiter hovering nearby.

'I see that damned German Jew, Monash, has been promoted to command the boys in France,' Sir Hubert said with a snort of disgust. 'It was bad enough that the King saw fit to knight him earlier this year. Sir John Monash, what will be next? At least he has a good second in command with Blamey.'

'Speaking of knighthoods,' George said quietly, 'is there any word about my being on the list to be submitted to the King?'

Sir Hubert put down the paper and looked at George. 'Old boy, you know that is a confidential matter.'

'How much?' George countered bluntly and the senior public servant scribbled a figure on a cardboard coaster, handing it to George, who read the sum and frowned. 'That bloody much,' he said.

George was silent for a while, then he sighed. 'I'll find the money. The Macintoshes have a family tradition of knighthoods. My great-grandfather was the first knight in the family, and I think it's only right that I re-establish that tradition for the sake of the Macintosh name.'

Sir Hubert nodded. 'Your great-grandfather was a man with an enviable reputation in the colonies. Knew how to deal with darkies and forge an empire in this country.' Sir Hubert did not elaborate as he might upset the moment by mentioning the scandals he had heard concerning the parentage of Michael Duffy, a Papist who had tainted the Macintosh blood line. But that was in the distant past and the Macintosh family was once again a pillar of Protestant virtues. Any taint of Irish heritage had been washed out by strong Macintosh blood.

'The money will be transferred to the usual account,' George said. 'It will be done before the end of next week.'

'Good,' Sir Hubert said. 'I'm sure your money will see to it that the family tradition is maintained.'

George felt a touch of exhilaration. Sir Hubert was virtually saying that the deal had been done and the announcement would be made at the next gazetting of the honours awards.

'Well, Hubert, old chap,' George said, throwing back the fine Scotch in the crystal glass, 'I must leave you.' With that, George rose and made his way out of the club. As he stepped onto the street a cold wind gusted rain into his face. He lowered his head and pulled up the collar of his expensive overcoat, making his way to the waiting car.

If only everything could be bought as easily, he thought as the chauffeur held open the rear door for him. Yes, he could pay for his nephew's murder, but purchasing that killing was a very risky business indeed.

15

Although the pitch-black night was warm for late summer, the ground was sodden from recent rain. Sergeant Tom Duffy was shivering uncontrollably as he gripped his rifle at the battalion jump-off line. He knew his nerves were stretched almost beyond the point of sanity, and he waited in dread with the rest of the battalion for the order to attack. He was thankful that in the dark no one could see how his body trembled and the sweat clung to him. The nagging thought that he would die this day had gone from a whisper to a roar, but there was no one he could tell of his fear for he was the man they all looked to for courage.

Tom was truly alone. For weeks he had pleaded for emergency leave, but with the big push coming his request had been denied. Juliet's fate had occupied his mind to the exclusion of everything else, and a letter he'd received from her parents had confirmed she was missing. They had accused him of being responsible for their daughter's disappearance and he'd received no more letters from the Joubert family.

The drone of Allied aircraft overhead helped suppress the noise of the big lumbering metal tanks moving into position, and only the occasional enemy flare swooshed up to illuminate the battlefield. Machine-gun fire came across in return but fortunately without inflicting any casualties on the men crouching with their weapons, awaiting the order to advance.

Tom had carried out his duties to ensure the men of his platoon were properly equipped for the attack on the German lines, and now he had a brief moment to reflect on what lay ahead of them all. On his inspection before midnight he noticed how many fresh faces were in the ranks, watching him eagerly for some sign that they would survive their first encounter with the horrors of an assault across open ground. These were the same fresh young men who had expressed their fears when they'd arrived two weeks earlier that they might miss out on any action as the rumour was that the Kaiser's army was on the run. Well, this day they would learn the hard way that the German soldier was second to none, and that every inch of ground taken would come at a high cost to the Australians.

Tom glanced at his watch and noticed that it was near 4am. A thick fog was rising all around them, cutting visibility to around twenty yards. Tom fought to stop the trembling. How much more could he take? He knew that to the men under his command he was some kind of legend, and it was said that if you stuck close to the sarge you would get through the war alive. How wrong that had been, Tom thought bitterly. So many faces had come and gone, and he had not got off scot-free himself. He had been wounded but not badly enough to be sent back to Blighty.

Sound was muffled in the fog but Tom heard the rustle in the wet grass behind him. He turned to see Lieutenant Sullivan crawling up to him.

'That you, Tom?' Sullivan asked, groping along the ground.

'Yeah, boss,' Tom replied and Sullivan was beside him.

'Are you ready?' Sullivan asked.

'As ready as I can be,' Tom said. 'Maybe this fog will help hide us when we hop the bags.'

'I bloody well pray so.' The platoon commander slipped his water canteen from his belt and took a swig, and then offered it to Tom, who shook his head. 'Orders came through that I'm to be sent back to a training battalion in England after this push,' Sullivan said, tucking the water canteen into his belt. 'The good news is that the company commander has nominated you to go with me. They need experienced senior NCOs to help train the new troops waiting to come over. I thought you might like to know.'

For a moment Tom digested the wonderful news – an opportunity to leave this hell behind for a training camp with good food, soft beds and no whiz-bangs howling over-head. Only a fool would say no to that.

'I wish I could accept,' Tom said. 'But maybe Sergeant Paddy Bourke might be a better bet than me.' Tom knew that by going to England he would be too far away to search for Juliet when the time came for him to be due extended leave.

'God almighty, man,' Sullivan exclaimed, 'why in hell would you decline an offer like that?'

'Personal reasons, boss,' Tom answered, leaning on his rifle and staring ahead.

'Well, I'm not going to ask but I suspect it has something to do with a matter of the heart. At least the members of the platoon will be pleased to have you stay on, and God knows they need you.'

'Thanks, boss,' Tom said and Sullivan reached over to grip Tom's shoulder. 'Good luck, old chap.'

'You, too, boss,' Tom replied and Sullivan slithered back to the main body of the platoon. A few minutes later Tom was able to calm himself enough to join the platoon waiting anxiously. It was a quiet time among them, a time to think about their own mortality. Some prayed silently, while others just sat on the grass and waited.

Then, around 4.20am, the big artillery guns opened up behind them, signalling that the battalion was to advance with fixed bayonets through the thick fog towards the enemy. Tom rose from the wet grass and the others followed.

'Follow me, boys,' Sullivan said, and they moved out in an extended line. Behind them they could vaguely make out the creaking sound of the tanks following, as shells poured overhead to soften up the waiting German soldiers.

So thick was the fog that the outermost sections of the platoon were out of sight, swallowed by the thick damp air within seconds of leaving the line of departure.

Their artillery rounds were landing to their front in a creeping barrage which helped shield them from enemy retaliation, and Tom was surprised to see that the machine-gun and rifle fire from the enemy was sporadic and unfocused.

The grass squelched under his boots as he walked, staying close to his platoon commander and keeping his eye on those soldiers nearby so that they did not get lost in the fog.

The ground shook and Tom felt the heat of an enemy artillery round exploding not far away. He sensed that the Germans were merely firing haphazardly as they could not see them advancing.

'Spread out,' Tom shouted, but few regarded the command. The instinct to be close to another human under such terrible circumstances was very strong. 'Don't bunch up.'

All the time through the artillery and small arms falling on them the Australians advanced, until after around a quarter of a mile the lips of the German entrenchments loomed up at them out of the mist.

Tom reached for a Mills hand grenade, pulled the pin and lobbed it into the trench ahead. He watched it explode and heard the cries of distress from its victims. Along the line others of the platoon were doing the same, and Tom was surprised to see that the Germans only had a meagre few strings of barbed wire as defence.

Seeing movement above the parapet, Tom squeezed off a shot and saw the head disappear with a jerk. With a fierce yell Tom charged the trenches, ready, like those who followed his lead, to carry out a vicious hand-to-hand fight to the death. But the German soldiers dropped their weapons and raised their hands. Tom ordered those close to him to round up the prisoners and get them back to their own lines as quickly as possible, nominating soldiers he knew were not likely to shoot the prisoners as soon as they were out of sight.

'See how bloody young they are,' Corporal Dan Frogan said. 'The Huns are scraping the bottom of the barrel now.'

Tom glanced at a German soldier not far from where they stood and noticed the boy did not look much older than sixteen. He was shaking and his eyes were wide with fear. Tom looked away. 'Do we have any casualties?'

'All accounted in my section,' Dan replied. 'We were bloody lucky.'

Tom saw Lieutenant Sullivan making his way along the trench towards them. 'Any casualties to report?' he asked.

'Not from Corporal Frogan's section,' Tom replied and saw the relief on Sullivan's strained face.

'None from the rest of the platoon either,' Sullivan said. 'But it seems the other companies have not been so lucky.'

As Sullivan spoke a machine-gun opened up from their front, pouring bullets out of the fog now starting to lift. None could see where the gun was firing from, but they located the direction of the sound.

'I have orders that we are to hop this trench and continue advancing,' Sullivan said. 'The Hun firing on us will have to be our next objective. Sergeant Duffy, assemble the men, and on my whistle blast we go over again.'

Tom quickly sorted out the platoon members and passed on the directions. In a minute or two the whistle shrilled the advance. Tom took up a position not far from Dan's section and they went over the rear of the German trench to move in the direction from whence they had heard the German machine-gun, now fallen into silence.

Suddenly it chattered into life again and all Tom remembered was nothing at all – not even the pain as the bullet took him in the head. Dan Frogan saw Tom crumple into the earth, and although he knew the procedure was to leave any man who had fallen, he disregarded the rule and rushed to Tom, who was now lying on his back, arms outstretched. Blood oozed from his head.

'Stretcher-bearers!'

Then Dan was hit as the unseen machine-gun sought out targets in the fog, as the platoon continued to advance into the sunrise.

'He's been head shot,' the voice drifted to Tom. 'A waste of time taking him back.'

'You bloody take him back or I'll shoot you lazy bas-tards myself,' another voice said, but Tom did not recognise the voice. The world around him was slowly fading into a peaceful world without care – except for the throbbing pain in his head. A voice was calling to him from down a long tunnel and somehow Tom knew that voice and was con-fused. The voice was so very distant and yet within hearing and it seemed to be a voice of his own blood.

Then all went as black as death.

Tom was suddenly awake, but was now completely confused as to where he was, and why he was looking into the face of a man wearing a white mask. A thumping sound shook the world he was in and he could see other faces hovering over his own – all wearing white masks and peering down at him. They would occasionally speak, and Tom wanted to answer but the words made no sense and the blackness came again. Glimpses of uniforms, and sounds of steam hissing; the smell of coal soot and the clatter of combustion engines. When he woke next he was aware of a smell of salt water, and the cool, crisp sheets beneath him.

'More water,' a gentle female voice said and Tom sipped the clear liquid while a hand rested on his forehead.

'His temperature is down,' the female voice said while Tom fought to remain conscious. But something called to him to return to the world of the dead where he was met by a spirit being. Time had lost all meaning.

'Tom,' the spirit being said, 'remember who you are.'

For some reason Tom sensed that the spirit being who met him in the corridor of light was an old black man with a long white beard shot with grey hair. Tom did not know who this man was, but it was as if this other world was better than the one when he opened his eyes. The terrible, crippling fear he had once known was gone and all he wanted to do was to remain here in the arms of eternal peace.

It was semi-dark and a smell of blood came to Tom. His eyes were open and he blinked, focusing on a high white ceiling. The sounds drifted to him from all around; coughing, whimpering and even sobbing.

'Hey,' Tom called weakly, and waited to see what would happen next. A ghostly figure glided to him from out of the dim light and bent, taking his wrist. Tom saw the angelic face of a young nurse, holding a fob watch and staring intently at it.

'How do you feel?' she asked, glancing up at him. 'You finally have a strong pulse.'

'Where am I?' Tom asked.

'You are in a military hospital in England,' the nurse replied gently. 'This is the first time in a month that you have been fully conscious and able to speak.'

'Month,' Tom echoed without any sense of time. 'What happened? Why am I here?'

'When you were brought in we didn't know what to make of it. Your vital signs were strong, and we were able to get you to swallow food and water but you didn't respond to any stimuli,' she said, lifting Tom's head gently and sliding a pillow under it, so that he could drink from a glass.

In the dim light of the ward he could just make out other beds and patients and guessed it was late night or early morning. He felt so weak that he had trouble moving his arm to support the glass the nurse held to his lips. 'I don't remember what happened to me. I don't remember anything about myself,' Tom said after a sip of water.

'That is to be expected,' the nurse said. 'You had a traumatic head wound – you were shot in the head – and the doctors had to replace part of your skull with a metal plate.'

Tom reached up to touch his head and felt a great swathe of bandages. How was it that he could remember nothing of the incident – or even who he was? He just knew that his name was Tom – because this was what the old black man had called him in the other world.

'I don't know who I am,' he croaked in despair.

'You are an Australian army sergeant, Tom Duffy,' the nurse said, taking a chair by Tom's side. 'You are a hero, and from what I was told by your friend, Corporal Frogan, a man who is sorely missed by his comrades.'

'Frogan,' Tom repeated with a frown. 'I don't recognise that name.'

The nurse took his hand. 'Doctor Mendelson will be very pleased to hear that you are back with us. He is a remarkable man and does wonders with cases such as yours. He pulled your scalp over the head wound; when it's healed, you won't even see a scar because it'll be covered by your hair – once it grows back, of course.'

Tom frowned. He was utterly confused.

'Now, you must rest and I must continue my rounds,' the nurse said, rising from the chair and leaving Tom wide awake to stare at the ceiling, desperately seeking through the dark corners of his mind to find the bits and pieces that defined him as a human in the living world. Nothing came to him; the past was a blank and the present a frightening reality.

Tom was still awake when the ward woke up with the clatter of bedpans, meals being served and men waking and talking to each other across the polished aisle and between beds.

'So yer finally awake, cobber,' said a voice from the bed beside him. 'The boys bet you wouldn't make it, but I figured you would, so I clean up today, thank you very much. I'm Sergeant Wilson Blackler from Mackay,' he continued. 'I copped a back full of Hun shrapnel at Mont St Quentin and I've been here since.'

Tom turned his head to see a pale face grinning at him. 'Sergeant Tom Duffy apparently . . . I'm not sure where I copped my wound . . . or where I'm from,' he said hesitantly.

'You must have lost yer memory,' Wilson Blackler said. 'I seen it before in a few of the boys when they went down with shellshock. It'll probably come back to you in time.'

Tom turned his head to stare at the patient lying in the bed on the other side of him. A sheet was drawn up over his face and the figure underneath was deathly still.

'Young Clarry died last night,' Wilson Blackler explained. 'He'd been stitched up by a Hun MG at the Somme Canal a few weeks ago. We never thought he's make it. They'll take his body away soon enough.'

That morning Tom sat up and ate a bowl of porridge, and after breakfast was visited by a doctor in a white coat. He was a short man with spectacles and thinning hair.

'How do you feel, Sergeant Duffy?' he asked, looking at his clipboard. He was accompanied by a gaunt, stern-looking woman wearing the uniform of a senior nurse. 'I am Doctor Mendelson.'

'Other than feeling weak, I feel fine,' Tom replied.

'I was informed by the night nurse that you had regained your senses, and that is a miracle in its own right,' the doctor said. 'I was also told that you have lost some of your memory.'

'I get snatches of memory, but none of it makes any sense,' Tom said. 'Like flashes in the mind.'

'That is a start,' Mendelson said, scratching a note on his board. 'I am going to have you shifted to another ward, where we can work on getting you back on your feet, and also on getting your memory back.'

Tom nodded, wondering what he would find in his past. He had had flashes of mud, blood and uncontrollable terror, which made his body tremble violently. He wasn't so sure he wanted to recover his memory.

That night Tom slept and a dream came to him of a cave and an old, bearded black man watching him with sad eyes. In his mind Tom could hear words echoing of a mission he had in life. What mission? Tom asked, but the dream faded and he woke up shivering.

The next day his recuperation began. He was transferred to a ward with more mobile patients and, with the help of a nurse, he sat up by himself. He felt the world tilt around him and his head pounded so hard he thought he might vomit. He struggled to stay upright, until the nurse gently laid him back down again. The next day it was slightly easier, and he placed his feet on the ground. It took a while, and a great deal of pain and discomfort, but eventually he could walk with the aid of a cane out into the gardens of the English manor house that had been converted to a recovery centre adjacent to the hospital. Slowly he started to put on weight. He pushed himself to work out with dumbbells after the bandages had been removed from his head and after a couple of weeks Tom felt his physical strength return – but not his memory. His old companion continued to haunt his dreams, until Tom ascertained that the cave was in a semi-arid place when the old man soared his spirit with his own over a sea of stunted scrub on red soil plains.

'Your dreams are extremely important,' Doctor Mendelson said to Tom one day. 'They may be glimpses into your past and may even assist us to recover your memory.'

Tom was about to say that they were not dreams but something more. But to say so would only infer that Tom had not only lost his memory but also his sanity, so he kept the thought to himself.

When Tom returned to the ward there was a man, a corporal, waiting for him.

'Tom, you old bastard,' the stranger said. 'I always knew you'd come good.'

'I'm sorry,' Tom responded, 'but do I know you?'

'Dan Frogan,' the stranger said and the grin turned to a sad smile. 'The nurses said you might not remember me. But that's okay. Give it time, old cobber, and it'll all come back. You and I copped it together, but all I got was a bullet through the shoulder, which was bloody good as it got me a Blighty. The whole mob back at the battalion will be pleased as punch to hear I saw you in good shape.'

'You must be the Corporal Frogan I was told about. I'm sorry I can't remember you, but I'm sure I will, in time.' Tom apologised.

'How about we go for a walk,' Dan said. 'It's a bit chilly outside, but hospitals give me the creeps.'

Tom nodded, grabbed his khaki greatcoat, and the two men wandered out into the garden, which was littered with rusty coloured leaves that had fallen from the trees. They walked in silence until they came to a bench and sat down.

Dan produced a silver flask from his pocket and handed it to Tom. 'Just a little something to take away the nip in the air.'

Tom unscrewed the lid and took a mouthful of strong whisky; it felt good – it warmed his body. He passed the flask back to Dan, who followed suit, taking a long sip of the fiery liquid.

'Enough to bring back a few memories,' Dan said but Tom looked blankly at him.

'I know I sound a bit stupid,' Tom said eventually, staring out at the garden. They had it to themselves; everyone else was inside, out of the cold. 'But tell me about the two of us.'

Dan shook his head sadly. 'Old mate, you and I survived some of the worst the Hun could throw at us over the last couple of years. You never spoke about your past in Queensland, but when I first met you in the old battalion, you were the best sniper we had. You used to work for Captain Jack Kelly until he got transferred, and then you were promoted to platoon sergeant. We've seen platoon commanders come and go, but you and I made a bloody good team.' Dan handed the flask back to Tom, who took another drink.

'Did I ever speak about a cave in Queensland?' Tom asked.

'Not to me – but maybe to Juliet,' he replied.

'Juliet,' Tom frowned. 'Who's Juliet?'

'You don't remember Juliet?' Dan looked sideways at his old comrade. 'God almighty! You really do have a bad case of memory loss. How could you forget the woman you were going to marry?'

'I don't remember her,' Tom replied bleakly.

'Ah, well,' Dan said, 'I suppose that will come with time. I bloody well hope so.'

The two men sat in silence, huddled in their greatcoats against the chill. Eventually it began to spit with rain, and the matron came looking to bring them in out of the approaching storm.

She stood over the two men on the bench. 'If I did not know better I would suspect that you have provided one of my patients with intoxicating alcohol, Corporal Frogan,' she said sternly.

'Er, sorry,' Dan mumbled. 'I was just going. Being sent back to France tonight, to rejoin the boys. I'll see you when I can, Tom,' he said, rising to his feet and slipping the silver flask in his coat pocket.

The matron looked down at Tom, who remained staring at the sky torn by a bolt of lightning and followed by the crack of thunder. The matron could see that he was trembling.

'Come along, Sergeant Duffy,' she said gruffly. 'I don't want you catching your death out here.'

Tom returned his attention to her words and stood stiffly to follow her back to the ward. The sleet and thunder had for the moment drawn him back to a place where death came in a loud flash to rip men's bodies apart, splattering the churned-up mud with entrails, blood and body parts.

16

The great rotating fan overhead made a clicking sound. Captain Matthew Duffy lay back in a comfortable leather chair and waited patiently in the foyer of the Cairo Hotel. It had been over three weeks since he had returned to Jerusalem with Saul Rosenblum, and after reporting to Allied HQ had once again been outfitted in an AFC officer's uniform, which Matthew had had to pay for. Matthew had expected to be sent directly back to his squadron but he had been diverted to Cairo for an intelligence debriefing.

A man dressed in the uniform of a British major strode across the marbled floor of the hotel foyer straight towards Matthew. Matthew rose from his chair and raised his right hand in a lazy salute, and the British intelligence officer returned the military compliment.

'Captain Duffy, I presume,' Wilkins said without

offering his hand. Matthew immediately sensed hostility in the English officer.

'Major Wilkins,' he answered.

'I pray that you have fully recovered from your ordeal,' Wilkins said. 'I only wish Miss Barrington had been so fortunate.'

At the mention of Joanne's name Matthew felt the now familiar pain of grief. He was surprised to see in the British officer's eyes outright anger. 'I am sure that you knew of our relationship,' Matthew countered. 'So you will also know that I have strong feelings about what occurred out there.'

'You cost me the life of a very talented agent and a personal friend,' Wilkins said.

Matthew's guilt was like an open wound. 'I would never have allowed Joanne to rescue me if I had known what she was up to,' he said. 'If I'd been able I would have traded her life for mine without any hesitation.'

Matthew's sincerity obviously touched the British officer, whose hard expression softened just a little. 'Miss Barrington was the most extraordinary woman I think I will ever meet, and I am just as responsible for her death as anyone. Maybe I should be directing my anger at myself for allowing her to take on a mission behind Ottoman lines. It is a decision I regret very deeply.'

There was nothing Matthew could say.

'Normally, you would have returned directly to your unit, but we need to know about the Turkish officer who took you prisoner,' Wilkins said eventually.

'Captain Barak?' Matthew said. 'Why do you need to know about him?'

'That is a question I cannot answer,' Wilkins said. 'But I think you would have noticed the man spoke fluent English. I don't know if you knew that his mother was English, and that his father was with the Turkish trade delegation to purchase our warships – before the outbreak of hostilities. Captain Barak grew up in England and attended the best schools. That is all I can say about him.'

'He's working for you,' Matthew said bluntly, but Wilkins did not reply. 'Too bad I didn't know that when I had the chance to escape by my own means.'

'We couldn't get a message to him,' Wilkins said. 'If I had, Joanne might be alive today.'

Matthew shook his head in despair. Intrigue had always been a part of Joanne's life but it had not helped her in the end. 'A bloody shambles,' he muttered.

'Joanne confided in me that you are the father of her children,' Wilkins said sympathetically. 'I am glad they still have a father.'

'I intend to visit them as soon as this bloody war is over,' Matthew said.

'That may be more difficult than you expect,' Wilkins said. 'Her father holds you responsible for all that has gone wrong in his daughter's life – including her death. He is a very powerful man, with contacts in our government, and probably a more dangerous enemy to you than the Turks. I expect him to stop at nothing to prevent you ever seeing your children.'

'That does not surprise me,' Matthew answered. 'But I am not a man without means myself. All I have to do is sur- vive this war, and then I will see to my son and daughter. Joanne would have wanted that.'

'Good luck,' Wilkins said. 'From what Joanne told me, I believe she would have wanted you to meet your children.'

'I'm surprised to hear you say that, sir,' Matthew said. 'I would have thought that under the circumstances you would have sided with her father.'

'Let's just say that I am not impressed by rich Yankee bankers throwing their weight around in my war,' Wilkins replied, and held out his hand. 'You have done your duty and I must share the responsibility for Joanne's death. You will be returning to your squadron in Palestine on tomorrow's boat out of Cairo, but I think it will not be the last time we meet. You, after all, are the only one in the Allied command who has personally met with Captain Barak.'

With that, Matthew saluted the British major and watched him stride out of the foyer and into the hot Egyptian sun.

The next day Matthew steamed for Palestine and rejoined his squadron. He was met with back-slapping from his fellow pilots on his miraculous escape from Turkish captivity and that night they celebrated his return in the officers' mess. He was glad to be back – he felt at home with these men – but he was subdued; he could not celebrate his life when Joanne had lost hers.

He and the rest of the Allied forces were unaware that General Allenby had carefully planned an all-out assault on the Turkish armies remaining in the Holy Land and the plan would prove to be brilliant in its execution. The British general had used deception to mass his forces and aimed to launch a lightning attack on the Turkish coastal flank, breaking through and rolling up what remained of the Ottoman defences. He would use his cavalry forces to speed towards Nazareth and the Upper Jordan region, in order to cut off the southern line of retreat of the Seventh and Eighth Turkish armies around Nabulus. From there the Allied cavalry were to make contact with the Arab guerrillas at Deraa and, by doing so, close the enemy's retreat via the eastern railway. If the plan succeeded, the Ottoman Empire was finished.

By a strange quirk of fate the main fighting would occur in a place with a name well known to many Christians. What was to come would be known as the Battle of Armageddon.

Captain Matthew Duffy would come to know the name well in the next few weeks.

Sergeant Tom Duffy stood to attention before the hospital's board of three medical officers. Weeks had passed and still his memory had not returned, but strangely his knowledge of military life had not been lost. Although he could not remember people or his past, he had proved he could still handle any weapon put before him and demonstrated his knowledge of tactics and military protocol.

'Remarkable, Sergeant Duffy,' said one of the senior military doctors – a major – as he flicked through the file on the table before him. 'I see you have badgered a training battalion nearby to assess you on your soldiering skills. It seems that your former platoon commander gave you some help, although I gather you do not remember him.'

'Yes, sir,' Tom replied. 'I was informed by a former NCO of my platoon that I might find Mr Sullivan at the camp, and he agreed to have me assessed before being paraded here this morning.'

'However, the decision as to whether you return to active duty must be made by this board and must take into account your physical fitness and your mental state,' the major cautioned.

He looked at Tom. 'You know, with the wound you received you are entitled to be shipped home and honourably discharged for your services to King and Empire. Your awards of the DCM and MM certainly prove your courage and many would say that you have done more than your bit for the war effort. To ask to return to France, and your old unit, borders on madness when any rational man would jump at the chance of going home. But when I also look at the decorations you have been awarded, I think I might understand why you would want to return to your comrades.'

'Yes, sir,' Tom answered dutifully. 'I have heard that the Hun is on the run, and I want to be with the boys of my battalion when the victory comes.'

The major glanced at the doctors either side of him and they nodded.

'I am going to approve your request to return to active service,' the major said, scribbling a signature on the file in front of him. 'And commend you for your obvious courage. Good luck, Sergeant Duffy. Your release papers will be processed today and, all going well, you will be taken to London this afternoon to embark on a ship for France where you will rejoin your unit.'

'Thank you, sirs,' Tom said and saluted smartly, turned on his heel and marched from the room.

Outside the room he thought about what he had done. A sane man would have jumped at the opportunity to be shipped home, but Tom knew that if he was to find his past he must return to the war he so badly wanted to avoid. There was one name that haunted him – Juliet Joubert. He could not remember what she looked like, or any detail of their relationship, yet he somehow knew she was very important to him. As for home – all he knew was that it was somewhere in the Australian state of Queensland. Perhaps after the war he would be able to retrace his life back from the place where he had enlisted. But for now he was returning to a world that he had lately remembered in his worst nightmares of exploding shells and men hanging dead and shattered on the terrible strands of barbed wire.

Tom returned to the ward to pick up the few personal items that had been brought in with him and there he was approached by the stern matron.

'I have come to wish you well, Sergeant Duffy,' she said. 'Doctor Mendelson would like to speak with you before you leave us. He will see you in his office now.'

Tom thanked the matron whose dour expression, he knew, belied a great compassion for the wounded men she tended, and for her nurses. Tom finished filling his kitbag with an issue of new uniforms and made his way to the doctor's office. He knocked and was told to enter.

'Sergeant Duffy,' Doctor Mendelson said, looking up from the copious papers scattered on his desk. 'I have been informed by the medical board that they have released you back to active duty – despite my objections. I think that I should close your file with the medical conclusion that you are totally insane.'

Tom shifted uneasily. He had grown to like and respect this small Jewish doctor, and could see in his face both disapproval and sadness. 'I have to go back, sir,' Tom replied feebly. 'I think my memory will come back if I am exposed to old comrades and cobbers.'

The doctor tapped his desk with the end of a pencil and motioned to Tom to take a seat. 'I have had the opportunity to evaluate you both physically and mentally, and I have to agree that, in theory, you are capable of resuming your duties with your regiment. But I feel there is a deep reason for you not remembering your past. It may be, as I have seen in many other patients, that you do not wish to remember the conditions you have lived under for the last few years – that is perfectly understandable – but it seems odd that you would be so determined to return. I think something else has disturbed you, something else has made you want to forget.'

The doctor sighed, placed the pencil on the desk and stared for a moment at Tom. 'I wish you well, Sergeant Duffy. God knows that we need soldiers like you to end this war, but I fear what will happen to you all once it is all over. I do not think you will be able to return to the same life you knew before the war, or that many people will ever understand the horrors you have experienced. I pray you survive your return to the fighting, and that you find what you're looking for in France.' He paused and rubbed his face. 'I suppose I should let you go and finish getting your clearances from here.'

'Thank you, sir,' Tom said, rising, and snapped a salute, surprising the army doctor.

'Not many of my patients have ever saluted me, Sergeant Duffy,' he said, 'but thank you.'

Tom left the office and made his way to the great entrance, passing stretcher-bearers bringing in new patients. He stepped out into the sleeting rain and strode along the driveway past ambulances and rows of green hedges. It was late September and he was about to return to hell.

Within the week Tom found himself moving up from the rear areas to his old battalion now stationed at the village of Frisse. He was met with enthusiastic greetings from many of the men. Although Tom could not remember them, he smiled and acknowledged their back-slapping and kind words of support. They were sympathetic as they had heard that their beloved Sergeant Duffy had lost his memory.

'You might not recognise me,' a tall lanky sergeant said to Tom as he searched for company headquarters. 'I'm Paddy Bourke. I heard you put in a good word for my promotion to sergeant.'

'Hello, Paddy,' Tom replied, a little bemused. 'Pleased to hear it – I'm sure you deserve it.'

'The company commander's glad to have you aboard again. He said he wanted to see you as soon as you returned, so I'll wander along with you and show you where our HQ is,' Paddy said.

'Any idea where I might find Corporal Dan Frogan? He came and saw me when I was in hospital and gave me a bit of news about the battalion,' Tom said.

Paddy Bourke slowed to a halt. 'I'm sorry, Tom, but you wouldn't have got the news yet. Dan went west a week ago. Hun sniper got him when he was on a courier run. I know he was a good pal of yours.'

Tom felt his blood grow cold. If there was anyone who knew about Tom's past, it was Dan Frogan, and now he was gone. 'Bloody shame,' Tom muttered and continued his walk to the company HQ with mixed feelings. How was it that he did not feel the pain of loss? He knew he and Dan were close friends, yet he felt nothing.

Paddy Bourke showed Tom to what was once a village shoeshop and was now occupied by his company's staff. He was met by the company clerk and he handed over his transfer documents.

'Boss wants to see you, Sergeant Duffy,' the clerk said, pointing to a room just off the small foyer of the shop. 'Good to have you back.'

'Thanks,' Tom said and lifted his kitbag.

He stepped through the doorway and immediately saluted. The man, who seemed to know him well, returned the salute. 'Welcome back, Tom,' Major Cooper said, rising from his chair and crossing the short distance to shake Tom's hand. 'It was touch and go but I made sure those rear-echelon bastards kept you alive.'

'Thank you, sir,' Tom answered. Major Cooper walked back to his desk, a battered table, and sat down. Tom knew he should remember his superior officer, but he didn't.

'You are just back in time for the big push on the Hindenburg line,' the major said. 'I am posting you back to your old platoon but you now have a new officer to break in – a former articled clerk from Sydney. He's just arrived and I'm depending on you to look after him so that he doesn't do too much damage in his first days on the line. Have you heard about Corporal Frogan?'

'Sergeant Bourke informed me that Dan caught it about a week ago,' Tom responded. 'I'm sorry to hear that.'

'I was going to promote him to platoon sergeant,' the major sighed. 'No bloody reinforcements coming from Australia and we need every experienced soldier we can muster. Your head wound should have had you shipped back home, but I'm very grateful you insisted on returning to the battalion – a very worthy effort indeed.'

'The battalion is the only home I remember, sir,' Tom said. 'I suppose you know that the head wound has made me to lose my memory, but I haven't lost my knowledge of soldiering, sir.'

'Yes, I was informed just after you applied to return to the unit,' the major replied. 'I was a bit doubtful at first, but seeing you here I am sure you will be all right among your old comrades. I will get Sergeant Bourke to take you to meet your new platoon commander, and give you a chance to settle in. You and he will be sharing a billet with Paddy. Good luck, Tom.'

Tom thanked his company commander and left the office to find Paddy Bourke lingering outside the former shop. 'Boss tell you that I'll be showing you around?' he asked and Tom nodded. 'We'll start with finding Mr Hopkins, and after you settle in, I know where we can get something to drink.'

The walk down the cobbled street brought fleeting memories back to Tom of other places he vaguely remembered, and he found that he was looking for a water fountain in the centre of the town. He did not know why, and he had no time to dwell on the fleeting memory as Paddy had brought him to a house on the main street. There were a few older French civilians out on the street but no young Frenchmen.

A very young officer wearing the rank of second lieutenant stepped from one of the houses.

'That's Mr Hopkins,' Paddy said and the two approached him.

'I have Sergeant Duffy with me, sir,' Paddy said.

'Haven't you forgotten something, Sergeant?' the young officer said haughtily.

Paddy remembered and saluted. 'Sorry, sir,' Paddy said sarcastically. 'I've been too long at the front – if I saluted you there, you might get dropped by a Hun sniper.'

'We are not at the front now,' Second Lieutenant Michael Hopkins retorted. 'I expect military courtesy to be maintained – along with discipline and good order.'

Paddy glanced quickly at Tom with an expression of sympathy.

'Tom Duffy, sir,' Tom said. 'I am reporting for duty with the platoon.'

The young officer looked Tom up and down. 'I see that you are correctly dressed but I expect a better shine on your boots as you are to set an example to the men.'

Tom felt his anger rise. What would this snotty-nosed young man know about soldiers? he thought angrily. Five minutes in the country and he thought he was General Monash. 'I'll see to that as soon as I can, sir,' Tom replied wearily.

'I did not want you in my platoon, Sergeant Duffy,' Hopkins said. 'You have been wounded, and from what I have been told, have little or no memory of your time with the battalion. What will happen if you break down under fire when I need you most?'

'With all due respect, sir,' Tom said, 'have you been under fire yet?'

The young officer looked uncomfortable. 'Not as yet, Sergeant Duffy, but I expect that I will do my duty in the face of the enemy.'

'With respect, sir,' Tom said, 'the best of men do not know how they will react when the bullets and shells start flying, but I reckon I was over here soldiering when you were probably still in school.'

'Careful, Sergeant Duffy, you are behaving insubordinately,' Hopkins said.

'You have the best sergeant in the battalion, sir,' Paddy butted in, trying to calm the situation before it escalated. 'I would trust Sergeant Duffy with my life – I have in the past.'

Michael Hopkins turned to Paddy. 'I can only take your word for that, Sergeant Bourke,' he said. 'You are dismissed for now.'

Tom threw a salute, turned on his heel and marched away with Paddy Bourke beside him.

'What a jumped-up little arse,' Paddy hissed under his breath. 'With any luck he'll cop it in the next push.'

'He's okay,' Tom replied with a shrug. 'He's frightened

that he'll stuff things up, and puts on airs to disguise the fact that he's frightened. I'll sort him out.'

'You have more faith in officers than I do, Tom,' Paddy said. 'I'd shoot the little bugger first chance I had. He's almost as bad as that bastard, Smithers, who was always causing trouble for you.'

'Smithers,' Tom echoed. For some reason the mention of the name made hate well up inside Tom. He struggled to remember why, but nothing came to him. He filed the name way; he'd ask questions later. Somehow, he felt the name was the key to many things he might not actually want to remember.

17

Lenny Johnson had good reason to look over his shoulder whenever he left Maude's flat. Detective Inspector Jack Firth was searching for him, and Lenny did not want to meet the feared policeman on the streets.

But he had to leave the safety of the flat to convince a colleague to assist him by driving his automobile to the residence of George Macintosh. He already had a down payment for the job, as Maude had been able to inveigle George into giving her a substantial amount of cash on the pretext of needing the money to buy more clothes and other female essentials.

'This the place?' Lenny's accomplice asked. He was a small man, with weasel-like characteristics, who sat behind the wheel of the car with a toothpick protruding from his lips. Lenny leaned out of the car window and stared at the big house behind the wall of high hedges and wide wrought-iron gates.

'Yeah,' he said and settled back in his seat. 'We park here so that we can see who comes and goes.'

'What's this job all about?' the Weasel asked, changing the position of the toothpick to the other side of his mouth. 'We gonna do it over?'

'You ask too many questions,' Lenny growled. 'But maybe that is not such a bad idea.'

Already Lenny was considering that he might be able to kill the woman and at the same time ransack the house to make it look like a robbery that had gone bad. He would ensure that Maude kept Mr George Macintosh occupied while Lenny broke into the Macintosh mansion. Lenny would use his sidekick to act as the driver on the job, and later the Weasel and the car might have an unfortunate accident, driving off the infamous Gap on Sydney's southern headland. It was not wise to leave witnesses to high-profile murders – Lenny knew from experience that only one person in a crime could keep a secret.

They waited, the driver reading the race form in the newspaper while Lenny continued to watch the house for movement. After a boring hour of surveillance Lenny was rewarded by spotting a very pretty woman emerge from the house, holding the hand of a toddler. Lenny frowned. Was this the nanny or Mrs Macintosh? He had not thought much about what she would look like and realised he was getting sloppy. He would have to rectify that and also learn how many servants might be on the premises at any given time.

'Okay, we can go now,' Lenny said, leaning back against the seat. The driver put down his paper and engaged the ignition as the woman wandered into the garden, following the laughing child.

★

'I don't know what his wife looks like,' Maude said. 'That's your job to find out.' She stood with her hands on her hips, wearing nothing but a flimsy nightdress.

'I need you to get me information on the layout of the house and how many servants live or work there,' Lenny said.

Maude looked thoughtful. 'I could get one of the staff to tell me about the house, maybe a nanny or a maid. I reckon it would just be a matter of accidentally meeting one of them away from the house, then getting them to talk. I wouldn't be seen as a threat. You identify the right one and leave the rest to me.'

'That could work,' Lenny said. 'You have a devious mind for someone so young, and that's a compliment, little sister.'

Maude broke into a mischievous smile and took Lenny's arm. 'I don't intend to live the rest of my life in this place – or until Mr Macintosh tires of me. One day I will be the lady of the house and maybe the new Mrs Macintosh.'

Lenny looked hard at his sibling and could see the expression of youthful determination in her eyes. He remembered that at her age he too had aspired to better things in life, but he hadn't had the opportunities. Having a sister so well placed could only improve his lot in life, so he'd do everything he could to carry out her plans to get rid of Mrs Louise Macintosh.

The sun was high when Giselle rode out across the plains of Glen View. An Aboriginal stockman had ridden to the house to inform her that one of the European stockmen had taken a fall from his horse and broken his arm.

Giselle immediately fetched her medical kit, then had her horse saddled, and quickly explained to Hector MacManus, the station manager, that she was riding out to see to the injured stockman.

'Take care, lassie,' said the stocky Scot as she hurried out of the house. 'Be back before sunset.'

On her mount, Giselle followed the Aboriginal stockman as he cantered through the scrub still damp after a sudden and violent spring storm. Already tiny shoots were sprouting that would herald the small but pretty wild flowers Giselle loved so much.

After an hour they slowed to a halt. Cattle stood grazing and the rest of the mustering crew had lit a fire to boil up a billy of tea. They greeted Giselle with great respect. One of the men sat with his back to a rotting tree trunk, holding his arm with an expression creased with pain.

Giselle could see that the bone was protruding through the flesh of his lower arm. She knelt and examined the injury.

'Hurts like buggery, missus,' said the stockman through gritted tobacco-stained teeth.

'I can only splint your arm and sling it until we get you back to Glen View, and then to a medical doctor for proper treatment,' Giselle said, reaching into her leather bag and retrieving a triangular bandage. Giselle turned to a couple of stockmen standing a short distance away, watching the procedures with enamel mugs of steaming tea in their hands.

'Please find me a couple of small sticks I can use as a splint,' she said and they shuffled away, returning moments later with suitable splints sticks, which Giselle used to immobilise the arm before applying the sling. All the time the injured stockman did not complain, although sweat glistening on his face belied his agony.

'Like a cuppa, missus?' one of the stockmen offered.

'Thank you, I would,' Giselle answered, rising to her feet.

'I need a couple of you to escort this man back to the house,' she said, accepting a battered mug from the stockman. The tea was hot, black and sweet.

'Horry and me can take Jacko back,' said the man who had offered the mug of tea. 'You comin' with us?'

Giselle shook her head. She knew that when the injured man was returned to the station house Hector would know what to do. As she was out on the plains she wanted to ride to the sacred hill, which was not far away from here. She did not exactly know why, but she felt as though the hill was calling to her. 'Tell Mr MacManus I will be home before sunset,' she said.

'Okay, missus, if that's what you want,' the stockman shrugged.

Giselle walked over to her horse grazing on the first shoots of spring. She mounted and rode away in the direction of the hill, leaving the cattle and the stockmen of Glen View behind.

Giselle rode for an hour, then pulled on the reins to bring her horse to a halt. *Funny,* she thought. *I should be at the hill by now.* She looked around her but could only see the monotonous stretches of tough and spindly scrub. A tiny suspicion crept into her mind that she was lost. The sun was starting to sink lower in the sky and Giselle knew that it would be wise to retrace her tracks. But she was not a trained tracker and after a few minutes she lost all trace of her horse's shod hoof prints in the sandy soil.

Giselle did not panic – she knew that if she had not returned by nightfall Hector would organise a search party – but she felt foolish for deciding to visit the sacred hill. This land was so vast and she had become complacent. This ancient land still had the ability to isolate one who was not born to it.

Giselle was not sure what to do but she felt that all she had to do was turn around and ride a little further and eventually the hill would loom up over the plains. At least from there she could make it back to the homestead.

It was late afternoon when Giselle finally dismounted, and she still had not found the hill. So it would mean an uncomfortable night camped out on the plains. She had a canteen of water and she reassured herself that she was not going to starve to death in the next few hours.

What she could do for the moment was gather rotting, termite-eroded timber and light a fire. Thankfully she always carried matches with her, and soon she had a small fire flickering away. A wisp of smoke rose but disappeared in the clear late-afternoon sky.

Giselle was glad that she was dressed in sensible riding jodhpurs and a long-sleeved flannel shirt as the night would grow chilly when the sun set behind the limitless horizon of scrub.

'Please, God,' she prayed, 'let them find me in the morning. I am a foolish woman but you need to save me for the wellbeing of my son.'

The night came and so did the cold. Giselle sat for some time watching the beautiful moonless night sky. She could not help but be awed by its magnificent serene beauty. Tiny shooting stars occasionally blazed streaks through the constellations, and in the distance Giselle could hear the dingos calling to each other. After some time she fell asleep, curled into the cooling soil, and began to dream.

In the sacred cave Wallarie sat by his fire. It had been a good day – he had been able to spear a small wallaby and the remains of his meal smouldered at the edge of his fire.

It would provide further meat in the morning. The fire kept the cave warm, and the nocturnal sounds of the bush were his lullaby. The dreams came again to him but this time it was not Tom's spirit that came to him, but the spirit of the little boy called David, who Wallarie knew was the son of Giselle Macintosh. The little boy smiled at Wallarie and held out his hand to him. Wallarie took the boy's hand, rising from where he slept to be led from the cave and into the dark night.

They walked through the scrub side by side, the old Aboriginal warrior and the little white boy. Wallarie did not know why the spirit boy had come to him but he followed anyway, knowing well that the ancestors always had a reason for what they did.

Then the boy was gone, and Wallarie could see a tiny light flickering through the scrub. He continued alone until he reached the point of the light, seeing that it was a camp-fire beside which lay the spirit boy's mother.

'Hey! Missus!' Wallarie called – just loud enough to wake Giselle but not to startle her. She stirred and sat up, rubbing her eyes, blinking away the sleep.

Wallarie stepped into the feeble light.

'Wallarie!' Giselle gasped.

'You bin lost,' Wallarie chuckled, squatting down on the other side of the fire, which was almost extinguished now. Wallarie reached for a small piece of wood nearby and stoked the fire into flames.

'How did you know?' Giselle asked, brushing herself down.

'You got no reason to sleep out here alone,' he said. 'You got any baccy?'

'Sorry,' Giselle replied. 'I don't smoke.'

'Mebbe you get some baccy and leave it at the cave sometime,' Wallarie said.

'I promise I will.' Giselle felt a great sense of relief to be in the old man's company. 'I last saw our stockmen around midday,' she continued. 'So I guess Mr MacManus will send out a search party at first light. I feel so foolish for causing all the fuss that a search will entail.'

'You orright, that is the main thing,' Wallarie said with a shrug. 'The ancestor spirits guided you here because I am not allowed to go to you and warn you that you must not go south to that other place where a *debil* lives. A bad man who would hurt you and the spirit boy.'

'Spirit boy?' Giselle queried. 'What spirit boy?'

'The one who is of your flesh and is called David. He got mighty strong powers if the ancestor spirits tell him to fetch me.'

'Fetch you?' Giselle asked, confused by the old man's strange conversation.

'Young David come to me in the spirit world and show me where to find you. You bin dreaming 'bout dark water,' he said.

'I have!' Giselle gasped. 'And so has my mother.'

'The spirit is in the blood and the old ones warn you with pictures in your sleep. Mebbe I help them but I also bin to the place of evil, and you and the boy must not travel south. Place *baal*, man there *baal*,' Wallarie growled, using an old word for bad. 'There is a terrible death coming to this land and we will not see it − 'cept in the bodies the crows and hawks come down to feast on.'

Wallarie's prediction chilled Giselle. Did it involve her family? 'What is this terrible death?' she asked and Wallarie simply shrugged his bony shoulders. 'Don't know. Just that the old ones from the Dreaming time say it a revenge on what the whitefella done to my people. Many will die.'

219

'You must mean that terrible war we are fighting on the other side of the world,' Giselle said.

'No, the death that will come to all this land in not a long time,' Wallarie replied. 'But now I will stay with you because you cannot go to the cave. No woman should enter the cave. It is a place for the men. Mebbe if you are hungry I will go back and bring you some cooked wallaby. But they will find you in the morning before the sun has reached the top part of the sky.'

'How can you be sure of that?' Giselle countered.

'Because I will fly to your mother and the pastor and tell them where you are,' he replied matter-of-factly. He began to chant a song and Giselle was fascinated by the melody that drifted on the sound of the old man's voice. She had been born on the other side of the world in Germany and yet it was in this land that she was drawn closer to her own spirituality. Giselle closed her eyes to absorb the hypnotic chanting.

It was sunrise and Giselle awoke to find herself alone. She sat up with a start and the only sound now was the tinkle of the horse bell on her mare grazing a short distance away. Where was Wallarie? He said that he would remain with her.

Giselle waited. She did not quite know whether she had dreamed the meeting with the elusive Aboriginal elder or whether he really had come in the night to warn her off accepting Louise's invitation to spend Christmas in Sydney with her. The small campfire was already cold and there did not appear to be any signs in the sand of his presence. But she put her faith in the words he had uttered – whether real or imaginary – and waited.

Midmorning she could hear the sound of horses and she called out. Hector MacManus, accompanied by two stock-men, appeared out of the scrub. Hector immediately flung himself from his horse and ran to Giselle. 'Lassie, are you hurt?' he asked urgently.

Giselle shook her head and smiled. 'I am perfectly well, Mr MacManus. I just seem to have lost my bearings out here.'

'Thank God we found you,' Hector said. 'Your mother and the pastor nagged me to look for you here. Your mother had a mad tale about seeing a wedge-tailed eagle flying over this spot, and she swore that if we searched near the creek we would find you unhurt.'

'Wallarie,' Giselle said softly.

'You dinna think the old blackfella guided us here?' Hector asked with a frown.

'Believe me,' said Giselle, 'I do not understand how, but Wallarie found me last night and said that you would find me before midmorning – and here you are. Wallarie is a strange man – with even stranger powers.'

'I'm with you, Mrs Macintosh,' the grizzled Scot said. 'Always said Wallarie was a magic man.'

'But if we told most people of his powers they would think us mad,' Giselle smiled. 'Is that not right, Mr MacManus?'

'We keep the secret to Glen View,' Hector said, guiding Giselle to her horse. 'There is magic in the rocks, hills and creeks of this land that few would understand.'

Giselle mounted her mare and the party set out to return to the homestead. As she rode she tried to recall every word that Wallarie had said to her. The warning; her son being a spirit boy favoured by Wallarie's ancestors, and the terrible death that would come to the land. No doubt time would prove Wallarie right, but for now all she could do was truly believe that the old man was unique in his spiritual powers.

Maude Urqhart stewed over her obsession. Mrs Macintosh had to go; George was not in love with his wife, he was in love with her. Maude was the one who deserved to live like a queen, not Louise Macintosh. That mansion should be hers, those servants hers to command. She would make it happen, no matter the cost.

Maude travelled across the city to the Macintosh mansion and, brazen as anything, entered the grounds and walked up the driveway to knock on the front door.

A young woman, only a few years older than Maude, wearing a white apron and her dark hair drawn up in a severe bun, answered the door. She looked Maude up and down with some disdain. 'What do you want?' she asked.

Maude, keeping her composure, answered, 'I was wanting to see the missus of the house, to see if there might be a chance for service under her roof. Is she in?'

'I am the governess here and I can tell you that Mr Macintosh is not hiring any staff,' the woman replied. 'So you can go away.'

'Who is it, Tabitha?' a female voice called from within.

'No one, Mrs Macintosh,' the governess called back. 'Just some young girl looking for work. I've told her to go away.'

Louise appeared behind the governess, and Maude felt her heart skip a beat. So this was George's wife, eh? Pretty, for her age.

'You must not be rude about rejecting the young lady's enquiry as to whether we have work, Tabitha,' Louise said sympathetically.

'Me dad was killed in the war,' Maude lied. 'And now

I am an orphan. I need to get work or I'll starve. Could I have a glass of water before I go?'

'Of course, young lady,' Louise said kindly. 'Tabitha will show you to the kitchen and serve you a cup of tea and fetch some biscuits for you.'

Tabitha reluctantly led Maude through to the kitchen and Maude could hardly believe her luck. Stupid woman for being so trusting.

As Tabitha boiled the water and prepared the tea things, Maude sat at an old, much cleaned wooden table, gazing around at the walls and ceiling. 'This is a beautiful house,' she said as Tabitha laid out a plate of biscuits. 'You are lucky to have service here. I bet it takes a lot of people to keep this place as pretty as it is.'

'It is a big house that requires a large staff,' Tabitha volunteered with some pride. 'Mr Macintosh employs a gardener, cook and a manservant – besides myself. I've the job of looking after Master Macintosh. The manservant is also Mr Macintosh's chauffeur.'

Maude picked up a biscuit and nibbled the edge. 'There must be a lot of rooms,' she said as if in awe of her sur-roundings, and this caused the governess to puff up in her pride. Before she could stop herself, Tabitha was providing a detailed layout of the residence, including where George and Louise had their personal quarters. She also explained that the gardener and manservant shared a cottage on the grounds near the former stables. Maude could not believe her luck and locked the layout of the house in her mind. She was an intelligent girl with a good memory.

After she had consumed her cup of tea and eaten two biscuits, Maude thanked the governess, who showed her out of the house and even smiled before Maude turned to walk down the driveway.

That evening Maude sketched out what she knew of the house layout, and the comings and goings of the household staff. 'If Mr Macintosh is with me, then his manservant will be in the car waiting for him to leave. That leaves the governess, cook and gardener. I think the cook only comes in through the day and goes home in the evening.'

Lenny stared at the sketch. 'I know where the entrances are,' he said. 'If your plan of the house is accurate, I know where to go when I do over the house. I'll make it look like a burglary, and the death of Mrs Macintosh an unfortunate consequence of disturbing the break-in.'

'When do you reckon you'll do it?' Maude asked, and Lenny thought for a moment.

'It'll take me about a week to get my plan worked out,' he replied. 'I will need to confirm the movement of the servants to ensure a clean run on the house. The Weasel will be my driver.'

Maude smiled her satisfaction. 'I'll make sure George is with me on the night you plan,' she said. 'It should be easy.'

'Should be,' Lenny echoed. 'Just make sure you pay up when the job is done or, sister or not, you'll cop it.'

Maude had the optimism of youth and she knew it would all fit into place. Nothing could stop her now from realising her wildest dreams of wealth and power.

18

The mission had been highly successful, and Captain Matthew Duffy brought his new Bristol two-seater fighter to a bouncing halt on the airfield on the plains of Palestine. The plan General Allenby had formulated relied heavily on air support, and Matthew, with his observer, Lieutenant Paul Goddard, and one other Bristol fighter, had been assigned to reconnoitre an area east of Jordan. They had found a Turkish camp and swooped down, strafing a Turkish unit exercising at Ain es Sir.

On their way home luck had still been on their side. They'd come across a column of fifty motor lorries carrying troops and supplies, driving south along the Wady Fara road. The fighters had dived on the trucks, dropping their bombs and scoring a direct hit on the lead lorry, which then blocked the road. Later that day a second wave of Bristol fighters would finish off the hapless convoy.

Matthew's ground crew rushed to the fighter plane now as he lifted himself wearily from the tiny open cockpit. Goddard did the same; he had just joined the squadron from Egypt, and today was his first mission. He had flown observer with Matthew. Like Matthew, his face was sunburned and covered in oil – except where he wore his goggles – and the cramped conditions of the flight had stiffened his body.

'How did it go?' the ground-crew supervisor asked as Matthew slid off the goggles, rubbed his eyes and stared around the airfield to see if he could recognise any of his comrade's aircraft safely home. 'We had a spot of good fortune, Sarge,' Matthew replied. 'Caught them napping in their camps.'

'Good to see that you're both all right,' the flight sergeant said.

'Thanks, Sarge,' Matthew answered and walked towards the operations tent to submit his report. Behind him, the second Bristol fighter was coming to a stop.

Was he all right? Matthew asked himself. Yes. In body – if not in spirit. He had written to Joanne's father weeks earlier, only to receive a letter from James Barrington's lawyers saying that he was not to approach Joanne's children or attempt to lay any claim to them as their father. Matthew's response to the legal letter had been to screw it up and throw it away.

When the war ended he would travel to America and confront Joanne's father, but for now all he could do was try to survive each mission and pray that what he did would help win the war. This thought kept him going.

'Jolly good show,' young Goddard said to Matthew as they approached a group of pilots hanging around outside the ops tent. Matthew did not reply. The young man was like an overgrown puppy, and that annoyed Matthew, who

226

felt old enough to be his father, despite the fact there were not that many years between them.

When they reached the tent they were greeted by the other aircrew, who had returned from bombing missions against Turkish troops retreating along the road between Et Tire and Tul Keram.

'We have them on the run,' Matthew overheard one pilot say. 'But the anti-aircraft fire was bloody heavy. Johhny Turk is far from beaten. I saw Dowling and Mulford cop it, but they were able to land okay. If the Turks are in a good mood, they might have taken them prisoner.'

Matthew experienced the gloom of losing two more comrades to the war but was brightened when a corporal clerk dashed out from the tent and shouted, 'Our boys in the Light Horse, chasing Johnny Turk, have just freed our two men shot down today.'

A cheer erupted from the pilots. Matthew joined in.

The squadron commander strolled to the entrance of the large tent. 'Well, boys, time for a cup of tea and a bit of a chat on how you went today.'

Like schoolboys summoned by the headmaster, the pilots filed silently into the tent to take their seats. Exhausted and numb, Matthew knew that, following the debrief, they would immediately be informed of the next job assigned to them. The pressure was on and usually the pilots barely had time to snatch a meal before becoming airborne again, seeking out more men to kill and supplies to destroy.

After a couple of sandwiches and a thermos of hot tea, Matthew and Lieutenant Goddard were once again in the cockpit of their Biff – as the Bristol was affectionately known to its crew – and soon soaring into the sky along with five other Bristols flying in pursuit of the enemy. They flew north of Kakon towards Baka and two of the Bristols peeled away to strafe a disorganised body of Turkish soldiers, while Matthew and the other three Bristols found a congested mass of men, towed artillery guns, carts loaded with wounded soldiers, and transport camels and horses making from Tul Keram towards Anebta. From their height the Australian pilots could see that the column had to pass through a narrow defile, surrounded on either side by steep, arid hills. The column entered the defile in their panic to escape the pursuing cavalry and Light Horse units. Matthew's flight pounced like eagles on a paralysed rabbit.

Matthew cocked his machine-guns to ensure that they were free to fire and brought his fighter plane down so low that he had fleeting images of terrified Turkish soldiers gaping up at him as he flew down the line of vehicles firing his guns. He knew that his bullets were tearing into men and animals, maiming and killing them without discrimination. Matthew had long trained himself to think of the victims below as simply targets in his gun sights; he knew that it did not pay to dwell on the death and destruction that he and his aircraft brought down upon the enemy. His Bristol was followed by the others, who raked the column with the high velocity .303 rounds.

Over his shoulder Matthew was alarmed to see one of the Bristols falter in the sky, trailing smoke. It peeled away to make a forced landing, hit by ground fire. Goddard was waving and pointing to the downed aircraft as if Matthew could do something to save them. The best he could do was turn, climb and swoop back down on the convoy until the firing pins clicked on empty chambers.

So far only a few bullets coming from the ground fire had ripped through the fabric of his aircraft, and Matthew realised it was time to rejoin the remaining airborne Bristols to return to the field with the forlorn hope that they would be stood down for a badly needed rest. He glanced over his shoulder at the small fires the deadly incendiary bullets from his guns had caused among the shambles of smashed vehicles, some already burning where fuel tanks had been penetrated. Black oily smoke rose in the clear sky of the late afternoon, and he saw another wave of Bristols approaching high and to his three o'clock. No doubt they would finish off the convoy with any bombs and bullets they were carrying. Matthew signalled to Goddard that they were going home, and he thought he saw a momentary expression of disappointment on the young observer's face.

'This is not a bloody game of cricket,' he growled, but his words were drowned by the roar of the engine and the *swoosh* of wind past his face.

He landed and brought the aircraft to a halt not far from where his ground crew sat at the edge of the strip awaiting his return. For the second time in a day he lifted himself from his cockpit and slumped wearily to the ground.

'What a damned fine thing we did!' Goddard whooped from his seat. 'We really showed Johnny Turk what for.'

Matthew felt like walking over and smashing his observer in the face. Maybe if he could take him back to the broken convoy and show him up close what the incendiary bullets did to a man's body – or how the bombs tore flesh like scissors through paper, then he wouldn't be so bloody cocky.

Matthew did not bother to wait for Goddard to join him but brushed past his ground crew to walk towards the ops tent for another debrief. God, he hoped they wouldn't be sent out on another mission today. The word Armageddon flitted through his head. Already the fighting was being referred to as the Battle of Armageddon after the plains that were being fought over, and Matthew knew that Armageddon had come to many young and old Turkish soldiers this day.

They were just people caught up in this terrible war because of ambitious politicians; men with mothers, wives, sweethearts and siblings, men who would most likely have died in agony with a burning bullet in their body.

Matthew tried to stop himself from thinking about the terrible carnage he had been involved in this day. A year earlier he had found himself literally sick with fear before flying the missions, but now he felt sick with disgust at the death he had inflicted on others. They might be the enemy, but they were people, not simply targets. How many men had he killed? He shook his head. Too many for one man's lifetime, but at least he had not seen all their faces as they died, as he had with the person he had loved most in this dangerous world.

It was late afternoon in France and Sergeant Tom Duffy sat alone under a shelter he had made from his gas cape. It had been an overcast and wet day but at least they were out of the front lines and bivouacked in the Hargicourt area.

Tom lay back against his field pack, smoking his pipe and gazing out at the fields where trees were already shedding leaves for the coming winter. Even now his memory had not returned, and he wondered how he was still able to function so well as a soldier. Gradually he was meeting some of his old comrades who, sympathetic to his condition, would gently remind him of his acquaintance with them. Sadly, they were only a few as many had been killed or badly wounded and sent home. He noticed Sergeant Paddy Bourke striding towards him across the field where the battalion had a tent.

'G'day, Paddy,' Tom said when he stopped in front of him.

'I got something that seems to be yours,' Paddy said, handing Tom a much worn photograph. 'It was found among a few of the items scavenged from the field months ago, and a couple of the lads said it was probably a picture of your fiancée.'

Tom took the photograph and stared at it. A beautiful cherubic face stared back at him in grainy black and white.

'Is it yours?' Paddy asked and Tom glanced up at him.

'Cobber, I wish I knew,' he said with a note of anguish in his voice.

'Keep it,' Paddy said. 'Maybe it will help prompt your memory. I have to go and sort out ammo issues. See you later.' He turned and walked away, leaving Tom gazing at the photograph worn by the toils of the battlefield. For a moment the picture of a water fountain flashed through Tom's thoughts and he strained to remember why. But the image disappeared and the beautiful young woman who smiled at him from the photograph remained a stranger. If she was Juliet Joubert, then Tom knew from which village she came, other than that, he knew nothing about her.

With great care he slipped the photograph into the top pocket of his jacket. It was near his heart and with time Tom would go to the village to look for her. He was sure that personal contact would bring memories flooding back. With any luck, all his past would come to him then. Everything he knew about his past had come from the official records the army kept. He knew that when he enlisted in Townsville his stated occupation was stockman. He was puzzled from his service record as to why his race should be described as Indian when he knew he was part Aboriginal.

Tom did not have much time to explore his memories, as the battalion was once again ordered up to the front lines in the big push to keep the enemy army reeling back towards

Germany. The weather was growing bitterly cold as winter approached.

In the first week of October Tom found himself face down on a sunken road. The attack had gone in against the German lines at 0600 hours, behind an artillery barrage dropped a mere four hundred yards in front of them to give them a wall of high explosive and shrapnel protection. By 0700 hours Tom's company and platoon had found themselves under heavy machine-gun fire, as well as coming up against a thick belt of barbed wire. While the Australians had been desperately attempting to find a way through the wire, German hand grenades had rained down on them. Potato mashers – as they were nicknamed by the Aussies – shredded flesh and killed any men unfortunate enough to be nearby when they exploded.

Tom had bawled out orders, knowing that above the din of rifle and machine-gun fire coupled with blasts of grenades he was barely heard. He had crouched, hearing the bullets crack beside his head, and watched some of his men double up as they were hit. Stretcher-bearers could not dash in to retrieve the wounded, and when Tom had cast around him to find his platoon commander he had not been able to find him. Maybe he had been killed; if so, it was Tom who must take command of the platoon.

'Get the wounded back!' he'd bellowed. 'Fall back!' He'd been able to see that his order had got through as a couple of the diggers had grabbed the jacket of a wounded comrade and begun dragging him along the ground away from the barbed wire.

Now Tom lay face down in the sunken road, desperately attempting to get the trembling that racked his body under control. 'Sarge,' a voice called out to him, 'what do we do now?'

Tom sat up, gripping his rifle, and pulled out his pipe.

'Have a smoke,' he called back. 'Time out for a smoko.' His answer caused a ripple of laughter from the men strung along the road. At least they were safe from direct-fire weapons, and Tom felt composed enough to drag himself to the edge of the road facing the enemy. He could see that the three wounded they had been able to drag or carry back to the road were being looked after and, with any luck, the stretcher-bearers would be able to come up and retrieve the wounded men.

From the edge of the road he could see a farmhouse scarred with bullet and shrapnel holes, and he could also see that the house was being used as a machine-gun nest by the Germans.

'Corporal Harrigan, to me,' Tom called over his shoulder. 'Have you seen Mr Hopkins?'

'Seen him when we stepped off, but he seemed to fall back as we advanced,' Harrigan shrugged.

Tom frowned. It was possible that the arrogant young officer had been wounded in the first bursts of enemy fire. Tom slipped a map from his pocket and quickly identified the location of the enemy machine-gun. He scribbled down a set of coordinates on a page torn from a notebook and handed the slip of paper to Harrigan. 'Get this back to battalion HQ. Tell them we need arty on the coordinates I have written down. Give them a brief of how we are holed up in this sunken road, and make sure they know where we are because I don't want to be digging our shrapnel out of my arse. You right on this?'

'Yes, Sarge,' Harrigan answered, and slithered down the slight rise to carry the message back to the battalion HQ, where it would be relayed to the field artillery regiment supporting their assault on the German lines.

There was nothing else Tom could do for the moment – except to growl at a few of the men who had lost equipment, and joke with others who were visibly traumatised by the effect of close combat. Moving among the members of his platoon lifted morale, although it did not dissipate anyone's fear.

While Tom waited for the artillery barrage he lay against the slope of the road and stared up at the sky. It was a fine crisp day and he could see a lark flying high. He was reminded of looking up into a clear blue sky where a great eagle soared on outstretched wings, and the name Wallarie came to him.

'It's comin'!' someone yelled and Tom could hear the distinctive sound of artillery rounds passing overhead to fall on the farmhouse with deadly accuracy. A cheer went up from the troops peeking very cautiously above the lip of the road. 'They got the bastard!' a soldier yelled as the house was ripped apart by a direct hit. It did not seem possible anyone could survive such an explosion and the threat of the concealed machine-gun was neutralised.

Even as the Germans were under the artillery barrage, a soldier scrambled down the road to Tom, who recognised him as being from company HQ.

'Mr Hopkins here?' he asked, moving from man to man until he reached Tom.

'Have you seen Mr Hopkins, Sergeant Duffy?'

'Sorry, can't say that I have since we jumped off this morning,' Tom replied.

'Well, that must mean you're in charge of the platoon,' said the private soldier acting as company runner. 'Got orders from the boss that when the arty lifts we're going in to mop up what's left. You clear on that?'

'Yeah, no worries,' Tom answered. The soldier nodded

and hurried away in a crouching run to inform the other platoon commanders of the order. Tom immediately passed along the order and ensured that all his able men had their bayonets fixed. This could require very close combat.

The deafening roar of explosions finally lifted at around 1030 hours and Tom glanced down his line of men and experienced a strange calmness. He noticed that his hands did not shake as much. Maybe having the lives of the men under his command to consider took his mind off his own mortality.

'Okay, boys, time to hop the bags,' he yelled down the line – and as one the men responded to his command, clambering to their feet and advancing on the system of trenches occupied by the enemy. Smoke curled in wisps from newly created shell craters, and the smell of death was heavy in the air.

Striding forward, his rifle outstretched, Tom could sense that the enemy had been broken by the artillery barrage. They were met only by scattered shots from sections of the trench system, and many surviving Germans surrendered rather than face the grim-faced soldiers with bayonets fixed. By midafternoon Tom's company had reached the slopes of a nearby range of low hills overlooking a valley, and immediately they began to dig in.

While his platoon were preparing their defences, Tom asked around for his platoon commander but no one had seen him. Tom was helping his men, belting in an iron picket to string barbed wire along, when the company commander and second in command approached him.

'Sergeant Duffy,' Major Cooper said. 'How are you coping with the platoon?'

Tom straightened and wiped the sweat from his brow with the back of his hand. 'I'm doing okay, sir,' he replied, before noticing the dark expression on the company commander's face.

'I am putting you in charge of the platoon – until the brigade sends us another officer,' Cooper said.

'Did Mr Hopkins stop one, sir?' Tom asked and the dark expression on Major Cooper's face turned to a frown.

'Let us just say, Sergeant Duffy, that Mr Hopkins is no longer with us,' he answered and Tom noticed the exchange of glances between Cooper and his second in command. 'That was good work today identifying the Hun position for our artillery,' the company commander continued. 'You'll get an MID out of that if I have my way.'

'Thank you, sir,' Tom dutifully answered, not caring much for military recognition. 'But maybe it should go to Corporal Harrigan for dodging the Hun fire.'

'I will mention Corporal Harrigan as well,' Major Cooper said, the frown disappearing from his face. 'I am confident that the boys are in good hands under your command. You know, if it was up to me you would be off to England for officer training and a commission.' Tom nodded, knowing full well that his Aboriginal blood prevented him from becoming an officer and entering the class known as gentlemen. 'If it is any consolation, Tom,' the major continued, 'I consider you one of the finest men I have had the honour of serving alongside, and I think the CO will consider you for a warrant and company sergeant major's job.'

Consideration for the company sergeant's position was an honour that touched Tom. He might not remember what his life had been like before he'd woken up in the English hospital, but at least he knew he had earned a lot of respect from those who served with him. 'Thank you, sir,' Tom replied, 'but I'm happy having temporary command of the boys.'

'Maybe after your replacement arrives you will take my offer seriously,' Major Cooper said and the company second in command nodded his agreement. 'I will expect you to attend my briefing for platoon commanders in an hour, Sergeant Duffy.'

Tom acknowledged the command and returned to finishing his job of hammering in the iron picket. Sergeant Paddy Bourke had only been a few feet away and had obviously overheard the exchange. He sidled over.

'I heard a rumour that Mr Hopkins lost it the moment we stepped over the start line this morning,' he said quietly. 'A couple of the boys said he just froze and went to ground, blubbering like a kid. I heard that after we cleared the Hun in the morning the boss had him hauled away to return to brigade. No doubt they'll say he had a serious breakdown and ship him back home, lucky bastard. The officers always look after their own. There is another rumour that he will be discharged because they found out he was underage when he joined up.'

Tom took his pipe from the pocket of his trousers and thumbed down a plug of tobacco into the bowl. 'They'll use that excuse to save face,' he said, searching for a box of matches in his webbing.

Paddy stared over the valley as Tom lit his pipe. 'I thought I was going to cop it today,' he confessed quietly. 'I don't know how much more I can take of this.'

Tom looked at his friend and fellow sergeant. 'You and I don't have the privilege of showing fear. Those poor bloody boys who fear this war have to fear us even more – or they wouldn't get out of the trenches and do the insane things asked of them. We can't show fear.'

'Cobber, every man in this battalion knows that you're a born fighter,' Paddy said. 'The number of men you killed as the company sniper last year still stands as a record. I don't reckon you get scared like the rest of us.'

'Paddy, I can't remember the last time I could hold a glass of beer without spilling it,' Tom answered with a weak smile, grey-blue smoke curling from his pipe. 'All I want to do is just bloody stay alive with two arms, two legs and a head so I can find out who I am.'

'You're a bloody blackfella,' Paddy said in a brighter tone, nudging Tom in the ribs. 'But you could almost be a whitefella.'

'If this is what whitefellas consider solving disputes over land, then I think I would rather remain a blackfella,' Tom grinned. 'Well, I have to get ready for an O group – so your mob can finish laying the wire.' With these parting words and a rude gesture to follow, Tom picked up his rifle and walked away, leaving Paddy feeling reassured that he was not alone.

As Tom walked away something clicked in his mind. What was it that Paddy had said? The reference to being a blackfella. Another name came to mind – Smithers – from a previous conversation. There was a link between the two matters and Tom thought that link might be the mysterious woman purported to be his fiancée. Tom felt a chill and it was not from the cold that came with the night.

19

It was one of those days that had gone very badly for the Weasel. The mugging should have been straightforward, but the victim had decided not to give up his money so easily, and as a result the Weasel had stabbed him in the stomach. The Weasel, whose name was Albert Cummings, had picked the middle of the day to carry out his crime, and the sound of the wounded man screaming bloody murder had brought curious witnesses from nearby shops and off the main street.

Cummings had fled but a description of him had soon led the uniformed police to his usual haunt in an inner city billiards hall where he was arrested and the knife seized as evidence.

That had been bad enough, but worse was to come when Cummings was passed on to Detective Inspector Jack Firth's section for interrogation.

Now Albert Cummings sat in a chair from which he had fallen many times, due to Firth's method of interrogation. Jack Firth was not a patient man.

'Okay, Weasel, stop stuffing me around and sign the statement in front of you,' Jack said, shadowed by one of his other detectives standing by smoking a cigarette. 'We both know you did the victim, and if things go real bad for you he might even die, and that means you swing at the Darlinghurst gallows.'

Cummings was terrified because he knew that the threat was real. He sat staring at the sheet of paper in front of him on the battered wooden desk and it was rather hard to see, as both his eyes were swollen from the blows. A good crim always had to have an ace up his sleeve, and in his desperation Albert Cummings had that ace.

'Yer still lookin' for Lenny Johnson?' he asked through split lips.

'I might be,' Jack answered cautiously. 'But that won't be enough to get you off the charges of robbery while armed and inflicting grievous bodily harm . . . maybe even attempted murder.'

'Yer know that Lenny is up to something big,' Cummings said. 'What if I threw that in too?'

'What's Lenny planning?' Jack asked. 'If it is any good I'll make sure you don't cop a further charge of attempted murder.'

'I think he's planning to do over that toff's place you see in the paper all the time,' Cummings said.

'What toff?' Jack asked.

'That Mr George Macintosh fella. Me and Lenny drove out to his place a couple of weeks ago to look it over. Lenny wants me to go back with him tonight in a car me mate owns.' Cummings prayed that the information would appease the detective inspector enough to halt the interrogation. Sure, he knew that he would go down for armed robbery, but that was better than murder. Cummings suspected that the knife wound was not as bad as Jack Firth made out and he could see a flash of interest in the policeman's eyes. 'I can give yer more details.'

'I need to know where Lenny is hiding out, and if you give me any rubbish I'm going to stick you with a charge of assassinating the Arch Duke Franz and starting the bloody war.'

'Promise you on me mother's grave that I'm tellin' yer the truth,' Cummings pleaded.

'Okay,' Jack sighed, as if he had just given up his pay for the year. 'I'll give your information a try – and if it pans out, maybe you won't swing after all.'

'Thanks, Mr Firth,' Cummings said gratefully. 'You'll catch a bigger fish than me, I promise.'

Jack left the office and walked out into the corridor of the police headquarters to think about the proposal. It was interesting that Lenny should be thinking of doing over George Macintosh's house. With Cummings's help they could catch him in the act, and that should make George Macintosh appreciate having such a good friend in Jack Firth. He knew that getting Cummings out of remand to help them would mean bending the rules, but that was never a problem for Jack.

He walked back into the dingy room. 'Got to get you cleaned up a bit,' he said to Cummings. 'Don't want you looking like you've been a round or two with Les Darcy. You're going to go ahead and meet Lenny tonight to do the job, but don't forget we'll be as close as maggots on rotting meat. Do anything stupid and all deals are off.'

'I'll do what yer say, Mr Firth,' Cummings replied, nodding his head vigorously.

'All right,' Jack replied and turned to the detective standing by the door. 'Let's get our man to a shower and see if we can line up a change of clothes.'

The detective escorted Cummings from the room, leaving the detective inspector to think about the job in silence. By letting the crime go ahead Jack would not only have the kudos of the arrest, but he'd also get his hands on Lenny. The murder of Mary Jackson was still outstanding, and maybe this time Lenny would realise just what trouble not showing up when and where Firth told him to could bring to his freedom. Jack was sure that Cummings would go along with the plan to nab Lenny, knowing how serious the charges he faced were. Jack was confident that nothing could go wrong, and now it was time to round up a few capable men to effect the arrest this night.

Maude lay on her back, a spent George beside her, fast asleep. She was pleased that her plan was working out. Over the weeks she had managed to wheedle enough information from George to work out which nights the staff had off. Tonight the governess would be out, and the manservant had taken leave to visit a friend. The gardener would be in the cottage, which left only George's wife and his son alone in the house. Maude had been able to take a key to the house from George's pocket while he was sleeping and had pressed it into wax to have a duplicate made, which she had passed on to Lenny.

Lenny had asked about the fate of the boy and Maude had said she would double his payment if he killed him too. If he was left alive, he would always be a reminder of his murdered mother. Lenny had been taken aback by her ruthlessness, but he'd shrugged and accepted the deal. Two dead got him double the pay.

Maude could hear the city growing silent as the night deepened. Soon she would be the mistress of George Macintosh's mansion and her future would be secured.

Lenny had been surprised at the state of Albert Cummings when he'd pulled over to the kerb to pick him up at their designated meeting place in the city. But Cummings had explained that he had received a beating from an SP bookie he owed money to, and Lenny had accepted the story.

Just after midnight Cummings drove them to the Macintosh house and stopped in the dark street outside the big iron gates. Lenny settled back to watch the house. There was only one dim light showing from an upstairs room.

'You a bit nervous, Weasel?' he said when he noticed Cummings fidgeting behind the wheel. 'Anything you want to tell me?'

Cummings had good reason to fear Lenny, as it was rumoured he had killed one of his girls for holding back on money from clients. Some said that the war had turned Lenny even more dangerous as he was known to succumb to explosive fits of anger, and his size usually meant he won any fights he got into.

'Nothin', Lenny,' Cummings replied. 'Get a bit like this before a job.'

'You'd better not let me down,' Lenny growled, lighting a cigarette and blowing smoke into the tiny cabin of the car. 'I am relying on yer to get me out of here real quick when the time comes.'

'Weight's right,' Cummings replied, gripping the steering wheel to prevent Lenny seeing how his hands were sweating. He wondered where the police were hiding out, and hoped that they were not seen by Lenny too early, otherwise he would suspect a trap. After all, only he and Lenny knew of the plan to break into the house, and any police in the area would make Lenny immediately suspicious that he had been betrayed.

'Time to go,' Lenny said, noting that the light had gone out in the window. He flipped his half-smoked cigarette into the dark and stepped from the vehicle. 'You just bloody well be ready when I come out,' he growled. 'You hear?'

'Got it, Lenny,' Cummings replied with a reassuring smile as Lenny disappeared into the shadows.

For a moment Cummings was tempted to start the car and drive away, but he knew that might mess up Detective Inspector Firth's plan to ambush Lenny when he broke into the house. Cummings feared the policeman more than his criminal colleague.

Jack had placed himself and another detective out of sight in the gardens of the house. He also had uniformed police standing by at the rear of the house, within a whistle call. Jack had moved his team into place late in the evening, and not even Mrs Macintosh was aware they were in the grounds of her harbourside home.

Jack squatted behind a flowering bush that gave off a sweet scent.

'What's this bloody bush, Dick?' he asked the young detective sitting beside him in the dark.

'Dunno, boss,' the detective replied. 'But it has a nice pong.'

Jack fingered the small pistol in his coat pocket. He badly wanted to light up a cigarette but he had forbidden everyone from smoking.

Just after midnight the monotony was broken by the sound of a car stopping outside the gates of the house, and Jack strained to see who it was. After a short time he could see the glow of a cigarette and then it spinning off like a small meteorite in the night sky. A dark figure stepped from the car and disappeared into the hedge to reappear moments later crossing the lawn.

'That's him!' Jack hissed softly. 'We let the bugger break in, then nab him inside the house with his hands full of the family goodies.' Both men watched as Lenny opened the door, with some kind of key by the looks of it. Lenny slipped inside, closing the door behind him.

As soon as he was inside both detectives left their place of concealment and hurried across the garden to the front door. Jack reached for the knob, presuming the door would now be unlocked.

'The bastard's locked the door behind him,' he said in surprise. 'We have to find another way in.'

Lenny discovered that a light had been left on in the foyer of the mansion, and he slipped the razor-sharp knife from his jacket, along with a flashlight. He moved towards the stairs and made his way up the steps until he came to a darkened landing, switching on the flashlight. Walking along another corridor he came to the room identified as the one where the little boy slept. Lenny paused and considered entering and killing the toddler first, but he had decided earlier that it would be better to eliminate the mother and then the child. Should the child cry out it might wake the woman. He flicked the flashlight off.

Lenny moved on and came to a closed door; he opened it cautiously and stared inside. Although the room was dark, light from an outside lamp illuminating the driveway disclosed the shape of someone in the bed. Lenny took a deep breath and crept into the room to stand beside the sleeping figure. For just a second he switched on the flashlight, and its beam caught the sleeping figure of Louise Macintosh.

Lenny shifted his balance to deliver the killing blow. He knew where to strike as he had been trained in the use of the bayonet by some of the best of the Australian army.

'Bloody hell, just smash the damned window,' Jack growled to his offsider, plain-clothes policeman, Richard Mawdsley, who was fiddling with the latches. Jack was armed with a flashlight and he used the brass butt to hammer the glass. It smashed and the crash of glass was followed by the tinkling as it hit the polished wood floor below. Sweeping aside jagged shards, Jack was first through the opening and he fell heavily to the floor, winding himself. He got to his feet quickly, though. Nothing was going to stop him catching Lenny in the act of carrying away stolen goods.

The breaking window woke Louise. There was a light shining in her eyes. Confused, all she could do was scream in fear as a knife swept down to draw first blood.

'You hear that, Dick?' Jack said to his colleague as he tumbled after him through the window.

'I heard,' said the young plain-clothes officer. 'Must be the missus of the house.'

'Blow the bloody whistle as hard as you can,' Jack snapped over his shoulder, stumbling in the dark for a doorway.

As soon as he found one he threw it open to find himself in the lit foyer. Behind him he could hear the whistle blasts alerting the waiting uniformed police to move in.

The razor-sharp edge sliced through Louise's upper arm but she hardly felt it. Pure instinct to survive made her roll away from the attack and then she screamed, 'My baby! Help me!'

Lenny swore viciously. It would have been a clean kill if the sound of breaking glass had not brought the helpless woman awake just as he was ready to strike. But now he could see her exposed back and knew exactly where to put the point of his blade to sever her spine.

Lenny raised the knife but something made him hesitate. What had broken the glass and why could he hear a whistle being blown? For a moment he was back in the trenches and the whistle was signalling an attack on the enemy lines. The sound chilled him with dread and he knew he was in dire threat of being killed by the enemy. He swung his arm down, still aiming straight for the point of her spine.

Jack was up the stairs and in the corridor and he could hear the woman's screams. There was a door open and he could see the light of a hand-held torch. Jack flung himself at the open doorway, pistol raised.

The blade came down and Louise howled as it bit into her flesh. The pain was excruciating but she had managed to twist around, which saved her spine, although she took the impact in her buttock. She was still confused and terrified, attempting to claw her way off the bed to the floor. A voice was shouting from the doorway.

'Drop it, Lenny, or I will drop you,' Jack screamed in the confines of the bedroom. 'Drop the bloody knife or I will shoot you now.'

Lenny had snapped out of the trenches and realised that he was in the beam of a flashlight. He could hear Jack Firth's commands and he knew he was an easy target. The knife slid from his hand and within a second a plain-clothes officer was on him, punching him senseless.

Jack found the light switch and turned on the bedroom light. He could see great splashes of crimson on the bedding and spreading across Louise's nightdress. By now, two uniformed police had forced the front door and followed the sounds of commotion to the bedroom.

'Get Mrs Macintosh to the nearest hospital.' Jack ordered, taking her hand.

'My baby,' Louise moaned, fighting the pain from the stab wounds.

'Check to see if Mrs Macintosh's son is all right,' Jack said to the second uniformed policeman, who reappeared a few minutes later with a crying toddler.

Louise reached up to touch her son as two burly policemen lifted her and carried her from the room.

Jack turned to Lenny, now handcuffed on the floor. 'You have really done it now, Lenny,' he said. 'By the time you and I are through, you're going to wish you had never been born.'

★

The sun was rising outside the police headquarters and the city was coming alive. But Lenny felt as if he had already died. His head lolled as he fought off badly needed sleep. The adrenaline had dissipated and left him feeling utterly exhausted. He had gone over the same questions time after time with the two police detectives sitting opposite him.

'No good denying you were trying to kill Mrs Macintosh, Lenny,' Jack said wearily. He, too, was exhausted and just wanted to get a signature on Lenny's confession. 'What I'm not clear about is why you would want to kill her.'

Lenny lifted his head and stared through bloodshot eyes at the detective. 'If I tell you, you will get me a cup of tea and a smoke?'

'Yeah, we can do that,' Jack replied, standing up and stretching his tired limbs. 'And we can get you a soft cell bed where you can have a good nap before appearing before the beak.' Jack had sworn the police in his team to secrecy until he figured out who would want Mrs Macintosh murdered in her bed. A terrible suspicion had come to Jack that George might have been behind the plot as he had been unable to contact him.

'So who put you up to this?' Firth said, sitting back at the table.

'The toff who owns the place,' Lenny lied, hoping to throw the hated policeman off the trail for a while. 'Seems he has a bit on the side and wanted his missus out of the way.'

Jack Firth paled. This would make matters very difficult. 'You're lying, Lenny,' he snarled. 'You decided all on your own to do away with the woman — just like you did to that working girl a few months' back.'

Lenny stared at Jack through eyes that felt as if sand had been poured into them. 'I thought Harry Griffiths did that one,' he said. 'Wasn't that what I was supposed to say at the committal hearing?'

'So, you're saying that you met with a respectable member of the community and he propositioned you to murder his wife?' Jack said, controlling his temper.

'That's exactly what I'm saying,' Lenny said.

'Who is this bit on the side that Mr Macintosh is supposed to have?' Jack countered and Lenny stared blankly at him.

'Don't know who she is,' he said eventually. 'Maybe you should ask him.'

Jack turned to his offsider. 'You never heard Lenny incriminate Mr Macintosh,' he said quietly and the detective nodded his understanding. 'I'll sort this out before we proceed any further. You get my meaning?'

The detective nodded again.

Jack found George at the hospital and took him aside in a quiet corridor, out of earshot of any hospital staff.

'The doctors have told me Louise should recover and that her pregnancy seems intact,' George said. 'I was told by one of the uniform policeman how you arrived to save the lives of my wife and my son life last night. I thank you for that.'

'The man who tried to kill your wife says that you hired him,' Jack said quietly. 'Is that true?'

George looked horrified. 'I may be responsible for what many might consider some despicable things in my life, but hiring someone to murder my wife is not one of them. This man of yours is obviously lying.'

Jack stared at George. 'He says that you have someone else on the side,' he continued. 'Is that true?'

'Of course,' George snorted. 'I have many women whose beds I go to, but my wife knows this and does not interfere.'

'Where were you last night?' Jack persisted.

'I was with one of those many women,' George answered calmly.

'I'll need to know who the lady is,' Jack said. 'In the meantime, the man I have in custody is someone you know – Lenny Johnson.'

For a moment George looked puzzled. 'Is he the man who was to give evidence against that Harry Griffiths chap?' he asked and Jack nodded.

'I can't keep this out of the papers,' Jack said. Not that Jack wanted to keep the matter out of the newspapers as he would be seen as a heroic figure who had saved the wife of a prominent businessman. His actions would be hailed by all. 'Questions will be asked and I will not be able to keep your name out of the enquiry – despite the fact I know Lenny is lying. My gut tells me that he is protecting someone else, and I intend to find out who. When I do, I have no doubt that whoever is behind this attempt on Mrs Macintosh will have no link to you.'

'I cannot thank you enough,' George said, extending his hand. 'You know that my gratitude is worth having.'

Jack did not take his hand but stared coldly at the patrician-looking man opposite him. 'You are not off the hook yet, and if I get any evidence that makes me doubt your innocence, I will have no choice but to investigate it.'

George dropped his hand. 'I am sure you will do your duty but I am innocent and trust in the law to see to that.'

'So, who were you with last night?' Jack asked again.

'A young lady by the name of Maude Urqhart,' George replied and he could see a strange expression on the policeman's face. 'Does that have any meaning to you?'

'Maude Urqhart,' Jack echoed. 'If I remember rightly, Lenny has a half-sister by that name. She used to work the streets when she was a kid.'

George paled and could feel a shiver of fear. If he'd had any hope that the murder conspiracy had no link to him, that had quickly evaporated. For the first time in his life he truly felt cornered. Maude's link with Lenny could see him accused of trying to kill his wife. Innocent men had been hanged before. How could life throw such a cruel twist against him? The echo of an old Aboriginal curse rebounded in the dreary corridor of the hospital.

20

It was the afternoon by the time Jack Firth had finished speaking to George Macintosh, who provided the detective with Maude Urqhart's address. Jack went to the address in the company of his faithful officer, Dick Mawdsley, and knocked vigorously on the door of the tenement house. Eventually it was opened and a middle-aged man stood glaring at the two detectives. It did not take long for Jack to realise that George had given him the run-around with the wrong address, and he returned to police HQ in a black mood. But why had Macintosh provided a wrong address? Jack pondered. He must have known that Jack would eventually catch up with Maude Urqhart one way or another. Something definitely smelled fishy about the attempt on Mrs Macintosh's life. Jack had still not crossed George off his list of prime suspects.

★

Maude was jumpy when George appeared at her front door. There had been no contact with Lenny and she was not sure if he had succeeded in their plot to kill Louise Macintosh and her child. Maude attempted to hide her strained nerves by flinging herself into George's arms when he stepped through the doorway.

'Oh, I've missed you,' she said, kissing him on the mouth and noticing how tense he was. 'Is something wrong, my darling?' she asked, stepping back to look at him with a frown on her pretty face.

'I've just come from the hospital where my wife is recovering from an attack on her only hours ago at our home,' he said slowly.

'Oh, how terrible,' Maude cried. 'Is she hurt badly?'

'She will recover – so I have been told by the doctors,' George said, taking Maude's hand and leading her upstairs to the bedroom. 'I know it's a terrible thing to say, but had the attempt succeeded, then you and I could have been together forever. You know, I even suspected that you sent the assassin.'

Maude blushed and bowed her head. 'Do you really mean that?' she asked softly. 'That if your wife had died, then we would be together?'

George reached the bedroom and led Maude inside, turning to begin stripping away her clothing. 'You know that I love you more than anything else in this world,' George said smoothly as Maude's clothes fell to the floor, revealing her young, smooth body to him. 'But I would need a gesture from you to prove your love for me – something that we could keep between ourselves, as a reminder of our everlasting love for each other.'

Tears welled in Maude's eyes as she let George push her naked body onto the bed. 'You know I would do anything for you, my darling,' she replied, gazing up at George who was still clothed. 'Just ask me.'

George leaned back, straddling her small body. 'I want you to write a letter saying how you planned to have my wife murdered. By doing that you will have proved to me just how much your love means, and then we will be together when I divorce my wife.'

Maude sat up and embraced George. 'If that's all it takes, I'll do it,' she replied. 'But why would you want me to write such a letter?'

George removed himself from the bed and stood over Maude. 'To do such a risky thing would prove you truly love me,' he said. 'No one would ever see the letter, of course, but I'm testing you, my little darling, and if you cannot write the letter then I know you do not love me.'

Confused thoughts swirled in the young girl's head. What she was doing was admitting to her part in a plot to kill a woman, and that was a dangerous, even deadly thing to do. But, on the other hand, she knew that George was a ruthless man and if she failed the test he would not hesitate to replace her. 'I have paper and pen, but I'm not a good letter writer,' she said eventually.

'It doesn't have to be perfect, and as soon as you have written it I will take the letter and destroy it in front of you.'

Maude thought for a moment. It was just a test; what harm could come from it if George intended to destroy the incriminating letter. 'What should I write?' she asked.

'I can help you there,' George said, running his hand down her breasts and to her thighs. 'Write that you and your half-brother planned to kill my wife.'

'How did you know that my brother is involved?' she asked in alarm. 'Has something happened to him?'

'No, no,' George reassured. 'The police have him, but

he didn't kill Louise, so he can't be charged with murder,' he said. 'I'll pay for the best legal defence in Sydney to represent your brother – anonymously, of course – so you have nothing to fear on that matter. Just go ahead with the letter and everything you want will be yours.'

Maude took the pad of paper and pen from her bedside cabinet. She dipped the nib into a bottle of ink and began writing painstakingly slowly in a childish hand.

'How do I spell "murder"?' Maude asked.

'It does not matter if you misspell words,' he said, glancing over her shoulder and stroking her nipples. 'Just write what I have told you and we can put the matter behind us.'

Maude looked up at George and smiled weakly. 'If this is what I have to do . . .' she said and returned to her laborious task of spelling out that she and her brother had planned to kill Louise, and that they had acted alone. As she did so she dreamed about life in the luxurious mansion overlooking Sydney Harbour. Eventually she finished, filling the page with her simple words, and handed the confession to George.

'Good,' he said, scanning the letter. 'All you have to do is sign it, and I can keep my part of the bargain.'

Maude smiled nervously. She hated to admit it but she was harbouring the slightest suspicion about George's motives and was starting to regret this self-incriminating act she was committing in the name of love. Still, she didn't have much choice now; she was backed into a corner. She took the letter and signed her name, then passed the document back to George.

'Now we seal our love the best way I know,' George leered, placing the letter on the bedside cabinet.

'Aren't you going to get rid of the letter now?' Maude asked.

'As soon as we have finished doing what you do best,' he said, climbing onto the bed and unbuttoning his pants. 'Just lie down on your stomach.'

Maude obeyed. She could feel his rasping breath on the back of her neck and felt his strong grip of her hair as he pulled back her head. But then she felt something else – a sharp stinging pain in her right arm.

'What is it?' she asked in alarm. She tried to roll over but he held her down.

'It is nothing,' George said and his voice was coming from far away. 'Just go to sleep.'

Maude felt a huge wave of euphoria and sighed as the darkness came to her.

George eased himself off the bed and pulled up his trousers. The syringe was still deep in Maude's arm and the dosage of heroin was enough to kill three people. He leaned forward to see if she was still breathing, and noted with satisfaction that her sleep was becoming deeper by the minute. Soon enough she would stop sleeping – and die.

He looked around the bedroom. The confession was on the bedside cabinet, near Maude's body, and it was not likely that anyone other than the police would be visiting her now. It was strange, George thought as he tidied himself to leave. This was the first time he had killed someone with his own hand, and he liked the feeling very much. It gave him an enormous sense of power; it was thrilling, almost ecstatic, and now he had done it once, he wanted to do it again.

A furious Jack Firth confronted George in his office the next day about the wrong address, and George responded by saying that it was his fault because he had been so distressed that he had given the wrong address.

Jack stormed from George's office and for the rest of the day George felt as if he was holding his breath. It was only a matter of time before the detective inspector stormed back through the office door when he found Maude's body. George contemplated whether he should go to the hospital to visit his wife or retire to his club until the next meeting with Jack Firth. He decided on the club so he could have a stiff drink to settle his nerves.

As it was Jack did not visit until the next day.

George had the secretary usher the policeman into his office and closed the door.

'We found her – just as you knew we would,' Jack growled, not bothering to remove his hat. 'We found the suicide note, and my only question to you is, when did you visit Lenny's sister last?'

George stood up from behind his desk and went to the window. He felt uncomfortable having the policeman staring down at him with his expression of contempt. 'I believe the last time I saw Miss Urqhart was the night my wife was attacked,' George replied, clasping his hands behind his back. 'I am shocked to hear that Maude has taken her life, but I am not surprised. She had such a miserable upbringing and I suppose no woman likes to think that she will spend the rest of her life earning a living on her back – yet what other option was open to the poor girl?'

'So, she was a drug user,' Jack said. 'I'm surprised that you would tolerate such a thing.'

George turned to the detective. 'I accepted the poor girl's wretched past and did not judge her,' he said sanctimoniously. 'I suppose I should do the right thing and arrange a decent burial for her.'

'I know you killed her, George,' Jack said. 'But I also know I could never prove it in light of the letter and your position in this town. Let's just say that we're square, and now we both go our own way.'

'I think that is impossible,' George countered. 'We know too much about each other's frailties and I suspect that you like my money too much to break our arrangement. You can rest assured that I am far too smart to make any mistakes that might embarrass either of us. I have it in my power to have you promoted to superintendent. So I expect you to steer the investigation into my wife's assault in the direction of a misguided young woman plotting to kill her lover's wife, because that is really what happened.'

'I can accept that,' Jack said, removing his hat and turning it round and round in his hands. 'But the death of your mistress is another matter.'

'She died from an overdose,' George shrugged. 'What more can we say?'

'I didn't tell you that she died from an overdose,' Jack said. 'How could you know?'

'You mentioned her drug use, and I presumed that is how she killed herself,' George answered quickly. 'We move on, and I trust in your influence to keep any mention of the link between myself and Miss Urqhart from the newspapers.'

'It'll cost you,' Jack said.

'As I said before, we need each other,' George replied, extending his hand. Jack took it reluctantly. 'It is a harsh world and one needs friends.'

Jack let the hand slip from his own and placed his hat on his head to leave.

★

'I have had a newspaper man visit me,' Louise said when George went to visit her in hospital.

His heart leapt into his throat at her words.

'It appears you have not been very discreet in your dalliances with other women. Or should I say, girls. What is your connection to the death of this Maude Urqhart?'

George shifted uncomfortably. He knew that his wife was aware of his other women, but she had tacitly agreed to turn a blind eye, so long as he did not interfere in her relationship with her son.

'What did the newspaper man want to know?' George countered.

'It seems that he does the police rounds, and the body of the girl was found naked in a tenement belonging to a Macintosh company. She was apparently a user of heroin, and he wanted to know if you knew anything about her, as he said he had sources that identified you as a frequent caller on her.'

'I think you and I are adult enough to realise that I have needs, and I will not lie to you – Maude Urqhart was a young lady I knew. But for the sake of our name I wish you to deny that to anyone in the press.'

'Of course,' Louise said wearily. 'For the sake of the good Macintosh name.'

'I had no connection to her death – if you are thinking that,' George added, and immediately regretted it when he saw the questioning look on his wife's face. 'It is just that the police have to carry out their routine of asking me as the owner of the tenement.' He changed the subject. 'Well, the doctors have informed me that you will be up and about before the end of the week. You will be well looked after at home.'

'Thank you, George,' Louise said and he could hear the bitter edge to her voice.

'I must get back to the office,' George said, and left without bothering to kiss his wife goodbye.

When he was gone Louise closed her eyes, drifting to the edge of sleep, only to awake to the sweet scent of flowers. She opened her eyes to see Sean Duffy's face smiling down at her and a bouquet of red roses in his hand.

'Hello,' he said. 'I thought these might brighten up the ward a bit.'

Louise broke into a smile, and tears formed at the corners of her eyes as she reached out her hand to take Sean's. 'Just the sight of you has brightened my world,' she said softly. 'How did you know I was here?'

Sean settled into a chair, still holding Louise's hand. 'Besides the attack being in every paper, and the fact that I am a practitioner of criminal law, it was not hard to track you down. I believe the police have a man, Lenny Johnson, in custody for the assault.'

Louise was silent for a moment. 'You are the first person to tell me his name,' Louise answered. 'Is he someone you know?'

Sean frowned. 'He was going to give evidence against a client of mine, Harry Griffiths. I think you've met Harry. I don't know why but I keep thinking that your husband has something to do with all of this, especially . . .'

'Especially in the light of the police finding the body of his young mistress.' Louise said what Sean had been too much of a gentleman to say. 'I had heard. My husband was here earlier and swore that he had nothing to do with the girl's death. Do you think he was lying?'

Sean sighed. 'I think your husband is a very dangerous man, and I wish you would leave him.'

Louise squeezed Sean's hand. 'I have grown up in a world where duty comes first, and my first duty is to my son,' she said. 'If only we could turn back time and start again, but I cannot leave George until my son is old enough to stand up to his father. I love you Sean, and I always will, but we cannot be together as long as George is alive.'

'I could kill the bastard myself,' Sean said with bitterness. 'God knows how many lives he has ruined over the years to consolidate his power in the family companies. If only Patrick and Alexander were still alive, matters would be very different.'

Louise had loved her father-in-law and gentle brother-in-law very much, and she missed them sorely. At least she still had the love of Alexander's widow, Giselle. 'I had a letter from Giselle recently,' Louise said. 'I was hoping that she would come down to Sydney to stay with me over Christmas, but she has declined the invitation. I can't help but be glad now. It's an awful business all round.'

The two chatted for a good hour, lifting Louise's spirits, until a disapproving matron came to inform Sean that visiting hours were over. Sean leant over and kissed Louise on the forehead before rising from his chair with the help of his cane. 'I'll come and visit again before you are discharged,' he said.

Louise watched him depart the ward before allowing herself to break down and sob. If only she could turn back time and have left George before she fell pregnant with Donald. But then she wouldn't have her precious son, and she couldn't regret his birth, no matter how much she hated his father.

Sean Duffy's entry to the hospital was noted by George Macintosh, who had been forced to wait for his chauffeur to bring around the Rolls-Royce. Recent events had distracted George from his plan of having the troublesome lawyer killed, but now that he had sorted out Maude he could turn his attention back to Duffy. He was quite sure Jack Firth would see to it that the coroner signed the girl's demise off as accidental death due to heroin overdose, and so long as the newspapers did not dig too deep, the matter would blow over in time.

George was also aware that as Giselle would not be visiting Sydney over Christmas, another plan would need to be put in place. Maybe it was time that he made a visit to Glen View. Accidents often occurred in the vast, lonely stretches of the Australian bush. All was not lost because his sister-in-law had not come to him to die. Now that he had tasted the forbidden fruit of murder, he could take death to Giselle and his nephew.

21

It was not the same, Tom thought, surveying his new platoon. The old battalion was gone, and he still remembered that day in September when the Australian army had mutinied. Not because they had refused to fight the enemy but because their casualties had been so high that the military authorities had decided to disband the decimated battalions and amalgamate men into new battalions. It was not within the scope of the military staff in their comfortable and protected headquarters to empathise with the men living and dying in the trenches. They could not understand the brotherhood between men who relied on each other for survival. A battalion was not just a military unit – it was a family.

A parade had been called to announce the new formations. The legendary Pompey Elliot rode onto the parade ground on his black mount, and the parade commander called the order to slope arms. The order was disobeyed by every man and officer on the parade, and Pompey Elliot was furious as he well knew that he was facing a mutiny.

'This nonsense must cease at once,' he roared and went on to explain in a furious voice that if the ringleaders could not be identified, he would use the old Roman army system of harsh discipline to have every tenth man executed by firing squad.

'We have bullets too,' came a voice from the parade, and the wily commander realised that threats against men who faced death on a daily basis was useless. To the war-weary men who had faced the terrible fighting on the Hindenburg line, seeing their battalions broken up was akin to deserting the dead who had given their lives wearing the cherished coloured patches denoting their family in the Australian army.

Elliot gave the men on the parade half an hour to change their minds, but when he returned, the stubborn diggers had not budged. They were, after all, volunteers and some had lived through shearer's strikes where comradeship had kept them going against the power of the government.

Pompey Elliot gave in and compromised, but it did not end there as in the following days other battalions took the same mutinous stance. As far as Tom knew, none had been punished for their stand and in their new battalions the diggers were allowed to keep their old battalion patches on their sleeves.

But mutiny was not confined to the Australians. On the other side of the front line the German army had also decided that the war was not worth the cost in lives and the misery of the civilian population back home, starving to death because of the British naval blockade. There was the fear of Bolshevism taking hold of Germany, and the

Prussian generals knew they could not win with the influx of the fresh troops from the USA.

As Tom rested up behind the lines on a late autumn day notes were already being exchanged between Berlin and Washington about the possibility of an armistice. Prince Max von Baden had already given an order to curtail unrestricted submarine war and hinted that the Kaiser Wilhelm would abdicated.

Despite the machinations by politicians on both sides, for Tom and the men of his battalion the war dragged on as artillery from the enemy still rained down hell on the terrified soldiers huddling in whatever shelter they could. Snipers still picked off the unwary and men still died, gutted by bayonets in hand-to-hand fighting while politicians on both sides continued to quibble over details of an armistice. For the moment Tom, and what was left of those he had come to know again in the old battalion, were relatively safe behind the lines, waiting for deployment back into the fighting.

Tom sat on an empty ammunition case, smoking his pipe, staring at the men lounging around but saying very little.

Paddy Bourke strolled across to him, a broad smile across his rugged face. 'We got some leave,' he said, plonking himself down next to Tom. 'As from 0600 tomorrow morning.'

Tom puffed on the pipe, pulling his greatcoat closer against the chill already in the air, and stared up at the gathering rain clouds sweeping across the wooded hills and ploughed fields. 'Where we getting our leave?' he asked.

Paddy mentioned the name of the village and Tom realised that it was the place his fiancée had lived. The mention caught Tom off guard. 'Juliet,' he uttered.

'What?' Paddy countered.

'Nothing,' Tom said, tapping the ash from his pipe on the side of the empty ammo crate. 'Just hope the rain holds off.'

'Bloody cheery bastard you are,' Paddy said, slapping Tom on the back. 'Our first bit of leave in ages, and not even that has brought a smile to your black face.'

'No, it's good,' Tom answered with a smile. 'It's just that when we finish our leave we come back to this bloody war. It's got so that I don't know how to do anything else any more, other than soldiering.'

'What did you do before you signed up?' Paddy asked.

'It says in my service record that I was a stockman,' Tom replied.

Paddy didn't ask any more questions, wandering away to share the good news of their leave.

Tom stared out through the smoke from his pipe. 'I just wonder if I can even ride a horse any more,' he murmured to himself.

Captain Matthew Duffy could see the deadly metal bombs falling from his Bristol into the packed columns of retreating Turks on the road to Damascus. Horse-drawn carts and riders on camels had little time to scatter, and exploding bombs tore apart man and beast without distinction.

Behind him, Matthew could vaguely hear the chatter of Lieutenant Goddard's Lewis machine-gun pouring bullets into the mass below, inflicting even more chaos and suffering. When Matthew swung his head he could see the other four Biffs also swooping on the shattered convoy.

Matthew dropped the nose of his Bristol to angle the machine-gun towards any target presenting itself. At such low level, as he swept over the scattered troops, he could see the expressions of terror on faces looking up at him. They were so vulnerable in the open to the fast flying death that came from the sky, and Matthew also noticed that few attempted to shoot back at their tormentors. He guessed they were too demoralised to do so.

The strafing run completed, Matthew pulled back on the stick to rise into the clear blue sky devoid of the blood beneath. He flew on to find another group of fleeing Turks pushed ahead of a pursuing British and Arab army.

It did not take long before he spotted another cluster of Ottoman soldiers sitting on the ground in the open. He signalled to Goddard and dropped the nose to strafe the Turkish soldiers, but as he swooped down he noticed the men below did not move. They sat as if they were too exhausted and demoralised to even make a run. Matthew knew he had enough ammunition left to kill or wound most of them but he was suddenly overcome by a terrible sense of futility. The nose of the Bristol rose and his guns remained silent as he turned and flew away, leaving the war-weary and dejected enemy soldiers to wonder why they had not been machine-gunned by the infidel flyer. Among their group was a Turkish captain by the name of Barak.

When Matthew and Goddard returned to the airfield, and the engine spluttered into silence, Matthew sat for a time in his cockpit. Behind him, Goddard also remained seated as the ground crew ran over to them.

'How was it, sir?' one of the crew called up to Matthew. 'Get a few Johnny Turk?'

Matthew did not reply, but eased himself from the cockpit and, with the help of the ground crew, jumped down onto the ground. Goddard was also helped from his cockpit and the two men stood facing each other. For just a brief moment they exchanged looks, and for the first time Matthew could see in the young officer's face an understanding he did not have before. Lieutenant Goddard knew that when a man was beaten, it was just not cricket to put the boot in.

Before going on leave, Tom had a visit from the company commander in his tent, where he was brewing a billy of tea. Tom could see from the expression on Major Cooper's face that something was wrong.

'I have just received some sad news,' the major said. 'Mr Hopkins had an accident with his service revolver while in England. You will be acting platoon commander for a while yet.'

'Like a cuppa, boss?' Tom asked.

'No thanks, Tom,' the major replied. 'Have to get back for a trip to battalion HQ. I just thought that you should know about Mr Hopkins's fate.'

'He shot himself, didn't he?' Tom said softly. 'Poor young bastard should never have been here in the first place. He's as much a casualty of the bloody war as any of the cobbers dead from Hun bullets.'

'He had an accident with his service revolver,' Major Cooper said, staring levelly at Tom. 'That is how it will be officially reported. The CO is going to see to that. I know Mr Hopkins was not very well liked by the men in his platoon, but he was one of us, and we look after our own.'

'I agree, sir,' Tom responded. 'I will inform the men of his tragic accident.'

'Well, time to head off, but I want you to know you're doing a fine job leading the platoon, Tom,' Major Cooper said as he turned to walk away.

Alone, Tom shook his head sadly. Maybe he should have done more to help the young officer settle in, he thought as he sipped his tea.

It was the fountain.

As Tom leapt down from the back of the truck the first thing he noticed was the tiny village's fountain. He suddenly remembered that it was near here that he had first met the woman in the photograph, whose name he knew was Juliet Joubert. She had been carrying a basket of eggs, and he had offered to assist her. With this memory came the realisation of their mutual and all-consuming love for each other.

Tom could feel the tears well in his eyes, and he walked away from the happy group of soldiers disembarking from the back of the truck, who spread out in search of their billets and a good grog shop.

Only Sergeant Paddy Bourke remained behind, keeping an eye on Tom. He didn't look quite right, and Paddy knew that shellshock came at the strangest times and places and he feared his cobber might be suffering an episode. He walked over to Tom and saw the tears streaming down his face.

'You okay, cobber?' Paddy asked, and Tom nodded, wiping away the tears with the sleeve of his battle blouse.

'Just remembered a lot about this place,' Tom answered. 'I need to ask the locals a few questions.'

'You want me along?' Paddy asked.

'Thanks but no,' Tom replied. 'I know some French. I think.'

'Okay,' Paddy shrugged. 'See you for a drink when you're ready.'

Tom nodded again and Paddy walked over to a gaggle of soldiers who had decided to go for a drink before seeking out their billets from a cleanly dressed junior British officer with a clipboard and pompous manner, who was already chiding the diggers for not saluting him.

Tom walked over to the fountain and sat at its edge, watching the water trickling over moss-encrusted stone. Juliet was the schoolteacher; he remembered clearly the day he had gone to her school on leave months earlier. He took a deep breath and made his way to a shop that was also a post office. There was little in the way of luxuries on the shelves and the owner was a stern-looking woman with her grey hair pulled back harshly into a bun. She saw his slouch hat and broke into a smile. The Australians had money to spend and were good for the local village economy – when they were sober and not brawling with troops from other Allied countries, or among themselves.

'Yes, monsieur,' she said, wiping down her dress for the handsome soldier.

'You speak English?' Tom asked.

'*Oui*, soldier,' she answered. 'A little.'

'I would like to know if you knew a Mademoiselle Juliet Joubert?'

'Certainly,' the woman replied. 'She was the school-teacher in our village.'

'Do you know where I might find her?' Tom asked, and the woman's eyes flickered uncertainly.

'I do not know where Mademoiselle Joubert is,' she replied. 'She left us very suddenly. But Pierre, our butcher, thinks she may be in Paris. His son was on leave there and he saw her in a street. He tried to speak with her but she rushed away from him. There is a rumour that she is work-ing in a . . .' The woman stopped and looked at Tom, her eyes wide. 'You are the Australian Juliet was to marry, *non*?'

Tom shifted uncomfortably. 'You said that she was

working in Paris,' he said. 'Do you know where in Paris?'

'Monsieur, I have only heard rumours and do not want to . . . how you say . . . tarnish Mademoiselle Joubert's good name, but it was said she was working in a brothel for officers. I am sorry. I do not know which one as Paris has so many.'

'Are her parents still on the farm?' Tom asked and the woman shook her head.

'No, monsieur, they have gone to stay with a relative in another village.'

'Thank you,' Tom said and placed a coin on the counter. He turned to walk out of the shop into the street. What the woman had said could not be true because Juliet was not that kind of woman. There had to be a mistake; besides, the French woman had said it was only rumour.

'Wait!' the woman said, following Tom from her shop. 'The butcher's son is now back with his father at his shop. I can take you to him, and he might know more.'

Tom was surprised at the kind offer and could see the sympathy on the woman's face. 'You are very kind but I do not wish to interfere in your work,' he said.

'It's no trouble,' the woman answered, reaching for keys to lock her shop. 'I lost my son in 1914, and from the little I know of you and Juliet, you loved each other. There should be some happiness left in the world. The butcher's son does not speak English so I will translate for you.'

The woman led Tom down a narrow cobbled street through a town that had barely changed since medieval days. She came to a small shop where a burly man was chopping pork chops on a wooden slab behind his counter. The postmistress and butcher greeted each other warmly and Tom sensed that she was saying something about him as he heard his name and rank mentioned. She turned to Tom. 'Phillipe is out the back,' she said.

Tom nodded to the butcher as he followed the postmistress through to the back of the shop. In the back room animal carcasses hung from hooks and there was a powerful smell of blood – a smell Tom was very familiar with.

A young man was sitting at a wooden bench outside, plucking the carcase of a hen, and when Tom glanced down at where his legs should be he saw that he had none. Tom guessed that he had lost them in the war and had been medically discharged to return to civilian life.

Phillipe paused in his work but did not bother to offer his hand when Tom thrust out his own. Maybe it was resentment, Tom reflected, that he was still in possession of his own legs. The postmistress spoke gently to Phillipe, who was a handsome young man in his early twenties.

'He and Juliet were childhood friends,' the postmistress explained. 'He said that he saw her in a Paris street known for its brothels about four months ago before he was wounded. He spoke briefly with her, but she was with a man, a deserter from your army well known in that part of the city as a bad man. Phillipe said that the man was once known as Smithers – before he received false papers.'

'Phillipe seems to know a lot about Juliet,' Tom said quietly.

'He once had, how you would say, a crush on Juliet, but knows that now he has no legs she would never look at him,' the woman said sadly. 'Phillipe says Juliet looked very sad and fearful of the man, Smithers, who was with her.'

Smithers . . . the name reverberated in Tom's memory. He already knew from what he had been told that Smithers had hated him; apparently the man had shot himself to avoid combat. Then he had deserted.

'Could Phillipe tell me the name of the street where he saw Juliet?' Tom asked and the postmistress translated.

273

She gave Tom the answer. 'There is little else Phillipe can tell us.'

Tom realised now that Phillipe had not offered his hand in greeting because he resented Tom for being Juliet's lover, but as they left he said something over his shoulder.

'What did he say?' Tom asked.

'He said that he prays you will find Juliet and return her to the village,' the postmistress answered.

Tom stepped onto the street and turned to the woman who had been so kind and helpful. 'Thank you for your help,' he said.

'Juliet would come every day in the hope of receiving your letters,' the woman replied. 'She spoke about you with love. I, too, would like to see Juliet return to us, and teach once again in the school. The children miss her; we all do. Adieu, Sergeant Duffy, and may God keep you well.'

Tom watched as the woman walked away to her shop. There was a bitter chill in the air and the surrounding open fields had long lost their pretty blue, yellow and red flowers. Another winter was coming to the trenches, and Tom wondered if Wallarie would still be looking out for him.

'You are planning to do what!' Paddy exclaimed in surprise. He and Tom were sitting in a corner of a smoky little café among the many other soldiers packed in to drink cheap red wine.

'I need to get to Paris,' Tom answered. 'No matter what the risk. I know where to start looking for Juliet.'

Paddy looked around, hoping that his cobber had not been overhead. 'You know you'll be marked as absent without leave, and that could be changed to desertion, depending how long you are away,' he said. 'Tom, you're the platoon commander now; you're the one we all look to.'

'I have to find Juliet,' Tom replied. 'She's my whole life, I know that now, and I would rather risk a long time in prison than not find her. We risk our bloody lives every day out there in the trenches, and for what? At least this time I'm risking my life for something that has meaning.'

Paddy took a sip of wine and screwed up his face. 'Wish this was a bloody cold beer.'

'So, you know a few tricks,' Tom said quietly. 'How would you go about taking a bit of unauthorised leave?'

Paddy thought for a moment. 'You need civvie clothes,' he said. 'In uniform every bloody red cap would be stopping you and asking for papers. That means you have to pass yourself off as a Froggie civilian, and for that you need papers. But that's not going to help much as you don't have a very good grasp of the local lingo.'

'I think I know where I might get papers,' Tom said, staring at the blood-red wine in his glass. 'As for the language, I might be a Froggie soldier discharged after suffering shellshock and unable to speak. We've seen that before.'

'At least in this country the colour of your skin isn't a problem,' Paddy added in a matter-of-fact way. 'You'll need a bit of money in the way of francs, and there I can help out. Our leave is up tomorrow morning so you will have to get your act together if you are going to go on this harebrained trip of yours to Paris.'

Tom smiled and Paddy could see a glitter in his eyes.

'Well, here's to Gay Paree – and I pray that you don't get yourself shot,' Paddy said, raising his glass.

Tom grinned, then downed the rest of his wine. It was time to visit the postmistress again. No doubt she would be in a position to get her hands on official papers; all he had to do was convince her that he needed them to find Juliet. Somehow, he felt that she would be sympathetic to his illegal and dangerous mission.

The door to the room Paddy and Tom were sharing in their billet creaked open in the early hours of the morning and Tom entered quietly.

'Got everything,' he said as Paddy came awake.

'You're a bloody fool, Tom,' Paddy said as Tom stripped off his uniform to dress in the garb of a French working man.

'I can hitch a ride on a cart to the next village, and catch a bus from there to a railway station,' Tom said, tying up the boots, which fitted nicely. 'Everything will be okay,' he continued. 'You can tell the boss that I must have gone mad – another bout of shellshock.'

'That will not hold up, Tom,' Paddy said, sitting up in bed. 'So get out of here and let me get some sleep. I'll be able to give evidence at your court martial that you were behaving like a nutter – and I won't be lying.'

'Thanks, cobber,' Tom grinned. 'I'd do the same thing for a white man.'

Then Tom was gone, walking along the cobbled streets of the town to a road junction just outside the village. The sun was rising when the promised horse and cart arrived to pick him up. He knew that he was now officially absent without leave, and if he did not find Juliet within days he would be marked on the roll as a deserter. That would mean a court martial and a long time in a military prison. He hoped that he would find Juliet quickly and then, when he had her safely away from Paris, he would be able to return to his unit of his own accord. With any luck he'd only face a charge of being absent without leave. Life was full of uncertainties, and all that Tom cared about for now was finding the woman he loved.

22

There was no way anyone could keep the attempt on the life of such a rich and famous family member out of the newspapers. George sat as he usually did reading the morning paper over breakfast.

'Damn the bastards to hell!' he swore. The facts were reported, but he was not that obtuse that he could not read between the lines of what the journalist was saying about his private life. Although the coroner had already declared Maude Urqhart's death an unfortunate overdose from heroin, that did not stop the newspaper article inferring a link with the attempt on Mrs Louise Macintosh's life.

In a fury, George slammed the paper down on the dining room table, knocking over his boiled egg in its sterling silver holder. This scandal could seriously jeopardise his chances of knighthood.

George was still fuming when Louise joined him in the dining room. She barely greeted him as she gingerly sat down at the opposite end of the highly polished teak table.

George held up the paper. 'Have you read the rubbish the paper has written about us?' he growled.

'No doubt your dalliance with the dead girl has raised questions,' Louise replied calmly as George pushed the paper down the table to her. She did not pick it up.

'Did Giselle tell you why she could not come down and stay with us at Christmas?' he asked, changing the subject.

'She did not give any reason, other than she would prefer to remain on Glen View with her mother,' Louise answered and nodded her thanks as the cook placed a plate of poached eggs and bacon before her.

'It will be bloody hot up there, and there aren't many comforts,' George said, 'but it's time that I visited to see how that damned Scot is managing my station.'

'Your station?' Louise queried. 'If I remember rightly, under the terms of your father's will you share the owner-ship with Giselle's son.'

George reddened. He did not like being reminded that he was not solely in charge of the Macintosh empire, and he knew that his wife had done so to annoy him. Without another word George rose from the table, threw his napkin down and stormed out of the dining room, leaving his wife to eat her breakfast alone.

A thousand miles north the sun was over the horizon and the Aboriginal warrior knew the day would be hot. But it had been worth the trek to the ancient creek course because the woman, Giselle Macintosh, had left the valuable sup-plies of tea, sugar, flour and tobacco by an old gum tree that she had marked for him weeks earlier. The ancestor spirits had forbidden him to seek out those at Glen View, but they had said nothing about them seeking him out, and Wallarie could see the woman sitting by the tree while her mare grazed on the drying clumps of grass nearby.

Wallarie approached, trailing his long spears, and smiled to reveal teeth blackened by the white man's tobacco.

'Thank you, missus,' he said as Giselle rose to greet him. He withdrew his battered pipe from a dillybag at his waist and immediately began plugging the pipe for a smoke. He sat down, cross-legged, and Giselle sat down opposite him.

'I've heard stories from the stockmen that this creek was a place where bad things happened to your people,' Giselle said.

Wallarie glanced around as if expecting to see his long-dead clan members sitting with them. 'Place *baal* at night,' he said quietly. 'Spirits of the dead come here and cry for what has gone from the land. Wallarie a very young man when the native police come and kill all. Wallarie escape and found his brother, Tom Duffy. Together we ride and shoot. Together the whitefellas hunt us until they kill my brother, and his woman, Mondo. But no one remember all that 'cept me, and soon I will join the ancestor spirits in the sky. My kin, Tom Duffy, he must know all the stories so he can tell his sons who will tell their sons and sing the songs of our people.'

'Who is Tom Duffy?' Giselle asked, drawn into the old man's world of memories.

'Tom . . . Tom is a mighty warrior, but I have lost him,' Wallarie sighed as the nicotine brought its rush. 'Sometime by and by, he comes to my dreams and we talk 'bout our people, but he is lost in another world. He is in a place where the rain always comes and the plains are always green.'

'Is he in Queensland?' Giselle asked and Wallarie glanced at her.

'Tom is in that place where all the whitefellas are fighting for their king.'

'France!' Giselle gasped. 'Tom is a soldier?'

'Mighty warrior who has killed more whitefellas than me,' Wallarie responded with pride. 'He steal the stars from the sky, and now richer than all whitefellas hereabouts. The spirits have told me that he will one day restore the land to them.'

The old Aboriginal's rambling did not make much sense to Giselle but she knew it was not her place to say anything. 'One woman, Kate Tracy, she my sister in the spirit world. She live in big house in Townsville. All these people share your son's blood – and so does Tom,' Wallarie continued.

Giselle recognised the name Kate Tracy as her husband had mentioned her. From what Alexander had said, his Aunt Kate was a very special woman and her son, Matthew Duffy, almost a brother to Alexander. Before the war the two had visited Giselle's father's plantation and she had come to know Matthew. As far as she knew from bits and pieces of news, Matthew was flying in Palestine, and she prayed that he would survive.

'Are you a man who has magic?' Giselle blurted.

'Some fellas think I am,' Wallarie replied and said no more.

'I have had dreams that only you seem to understand,' Giselle sighed. 'That seems a little bit like magic to me.'

For a moment Wallarie stared at the creek, now a mere muddy trickle. 'Magic stuff is what whitefellas don't understand,' he said. 'Magic stuff all around here. The water goes and the water comes back. The eagle can see further than any whitefella, and that is the eagle's magic, but the eagle does not know he has the magic.'

Giselle could see that she was going nowhere with this line of questioning. 'I must return to the homestead,' she said, rising to her feet. 'I will make sure that there is always a supply of goods left here for you.'

'You are a good missus,' Wallarie said. 'When the big death comes to all the lands soon, I hope that the ancestor spirits will protect you.'

Giselle turned to ask Wallarie what he meant by the big death but he was staring with cloudy eyes into the bush, and she could see that he was in some kind of trance. She walked over to her mare and threw her leg over her saddle. When she glanced back at the bank of the creek she noticed that Wallarie and the supplies were already gone. Giselle shook her head. He was an exasperating man and she did not know whether he was truly magical or simply an old rogue who liked to have people think that he had spiritual powers.

It was night-time in Paris and Tom Duffy huddled under the shelter of a stone bridge. It was raining and he drew up the shabby coat to protect himself against the cold. Tom was not alone under the bridge. Three other men also sought shelter there, and they watched him warily. They wore ragged civilian clothing and the Australian wondered if they were French army deserters, or simply homeless veterans, because they were all of military age.

Tom slipped his hand around the knife he carried which had once been a bayonet until a soldier in the battalion had cut it down and attached a brass knuckle-duster hilt. The razor-sharp knife was a dual purpose hand-to-hand weapon.

Tom's instincts warned him that the three men were not to be trusted as they watched him with keen eyes.

The journey to Paris had gone well, with only one close call when French military police stopped Tom as he stepped onto the railway station. Tom had produced his falsified papers and to emphasise that he was a truly shellshocked veteran of the French army had fallen to the ground to scream and roll up into a foetal position. The military police, embarrassed by the spectacle of one of France's heroes being stopped for an identification check in front of the many civilians waiting for the Paris train, moved away, leaving his papers on the ground beside him.

By the time he had reached Paris it was late, and Tom had not been sure how to find the street Phillipe had told him about. For the moment he had needed sleep and a place to get out of the rain. As a soldier used to living in muddy trenches, the shelter provided by the bridge was like accommodation in a mansion. At least under the bridge no one was trying to kill him, and his companions were now passing around a bottle of some fiery liquid. One of the men spoke in French and reached out with the bottle to Tom, who accepted it and thanked them in the few words of French he knew, before passing it back.

Eventually sleep overtook Tom and he dozed off, gripping the handle of his knife close to him under his jacket. He was suddenly awoken from a deep sleep by one of the three men shaking his shoulder and holding a knife against his throat.

'English,' the man snarled and Tom could smell the rancid odour of cheap wine on his breath. 'You call out in your sleep in English. *Non?*'

'English, no, Australian, yes,' he replied, realising that they had already gone through his pockets and removed his

283

official papers and money, along with his knife. There was no sense lying when they had the drop on him.

Unexpectedly, the young man holding the knife to his throat withdrew the weapon and sat back on his heels. 'You deserter like us,' he said. 'You know they will kill us if they catch us.'

Tom did not tell the French former soldier that the Australian government was virtually alone in forbidding the death penalty to its troops. 'I am not a deserter, I'm looking for someone and I will return to my battalion when I find them,' Tom said, seeing that it was safe to sit up and doing so.

The young Frenchman looked at Tom with surprise. 'I have heard that the Boche is reluctant to fight you Australians. Maybe the war end soon, *non*?'

'I hope you are right,' Tom said. 'You intend to give me back my things?'

The Frenchman didn't answer. Tom guessed he was in his late twenties, but he had the haunted eyes of a man who had already seen far too much. He was handsome in a Gallic way and Tom guessed that he was mixed race like himself. Maybe Algerian and European parentage. 'You speak bloody good English,' he said in an attempt to gain common ground with the man. 'Where did you learn?'

'I was a seaman before the war and travel much,' the Frenchman said. 'I like England. I even travel to Australia. I see that you are like me, not all white.'

Tom was surprised at the man's perceptive observation and guessed that as a former sailor he would have been in contact with many races. 'I have Aboriginal blood,' Tom answered and saw the beaming smile on the other man's face.

'You are half-caste like me,' he chuckled. 'We fight for the white man who does not care if we die for him. That is why I desert. My name is Chason, and I was a gunner. My comrades wish to cut your throat, but I say no. We just rob you instead, and let you live.'

'How about you give me back my papers and keep the money?' Tom said. 'Then we can go our own way.'

Chason frowned and used the pointed tip of his knife to clean under his cracked nails. 'I do not steal from comrades. I give back your papers and keep the francs. But I will help you so that you cannot say Chason is a thief.'

Tom was bemused by the man's logic but he was grateful to have his help. He told the man the name of the street he was looking for and Chason beamed.

'I know it,' he said. 'It is a place where officers go to find woman. You know a woman there?'

Tom did not know how to answer that question. 'I don't know. Maybe.'

'We go there today,' Chason said, standing and addressing his two companions in French before turning back to Tom.

'They say they will go but they will take their share of your money. I cannot stop them but I will work for my share. I meet *mes amis* later. I have friends in Marseilles who can get me a berth on a merchant ship back to Africa. Maybe if you have money you can go with me.'

'When I find the woman I am looking for I will be returning to my battalion at the front,' Tom said. 'All they can do is throw me in prison.'

'Okay, we go,' Chason said. 'I know a café on the street and we will spend your money on breakfast there.'

Tom rose from the ground and brushed himself down. He followed the Frenchman, who waved to his companions as they sauntered away.

'Here are your papers,' Chason said, handing back the

crumpled pieces of valuable paper reproduced by the post-mistress of the village. 'They are very good forgeries.'

Tom did not comment but felt uneasy that Chason had spotted them as forgeries. They stepped onto a broad avenue lined with trees and already filling with civilians on bicy-cles, as well as a scattering of soldiers in the uniforms of many nations. What made Tom nervous was the occasional sight of a British red-capped military policeman or a French gendarme.

Chason turned into a narrower side street on either side of which were double-storeyed buildings that looked almost as old as Paris itself. Now it became busy with more uniformed soldiers bumping each other and walking off the excesses of sex and alcohol from the night before. They ignored the two filthy men wearing long civilian coats.

'Here is the café,' Chason said, indicating a small shop that smelled of coffee and croissants. Tom realised just how hungry he was and, despite being anxious to seek out Juliet, realised he needed to eat.

The two men went inside and Tom noticed that the pro-prietor cast them a disparaging look as he poured a cup of coffee for an American officer. He was about to say some-thing to Tom and Chason when Chason produced a fistful of Tom's francs, placing them on an unoccupied table by the large glass window. The proprietor sniffed and turned his head as both men sat down.

Chason ordered and their breakfast appeared minutes later.

'Better than damper,' Tom said, biting into the butter rich pastry and swilling down a mouthful of hot coffee.

'What is damper?' Chason asked, halfway through his pastry.

'It's bread we make in the campfire back home,' Tom

286

replied and surprised himself with a flash of a memory of another place and time. 'This is pretty bloody good.'

They ordered a second round of breakfast and Tom glanced out the glass window onto the street. 'Bloody hell!' he gasped, startling Chason.

Tom scraped back the chair as he leapt to his feet and pushed past the American officer leaving the café. 'Juliet!' he yelled, running towards her down the narrow street. But she was not alone and the burly man with her was vaguely familiar. When Tom reached Juliet she was standing frozen in surprise. She was carrying a basket just as Tom remembered from their first meeting, and it was obvious that she was pregnant. For a moment Tom struggled for words.

'Juliet.' Tom reached out and touched her arm. 'I have been looking for you.'

'Get back, you black bastard,' said the burly man accompanying Juliet, shoving Tom in the chest. 'This woman is my property.'

'Smithers,' Tom said, putting a name to the man. 'Now I remember you.'

'Tom,' Juliet said and he could see that all colour had drained from her face. 'I . . . I am not free . . .'

'If yer know what is good for you, Sergeant Duffy, you will piss off real quick before I call a copper. From the way yer dressed I doubt that the army knows yer here. Me now, I have a good workin' relationship with the local gendarmes.'

'Get out of the way, Smithers,' Tom growled, preparing himself to strike with all his force, but he hesitated when Smithers produced a long dagger in his hand. Damn! Tom cursed himself. Chason had not returned the knife to him and he was virtually defenceless against the blade.

'Here, *mon ami*,' a voice said close to Tom's shoulder and he felt the knife slipped into his hand.

'Yer mate ain't goin' to be much help,' Smithers snarled, seeing the Frenchman approach and provide Tom with his defence. 'I'm goin' to gut yer.'

Smithers lunged and Juliet screamed.

Tom stepped back, avoiding the wicked blade, but he was also aware of shouting and a whistle blowing. Before he could counter Smithers, Tom felt his arms pinned and a voice shouting at him in French. Two nearby French police had been alerted to the confrontation and were on Tom before he could react. He was slammed into the ground and hit the stone road so hard that he saw a red haze of stars. The last thing he remembered was the terrified expression on Juliet's face as she was dragged away by Smithers.

'You should bloody well be court-martialled and the key thrown away,' the commanding officer roared as Tom stood hatless and to attention before him. It had been over a fortnight since Tom had been arrested by the French authorities and handed over to his battalion on the insistence of the brigade commander. 'I have had to stretch a lot of favours with our French allies to have you released to us when you should be facing criminal charges in Paris,' he continued and Tom winced. 'If it were not for the sworn statement by Sergeant Bourke that you had not set out to desert but to look for your fiancée, I would have left it in the hands of the French. Sergeant Bourke's statement and your sterling record as an NCO has got you back to us, but I cannot dismiss the affair without our own charges of you being absent without leave. What have you to say, Sergeant Duffy?'

Absent without leave was not as serious as the crime of desertion. Tom might be stripped of rank and face a short period confined to barracks, but he would not face a hefty prison sentence.

'Sir, I know that I acted outside regulations but I had to find my fiancée. I accept any punishment I have coming.' Tom saw that the stormy expression on his commanding officer's face had dissipated a little at this answer.

'I am not sure if you have heard the rumours going around that the Hun is on the verge of capitulating, Sergeant Duffy, but it seems that I have the power to deal with your offence at my level,' the CO said. 'As it is, I am busy and may not have the time to deal with you, so in the meantime you are to return to your duties as platoon sergeant as we have not had a replacement officer sent to us. If it were not for the fact we need you to lead the platoon, I would hand the charges to the adjutant, who would no doubt deal severely with the matter.' Tom was not sure but he thought he saw just the slightest flicker of a smile on the CO's stern face. 'As it is, if the rumours prove to be true, no doubt your indiscretion will be forgotten in the administration of the battalion preparing to go home. In fact, you would not have a black mark in your service record. That is all, Sergeant Duffy, you are dismissed to resume your duties with the company.'

'Thank you, sir,' Tom said, replacing his slouch hat and saluting smartly. 'March out, Sergeant Duffy,' the RSM roared behind Tom. Both men marched out with a crash of boots and in the hallway the RSM brought Tom to a halt.

'You can count yourself bloody lucky . . . again, Tom,' he said quietly. 'It just shows the high regard the army has for you. The CO would normally have any other soldier in the clink faster than you can say Jack Robinson, but you have done your duty more than any NCO I know. Let us hope that the rumours are right and not just furphies.'

Tom returned to his company and his platoon. He was visited by the company commander, Major Cooper, and nothing was said about his absence without leave. All went on as if it had never happened – except that the pale face of Juliet haunted Tom. It had brought back all the memories of the only true love he had ever known.

23

The Ottoman Empire had surrendered to the Allied advance on 31 October 1918, and now Matthew's war in the skies of Palestine was over. He did not know whether his squadron would be transferred to the fighting on the Western Front, which continued with its usual ferocity. He was sitting on his camp bed in his tent, staring out at the rugged arid hills on the horizon, when the leading ground-crew NCO popped his head around the entrance.

'Got some mail for you, boss,' he said.

'Thanks, Archie,' Matthew replied, accepting two envelopes from the soldier. He could see that one of the letters was from his mother, writing from Townsville, but the other letter bore the embossment of an American legal firm. Matthew immediately opened the American letter and read the contents. It was a demand on behalf of a Mr James Barrington Snr that Captain Matthew Duffy AFC provide all assistance to a team being sent to Palestine to search for and recover the remains of one Miss Joanne Barrington so that she could be returned to her home in the USA for a Christian burial.

Matthew stared at the letter and his first impulse was to screw it up and toss it to the desert winds. Joanne had loved this land and probably would have wanted to be buried in its soil, he thought. Then he remembered they had two children growing up in America and that it would be better for them to have a gravesite they could visit when they were older. And maybe by conceding to Barrington's wishes might help Matthew gain access to his son and daughter.

The letter went on to mention certain high-ranking names in the British forces in Palestine, and the Australian flyer could see the extent of Barrington's influence on international politics. Matthew would arrange to speak with his commanding officer and explain the situation, producing the letter as evidence. Now the fighting had ceased in the Holy Land the CO would more than likely release him from his duties to assist the American search and recovery team.

According to the letter, the team would arrive in Jerusalem within a month, and a contact had been left for Matthew there. When Matthew looked at the date on the letter he saw that a month was actually within a week.

A fellow officer appeared at Matthew's tent and poked his head in. 'The bar has been opened, old chap,' he said. 'We're celebrating the victory, and young Goddard's promotion to captain. It came out in the gazette yesterday, and the PMC has said Captain Goddard will be shouting the mess.'

Matthew glanced up and acknowledged the invitation as he well knew that when the president of the mess committee made an invitation it was virtually an order. He read the letter from his mother before changing out of his flying suit into his dress uniform. Joanne, and the guilt and grief that came with her memory, was never far from his thoughts. Maybe this was a way to start to lay the past to rest and look to the future with hope.

A week later, Captain Matthew Duffy sat in the foyer of British military headquarters in Jerusalem. The building had cool marble floors and overhead fans that clacked and rattled. High-ranking officers wearing red flashes on their collars passed without noticing Matthew, although he was careful to stand and salute if one of them did catch his eye.

Eventually three men dressed in expensive suits entered the foyer, chatting with a British Army brigadier armed with the traditional swagger stick tucked under his arm. Matthew rose to his feet, sensing that the men might be those he was to meet. The brigadier strolled over to Matthew with the three civilians in tow. Two were in their mid-thirties, but the third man was in his late forties. Immediately Matthew knew that the older, aristocratic man was Joanne's father; he had her eyes.

'Ah, Captain Duffy,' the brigadier said when Matthew saluted him. 'I have the honour of introducing Mr James Barrington from America.'

Slowly, Matthew extended his hand to Barrington who looked at him with open contempt and hate.

'I don't think we need introducing, Brigadier,' Barrington said, ignoring Matthew's conciliatory gesture. 'Captain Duffy and I have an understanding.'

'Good show, then,' the brigadier said, flushed by the

chill he could hear in the prominent American's tone. 'I will leave you chaps to discuss the matter in hand.'

He departed, leaving Matthew in the company of what were obviously three very hostile men. It was Barrington who opened the conversation. 'I am led to believe that you were with my daughter when she was killed, and you had her buried somewhere out in the wilderness,' he said in a cold tone. 'That must mean you know where I can find my Joanne.'

'Yes, sir,' Matthew answered, his eyes flicking to the men standing either side of Barrington. They were tough-looking men with eyes as icy as Barrington's, and Matthew sensed that they were not the usual run-of-the-mill clerks employed in banking. They had the look of soldiers – or thugs. Neither attempted to introduce themselves but remained silent, allowing their employer to do all the talking.

'My daughter died because she was foolishly attempting to rescue you,' Barrington said bitterly. 'She would still be alive if you had not come into her life.'

Matthew did not respond to the accusation. War made no discrimination in those it took from the earth. 'If I am to lead you to where Joanne is buried I will need the services of her guide at the time, Mr Saul Rosenblum,' Matthew said, returning Barrington's hard gaze with his own defiant expression.

'That is a Jewish name,' Barrington said. 'From my experience you can't trust Jews.'

'Saul was one of your daughter's best friends in this part of the world, Mr Barrington, and Joanne trusted him with her life,' Matthew retorted.

'I would rather you not use my daughter's name with such familiarity, Captain,' Barrington said. 'I am sure you know that if I had my way your kind would be wiped from the earth.'

'My kind, Mr Barrington?' Matthew asked coldly.

'Jews, Negros and Papist Irishmen are destroying the American way of life, Captain Duffy, and now your blood has contaminated my line,' Barrington said. 'Our Anglo-Saxon heritage is under threat from the insidious cancer your kind bring upon America. But this is neither the place nor the time to discuss such matters. I have arranged to put you up in this hotel until we leave to find my daughter. If you think the Jew you mentioned can help, I will pay for his services. My men will check upon your progress here each day. I have already cleared your secondment to me through our ambassador in London – and your military staff in Jerusalem. You are for the moment – how you would say it in your military protocol? – under my command. Good day, Captain.'

Matthew watched as the three Americans turned and walked away. He was shocked to hear that he had been seconded to Barrington without having had any say in the matter. Then he remembered something he had seen tattooed on the right hand of one of Barrington's men. It was three letters – *KKK* – Klu Klux Klan. Matthew also remembered a trip to the USA before the war, and how he had heard of the infamous organisation while travelling in America's south. It was hardly believable, he mused. That the rich and powerful Barrington patriarch was a supremacist bigot, when his daughter had believed that all humans were equals.

It was time to seek out his old friend and comrade in arms, Saul Rosenblum. Matthew had the feeling that he would need someone to watch his back. He had survived a war and was not ready to be quietly murdered in the lonely and isolated holy lands of the Bible.

★

An hour or so later, armed with a bottle of good Scotch, Matthew found a nearby airfield occupied by British airmen. He introduced himself to the commanding officer and explained that he needed to borrow an aircraft for a few hours. The CO made some enquiries to clarify that Matthew was a man to be trusted and, after he'd been cleared, accepted the bottle of Scotch across his desk.

Before long Matthew was in the air in a Bristol with a British officer as his observer to ensure that the aircraft was returned. After a couple of hours of flying Matthew circled Saul's village and set down on an airstrip he knew had been constructed the year before. He was met by a crowd of curious Jewish settlers, who directed Matthew to the village where he found Saul with his family. The British officer remained with the aircraft and soon found himself the centre of attention from many little boys who crawled over his aircraft asking questions in a language the airman did not understand.

'Ah, it is good to see you,' Saul said, embracing Matthew in a giant bear hug.

Matthew disengaged himself and stepped back. The two men stood outside Saul's modest stone house watched by passing villagers. Many remembered Matthew as the brave airman who had helped save their village.

'Come inside,' Saul said. 'I will make us real coffee. My family are away so you will have to trust my skills in the kitchen.'

Matthew went inside the house and the familiar, homely scents assailed him with memories of a time when he and Joanne had clung to each other in his tiny bed before a dangerous mission. He sat down at a wooden table while Saul fumbled around in the kitchen, preparing the thick, black coffee he had acquired a taste for, although Matthew found it overpowering in the small cup it was served in.

'We have a mission,' Saul asked, making it a statement, and Matthew related the story of James Barrington Senior and his cronies back in Jerusalem.

'They plan to kill you when you show them where Joanne is buried,' Saul said, sipping his coffee and stroking his long beard. 'We will have to prepare for that situation when it comes.'

'Thank you, my old friend,' Matthew said. 'You are truly my brother.'

'We have been through a lot,' Saul smiled. 'I remember a boy shaking with fright at Elands River, but he left a man and with his head high.'

'You were not there when we were relieved,' Matthew reminded him. 'If I remember rightly, you were off with the Boers, and I was still shaking with fright when the British relief force arrived.'

Saul shrugged, as if the details did not matter. 'I will meet with you in three days at your hotel, and by then you should have been able to secure all the supplies we will need. Trust me, Matthew my brother, I will not allow anyone to kill you.'

Matthew made his farewells and returned to the airstrip to rescue the British observer from the admiring young ladies who had joined the children to examine the curious flying machine.

Matthew took off and returned to the British airstrip early in the afternoon, bringing both observer and Bristol fighter intact. Back in the hotel he ran into Barrington himself in the foyer.

'I was informed that you flew south this morning,' Barrington said from the cane chair he was occupying.

Bloody man had eyes everywhere, Matthew thought. He had obviously been waiting for him to return.

'I went to meet the man who will accompany us in our search,' Matthew replied. 'He will join us in three days and has left the organisation of the supplies to me. We will need to go armed. The territory we will be in is home to several groups of Bedouin bandits.'

'You will not be required to carry arms. The two men I have with me are more than capable of defending us.'

'I am an officer in the Australian Flying Corp and we carry a sidearm as a matter of protocol,' Matthew countered.

'Very well,' Barrington conceded. 'You are permitted to arm yourself with a pistol – but no other arms. If that is all, I expect that we will leave from here at 6am sharp, three days from now.'

The imperious American rose from his chair and left Matthew alone in the foyer pondering Saul's plan to keep them both alive. 'I hope you have a bloody good plan, old son,' he muttered. 'Or we will end up as bleaching bones out there.'

On the Western Front the war dragged on, although rumours of an imminent armistice filtered down to the trenches, where men huddled in the safety of bunkers and the gashes in the earth, waiting for another winter of barbed wire, bombs, bullets and bandages.

For Sergeant Tom Duffy time in the rear of the trenches training the newcomers to the platoon meant another day away from the death he knew stalked him. His students formed a semicircle around him as he went through the drills of fusing and preparing the Mills hand grenade, while in the background the steady *crump crump* of exploding artillery shells drifted to him from the direction of the front line.

'The preferred method of throwing the bomb is the overhand toss as if you were back home bowling for the pub team,' Tom said, adopting the stance of a cricket bowler. He paused. There was something different in the air and he lowered the unfused practice grenade to his side. He could hear a lark singing when at this time of year they should not be heard, and there was a steady growl of men's voices shouting and hollering from the cluster of tents nearby.

'Sergeant Duffy, Tom!' a voice called and Tom turned to see Sergeant Paddy Bourke running and stumbling towards him across the grassy field, waving his arms. The frantic approach by the platoon sergeant caught all in Tom's class attention. When Paddy reached Tom he was out of breath but his face was lit with a broad smile.

'It's all over,' he gasped. 'The war is over. The Huns signed the armistice and in half an hour,' Paddy said checking his fob watch, 'at 1100 hours today, the fighting stops.'

Tom stared at his cobber, trying to register that all he had to do was live another half-hour and it would be all over; then, as if all the demons of hell were mocking them, the silence was interrupted by a steady series of explosive crumps of artillery shells exploding.

'The bastards!' Tom swore. 'They're using up as many of their shells as they can before the war ends.'

Paddy looked at Tom and his smile disappeared. Both men knew that the Allied gunners were pouring in every round they had as fast as possible, and German soldiers would be dying as the earth shook under them and the red-hot fragments of steel tore away flesh and limbs. Even with only minutes to the cessation of hostilities the Allies were wreaking a terrible revenge on their foe. There would be mothers, wives and sisters in Germany who would lose their beloved with only minutes left to the end.

Tom turned to his class and gave the order for them to fall out to their tents. When they were gone he and Paddy sat down in the field to light their pipes and wait for the silence of the guns, and for the lone lark to return with his song.

At 11am on the eleventh day of November, 1918, sergeant's Tom Duffy and Paddy Bourke were discussing the future when the war finally ended on the Western Front. Tom knew where he would go on his first leave. The war had brought Juliet Joubert into his life and also taken her from him, but in peacetime she would be with him forever. Before then, he and Paddy Bourke would get falling down drunk and try to forget the last four years of hell.

24

The faces of the men sitting around the huge teak table were grim. George Macintosh sat at the top of the boardroom table; his assembled directors puffed on cigars and cigarettes, filling the room with smoke.

'I know that the end of the war will effect profits from our government contracts,' George said. 'But the companies have to now diversify and cater to the changing situation peace has brought to the world. We will have our troops returning and I see a market in that. Gentlemen, I expect you to come up with ideas as to how we can make money from the returning servicemen. Many will find that they no longer have jobs, and I foresee an unemployment problem. The government has promised land to returning soldiers, and from what I have learned through confidential sources, the farmland to be allocated will not be the best. Much of it will be scrub and the recipients will need to invest in clearing that land before it can be farmed. There is an opportunity in picking up what's left when they find themselves in debt after they improve the land.'

'That is a bit rough,' a board member protested. 'Those men have suffered enough, and to exploit them seems ruthless and immoral.'

George did not lose his temper at the protesting board member; he knew the man had a nephew returning to Australia from France. 'It is not immoral, Mr Beadsley,' he responded. 'It is simply a matter of good business to take advantage of any bad decisions made by the government, and by buying out those who are not able to make money from their allotments, we will be doing them and the country a service.'

George could see that his response had not satisfied all his board members – especially Beadsley – but he knew that they were smart enough not to challenge him if they wished to continue prospering under his leadership.

The meeting continued and ideas were passed around the table for the future of the Macintosh companies. To the businessmen sitting in the boardroom peace simply meant reassessing the business environment. War had proved to be a bonus to the Macintosh financial empire and George believed that peacetime would bring its own profits. Thank God his father and brother had been killed off by the war, or they might have returned with charitable ideas of distributing the wealth to those in need. He surveyed the men down the table and knew he was among like-minded people. They had not been touched by war, sitting safely in their Sydney mansions and ensuring that their sons remained out of uniform or had been allocated desk jobs away from the fighting.

Now George had the board onside, he could get on with scheming the demise of his only real competitor – David Macintosh.

On the other side of the world Matthew Duffy and Saul Rosenblum were already trekking east from Jerusalem. They rode well-fed horses and so did Barrington, but his two assistants were forced to ride donkeys. The allocation of donkeys to the two surly men had been Saul's idea. He had told them that horses were in short supply, and that if they did not wish to walk the three days it would take to reach their destination, they would have to ride the donkeys. They weren't happy about it but there wasn't much they could do. All supplies were packed and carried in saddlebags and when Matthew had asked Barrington about a means of transporting Joanne's body he had said that this had been already worked out. Matthew thought this odd as there were no spare mounts, unless of course someone no longer required theirs.

Matthew was surprised at how tough Joanne's father was in the harsh conditions of the journey. He did not show any signs of fatigue or discomfort, and rode with a straight back and in silence.

The country became more isolated and rugged as they rode on, until the last of the large villages was behind them. They were fortunate with the temperate weather and clear skies. That night they set up camp in a ravine bordered by arid hills.

Matthew and Saul made the excuse of seeking wood or camel dung for a small fire and left Barrington and his men at the camp.

'What is your plan if things start to go wrong?' Matthew asked as they foraged in the gully, out of earshot.

'Don't worry,' Saul replied, finding a small dried stick washed down the gully when the rains had come. 'Just trust me – we are being looked after.'

'Yes, but how?' Matthew frowned. 'Barrington obviously intends to use our horses to convey Joanne back to Jerusalem. That means we will no longer need our mounts and that means we will be left out here – most probably corpses.'

'We have our pistols,' Saul said. 'And we won't be in danger until we find Joanne's grave.'

Matthew agreed and decided to trust in Saul's contingency plan – whatever it was – although he resented Saul's evasiveness on the subject.

When they returned to the campsite with a small bundle of sticks they could see that Barrington and his men were already eating from cans of cold meat. No provision had been made for Saul and Matthew so they decided to set up their small fire a short distance away. At least they would have hot coffee with their cold meat.

'Hey, Jewboy!' called one of Barrington's men. His name was Gruber and he was the least pleasant of the two men Barrington had hired for the expedition. 'You boil up some coffee for us.'

Matthew noticed Saul reach for his revolver but he glanced a warning at him.

'Get your own kindling,' Matthew replied.

Gruber stood and walked belligerently towards Saul, who was squatting by the small fire sipping his coffee.

'You know what me and Peabody over there did to a nigger a couple of months ago in Alabamy, we cut out his balls, strung him up and set him alight so we could hear him squeal. The whole county turned out to watch.'

'This is not Alabama, my friend,' Saul said in a low,

304

dangerous tone. 'Here you are in my land and we have far more imaginative ways of killing a man slowly. I suspect that you have never faced a man who is armed and dangerous.'

Gruber was standing over Saul, but backed off when he saw the expression on Saul's face.

'Nice bastard,' Matthew said quietly. 'I bloody well hope that whatever plan you have is bloody sound.'

'You have the papers I recommended you have drawn up by my wife's cousin in Jerusalem?' Saul asked, glancing over his shoulder at Gruber and Peabody, who were now cleaning military-issue Springfield bolt-action rifles.

'Yes, in my saddlebag,' Matthew answered. 'But I can't see how they're going to help us out here.'

'Trust me, Matthew,' Saul said. 'Have I ever let you down?'

'No,' Matthew smiled. 'But you have led me into some damned dangerous situations where I was lucky to get out alive.'

Saul laughed out loud, but said no more.

That night both men slept away from the three Americans and took turns to keep watch. The night was uneventful, however, and so was their journey the next day.

Midmorning on the third day Saul led the small party to the hilltop where Joanne was buried under a cairn of stones. The five men stood around the small pile of rocks in silence as a breeze wafted from the north-east.

Matthew felt terrible grief for what he had lost, for the mother his children would never know, and he did not attempt to hide the tears that ran down his cheeks.

Barrington looked apprehensive, but he showed no signs of the grief he might be feeling. Instead he asked gruffly, 'You sure this is my daughter's grave?'

Matthew nodded.

'Get the shovels and the canvas,' Barrington commanded his two men. They returned with shovels and a sheet of canvas to wrap Joanne's remains.

'I am sorry, Mr Barrington, but I do not wish to be present when Joanne's body is disturbed,' Matthew said, wiping away his tears with the back of his hand.

Barrington cast Matthew a sharp look. 'It was you who brought her to her grave, yet you do not have the guts to see what you have done to my little girl.'

'It was the war that took your daughter's life,' Saul growled, 'not Captain Duffy.'

Barrington did not answer but watched as Peabody and Gruber stood by waiting for the next order, their rifles slung casually over their shoulders.

'You know what, Peabody,' Gruber said, throwing the shovel on the earth in front of Saul and unslinging his rifle. 'I think the Jewboy and Papist should do the work.'

Gruber had hardly levelled his rifle before both Matthew and Saul had their revolvers in their hands, pointing at him. Gruber, however, did not appear to be alarmed.

'Your pistols have been unloaded,' Barrington said. 'I know you are a smart man, Captain Duffy, and always knew that you knew that you would occupy my daughter's grave.'

Matthew pulled the trigger, but the hammer clicked on an empty chamber. Barrington had not been bluffing. By now Peabody also had his rifle off his shoulder and was aiming it at Saul.

'Seems you got the drop on us, Barrington,' Saul said with a nonchalant shrug of his shoulders, and raised his right arm.

'Pick up the shovel, Jewboy,' Gruber said, stepping forward to lash out with the butt of his weapon. Saul stepped back quickly, avoiding the blow.

'Hit me, you piece of scum,' Saul said, 'and I will kill you.'

Gruber hesitated, then burst into laughter. 'You know how we told you about what we did to that nigger in Alabamy, well, you're going to find out what it feels like to have your balls cut out and stuffed in your mouth. I —' Gruber paused when he saw the look of shock on Peabody's face. 'Goddamn!' he cursed, following Peabody's gaze. 'Who are they?'

All turned to stare at a ridge only a hundred yards away to see a line of seven mounted men on horses pointing rifles at them. They were dressed in the garb of Arab Bedouins and Matthew broke into a broad smile. So this had been Saul's secret plan, he thought.

'They are men from my village — led by my son,' Saul said. 'And if you don't lower your guns, they will ensure that you die a slow and very painful death.'

Matthew could see that Barrington had paled, and when they caught each other's eyes Matthew could see an almost grudging respect.

'Put down your rifles,' Barrington said. 'There is no need for bloodshed.'

Reluctantly Gruber and Peabody placed their rifles on the ground as Benjamin, leading a band of six men, rode down a steep slope and up onto the top of the hill.

Benjamin leapt from his horse and approached his beaming father.

'You have done well,' Saul said with pride. 'You did well to remain out of sight and still keep course with us.'

'You trained me well, Father,' Benjamin said, grinning.

Saul turned to Matthew, who took Barrington aside. 'I have legal papers in my saddlebag,' he said. 'And if you wish to leave here alive, you will sign them.'

'What papers?' Barrington asked suspiciously.

'Papers that verify that I am the father of Joanne's children. And that I will be able to see my son and daughter in the future.'

Barrington glared at Matthew. 'What is the alternative?' he asked in a cold tone. 'I'm not afraid of you.'

'You and I will never be friends, but I expect you to recognise that I am your grandchildren's father,' Matthew said. 'I am also practical enough to know that my children will benefit from your wealth and influence in the years ahead, and that I would be a very poor father given the kind of life I lead. So I offer you the children to raise but insist that I be able to visit them when I choose. If you sign the papers I will also spare your life.'

The slightest of smiles crossed Barrington's aristocratic face. 'I certainly underestimated you, Captain Duffy. Of course I am fully aware that no American court of law would release the children into your care, but I appreciate your generosity in allowing me to keep them. Now, they're all I have left of my Joanne,' he said, motioning abruptly to the grave marker. 'I am very attached to them and I can promise you that they will want for nothing that my money can buy. In our contract you will add that I am to raise my grandchildren without any interference from you.'

'Fair enough, Mr Barrington,' Matthew said extending his hand, which Barrington accepted with a strong grip.

'Had you been a Protestant, Captain Duffy, I might have thought you a suitable man to share Joanne's life. I might have even placed you in my family business.'

'I have no doubt that you and I will never see eye to eye, Mr Barrington, but I also suspect that you are a man of your word.'

'What is going to happen now?' Barrington asked.

'We will retrieve Joanne's body and return to Jerusalem,' Matthew replied. 'But your men will remain here.'

'Are you are going to murder them?'

'No, they will be given my revolver and two rounds – along with a couple of water bottles. It will be up to them to make their way back.'

'That is a death sentence,' Barrington said.

'Considering what the three of you had in store for Saul and myself, I am showing mercy. They may get lucky and find their way back, and if they don't, they have a round each to put themselves out of their misery.'

'You are far more ruthless than even I anticipated,' Barrington commented with grudging admiration.

'I have spent the last three years killing men from the air,' Matthew replied. 'Those men were honourable and fought to defend their lands – your two men are scum.'

Barrington did not respond, only turned his back and walked away.

Matthew did not want to see Joanne's body as she was raised from the earth. The pain was too much to bear. He noticed that Barrington, too, walked a short distance away, not wanting to look upon what remained of his beloved daughter. Saul supervised the digging up of the grave and the wrapping of the body in canvas and sewing it up for transportation on one of the donkeys.

When the task was completed he joined Matthew. 'It is time to go,' he said gently, placing his hand on his friend's shoulder.

The caravan set off from the hilltop in the late afternoon, leaving Gruber and Peabody standing forlornly watching them depart. Matthew knew that he would never see the two KKK men again.

★

Paris was a city that had thrown off the shroud of gloom with the announcement of the Armistice. Tom had been able to secure a forty-eight hour pass and he wasted no time in getting himself back to the street where he had last seen Juliet. This time Paddy had insisted on coming with him, and both men, dressed in uniform and slouch hat, mingled with the men of many nations who were seeking alcohol and women in this part of the city.

Tom was fortunate that Paddy had a decent grasp of the French language, picked up during the war, and acted as his interpreter when Tom questioned shopkeepers about Juliet and Smithers. Most shrugged, but the owner of the café where Tom and Chason had gone for breakfast knew both.

'He says that the woman you ask questions about has gone from here with Smithers,' Paddy said. 'The gendarmes were closing in on him and he took the girl with him.'

'There must be someone who knows where they went,' Tom said desperately.

'Maybe the madam of the brothel where Juliet worked,' Paddy suggested hesitantly, knowing what this inferred.

'Okay, we speak to her,' Tom said, grim-faced, and they set off.

Entry to the brothel was secured with a hefty wad of francs; as the premises had been designated for officers not enlisted men, but now the war had ended the qualifications for entry had been lowered – all anyone needed was money.

Paddy approached the madam, a hard-faced woman in her late fifties, and explained that they were looking for a Mademoiselle Juliet Joubert.

'I speak English,' the woman replied haughtily. 'Juliet worked for me as my cook and cleaner – until she got herself too much with baby to work any more. I fired her and the lazy man, Smithers. I do not know where they are.

One of my girls, Denise, thinks they have taken a ship to England.'

So Juliet had not been forced to work as a prostitute, Tom thought with great relief.

'What do we do now?' Paddy asked as they left the brothel and pushed their way through the crowds on the narrow cobbled street.

'The army will probably send us to Blighty before we return home,' Tom replied. 'I'll search for Juliet in England.'

A week later both Paddy and Tom found themselves standing in line on the docks of London, awaiting processing for a berth on a ship home. They were given three days' leave and, again, Tom did not waste time.

Using his back pay he bribed a fellow Paddy knew in Customs and Immigration to ascertain whether either Smithers or Juliet had entered the country, but the department had no documentation in either name. The world was a big place, and Tom despaired that the woman he loved could be anywhere now that shipping lanes were free of the dreaded U-boats. He knew he would not be allowed to remain in England and would have to go home to be honourably discharged from the army. Besides, he wanted to recover the missing fragments of his past back in Australia.

Within the week Tom had boarded a troopship steaming home to Australia. Juliet was lost to him for now but not the nightmares of war or of his lost memory. He was a stranger sailing to a strange land, and all he knew was that he had enlisted in Queensland with the origin of his race being listed as Indian. When he was demobbed he knew he would once again be another blackfella to the society that only prized his abilities to fight and kill their enemies. Tom was not sure where he would go and what he would do when he returned. At least working the cattle properties of Queensland his colour did not matter and it said on his papers that he was once a stockman.

At nights aboard the ship in the crowded quarters below decks Tom would slip into a troubled sleep to dream of a strange cave and see the face of an old Aboriginal man whose name he somehow knew was Wallarie. What the dreams meant, Tom did not know. Nor did he know where the old man and the cave were. Australia was a big country and Queensland a big state.

Part Two

1919

Peace and Pestilence

25

George Macintosh had received disturbing reports from Melbourne that the influenza outbreak killing so many around the world had reached the shores of Australia. The insidious disease could strike down a young and healthy person in the morning and by the time the sun set they would be dead, drowned in their own bodily fluids.

George called to his manservant to fetch Mrs Macintosh. Louise appeared in the dining room.

'What is it, George?' she asked when she saw the serious expression on his face.

'Those damned returning soldiers have brought that Spanish flu to us,' he growled. 'I think you should reconsider joining Giselle at Glen View for the Christmas break.'

Louise sat down at the end of the table and considered what her husband had said. 'She will be very disappointed. I have not seen my dear friend for such a long time.'

'War news seemed to overshadow news about the sickness killing so many overseas that now it has appeared in Melbourne I think we would be better staying here until it passes. I do not like the idea of being exposed to the public who could be carrying the wretched disease. Besides, we have my son's safety to consider and travelling could expose him to the disease.'

Louise could not argue with her husband's reasoning, and agreed that they would put off the trip until the epidemic had passed. She knew Giselle would be disappointed, but Donald's health was her main concern. How ironic it was, she thought, that peace had brought in its wake the apocalyptic horseman of pestilence.

Tom Duffy celebrated the new year drunk in a gutter of a Brisbane street. He had been discharged with a record of distinguished service, but as soon as he had taken off his uniform and bade farewell to his battalion comrades he had became once again one of the lost generation of mixed blood in his own country.

Tom had been able to procure the beer through a sympathetic returned soldier as he had been refused service by a publican who had told him it was against the law to serve alcohol to blackfellas – even ones that did not look or act if they were blackfellas. The publican had not been interested in the fact that Tom held the Distinguished Conduct Medal – as pointed out by the returned soldier with him – and both men had been forcibly ejected after a brawl. The white soldier had bought beer from a pub down the road, then the two men had gone to a small park along the river and drunk until they were oblivious to the civilian world around them.

Tom was awoken in the morning by a savage kick in the ribs. When he opened his eyes he was staring up at two blue-uniformed policemen glaring down at him.

'Get up, blackfella,' the older police officer said. 'You're off to the watch-house for being drunk in a public place.'

Tom, groggy from the effects of the night's binge, did not resist and was marched into the city to the watch-house where he found himself standing before a stern watch-house keeper.

'Empty your pockets on the desk,' he ordered and Tom did so. He had some small change, which he took out, and had been carrying his medals for bravery. When Tom put them down beside the coins the watch-house keeper picked up a medal and examined it.

'Who did you steal this from?' he asked angrily. 'This is a medal given for courage. How did a blackfella get this?'

'It's mine – they both are,' Tom mumbled, his head ringing with the ache of a hangover. 'You will see my name is engraved on the edge – along with my regimental number.'

The watch-house keeper turned the medal on its edge. 'Tom Duffy it says is the owner of the medal. What is your name?'

'Tom Duffy.'

The expression on the watch-house keeper's face softened and he looked closely at Tom. 'You served in the war,' he said. 'My son was killed at Mont St Quentin last year. He only had to survived a couple of months more and he would have come home to me and the missus.'

'A bastard of a hill,' Tom said. 'The Huns had their best waiting for us there.'

'I didn't know blackfellas were allowed to enlist,' the watch-house keeper said.

'As far as I know I was enlisted as an Indian, and that's all

317

I remember about my life in Queensland,' Tom explained. 'I copped a head wound last year and it made me lose my memory.'

The watch-house keeper handed the medals back to Tom. 'It's against the regulations but I don't believe a man should be parted from something he earned for his country. I'm sorry that you've ended up in this place but I'll make sure you get a cell for yourself instead of joining the others in the drunk tank.'

Tom was grateful for the man's compassion. After the paperwork was complete he was escorted to a dingy cell but at least he had privacy to lie down on the concrete floor and sleep off his hangover. In the afternoon he was released, but he had nowhere to go.

For the next few weeks he wandered aimlessly, cadging beer and getting drunk. He was lost in a world unfamiliar to him, and there were days when he yearned to be back with his cobbers in the battalion, even if they did have to live under the terror of active service in the front lines. When he slept it was not a respite from his new life. The shells rained down and the chatter of machine-gun fire caused him to cry out and thrash around under the night skies. His money from his army pay was running out, and soon he would be just another destitute man on the streets of this city. Brisbane was no bigger than a large town really, and it was struggling with the terrible flu epidemic taking a toll on its population. Tom was almost oblivious to the faces in the streets masked against the spread of the dreaded illness; the alcohol kept him in a blurry half-world where he didn't need to think or feel or remember.

One afternoon, as Tom stumbled along the banks of the Brisbane River, he met an old Aboriginal man who asked him for beer and tobacco. Tom slumped down beside the old man, who was dressed in rags and had grey stubble on his face. The old Aboriginal still had the black skin of his people and in his fractured English he told Tom he was from central Queensland and had drifted south when his people went to the ancestor spirits through disease and the whitefella's alcohol.

The sun was sinking and Tom had one bottle of beer left, which he passed to the tribal man along with his pouch of tobacco.

'Thank you, brother,' the old man said. 'Where you from? What your people?'

Tom rolled himself a cigarette and stared across the river where a cargo steamship was anchored in the muddy waters. 'Don't know, old man,' Tom replied. 'Been away too long fighting the whitefella war.'

The older man took a swig and handed the bottle back to Tom. 'You bin look like a Nerambura blackfella,' he said. 'Your people all gone now – 'cept Wallarie.'

Tom started at the mention of the name so familiar to his dreams. 'What do you know about the blackfella, Wallarie?' The old man licked the edge of a thin cigarette paper and rolled it up around the tobacco. 'Wallarie older than me,' he replied. 'He bin live up in the brigalow scrub, where he sometime turn into a big eagle and fly away. He bin live in the sacred cave of the men at a place the whitefella call Glen View. I met Wallarie long, long time ago and we hunt together. He bin got a whitefella sister, Kate Tracy, who kind to me when I go to whitefella town of Townsville.'

Townsville – the name was familiar to Tom but he was not sure why. 'Brother, you keep the bottle and baccy,' he said, rising to his feet.

'Where you go, young brother?' the old man asked.

'I'm going home . . . I think,' Tom replied. He would use

the last of his money to purchase a fare on a boat going north, and then he would seek out the place with the vaguely familiar name of Glen View. Maybe there he would find out who he was and why this sacred cave haunted his dreams.

The old Aboriginal watched Tom walk away and chuckled. Hadn't Wallarie come to him in a dream and said that a brother who had been in the white man's war would meet him in a place near water and give him gifts? Old Wallarie was never wrong, and so he had met the Nerambura man who was lost but was now going home, just as Wallarie had predicted.

The postman came to Glen View on his weekly rounds. He drew up his horse and sulky to take to the homestead the bag of mail that connected the isolated property to the civilised world.

Giselle met him at the front door. 'You don't look well, Herb,' she said when she noticed that he was pale and shaking.

'Just a bloody cold, Mrs Macintosh,' he said. 'I'll be all right in a day or two.'

Giselle frowned. It was obvious to her that Herb was seriously ill, and she begged him to stay and rest, but he insisted he would come good that evening when he camped over at the next homestead. Giselle watched as he took hold of the reins again and clucked his horse to move on into the hot haze of the early afternoon.

Two days later Giselle started to feel ill. She had trouble breathing and so did Angus MacDonald, the stalwart servant who had followed his best friend Patrick Duffy on the desert campaigns in Egypt almost forty years earlier.

Karolina Schumann sat by her daughter's bed throughout

the night and cooled her fevered brow with a wet cloth. From time to time, Pastor Karl von Fellmann came to sit with Giselle and Karolina.

'It's the flu,' he said quietly in the early hours of the morning. 'I will pray for her.'

The sun was rising on another sweltering day when Giselle opened her eyes. Karolina watched as her daughter turned her head and looked to the window where the first rays of the sun were softly kissing the earth before they became a savage bite.

Her smile was weak and she reached out to something Karolina could not see. 'Alexander,' she croaked. 'You have returned to me.' The weak smile turned to a glow and then Giselle suddenly struggled for breath.

Karolina leaned over her daughter, frantic with grief for what she knew was coming. She wrapped Giselle in her arms and rocked her as the young woman's life left her. Her daughter was dead.

In the room next door David burst into a crying fit while his grandmother held her dead daughter's body to her bosom. Elsewhere in the house Angus MacDonald fought his last battle and passed from the dry lands he had come to love to the cold, misty hill and heather of his childhood in Scotland. His old friend Hector MacManus sat by his bed and watched him die.

Hector struggled on the next few days, managing to ward off the sickness that would take over ten thousand Australian lives before it abated. But within the week, new graves were dug to bury the dead of Glen View.

Pastor von Fellmann and Karolina had escaped the epidemic and now stood by the graves of Giselle and old

Angus MacDonald. The Lutheran pastor found a passage from the Torah to recite over Giselle's grave while David clung to his grandmother's long skirt, staring with confused eyes at the mound of red earth.

That night Karolina sat on the small verandah of the missionary house, her grandson asleep in her lap, and gazed up at the sky brilliant with sparkling light. Karl brought her a coffee and they sat side by side, absorbed by the vastness of the universe.

'Old Wallarie says that each star is a person's soul,' Karl said gently. 'That would mean the brightest we can see is Giselle.'

Karolina turned to him and reached out in the dark to touch his arm. 'The people of this land understand a greater and simpler spirituality then we give them credit for. We come from the very earth itself and to the earth we return.' She ran a hand tenderly over David's head, staring at his sleeping form for a long moment. 'But it is the living that I must look to now. David is an orphan by law but I am his next of kin. He will stay with me.'

'Are you sure this task is not beyond you?' Karl asked cautiously.

'He is my flesh and blood,' Karolina said, turning her sad smile from David's sleeping form to Karl. 'He is a wonderful little man, and I wished that in his life I had been a little less hostile to his father.'

'War took Alexander's life. Now pestilence has taken Giselle. We can only pray God protects us from any other plagues.' Karl sighed. 'We will have to contact Mr Duffy in Sydney to inform him of Giselle's passing, and see if we can receive financial assistance from the Macintosh estate.'

'That evil man, George Macintosh, he will never approve support. But I do not care. I have means to raise

David in the manner he was born to,' Karolina said. 'I still have my plantation in New Guinea and my late husband's financial estate. David will not be a beggar at the Macintosh table. He will be independent – until he comes of age and returns to take his rightful place at the head of the family.'

They fell into a silence and sat sharing the serenity of the night far from the comforts of civilisation.

It took a week for the glorious news to reach George Macintosh. His sister-in-law was dead. Sadly, her brat had not died with her, but at least it spared him the headache of plotting a double murder. The boy was very vulnerable now, and George had a perfect excuse to travel to Glen View – he must see to the boy's future now his mother was dead. And see to it he most certainly would. George was at home, seeing to some business matters that required utmost privacy. A few friends had accepted an invitation for tennis and afternoon tea and they were due to arrive soon. He yawned at the prospect; he would have much preferred to be in the bed of the girl he had procured to take Maude's place. Mavis was a year younger than Maude and came from an impoverished family; the mother had lost her husband to the war and had seven children to feed. The girl was the oldest and George had discovered her through his agency that rented out his houses in the inner city. It did not take long for the handsome and charming George to discuss with the widow her options of being put out on the street because she could not pay the increased rent or sending her eldest daughter to live in a flat he owned in order that she look after his domestic needs when he was away from his family home overlooking the harbour.

Mavis was pretty and George soon demonstrated what he meant by his domestic needs away from home. Her mother was paid a generous allowance that she did not dare jeopardise by asking questions.

George was thinking about Mavis when Louise entered the living room where he was working.

'I have some news from up north,' he said. 'I'm afraid your sister-in-law has died as a result of the flu. They buried her on Glen View about a week ago.'

Louise paled and almost collapsed. She staggered to a divan and slumped down on it.

'Do you need me to fetch the housemaid with a brandy?' he asked matter-of-factly.

Louise shook her head and waved away his offer. 'When did you learn?'

'I received a letter from the station manager, a Mr Hector MacManus. It was in the mail delivered to me today,' George said, fighting hard to conceal his delight. 'It seems the good news is that young David is well and being looked after by his grandmother. I feel that I should travel north as soon as I have the opportunity in order to see to David's welfare.'

Louise looked sharply at her husband. 'I am surprised that you would do that, knowing your bitter hatred for both your brother's wife and his son.'

'I do not hate young David,' George said, getting out of his chair and walking over to his wife in order to display concern for her distressed state. 'He is, after all, a mere boy and has never done me any harm. I am surprised that you should think I hate him.'

'He is the only person between you and your unholy lust for sole ownership of the family companies,' Louise said, looking up with suspicion at her husband standing over her.

'You forget that our son Donald is also a part of the family ownership,' George said, looking out to the driveway where he could see a car pulling in. 'Ah, I see the first of our tennis guests have arrived. And look at you, the perfect wife in the bloom of motherhood. What a perfect couple we make.' He smiled savagely at her and left the room.

Louise was not in the mood to be cordial to her husband's guests but knew she must put on an act for the sake of keeping the peace between them. This was the only way she was able to keep her son and that meant more to her than her own happiness. Louise struggled to her feet. She put on a brave front, and waited until she was safe in her lonely bedroom to grieve for her friend.

Tom Duffy had finally made it. Weeks of travelling, first by coastal steamer north and then by a horse he had been able to purchase in the Queensland town of Mackay, had brought him to the cattle station of Glen View. He could see the house with its corrugated tin roof and verandahs and he kicked his mount into a trot up to the front steps.

When he dismounted he was met by a tough-looking man wearing the garb of a stockman.

'Can I do something for you, lad?' the man asked with a distinctive Scottish accent.

'I'm looking for work,' Tom said, taking off his broad-brimmed hat and wiping his forehead with the cuff of his long-sleeved shirt. 'Bloody hot one.'

'You worked cattle before?' Hector MacManus asked, eyeing him closely.

'I worked up in the Gulf country on a few properties before the war,' Tom replied. 'The name's Tom Duffy, and I have just got out of the army after service overseas.'

'Tom Duffy, eh?' Hector said and looked at him curiously. 'Hector MacManus, Mr Duffy.' Neither man offered their hand as in the country personal space was rarely invaded. 'I'm the boss cocky around here.'

'Mr MacManus,' Tom said. 'Pleased to meet you.'

'You're in luck, Mr Duffy. I lost a couple of my men to that damned flu and could do with an extra man for the mustering this week,' Hector said. 'Where were you during the war?'

'I served in France,' Tom answered and gave his battalion designation.

'I read about your battalion,' Hector said 'Saw a bit of action then?'

'Yeah, we saw a bit,' Tom replied and noticed that the hard look had softened a little. Hector took some steps forward and came within a pace of Tom. He held out his hand and Tom accepted the gesture. Both men had iron grips.

'You have the job,' Hector said. 'I'll take you over to the shed and introduce you to the boys.'

'Thank you, Mr MacManus,' Tom answered. 'I won't let you down.'

'Got a feeling that you won't, lad,' Hector said.

They strode across the dusty yard past and Tom suddenly stopped and stared at the old bumbil tree.

'What is it, Mr Duffy?' Hector asked. 'You look like you've seen a ghost.'

Tom shook his head and looked at Hector with a touch of embarrassment. 'I'm fine, Mr MacManus, it's just that I had a strange feeling when we came to this tree.'

Hector's face broke into a smile. 'Not surprised, lad,' he chuckled. 'Old Wallarie spends a lot of time under that tree.'

'Wallarie!' Tom gasped. 'Then I am in the right place. I have been here before . . . I remember. Before the war.

I met Wallarie and he told me strange things. Something about the stars in the sky.'

Hector's smile faded. He, too, was experiencing a strange sensation of deja vu. This was no ordinary stockman. Even his name was familiar – Tom Duffy had been a legendary bushranger around these parts many years ago. The old Scot felt a cold shiver down his spine.

26

The soldiers were returning from five years of war and dispersing to families who soon found out their husband, son, brother or lover was no longer the man they remembered. How could they be after they had been through hell? They could not tell their families about the horrors they had endured, so it was to old comrades they turned.

Tonight's dinner had been organised by Sean Duffy's former commanding officer and was open to all officers who had served. Sean had been pleased to be remembered when the invitation had arrived at his office. As most members had enlisted in Sydney, the former CO had organised for the dinner to be held in an upmarket city hotel. Candles flickered along tables set with crisp white linen and shiny silver, and gilt-edged table tickets had been printed with the guest's rank and decorations.

Sean wore a dinner suit and his medals in miniature as he limped towards the place allocated to him at a table already filling with faces he remembered from his time in the front lines. He noted that he had been seated next to a former captain of the battalion who had been a lieutenant when Sean had been invalided out.

'Sean, old chap, good to see you again – and in good health,' the former captain said. Sean accepted the man's handshake. He was in his late twenties with thinning hair and haunted eyes. He had a tic at the side of one eye.

'Good to see that you came back in one piece . . . er . . .' Sean stumbled.

'Horace Davis,' the former captain said. 'Don't blame you. We lost so many good chaps in France and Belgium, but I have always remembered how much you taught me and have always been grateful.'

'I doubt I was much of a teacher,' Sean said modestly.

'You were very supportive of all us new officers who joined the battalion,' Horace said as they sat down after the CO had taken his seat at the head of the long table.

The dinner followed the format of an officer's dining-in night, and after the former battalion padre said grace, the first course of vegetable soup was brought out by white-jacketed waiters. Chatter rose in a crescendo and so did the laughter as old comrades shared stories of misfortunes behind the lines and of characters colourful and otherwise among the ranks they had commanded. Occasionally a silence fell between men when names were spoken of those who had not returned to share this evening of goodwill and memories.

'So, old chap,' Horace said. 'How is your law practice fairing?' he asked and Sean told him that he had his fair share of criminal cases to keep life interesting.

'Where are you now?' Sean countered politely.

'Won back my old job in parliament working in the Premier's Department,' Horace said. 'Rather dull after what we've been through but at least I am not trying to dig holes in the carpet.'

'So you would be privy to all sensitive files sent to parliament,' Sean said.

'I suppose I am,' Horace replied, waiting for the CO to commence the second course before he started eating.

'There was a file transferred from police HQ to the Premier's Department some months ago concerning a matter of an enemy alien investigation back in '17,' Sean said cautiously and went on to explain about the investigating officer's possible misconduct. 'I would be eternally grateful if that file could somehow find its way back to the inspector general for further investigation.'

'Are you sure that doing so would not compromise the Premier's Department?' Horace said.

'Not at all,' Sean reassured, knowing that he was asking a lot of his former comrade. 'This Detective Inspector Firth has a few powerful friends – but not strong enough to back him if the file is investigated properly.'

Sean took a sip of red wine from the crystal glass while Horace considered his proposal. He waited in silence, almost holding his breath.

'I will see what I can do,' he answered. 'Leave it with me.'

Sean exhaled in relief. 'Thanks, Horace, I owe you one.'

After dessert came port wine decanters and toasts to the King, the battalion and those who remained behind buried under the soil of foreign lands. Eventually the dinner was over and the men retired to continue drinking, talking and smoking in an adjoining room.

Sean mixed with old friends and for the first time in his

civilian career felt a warm communion with kindred spirits. The night wore on and finally he bade goodnight to the president of the mess committee, and then the CO, who shook his hand warmly.

'You were a bloody good officer, Major Duffy,' the former CO said. 'You did the battalion proud.'

Sean returned to his flat in the city much the worse for the wear, but before he laid his head down on his pillow he thought about the file. Everything depended on whether Horace would put battalion loyalty before civilian political concerns. Sean could only wait. It had been a chance meeting, but life on the front lines had taught him that chance was everything – after all, it decided whether you lived or died out there on the battlefield.

A week after the officers' dinner Detective Inspector Jack Firth reported to work at police headquarters after a weekend off duty. As he walked into the office he shared with his small crew of men he noticed a sombre feeling in the air as if someone had died.

'Well,' he growled. 'What's up?'

'You're wanted upstairs,' one of his men volunteered quietly.

Jack frowned. Upstairs meant the inspector general's office and that was never a good thing. He made his way to the waiting room outside the top policeman's office and was met by a male assistant.

'The boss wants to see me,' Jack said and the assistant looked decidedly nervous.

'Just take a seat, Detective Inspector Firth,' he said, motioning to a lone chair at the corner of the reception room. 'The inspector general won't be long.'

PETER WATT

Jack waited for a good half-hour and with each passing minute he grew more and more anxious about why he
had been summoned upstairs. Perhaps it was because he had
not got a result on his case about the dead prostitute that
Jack had tried to lay on Harry Griffiths. Well, that could
be explained away by lack of resources and still gathering
evidence against Lenny.

Jack almost jumped when the door opened. 'Come in,
Detective Inspector Firth,' the inspector general said in a
cold that Jack immediately recognised as containing bad
news for him.

Inside the office he was surprised to see that the inspector general was not alone. A man in his late twenties and
wearing an expensive civilian suit sat in one of the chairs.
Jack vaguely recognised him as a public servant from the
Premier's Department, and Jack's blood ran cold when he
noticed a well-thumbed file sitting on the inspector general's desk. The bloody Schumann file, he thought. It never
seemed to go away.

'This is Mr Davis from the Premier's Department,' the
inspector general said. 'Last week he returned the Schumann file to my office, and since then I have had a good
chance to read its contents. You assured me that nothing
improper occurred, but I am afraid I disagree with you,
Inspector Firth, and so does the premier. Your dereliction of
duty in the matter is in contravention of police regulations.'

'Sir,' Jack said desperately, 'that all happened during
the war and a long time ago. I may have made one or two
mistakes but that's to be expected.'

The inspector general sat down at his desk and stared
hard at Jack, who was now sweating. The public servant
remained silent but watched Jack intently.

'You were attached to military intelligence when you

were given the Schumann case,' Davis finally said. 'You are also in breach of military regulations.'

Jack turned to the public servant and had the urge to cross the room and punch the man in his smug face. 'What would you know of my work with intelligence?' he said, trying to intimidate the public servant.

'I was soldiering in the trenches and we expected the best from those vested with protecting the home front, Inspector,' Davis said, rising from his chair. 'The premier concurs with the inspector general that you should answer to serious charges of obstructing military regulations.'

Jack turned to his boss. 'What if I resign?' he blurted. 'Would that prevent any embarrassment to the department?'

Jack knew he was cornered. How in hell had the file made its way out of the archives?

'That may be in all our interests,' the public servant said, turning to the inspector general. 'The premier does not want any scandals at a time when we need to rely on the public's faith in law and order. I think, given Detective Inspector Firth's otherwise fine record, that he be allowed the opportunity to hand in his resignation.'

The inspector general nodded. The resignation would save face all round. Jack Firth was getting off easy. 'Inspector Firth, you will have your resignation on my desk by the end of your shift today, and I will then place you on annual leave with your discharge becoming effective as from the end of your leave. I doubt that you have any questions.'

'No, sir,' Jack said in a beaten voice. 'I will write out my resignation request as soon as I return to my office.'

'Well, if there is nothing else, you are dismissed, Inspector,' the top policeman said, and Jack turned and walked away in a daze. It had been so brief and yet many years of serving his community had just been obliterated to the whims of a political system that understood nothing about law and order.

When he returned to the office he could see from the expressions on the faces of his men that they already knew of his fate.

Jack's offsider, Dick Mawdsley, approached. 'Bad news, boss?' he asked nervously.

Jack shot him a withering look and stormed from the office. He would make his way to see George Macintosh, who he held responsible for his sacking. As Jack Firth strode along the street the thought dogged him that behind the re-emergence of the incriminating file was the bloody solicitor, Sean Duffy. Jack did not have proof but that had not stopped him in the past from convicting known criminals on fabricated confessions. As Jack approached the company offices of Macintosh Enterprises his rage was building and George would feel the full brunt of it.

Jack brushed past the protesting male secretary in the anteroom to George's office and flung open the door.

'What in hell are you doing in my office?' George demanded, rising from his chair.

'This morning I reported to work and now I am facing an early retirement because you did not ensure a certain file was buried for good – as you firmly assured me it would,' Jack exploded. 'A bloody civil servant by the name of Davis had it dug up and sent back to the inspector general's office.'

The news took George by surprise. 'Davis?' George said thoughtfully. 'I know him. I met him at the Australia Club. He served in the same battalion as Sean Duffy. There has to be a link. The bond between these damned returning servicemen is as strong as any in a family.'

'That does not help my situation,' Jack said, calming a

little. 'You always said that if things went wrong you would ensure that me and my family would be looked after.'

'I do not renege on a promise,' George answered quickly, and hoped that no one of influence had seen the notorious police officer come to his office on the day of his 'resignation' from the police. It did not bode well for a man aspiring to a knighthood. 'I always have a position for a personal assistant on my staff.'

Jack rolled his eyes to the ceiling. 'What, a lowly paid secretary like the bloke you have outside. No, I want more than that. You owe me my job, and when it gets out on the streets I'm off the force, I'll be a marked man by every spiv with a knife and grudge.'

'I am planning to travel to a family property in Queensland next week,' George said. 'I can employ you to travel with me as my personal assistant. I can promise that the money you are paid will be more than you have earned as a police inspector.'

'What do I have to do for that amount – kill someone?' Jack said with a smile of amusement at his own joke.

'Only those who threaten my position in the family business,' George replied calmly, watching the smile fade from Jack's face. 'Such a job would naturally incur a generous bonus, not to mention shares in one of my real estate developments. I can promise that you will become a very rich man.'

Jack stared at George with an expression of fascination. 'Did you kill that actor bloke, Guy Wilkes back in '14?' he asked on impulse.

'No. But now you're no longer a police officer I can tell you who did,' George replied. 'It's no secret that the Wilkes case has haunted you the last few years. It was my father, the respectable and honourable Brigadier Patrick Duffy, who shot Wilkes.'

'Bloody hell!' Jack hissed. 'How do you know?'

'I was there, although my father did not know at the time,' George answered, sitting down at his desk. 'The shooting was an accident as a result of Wilkes pulling a gun – a derringer, if I remember rightly – on my father who attempted to disarm him when the gun went off. But the family name had to be protected, so I convinced my father not to confess.'

'Even if I am out of the force, I could still pass on what you've told me and have you brought up on charges for being an accessory after the fact,' Jack said.

'You could, but I think by telling you what happened I have proven my trust in you to do the right thing and accept my offer. Business is business – and after this flu epidemic passes, we will be back to a world that will not want to remember what happened before – or during – the war.' George shrugged. 'After all, Wilkes was not a very good actor anyway.'

'You're a ruthless bastard, Macintosh,' Jack said. 'But if you stick to your side of the deal, you will have my loyalty.'

George rose from his chair and went around his desk to stand before Jack. He thrust out his hand and Jack accepted. The former policeman had now sealed his pact with the devil.

First came the boiling black clouds that blotted the sun, and then came the deadly stillness in the air. Wallarie stood among the scrubby trees and stared to the west, where the storm was coming from. The world around him fell into an expectant hush. Would the storm rolling in with a purple tinge, like a massive bruise to the sky, bring a torrential downpour to cool the sandy soil parched under the summer sun, or would it be filled with fiery forks of lightning that set the earth alight? Whatever was to happen, Wallarie knew it was a message from the ancestor spirits, and he cringed, knowing that he had lately been a little disrespectful to their voices in the night.

Whatever it was, he decided the best place to be was off the plains and back in his cave, safe from the coming fury.

A few miles away, Tom Duffy sat astride his mount, watching the approaching storm. Beside him an Aboriginal stockman muttered in a language Tom did not understand.

'What are you saying?' Tom asked, feeling the sweat creeping down his chest and back as the hush fell over the plains.

'Ol' Wallarie, he do this,' the stockman said. 'Wallarie sing up dis storm.'

Tom shook his head. The name of the legendary Nerambura warrior was ever present on Glen View. Tom had still not fully recovered his memory, but it was coming back in bits and pieces, sometimes as flashes and other times as long stretches of memory. Tom had put together the pieces concerning Wallarie and knew that he was a kinsman whom he needed to find and speak with. But the old Aboriginal had not been seen for many weeks and Tom had thrown himself into his work of mustering cattle and the other tasks expected of his position.

Hector MacManus had proved to be a fair boss and he treated all his men with an equal hand, whether European or Aboriginal.

Although Tom had not known Giselle Macintosh, he could see the impact her passing had on one and all, from the station manager to the Aboriginal families who lived on the land of Glen View. She was sorely missed for her compassion and practical administration to their needs. It was very strange how her little boy had taken to Tom and followed him around whenever he visited the homestead.

'Don't know about Wallarie being behind this,' Tom replied. 'But we might be wise getting some shelter. The hill is not far away – and it's about time I visited,' Tom said, pulling his horse's head around and pointing it in the direction of the craggy rock outcrop he could see a few miles away where he knew from his memory the sacred cave was.

'Not a good idea,' the stockman said. 'Ol' Wallarie live there an' he might get cranky. Mebbe we ride to house.' Tom had noticed that all the stockmen seemed to avoid two places on the property. One place was the craggy hill, and the other was a stretch of creek where, so he was told, the bleaching bones of a people past appeared in the earth after flash floods.

'You can do that,' Tom said. 'Tell Mr MacManus we have around forty head here and we'll get back to them when the storm passes.'

The Aboriginal stockman nodded and kicked his mount into a trot, sensing that this was no ordinary summer storm, and as he set off the first crack of lightning struck the dry earth causing a flare of fire to crackle in the scrub. The thunder now rolled and crashed all around the plains and for a moment Tom was thrown back to the Western Front as the artillery rained down on the trenches. He closed his eyes and gritted his teeth, forcing himself not to fling himself from his horse onto the ground to seek cover.

He spurred his horse on and made his way to the landmark hill dominating the plains. Lightning and thunder were simultaneous – but there was no sign of rain to quench the parched earth.

Tom could smell the acrid scent of fire on the still air, and then the wind came in a howling burst to sweep across the tinder-dry scrub. A bushfire was now in its infancy and growing rapidly. Tom dug in his spurs and the horse broke into a gallop, heading for the safety of the hill. At least the fire was behind them, and when they reached the hill Tom leapt from his horse and led it along a narrow rocky track towards the summit. At the entrance to the sacred cave he tethered his horse to a stunted, gnarled tree. When he turned to gaze back over the plain he could see the wall of fire creeping towards the homestead. Tom was torn between remounting and galloping to warn the residents of Glen View homestead, and seeking out Wallarie.

'You come inside,' a voice he recognised commanded. 'Brother fire will go away by and by.'

Tom turned to see Wallarie standing in the entrance of the cave. Tom followed the old man into the shelter and was assailed by the musty odour of a place used by his father's people for countless centuries. It brought back memories of a time before he went away to fight in the European war.

'You come back,' Wallarie said in a sombre voice. 'Got any baccy on you?'

Tom smiled. He felt curiously at home here and the distant sound of the raging fire drifted into the background, as did the terrifying crash of lightning. Here he was surrounded by the earth as if he had returned to the primeval womb of creation.

'Wallarie,' Tom whispered. 'You were always with me when I was frightened and alone over there.'

Wallarie settled down in the centre of the cave and crossed his legs. He beckoned to Tom to do the same.

'You, me sing,' Wallarie said as Tom sat down. 'Tell brother water to come and fight brother fire.' Wallarie broke into a chant that filled the cave. Tom could not understand the words he used and remained silent, still fearing that the fire would sweep down on the homestead before they could adequately prepare. Sitting here listening to Wallarie sing his song seemed so inane, Tom thought and became restless. He was about to say that he must go but would return when Wallarie stopped chanting his song and looked directly at Tom.

'You found the stars that live under the earth,' Wallarie said after he'd finished. Tom did not know what he was talking about. What bloody stars? The old man was deranged.

Hector MacManus stood at the front gate of the homestead and felt the hot air whip at his face. He could smell the burning scrub before he saw the billowing smoke blend with the black clouds of the dry storm.

'God almighty!' he whispered. 'It's comin' straight for the house!'

Hector turned and hurried back to the homestead, calling the names of all those who resided within, from the Aboriginal cook to the Chinese gardener. They would have to evacuate. Already burning cinders were falling all around the house and the explosive crackle was audible above the fury of the lightning.

Hector realised that the mission station would be next, and the lives of the pastor, Mrs Schumann and young David were at stake. When he was assured that the house was evacuated and his small staff headed for a dam nearby, he quickly dragged a horse from the stockyard, leaving the gate open to allow the rest of the horses to escape.

Hector flung himself on the bare back of the horse and

with only the reins leaned over the animal's neck to avoid choking cinders. He turned the horse in the direction of the mission station and urged it into a gallop. The fire was on one flank, but in the distance he could see a second fire front forming which directly threatened the Lutheran outpost.

In the cave Tom grew more restless. Lives were in danger down at the homestead. He couldn't wait here any longer.

'The stars that grow under the ground,' Wallarie repeated. 'The spirits of the old ones told me you found them. My sister Kate Tracy now holds the secret.'

Tom stood up impatiently. 'I have to do something,' he said in an anguished voice. 'Ill come back later.'

'You stay,' Wallarie said. 'Brother wind and water will come.'

Tom turned to Wallarie, who remained sitting cross-legged with a serene expression on his face. 'You gotta trust the blood you have.'

Tom was confused. Brother wind and water? Superstitious stuff of an old blackfella.

'You got any of that baccy?' Wallarie asked again.

Frustrated, Tom slumped back to the floor of the cave and searched through his pockets for his pouch of tobacco. He handed it to Wallarie, whose eyes lit up. Wallarie pulled out his battered clay pipe and stuffed the precious dry leaf into it.

'You got a match?' he asked and as Tom was pulling out the box he carried with him, his own pipe fell from his pocket. Wallarie reached for it, putting aside his own pipe. Tom had a finely made pipe that he had purchased in England and Wallarie looked with delight at the beautifully crafted smoking implement.

'You can have it,' Tom said. 'I have another one in my swag.'

Wallarie smiled, immediately going to work on filling the bowl of his new possession and lighting up. Wallarie sucked on the pipe and puffed out grey smoke contentedly.

'Ah, brother wind and water come soon,' he sighed. 'Then I tell you 'bout Auntie Kate.'

What the hell, Tom thought. After the fire he would probably be doing a body search and burying the charred remains. He had left one war only to be caught up in the eternal war fought between those working the land and nature's fury. Tom was long hardened by the loss of life and accepted that in a chaotic universe he had little control over events around him.

Hector MacManus reached the mission station and could see that already Karl, Karolina and David were in the horse and sulky ready to leave. The wind had become a roaring voice from hell and Hector pulled his horse up as close to the sulky as he could so as to be heard.

'Never seen anything like this before,' he yelled. 'We have to get to the dam – it's our only hope.'

Karl nodded his understanding. Karolina was holding David, who was wrapped in a wet blanket as protection from the glowing embers falling all around. Hector could see a gap in the flames and thought to ride through there to the relative safety of the dam, but even as Karl struggled to convince the terrified horse to move, the break disappeared as the flames closed the gap. No matter which direction Hector looked they were surrounded by fire. He wished he had snatched up his gun before leaving the homestead. A quick death from a bullet was better than being burned alive.

The fire came on with the spirit of an avenging demon, and just for a moment Hector wondered if the curse he had so often heard of from those who had lived longest on Glen View was real and had finally come to purge the land.

With horror, he watched as the flames caught the mission station house and roared with fury into the sky. Hector began to recite an old Presbyterian prayer he remembered from his boyhood in Scotland. The flames crept inevitably towards the small huddle of people desperately sucking the little oxygen left in the burning air. Death was coming to them in one of its most horrible forms. Soon, it would all be over as the flames licked the flesh from their bodies.

27

The fire lashed and coiled in red–hot tongues towards the evacuated homestead, searing all in its path. Burning cinders rained down as the winds whipped up long fingers of red and black. Flames crept closer and closer to the bumbil tree. But then, as if it were a living being, the fire hesitated – and recoiled. Brother wind and water came in defence of the bumbil tree, changing the direction of the fire and thundering down from the sky torrents of quenching rain.

A few miles away Hector, Karl, Karolina and David had crawled under the sulky after releasing the terrified horse from its harness. The unfortunate animal stood a short distance away, shivering in fear, as the flames closed in.

Hector felt the shift in the wind and suddenly the rain

came, falling heavily from the dark sky. The ground sizzled and steamed from its saving touch. The fire was desperately attempting to fight back, but the heavy downfall was winning.

Hector crawled out from under the sulky and stood to let the water soak his clothes.

'A bloody miracle!' he screamed to brother wind and brother rain.

He was joined by Karolina and Karl and the three hugged one another. David stood beside them, staring at the steam rising from the tortured earth and scrub. Karolina lifted him into the air, allowing the water to soak his clothes with its soothing coolness.

Tom Duffy could smell the change from within the cave even before he heard the rain. He glanced at Wallarie, who was contentedly puffing on his new pipe.

'Brother wind and brother water come,' the old man said, the pipe clenched between his tobacco-stained teeth. 'Said they would come.'

Tom shook his head, rose and went to the entrance of the cave. Rain fell in great sheets, whipped by a wind countering the fire's progress. Flames were rapidly being replaced by billowing steam, and the world Tom knew was saved.

He turned back to Wallarie. 'What is it about this lady Kate Tracy?' he asked.

'Kate my sister, your aunt,' Wallarie replied. 'She has secret of stars that grow under the ground. You must go to her in the whitefella town of Townsville and she will tell you.'

'Kate Tracy,' Tom frowned and suddenly as if he had been hit by lightning he saw a picture of her in his mind.

'Aunt Kate,' he gasped. 'I remember. She helped me enlist. Told them I was of Indian blood because the army could not enlist Aboriginals. She's a good woman.'

Wallarie nodded his agreement. 'You go to her. Tell the station boss you gotta leave. I have to go and find what brother fire left for me to eat. Mebbe a fat goanna – or young wallaby. You get goin' now.'

Tom smiled at the old man. 'You're a cunning old black-fella, Wallarie,' he said with affection. 'Maybe we meet again soon.'

Wallarie returned the smile. 'Mebbe.'

Wallarie watched Tom leave. He knew it wasn't over for Glen View yet. That *debil debil* was coming in the wake of the fire he had sent to kill the boy.

When Hector returned to the homestead he expected the worst, but was overjoyed to see that it stood intact and that the staff had returned without any injury.

'Praise be to God that He has listened to our prayers and saved the house,' Karl said, standing beside the Scot.

'Do you see notice anything queer?' Hector asked.

'What do you mean?' Karl said.

'Well, you see how the ground is scorched around the bumbil tree where Wallarie always sits, and that the fire skirted round the graves of Giselle and Angus, maybe we should be thanking him for saving us all.'

Although Karl knew that such a statement bordered on being blasphemous, he had lived too long in the isolation of Australia's outback not to respect the beliefs of its indigenous people.

'It is possible that God works through one of His children,' Karl acknowledged.

'I just pray the lads out mustering have fared well,' Hector said, observing the anguished Chinese gardener kneeling among what was left of his precious vegetable garden. As if in answer to his prayer, Hector saw a file of horsemen approaching the homestead. He counted them in, none were missing or injured. Although Tom Duffy was not present, Hector was reassured he had been last seen seeking the hill for shelter. In all, it was nothing short of a miracle, although whether Wallarie or God was responsible, he couldn't say.

Sean Duffy and Harry Griffiths met in an inner-city hotel for a counter lunch. It was Sean's shout to celebrate their victory in having Jack Firth brought to heel. The beer tasted especially good when they raised their glasses over their lunch of lamb stew and potatoes. However, they had hardly taken a mouthful of the cold beer when the man himself appeared behind them.

'Think you two are smart,' Jack snarled. 'It had to be you, Duffy, who had that bloody file sent to the inspector general.'

Both men turned away from the bar to see the cold fury in Jack's eyes. 'I wouldn't consider doing anything rash, Firth, if I were you,' Sean said. 'After all, there's nothing more ex than an ex-copper.'

Jack flinched but did not lose his composure. Sean could see that he was in a very dangerous mood.

'Push off, Firth,' Harry growled, clenching his fists. 'Now you know what it's like to be out on the streets as a nobody.'

Jack appeared to back off, a bitter smile crossing his face. 'It's not over, you know,' he said. 'I have a long memory, and I wouldn't be too cocky if I were you two.'

'If that's a threat,' Sean said, lifting his glass of beer, 'put it in writing, and send it to my office.'

Firth did not reply but turned on his heel and walked out of the hotel, leaving Sean and Harry to stare at his departing back.

'The bastard might have been kicked out of the police, but I know Firth,' Harry said. 'He's still as dangerous as he ever was.'

'I agree,' Sean answered. 'I've heard he's working full-time for George Macintosh now, which can't bode well for us.'

'While Firth is alive he will always be a danger to us both,' Harry said menacingly.

'I know what you're thinking, Harry, but he's not worth it,' Sean cautioned. 'We survived too much to throw away what's left of our lives on rubbish like him.'

'Just dreaming, boss,' Harry sighed and the two men returned to their plate of stew and cold beers. But Firth's veiled threat echoed in Sean's mind. George Macintosh and Jack Firth together were a formidable and extremely dangerous duo.

George informed his wife over dinner that he was booked to travel to Glen View with Jack Firth.

'That man,' Louise said, raising a spoon of leek soup to her lips. 'Why would you wish to have him travel with you?'

'He will act as my assistant,' George replied.

'I have heard rumours that Inspector Firth was known as a brutal man when he was in the police force. What use could he be to you if you are simply going to Glen View to review the management of the property?'

George looked irritated by his wife's persistent questions. 'Just remember who puts the food on the table and pays for your extravagant lifestyle,' he snapped. 'You should learn not to question how I choose to run the family companies.'

After finishing dinner in silence, Louise excused herself to go to her room. She was troubled by her husband's employment of the disgraced police officer, but even more troubled by the fact that Jack Firth would be travelling to Queensland with George. Louise remembered the stories she had heard of a curse on the family incurred by a terrible massacre of the Aboriginal people who had once roamed the lands now known as Glen View. It was said that the curse reached out to take the lives of the Macintosh men, and it seemed the curse did not discriminate between those who were good and those who were evil.

Louise lay on her bed. She could feel the sweat from the warm summer's evening drip between her breasts. She was heavy with child now and found the endless heat trying. She tried to shake the premonition that Giselle's young son's life was in danger, but she could not.

Tom sat on the front verandah of Glen View with his hat on his lap. Hector MacManus gazed at the blackened plains around the homestead.

'So old Wallarie is a kinsman of yours?' Hector said. 'Can't say I'm surprised. Nothing about that old magic man would surprise me.'

Tom shrugged. He didn't know whether Wallarie was a magic man, but strange things certainly seemed to happen around him.

'Go to Townsville, Tom. There'll still be a job here when you get back,' Hector said. 'It'll take some time to get to Townsville to see Mrs Tracy. She's a grand lady, and the property adjoining this one is owned by her. For years, she's been at the Macintosh family to purchase Glen View – curse and all.'

'I've heard about the curse,' Tom said quietly. 'There's not a man on Glen View who doesn't believe this property has some kind of cloud hanging over it.'

'It all goes back to when old Sir Donald Macintosh carried out a so-called dispersal – with the help of the Native Mounted Police. That must have been over a half-century ago. They slaughtered pretty well every man, woman and child they came across. Wallarie and a handful of survivors got away, and with the help of a whitefella, your namesake Tom Duffy, lived out in the scrub and exacted revenge on the Macintosh men employed in the massacre down at the creek. Every now and then the bones of the blackfellas turn up after a flood.'

'Tom Duffy was my grandfather,' Tom replied. 'My father, Tim, named me after him.'

Hector glanced at Tom. 'It all makes sense,' he said with a sigh. 'I feel it in my bones that the curse hasn't run its course yet. Maybe it's my Gaelic blood that makes me superstitious about these things. On that subject, I have received notification that Mr George Macintosh will be arriving next week to inspect the management of Glen View. It's possible I won't be here when you return.'

'He'd be a fool to fire you when there's no better person to run this place,' Tom said with genuine praise for the man he had come to respect and like.

'He's no fool from what I know of him, but he is a money-grubbing bastard who exiled his dead brother's wife and son to this place so he could take possession their home in Sydney. I don't know what he wants up here, but it can't be good.'

'Well, I'll be back, Mr MacManus,' Tom said. 'I like it out here, and I like the work. Besides, there's not much else a broke blackfella like myself can do for a living in this country. What I did for the country in the Great War doesn't count for much now.'

Tom rose and placed his hat on his head. His horse was saddled and Hector had generously provided him with supplies for the long journey across the semi-arid lands between Glen View and Townsville.

'I was a soldier once,' Hector said, rising from his chair and extending his hand. 'I don't care who you are. What counts is the heart a man has – and yours is a big heart, Tom Duffy.'

Tom accepted the firm grip and then walked down the stairs to his horse tethered in the yard. He made final adjustments to the girth and leapt astride his mount. 'See you when I see you, Mr MacManus,' he called. Then he turned his horse's head north-east to Townsville.

'There's a man coming up the driveway,' said Kate Tracy's young Aboriginal housemaid as she stared out the flyscreen door at the late afternoon shadows softening the hot day.

Kate put down her sewing and rose from her chair. She could see a young man with a kitbag over his shoulder striding towards the house. Kate quickly put on her spectacles to get a better look.

'Oh, my God!' she exclaimed and flung open the door, brushing past her housemaid with her arms outstretched.

'Hello, Mother,' Matthew said, dropping his kitbag and embracing her, lifting her from the ground and swirling her about. 'Sorry I didn't write that I was coming. You know I've never been much for corresponding.'

Kate did not answer because she was crying with joy. It had been four years since she'd last seen her son, and every day that passed had been agony, not knowing the fate of her one and only son. She did not know where to start with the many questions she had for him, but when he put her down she gripped his hand as if never intending to let it go.

'Oh, Matthew,' she said and led him toward the house where the young maid was watching with curiosity.

'Mary,' Kate called. 'Put on the kettle and bring out the biscuit tin.' The girl disappeared into the house as Kate and Matthew walked up the stairs. Kate led her son to the cane chairs he was so familiar with and sat him down. She was still at a loss for words and stroked his hair instead.

'It's been a long time,' Matthew said and Kate could see the colourful ribands on his uniform jacket awarded for his courage and service to his country. 'And I'm afraid I'll have to leave again soon.'

'But you've just returned home, and there is so much that we have to catch up on,' his mother protested. 'Why do you have to leave?'

'To return to Mesopotamia,' he replied gently. 'I can see an opportunity to establish an aircraft business to supply the oil men who will be arriving there.'

'What of my grandchildren?' Kate asked hopefully and Matthew shook his head.

'I am afraid I made a deal with their grandfather,' Matthew answered and went on to explain the terms of the contract that James Barrington and he had signed in Palestine. 'But, when they are older, we may see to making other arrangements,' he said. 'I am sure that the formidable Kate Tracy will find a way to use her power and influence – and substantial fortune – to do that.'

Kate frowned. Oh, but she would move heaven and

earth to see her only grandchildren, and already the germ of an idea was forming in her mind.

The tea arrived on a silver platter and Kate poured her son a cup. 'Wallarie told me that I would be a grandmother before it happened,' Kate said, pouring her own cup. 'He came to me one night.'

'Wallarie,' Matthew frowned. 'I thought he was still at Glen View.'

'Ah, he came to me in a way you would scoff at, because you have become a man of engineering and science,' Kate smiled. 'But I knew.'

The two sat talking until the sun went down behind the eucalypt trees and the white cockatoos began swirling noisily in the cloudless sky as they looked for a tree to roost in for the night. Matthew told his mother of Joanne and her death. She cried for his pain and they reminisced about friends lost to the war, such as Randolph Gates, the American who had worked for Kate on the property adjacent to Glen View. The war had taken so much, but at least it had returned Kate's son to her.

Over a dinner of corned beef and cabbage Matthew talked to his mother about his plans for a flying service on the other side of the world, and when the dinner was over and they had retired to the front verandah to finish the evening with the best whisky Kate had in her liquor cabinet, she agreed to become a silent partner and use her considerable wealth to capitalise Matthew's dream. Matthew pulled out a packet of Cuban cigars and lit one. The night was warm with no breeze as they chatted. Suddenly Matthew rose to his feet and stared into the night beyond the house.

'What is it, dear?' Kate asked.

'We have a visitor,' Matthew replied.

It was a man astride a horse; he was illuminated by the verandah's lantern-light.

'My God!' Kate gasped. 'It's Tom Duffy!'

Matthew turned to his mother with a questioning expression, but she was already picking her way down the stairs to greet Tom, now on foot and leading his horse. She gathered him to her in a warm embrace. Tom tethered his horse and was led up the stairs to meet his cousin.

'Matthew, this is Tom, your cousin on my brother's side,' she said and the two men shook hands.

'My mother's told me about you,' Matthew said warmly. 'She said you served in France and Belgium.'

'I see from your uniform that you saw a bit of the war too,' Tom said.

Matthew waved off the compliment. 'I was over in Palestine flying with the AFC,' he said. 'Our war was not as bad as yours though.'

Kate poured a tumbler of whisky for her long-lost nephew and sat him down on one of the chairs. As former fighting men will, Tom and Matthew fell into a conversation about their experiences, and Kate sat listening patiently, realising that what was happening was necessary for both men. The night drew on and Kate left her son and nephew to continue until the bottle was empty and they stumbled off to bed.

Over a hearty breakfast Matthew and Tom sipped at their tea bleary-eyed with the toll the whisky had taken on them. Kate buttered toast and spread on Rosella jam.

'You mentioned last night that Wallarie sent you here,' she said to Tom.

'He said that you would know about the stars that grow under the ground,' Tom replied, his head aching.

Kate frowned. 'I'm sorry, but that is something I don't

know about . . . stars that grow under the ground? Whatever does he mean? You sent me an envelope from France last year with instructions that I was to open it if you did not return.' Kate scraped back her chair and went to a sideboard, opened a drawer and took out a small but thick brown envelope. 'It has remained sealed and I can now return it to you unopened.'

Tom took the envelope, recognising his own handwriting, and stared at it for a moment. 'I don't remember sending this,' he said. 'I lost my memory after being wounded last year.' Both Matthew and his mother expressed their concern as Tom stared at what was his own handwriting.

Tom slipped open the envelope to reveal a bank passbook in his name. There was a letter with the passbook and some fancy-looking folded certificates drawn on a Swiss bank. Tom glanced at the letter and went directly to the signature before reading the contents. It had been written by a Captain Jack Kelly and the name brought memories tumbling back, of lying out in no-man's-land and sniping unsuspecting German soldiers. Tom had a vague recollection of the officer who directed him in his one man operations.

'Jack,' he murmured and Kate and Matthew watched him with curiosity.

'A letter from an old cobber?' Matthew asked, now bravely attempting to consume the fried egg and bacon on his plate.

Tom glanced up at Matthew. 'He was a company commander I had and he became a friend – despite the fact he was an officer. He worked up in New Guinea gold pros–' Tom's voice trailed away. That was the link! He flipped open the bankbook and stared at the balance of his untouched account. 'Bloody hell!' he exclaimed.

'Not some kind of bad news, is it?' Kate asked, and Tom simply passed her the book.

'Goddamn!' Kate said, echoing one of her American husband's favourite curses. 'You're rich beyond imagining.'

Matthew forgot about his breakfast and rose to stand behind his mother and look over her shoulder at the balance. 'Cobber, there's enough money there to buy half the properties around Townsville.'

'The stars that grow under the ground were diamonds,' Tom said quietly. 'I came across them when I was with our unit advancing on a French village. Captain Jack Kelly helped me convert them to cash through sources he had in the gem business. If I did not return the money was meant to buy Glen View from the Macintosh family and help out the mission station. It would have ensured Wallarie would always have his land – our land. Aunt Kate, you were meant to make the purchase and the property would have gone into the Duffy name.'

Stunned, both Kate and her son stared at Tom.

'What are you going to do?' Matthew asked.

'I'm going to ask you, Aunt Kate, to manage the money for me,' Tom replied. 'It seems that I have some kind of certificates for shares. I'm not good at managing money and I trust those of my own blood. I have something urgent to attend to in England, and when I return I'll try to buy Glen View from the Macintosh family.'

'I'll ensure that your money is invested with the best returns,' Kate said, touching Tom on the hand affectionately. 'But you have enough money there never to have to work again, and I can tell you from my own experience that purchasing Glen View will not be easy. I have tried in the past, offering a good price, but the Macintosh family will not sell. Besides, you have enough money to buy any other property; two or three if you like. As for travelling to England – you can certainly do that – and travel first class,' Kate laughed. 'When you find her I hope to be at your wedding.'

'I will be able to afford to have an old cobber from the battalion act as my best man,' Tom said, forcing back tears. 'Paddy Bourke and I saw out the war together and he is down in Sydney.'

It was like a dream, Tom thought. It was the means to right so many wrongs in his life and that of those he cared for. He guessed that his old friend Paddy would have struggled when he returned home with his large family to care for, and times were tough for returned soldiers.

Kate and Tom stood in the bank with its stuffy staff and smell of polished wood. Tom was dressed in his stockman's clothes, and he and Kate were waiting to see the bank manager. As this was not Kate's normal bank, she was not recognised by the staff. When Kate had requested to speak with the bank manager she had been treated in a very offhanded manner by the clerk behind the counter. He had made it plain that bank managers were beyond the requests of mere customers, and had only agreed to speak with the manager in his office when Tom had glowered at him ferociously.

'A long time ago when I was a young woman in Cooktown during the gold rush,' Kate said quietly so that only Tom could hear, 'I had a similar experience with a bank manager who thought I was not worth the effort of seeing, so I bought his bank from under him and had him fired.'

Tom burst into laughter, causing the staff behind the counter to glance at him nervously.

Finally, the bank manager came out of his office. He was a small rotund man wearing a three-piece suit with a fob watch at his waist.

'Yes, madam, what can I do for you?' he asked in a condescending tone, eyeing Tom suspiciously.

'I am Mrs Kate Tracy and this is my nephew, Mr Tom Duffy,' she said. 'I believe my nephew has an account with your bank.'

The manager took a second look at Tom. 'We have an account in the name of Tom Duffy, but it could not be the same person, Mrs Tracy,' he said frowning.

'Why do you say that it could not be my nephew's account?' Kate countered.

'Because the account is the largest we have in the district, and couldn't possibly belong to a half . . .' He hesitated as the Tracy name struck a familiar accord. 'I am terribly sorry, Mrs Tracy, I did not mean to infer that your nephew is of mixed blood.' The manager remembered from reading the local paper the wealth and influence of the woman standing in his bank and it did not pay to upset her.

'I am part Irish, part Nerambura,' Tom said quietly. 'I have in your bank a considerable fortune, and if my half-caste blood offends you I can take my money to another bank.'

The manager was now experiencing a rush of blood to his face and could feel his heart beating faster than was good for him. The very thought that the money might be withdrawn was horrifying.

'I am sorry, Mr Duffy,' he said extending his hand. 'I did not mean to upset you.'

Tom glanced at Kate with a wicked grin. Maybe he should buy the bank, he thought. 'I'd like to arrange the following amount withdrawn in five pound notes,' he said, handing the manager the form he had filled in when they first arrived. The manager looked down at the amount.

'I will have the money arranged by late afternoon, Mr Duffy, and I would like to discuss with you the many ways you can accrue interest on your deposit with us.'

'Mrs Tracy handles my affairs,' Tom replied. 'You may speak with her at a later date. Just have the money ready by this afternoon.'

With that, Tom and Kate swept out of the bank, leaving the manager standing gaping at their backs.

Even as Kate was taking Tom to the best clothes stores to purchase garb befitting a wealthy man planning to travel to England, George Macintosh arrived at Glen View station with murder in mind.

Wallarie's worst fears were being realised – the ancestor spirits had told him the devil would follow his fire, to finish off the last innocent.

28

It was bitterly cold in London, and the young woman screamed her pain in the dingy room. Outside the brooding building, snow flurries whipped around the legs of those unfortunately enough to be out on the streets.

Juliet lay on a table and a young doctor, assisted by the institution's nurse, washed his hands in a bowl of liquid antiseptic. Although the British workhouses had changed their name in an attempt to give the establishments a better reputation, Juliet had found herself at the door of one such 'institution' after being evicted from the slum rooms she had shared with her brutal master, Smithers.

Smithers had controlled her from the moment she had been employed by the French madam in her brothel. His mere physical presence and her lack of means outside the brothel had ensured that she remained under his control while she scrubbed floors and prepared meals for the staff.

His beatings ensured her subservience, as did the fact that Juliet did not know whether the child she carried was his. She was certain that Tom Duffy would never be able to accept her back into his life if she bore the child of the monster who had raped her, yet she could not give up the child. Alone and virtually destitute, Juliet had allowed herself to be used by Smithers; in truth there had been nothing she could do to stop him, save run away again, and she had nowhere to run now. Her only hope had been the fleeting sight of Tom the day the gendarmes had beaten him and taken him away. He had not returned and Juliet had lost all hope after that and submitted to Smithers's will.

They had fled Paris for London near the end of the war as the authorities were closing in on the Australian deserter. Smithers had taken up with the local London criminals when he reached English shores. However, he had proved to be a failure in his criminal enterprises and they had lived in a slum tenement as Juliet approached her time to give birth to what Smithers considered was his child.

But the night had come when Smithers had got drunk, gone to bed and choked away his life in a flu-fevered condition. Juliet had sat in the corner of the room staring at the corpse, wondering what on earth she was going to do now, when she'd felt the first of her labour pains coming to her. She felt no pity for the man who had degraded her, but she also realised that she had no money for food and lodging and would not be able to earn any with a new baby to take care of. In her despair the young woman had sought admittance to the place that attempted to care for those with no hope. At least it had an infirmary to deliver the baby she carried.

The stench of rising damp pervaded the room and the young doctor frowned when he examined his patient.

'You are French?' he asked and Juliet nodded, sweat rolling from her brow as she fought the waves of pain.

She reached out, grabbing the doctor's hand. 'You must register the father's name,' she gasped. 'You must say where my child was born. You must swear an oath that you will.' Juliet knew of the policy to save future embarrassment to those born in the institutions by registering a fictional address as their place of birth.

'I promise,' the doctor said to placate his patient. This was a very problematic delivery and he did not think the young woman would survive it.

'There, there,' the nurse said soothingly, stepping forward to release Juliet's iron grip. 'You must assist the doctor with your delivery.'

Juliet stared up at the wrought-iron roof with its fancy scrolling and felt the life move within her body. The delivery took a long time and it passed in a haze of pain, but eventually a squalling, red creature emerged.

'You have a girl,' the nurse said as the doctor walked over to the sink to wash the blood from his hands.

'It is Tom's daughter,' Juliet whispered hoarsely with relief as the tears of pain and joy flowed down her cheeks. She had only to look into the baby's eyes and see the golden sheen of her skin to know who her daughter's father was. 'You must register my daughter Jessica as the child of Tom Duffy, an Australian soldier. You must promise me that you will do that.'

The nurse glanced at the doctor, who was wiping his hands with a dry cloth. Juliet saw the exchange and turned her head to the doctor. 'I know that I am dying,' she said. 'Please promise me that you will register my baby's father as Tom Duffy.'

The doctor walked over to the bed. 'I promise. Was Jessica's father killed in the last days of the war?'

'No, I don't think so,' Juliet answered. The pain was still racking her body and the doctor could clearly see that, despite his desperate attempts to stem the bleeding, she was haemorrhaging. He turned to the nurse with a knowing look. 'Please make the patient comfortable, sister,' he said and she nodded her understanding.

The squalling bundle of new life was placed on Juliet's breast. Tears welled in her eyes as she fought the pain in her body. 'My beautiful baby,' she murmured as a peaceful darkness descended on her. She was once again in the flower-covered fields of her village, and Tom was walking towards her with a broad smile on his face, dressed in his uniform with his slouch hat set at a jaunty angle. The pain was gone and so were her tears.

'She's dead,' the doctor said in a flat voice. The nurse wrapped Jessica in a thick, warm blanket after the doctor had cut the umbilical cord and wiped the mucus from the baby's mouth.

'Whether the baby's father is dead or alive,' he said to the nurse, 'make sure that the young woman's final request is kept.'

'But Doctor . . .' the nurse protested.

'Make sure that the child is registered as Jessica Duffy, and that it is recorded her father is one Tom Duffy of the Australian army. It is the least we can do for that poor unfortunate woman.'

Reluctantly, the nurse obeyed the doctor's orders when she filled out her paperwork. 'Highly unusual,' she muttered but the doctor was a man not to be crossed.

Jessica Duffy was born the day her father set out for his long journey to England.

★

The funnel of air swirled up the ash from the fires and twisted in a dance across the brigalow plains. Wallarie stopped to stare at the twisting, twirling column of air he had heard the white man called dust devils. It slipped away and Wallarie mused on its appearance. Had it tried to speak to him? He had been feeling uneasy these past few days. It was as if a dark shadow had fallen across his consciousness but he did not know why.

Wallarie reached down to pick up the dead echidna. The fire had caught it and it would now provide a tasty treat for the old warrior.

That night, with a full belly, Wallarie sat by his fire and chanted his song until the shadows shifted to reveal the other world of his ancestors. What he saw chilled him to the core, and he cried out, breaking his link with the shadow spirits. Giselle's son's life hung in the balance, and there was no one who could save him from the clutches of the devil. If the boy died, then the ancestor spirits had played a cruel joke on Wallarie.

Hector MacManus disliked Jack Firth on sight, just as he had disliked George Macintosh when he'd first met him. Both men arrived covered in dust after the long journey by Cobb & Co horse-drawn coach and were picked up in a sulky Hector had sent to the crossroads fifty miles away. They carried little more than a carpetbag each, and George demanded a hot bath as soon as he step inside the homestead.

Hector sent a couple of his stockmen off to fetch water from the dam, and the bath was prepared for the city visitors.

That evening, Hector ensured a good meal was placed on the table, and he had as his guests Karolina and the pastor, who rode in from the wreckage of their mission station where they had erected a tent until the buildings could be resurrected. Despite the heat of the evening, the air had a chill as they all took their places at the table.

The food was brought out by the housemaid and Hector carved a tender haunch of beef. Slices were placed on the fine china plates kept for such important occasions.

Karl said grace and they commenced eating.

'You can see that we suffered a bad bushfire some weeks ago, Mr Macintosh,' Hector said. 'You are not seeing the property in its best light.'

George ignored this comment. 'I note from the figures in Sydney that your production quota was down for head of cattle,' he said, picking at his beef with a fork while Jack, sitting next to him, ate heartily.

'We lost a few in the back blocks,' Hector replied. 'The lads are chasing them down, and it will put up our figures in the next head count.'

'You must know my reputation for efficiency, Mr Mac-Manus, and know that I do not suffer fools,' George said coldly, causing the tough Scot to bristle at the insult. 'I expect to see the head count improve by at least twenty percent before winter.'

'That will be done,' Hector answered. 'In the meantime, how long do we have the pleasure of your company?'

George paused, looked around and returned his attention to Hector. 'I do not see master David here tonight. I hope nothing is wrong.'

'My daughter's son is with one of Pastor von Fellmann's parishioners back at the mission station,' Karolina answered. 'He is in good hands.'

'I did not know that you had any European help at your mission station,' George said.

'We don't, Mr Macintosh,' Karl said. 'The tribesmen and their families are looking after David. As Mrs Schumann has said, David is in good hands.'

George raised his eyebrows in disapproval. 'If you say so,' he said and raised a slice of beef to his lips.

'I am surprised that you have come to Glen View, Mr Macintosh,' Karolina said coldly. 'Considering that you must know about the curse on your family.'

George placed his fork beside the plate and wiped delicately his mouth with the edge of a starched linen napkin. 'I have heard the old wives' tales,' he scoffed. 'As far as I can see, the curse seems only to have taken your daughter and that doddering old manservant of my father.'

Karolina rose to her feet and stormed from the room; Karl excused himself and followed her, leaving Hector ready to punch his employer. But he held his temper.

George shrugged. 'I meant no disrespect for the dead, Mr MacManus.'

'Mrs Macintosh was much loved and respected here, Mr Macintosh, and your comment was inappropriate under the circumstances,' Hector growled.

'I apologise, Mr MacManus,' George shrugged, savouring the tension he had caused more than the meat he was eating.

'It is to Mrs Schumann that you should apologise,' Hector said. 'Not me.'

'I will do so in time,' George answered. 'But, in the meantime, you must know that your position as station manager is at risk if my inspection of the property proves any incompetence.'

The trio ate the rest of the meal in silence, and Hector was glad when it was finally over and he had an excuse to retire. He was seething at the insults thrown at him and his friends during the meal but there was very little he could do – George had the controlling share of Glen View. He could hear the two men start in on the bottle of good whisky he had set aside for them; after a while the two unwanted visitors went onto the verandah to finish off the bottle. Hector could hear the faint murmur of their voices, but that was all. He tried to sleep but could not; George Macintosh's arrival at Glen View did not bode well for anyone.

George indicated to Jack that they should take their drinks and walk a short distance from the house to discuss their plan.

'If the boy is left in the care of the savages here, it will make it easier for us to get rid of him,' George said.

'How do you plan to do that?' Jack asked, staring up at the brilliance of the night sky.

'Well,' George said, 'what if young master David was to wander off into the scrub and get lost. In this heat he would not live long. It would be a case of saying the blacks were careless and let him slip away.'

Jack remained silent for a short while contemplating the idea. 'How do we get the boy out of the clutches of the blacks – and his grandmother?'

'That is what I need to consider, but the idea of the boy dying in the wilderness has a certain romantic twist about it, don't you think?' George said.

'I stop short of being present when the boy dies,' Jack said. 'Your money only buys so much, Mr Macintosh.'

George turned on Jack. 'This is not personal,' he said. 'Simply a case of basic financial consideration – as there can only be one captain of a ship.'

Jack took a long swig of the fiery liquid in his glass. He did not like what he was being asked to do, but he was now totally reliant on George Macintosh's patronage.

'We'll sleep on it,' George said, turning to walk back to the house, which was lit by kerosene lanterns. 'I expect that with your experience you will be able to find an opportune moment to snatch the boy and carry him into the wilderness.'

'You're a cold bastard, Macintosh,' Jack said.

'And you will be a rich bastard, Firth,' George countered.

Hector assigned one of his experienced Aboriginal stockmen to take George and Jack on a tour of the property. As neither were riders, a sulky had been readied and the stockman took the reins.

'Where you want to go?' he asked. He was a wiry man in his midthirties and had been born to a tribe north of Glen View, but had drifted with his clan south to settle on the fringes of the property. As a young boy he had been recruited to work around the stock and given the name Billy. Billy eventually found himself in the saddle as a stockman where he had proved himself an excellent manager of cattle.

'I would like to see the hill on the property first,' George said. He knew that it was time to confront his hidden fears but he was not about to explain to a mere cattle manager.

'That not a good place to go, boss,' Billy said. 'Ancestor spirits live there. Bad place to go.'

Hector, standing a short distance away, broke in. 'I would take Billy's advice, Mr Macintosh. The hill is a sacred place to the Nerambura people.'

'Are you telling me, the owner of this place, that I cannot go and look at a piece of volcanic rock on my own land?' George said coldly.

'You boss man,' Billy said. 'I take you there but ol' Wallarie, he still alive an' he still live there.'

George shuddered inwardly at the mention of Wallarie's name. He was like some living ghost haunting the family with the memory of the massacre.

'The idea of some old black savage does not worry me,' George said arrogantly. 'After all, this is the twentieth century, and my friend Jack is carrying a reliable revolver. I am sure if he hobbles at us waving a stick, we are more than capable of dealing with him.'

'Ol' Wallarie uses magic,' Billy said. 'No whitefella bullet can kill 'im.'

'Just take us to the hill,' George commanded.

Billy shrugged. He had warned them.

The day was hot and the sun blazed down on the sulky as the horse plodded through the blackened scrub. They reached the hill by noon, and even George had to admit this place that had featured in family folklore for generations was impressive. He knew from his schooling that the lone and prominent feature on the plain was probably an ancient volcanic plug, eroded over the millennia by wind and rain.

Billy brought the sulky to a stop and pulled out the picnic basket Hector had asked the cook pack for his employer's sightseeing tour. It contained beef sandwiches with chutney and some cake to follow. Jack had ensured that they take a bottle of gin as refreshment.

They dismounted and Billy placed a feed bag on the horse's nose. George sought out one of the few trees that provided some semblance of shade against the blistering sun.

'Bloody arse end of the world out here,' Jack grumbled, brushing the flies from his face. 'The bloody blackfellas can keep this land.'

Although George agreed the place was hellish, he also knew that Glen View, along with the other Queensland properties the Macintosh family owned, provided a respectable income. He had no idea what had prompted his brother to live the life of a cattleman out here on the outskirts of civilisation, although much was changing even in this part of the world. The Cobb & Co coaches were almost all gone, replaced by trucks and buses. Telephone wires were reaching out to far-flung properties, and the nomadic Aboriginals were being pushed onto mission stations. The frontier his great-grandfather faced was a half-century in the past, and the warrior tribesmen who had stood and fought pitched battles against the white settlers were a distant memory now.

George opened the packets of sandwiches and handed one to Jack but ignored Billy. The two men ate, brushing constantly at the annoying flies that had been attracted by the scent of meat.

'All right I go for a walk down the creek, Mr Macintosh?' Billy asked. 'Boss wants to know how much water we got there.'

'I suppose so,' George replied. 'Be back within the hour.'

'All right, boss,' Billy said and walked away, leaving the two men in the sparse shade of the stunted tree.

'I thought we might go for a walk up the hill,' George said. 'I believe there is some sort of cave up there.'

Jack had taken the bottle of gin from the sulky and poured himself a generous drop in a glass. 'Not my kind of thing to go waltzing around this godawful country,' he said. 'But you go – if you want a case of sunstroke.'

George frowned. 'Just don't drink the whole bottle,' he said, turning to take a track he could vaguely see imprinted into the rock and earth at the foot of the hill.

George climbed for what seemed a long time; the back

of his legs were beginning to ache. He was not used to hard physical exercise and soon had to sit down on a rock about a hundred yards from what he thought was the summit. He wished he had brought the canvas water bag hanging from the side of the sulky. George was hot and thirsty and thought he might have had a touch too much sun. He removed his floppy wide-brimmed hat and waved it in front of his face to create a cooling breeze. Maybe he should have listened to Jack, he mused.

As George sat on a rock gazing back across the plains he experienced a ringing in his ears. It was the silence, he thought. He was so used to living in a city with its honking horns of automobiles and clip-clop of draught horses pulling wagons and din of constant voices that this silence was eerie. The sun was a blazing ball of fire and his vision blurred as the plains danced in shimmering swirls.

'Got to get back for water,' he muttered, attempting to rise, but he found he could not. And then all the terror he could ever have imagined took shape before him. George immediately sensed that his life was in dire peril, and he knew from whom.

'Wallarie!' he gasped as the swirling image of a war-painted warrior loomed before him. The warrior was holding high a long hardwood spear balanced on a woomera – the means to give the spear leverage when hurled at its target. But the man could not be Wallarie, could he? This was a hard-muscled young warrior at the peak of his fighting prowess. The distance was only about twenty paces between them, and George knew that within seconds he would die a slow death, pieced by the long spear just like his illustrious ancestor, Sir Donald Macintosh, all those years earlier. George tried to scream but no words came. Instead it was as if he was hearing a warning in his head to leave Glen View immediately and never return. For him to remain meant certain death. George knew that he had soiled himself in his abject terror and fell to his knees before the fearsome spectre to beg for his life.

With great difficulty George lifted his head and was stunned to see that the young warrior was gone but George could still sense his presence close by. For the first time ever he prayed for his life and for minutes he remained kneeling, waiting for the spear to pierce his body. The fatal wound did not come and eventually George rose cautiously to his feet.

The smell of his fear still with him, he stumbled blindly down the track to the spot where he had left Jack. The man was asleep propped up against the sulky, gin bottle in his hand.

George stopped and the fear returned with a sudden rush. Within a foot of where Jack dozed was a long spear protruding from the earth.

'Wake up, you stupid bastard!' George screamed. 'We've got to get out of here.'

Jack stirred, blinked and forced himself to his feet. It was then that he noticed the spear sunk in the dry earth inches from where he had slept. 'What the bloody hell is this?' he said but did not touch the terrifying object.

'It could have been your death,' George snapped, casting around for their guide, who he spotted walking back to them through the scrub.

Jack was not completely drunk and George's dishevelled appearance startled him. 'Bloody hell,' he sniffed. 'Did you step in something bad?'

'You, Billy, get over here quick, and get us out of here,' George shouted, clambering aboard the sulky.

Billy joined them, and his attention was caught by the

sight of the spear. '*Baal,*' he said. 'Very bad. Wallarie angry. We must go now.'

'As quick as you can,' George said, glancing all around him at the lengthening shadows. He did not want to be out here when the sun went down.

'What happened?' Jack asked, following George into the sulky.

'Nothing I want to talk about. But we will be leaving Glen View first thing in the morning.'

'I hate to say it, but you stink like you shat yourself,' Jack said, wrinkling his nose. George glared at him, discouraging any further questions about his physical state. 'What about the boy?' Jack asked.

'Another time and another place,' George replied. 'Anywhere but here.'

29

The following day a still pale George Macintosh had his carpetbag put in the sulky.

'I am surprised you are leaving so soon,' Hector said, attempting to keep his pleasure under control at seeing the odious man departing. 'You have not had a chance to inspect the workings of the property.'

Jack Firth was already seated in the sulky and George climbed up beside him.

'I have seen enough, Mr MacManus, and I am satisfied that you are managing well enough to retain your position here,' George replied.

'Thank you, Mr Macintosh,' Hector replied just as Karl, Karolina and young David approached the homestead in their sulky. George saw the three and scowled.

'I see that Wallarie is watching over you for your trip, Mr Macintosh,' Hector said.

George looked up in alarm. 'Where?' he asked, suddenly fearful again at the mention of the old Aboriginal's name.

'Up there,' Hector answered, pointing to the sky where a huge wedge-tailed eagle soared in the azure skies above the homestead. 'My men believe that Wallarie can turn into an eagle and take to the skies.'

Shielding his eyes with his hand, George looked up at the majestic bird circling overhead. 'I do not believe in such superstition, Mr MacManus,' he said unconvincingly. 'We will be going now.' He indicated to the driver to set off and as the sulky disappeared down the track Hector could swear that George Macintosh was still warily watching the eagle in the sky.

Hector turned his attention to the pastor, who had brought his sulky to a stop in the front yard of the homestead.

'I see that Mr Macintosh has left suddenly,' Karl said with a slight smile. 'I wonder why.'

Both men passed knowing looks, but did not need to mention Wallarie's name. Some things in the vast inland stretches of Australia's rugged land defied logical explanation.

In a hospital in Sydney, Louise Macintosh gave birth to a daughter.

She lay back holding her infant and tears of joy flowed down her cheeks at the sight of the tiny creature squirming in her arms.

'You will be mine,' Louise said softly as the infant reached up with a tiny balled fist to touch her new world of strange sounds and scents. 'Your father will have no interest in a girl. A daughter will play no part in his ambitions.'

George was still away in Queensland, and her first visitor was Sean Duffy carrying a huge bouquet of flowers.

'She's as beautiful as you,' Sean said, gazing down at the baby girl Louise was cradling in her arms.

Louise could not express her deepest wish that the child had been Sean's.

On a wharf in Brisbane two very well-dressed young men stood side by side waiting to board the ship to take them to Sydney and then on through the Suez Canal to England.

Matthew and Tom Duffy turned the heads of more than one young woman also waiting to board. Well-dressed and handsome, both men stood out for their manly bearing.

Matthew's journey would end at Suez where he would disembark to make his way to Jerusalem to organise his new enterprise in the territory the British controlled in the former Ottoman Empire. Black gold was drawing the big companies to the desert lands in search of deposits beneath the sands, and Matthew knew they would require air transport to prospect and move supplies to remote areas. By doing so he would be able to continue flying and be close to the land Joanne had loved so much.

For Tom it would be a case of disembarking in England and using his wealth to search for the woman he loved. The war was over for the two men who had lost four years of their lives to fear and death. Now was a time to use their courage and initiative to find a new life in the peace that followed the Great War.

Once a year, Kate Tracy attended a meeting of her directors in Brisbane to review the progress of her many investments nationally and internationally.

Her Brisbane office had a small but lavish boardroom

with a great teak table and the walls adorned with expensive paintings. When Kate entered the room the directors rose as if the queen herself was in their presence.

Kate sat at the head of the table as each director delivered his report and listened to the drone of facts and figures. However, her mind was not on the delivery of the good news that the war had increased profit for most of her diverse enterprises. Instead, she found herself gazing at a painting that her former cattle manager, Randolph Gates, whom she had respected and liked, had recommended she buy. It was a scene of cowboys in Montana mustering cattle, which had a nostalgic meaning to him as he had been hired by her years earlier to manage the breeding of a strain of cattle better suited to the tropics before leaving the American state.

'In all, Mrs Tracy, we have an overall increase in profits of thirty-five percent,' the vice president of the board announced.

'Thank you, Mr Howard,' Kate responded. 'I must extend my personal congratulations to you all for your sterling service over the past twelve months and inform you that Mr Howard will be acting in my place for the next six months. I am sure that you will welcome this decision as we all know that Mr Howard has proved himself more than capable over the years. Now, I think it is time that I closed this meeting and allowed you gentlemen to retire for cigars and a well-deserved drink.'

All stared with surprise at Kate's announcement; she had never handed over control like this before. It was most unlike this gentle but iron-willed businesswoman. Kate could see their looks of surprise and smiled. 'Gentlemen, I have decided that money is not as important as those we cherish in our lives. I know that two of my board members lost sons in the Great War, and also know that all the money in the world cannot bring them back. I have booked to journey to America, which, as you know, is the homeland of my late and much loved husband, Luke Tracy. The years are passing so fast that I feel it is time I saw his land before I pass on. I also have other reasons to visit America. Be assured, however, that I will be back before the end of the year.'

Wishes of goodwill came from the members of the board, who not only respected but liked this astounding woman who had built a financial empire from the dangers and trauma of her youth.

Kate thanked them and then said, 'Mr Howard, if I could have a word with you in your office.' With this, she left the room.

In his office, Mr Howard thanked Kate the trust she had placed in him.

'I need to know more about our American investments,' she said, taking a seat and accepting a cup of tea. 'Do we have any links to the banks?'

Howard was very well versed in the company's portfolio of offshore investments. 'We have a considerable share base in certain banks,' he replied.

'Good,' Kate smiled. 'I would like you to prepare a report before I depart for America.'

'May I ask your interest in our US banking interests?' Howard asked and Kate paused for a moment before answering. Then she explained what she planned to do and Howard sat down at his desk in his utter astonishment. He could see that Kate was deadly serious and could not help but break into a broad smile. He shook his head and his smile became a chuckle.

'Bloody Yanks – excuse my language, Mrs Tracy – won't know what's hit them.'

Kate sipped her tea and smiled.

Now that Matthew had chosen to return to Palestine Kate was once again alone. Oh, how like his father Matthew was. He was born to roam the world in search of purpose and fortune. But at least he had given her the greatest gift she could have wanted – grandchildren. Nothing would stop Kate now. As a young woman she had made her fortune on the goldfields of the Palmer River. She had known two husbands and lost them both, stood and fought the wild and courageous Merkin tribesmen in a pitched battle, and survived the terrible hardships of the wild frontier of north Queensland when the state was still a British colony. She had slowly built a financial empire and had done it as a single woman raising a son. Although he did not know it, James Barrington Snr was about to confront the most formidable foe he had ever encountered.

EPILOGUE

June 1919

Today was the day George Macintosh expected to hear from Sir Hubert that he was to be knighted by the king. George hurried to the exclusive Australia Club to meet Sir Hubert and found that in his eagerness he had arrived first. George settled back in a deep and comfortable leather chair, Scotch in his hand and smile on his face. When Sir Hubert arrived George rose to greet him.

'Well, old chap,' he said without any of the polite pre-liminaries. 'Do you have the news?'

Sir Hubert settled in a chair facing George and ordered a whisky from a passing waiter. George had to admit he was feeling a little nervous. At least nervous was better than the nightmares that still haunted him in the darkness of the night since his return from Glen View.

'I'm sorry, George, old chap,' Sir Hubert said. 'But the past year there has been too much scandal associated with you and your companies. The bestowal of your knighthood has been deferred.'

The news struck George as painfully as if Wallarie had pieced his chest with his fire-hardened spear. He sat stunned. The bloody curse, he thought.

'However,' Sir Hubert continued, 'given time, I am sure that you will be renominated.'

'I bloody well better be,' George snarled. 'Considering how much has gone into your party's coffers and your own pocket. How long . . . a year, two years?'

Sir Hubert looked uncomfortable. 'Two years should see things settle down. I am sure it will eventually be approved.'

George swallowed the remaining whisky in his crystal tumbler and glared at the senior public servant. 'Two years,' he said firmly. 'After that, if it has not been approved, you and your party can go to hell.'

'Don't be like that, old chap,' Sir Hubert protested. 'You have to look at it from our point of view. A knighthood now would raise questions in the house, but the newspapers will move onto some other scandal and the death of that unfortunate girl will be quickly forgotten.'

George had heard enough. He stood up and left, without bothering to shake hands with Sir Hubert.

George stepped out into the bitter cold of the day and glanced up at the scudding clouds whipped through the sky by a southerly gale. Nothing seemed to have gone well since his visit to Glen View, he thought morosely, pulling up the collar of his overcoat as he walked along the street. His wife had given birth to a useless daughter when George had hoped for a boy to strengthen his future hold on the family name. George could have nurtured a fierce competitiveness among two boys to see which would emerge the stronger.

A girl was of no use to him. His wife had given his daughter the name of Sophia – not that George cared much.

Worse still was the death of Jack Firth, whose violent and mysterious death still caused talk on the streets. Drunk one night, Jack had been returning home when it appeared he had been confronted by a robber and stabbed to death in the dark. The police thought the killing had been done by an ex-serviceman with experience in using a bayonet. Although neither the murder weapon nor a suspect had been located, the single thrust under the ribcage and into the chest cavity was remarkably like that of a killing thrust from a soldier armed with the long, deadly blade of the bayonet.

Although the name of Harry Griffiths had been pandered about among investigating detectives, it seemed the man had an airtight alibi at the time Firth was killed. Harry Griffiths was playing cards with the well-known and respected Sydney solicitor, Sean Duffy. There were no other leads, and it seemed that the murder of the former detective inspector would remain unsolved.

Without Jack Firth in his employ, George felt vulnerable. He had no one to do his dirty work for him now, nor did he have anyone within the police force to watch out for his interests.

George was sure that his wife had renewed her affair with Sean Duffy, as she disappeared for long periods and was haughty in her responses to his questions of her whereabouts. He was sure people were talking behind his back about the affair. He was angry and humiliated, but he could not afford to alienate Louise – she knew too much about his private life and he could not afford the public shame and scandal of a separation, not after all the business with Maude Urqhart.

It was as if all George's power was slipping away; he felt old and weak and powerless.

As if to add to the weight of misfortune weighing him down, the sky burst asunder and rain poured down. George hunched against the rain, knowing that when returned to his office he would have to deal with the German chemical company and the huge loss the company was having to carry as a result of his investment. Somehow, he would have to find a way of keeping the loss from the company directors. It was just another nail in the cross he found himself hanging from. Damn the curse!

On the other side of the world, Matthew Duffy stood on a newly constructed airstrip outside the former Ottoman city of Basra where the two great rivers of the Tigris and Euphrates met. Nearby, in the searing heat of the day, a couple of his flying service's British fighter aircraft were waiting for a ground crew, due to arrive any minute.

Behind Matthew was a vast shed of corrugated iron and timber housing the two civilian versions of the Vickers Vimy bomber he had purchased. He had painted on the nose of one the name *Joanne* and on the other, *Kate* – the two women in his life.

Matthew was aware that a people called the Kurds living in the north of the country were in rebellion against the British occupation, and the Royal Air Force was flying bombing missions against their villages. There was talk that chemical weapons should be deployed against the rebels, and that idea was backed by Winston Churchill. Matthew was saddened by the continuing unrest as he wanted the war behind him, but in many places around the world, from Russia to the newly emerging Arab states, war still raged and many of the innocent were still dying. The complexities of political manoeuvring to secure resources ensured that the killing would go on, despite the Western world looking forward to a bright and prosperous new decade.

Matthew's appointed agent in Jerusalem, Saul Rosenblum, had advertised for a ground crew and interviewed the potential employees of the company Matthew had registered as Desert Airlines with the British civil service in Baghdad. Saul had grudgingly accepted Matthew's request to act as his agent in Jerusalem; he had felt that he would be better off leading his people at their settlement but the generous pay had proved a compensation for the task. He had whittled the prospective employees down to five and they were expected very soon.

When the lorry finally arrived at the airstrip, five new employees tumbled from the back to stretch their legs.

Matthew strode over to the small cluster of people gazing around them at their new home. They had answered the advertisement published in English newspapers that promised adventure and good money.

Matthew scanned their faces and stopped at the last one. 'Bloody hell!' he swore under his breath. The fifth member was a young woman, wearing overalls and a cap.

'Welcome to Basra,' Matthew said. 'I am Matthew Duffy and, as you can guess, I am an Australian. Any of you Poms have any trouble with that?'

They grinned and shook their heads. 'Only if you don't pay us,' a voice said from the group, and they broke into laughter.

'You will be paid if your work is up to the high standards I expect of you. I have housing organised for you and you can settle in after I take you for a look around the strip and its facilities. As you can see, the conditions are harsh but the money you make will compensate for that.' Matthew's eyes fell on the only female in the group and could see that she was strikingly beautiful. Her raven hair was cut short and her emerald eyes dominated a peaches and cream complexion. She noticed him staring at her and looked back defiantly, as if challenging him to question her right to be in his team.

Matthew escorted the cluster to the vast shed and they inspected the two aircraft inside. A young Iraqi man stepped forward with a platter of fresh sandwiches and indicated a small table with a big teapot and china cups laid out. Matthew invited the group to take refreshments while he interviewed each one at a desk in the corner of the hangar.

Each man came forward with his papers and Matthew was satisfied that Saul had chosen well. The last to be interviewed was the young woman and she placed her papers on the desk in front of Matthew.

'Take a seat,' Matthew said, flipping open her dossier. 'I see that your name is Diane Hatfield and that you are eighteen years old.' Diane nodded her head. 'Why in hell did Saul accept you onto my team?' Matthew said in a pained voice. 'You are both very young – and a woman.'

'I worked in the factory where we built the Rolls-Royce Eagle engines that your aeroplanes are equipped with,' she said. 'As my parents were killed in a Zeppelin bombing raid and my fiancé did not come back from the war, I had nothing to lose by applying for the position, Captain Duffy, and Mr Rosenblum seemed to think I was perfectly capable of carrying out the job.'

Matthew relented. 'My first instinct is to pay you off and send you back to England,' he said. 'But you remind me of someone I once knew who had the same adventurous spirit you seem to possess.'

Diane turned her head to gaze at the two big aircraft in the hangar. 'Was it Kate or Joanne?' she asked.

'Both,' Matthew replied with a smile. 'So long as you prove your worth, you have a job. I will arrange separate housing for you in Basra. Welcome to Desert Airlines.'

'You will not regret your decision, Captain Duffy,' Diane said gratefully. 'I can work as hard as any man in the team. One day I hope to fly too.'

Matthew glanced at the young woman. The world had certainly changed with the end of the war. He had no doubt that this slip of a girl would end up flying one of his Vimys one day.

Outside the hangar Matthew could hear the two British light bombers roaring into life for a bombing mission over the desert in search of rebel formations. The sound was a reminder that the war had not really ended and the future was far from certain. The memory of Joanne was always with him in the silence of the beautiful desert nights, and on the other side of the world were his son and daughter who he had not yet held in his arms. Matthew swore that when he was settled he would go to them, but for now he had a job to do in establishing his airline in a very troubled part of the world.

In England it was a warm summer's day and Tom Duffy was glad to be out of his expensive hotel room and down in Hyde Park, watching a brightly uniformed military band playing for the well-dressed strollers in the magnificent gardens. He had been in London for over three months now and he missed the vast open plains of Queensland. His money had brought him respect from those he dealt with and provided funds for a firm of private investigators to find Juliet.

Day after day he had waited for their reports, until this morning Mr Greaves, the head of the firm, had rung to say they had made a breakthrough.

Now Tom stood in his tailored suit and bowler hat watching the band perform, waiting impatiently for the private investigator to arrive. He had said on the telephone that it would be better that they make contact this way and his news was both good and bad.

'Mr Duffy,' a voice said behind him. Tom turned to see the smallish, balding man in his late fifties. 'I have some news for you.'

'You have found Juliet, Mr Greaves?' Tom asked, holding his breath in his excitement.

'Sadly, I have some bad news on that front, Mr Duffy,' the investigator said. 'We were able to trace your fiancée to a poorhouse where she died in childbirth earlier this year.'

Tom paled and fought to remain on his feet. 'Where?' he asked. 'Is the baby alive?'

'That is why I arranged to meet you here, Mr Duffy,' Greaves said. 'The institution is a cab drive away and I have arranged to have us taken there to meet your daughter.'

Tom was too stunned to speak and tears welled in his eyes. Juliet was dead, but he had a daughter. It was too much to take in at once. With a gruff attempt to wipe the tears away, Tom let the investigator lead him from the park to the street where a taxicab was waiting. They drove in silence along busy streets until they were almost at the establishment Greaves had located.

'I have had to pay a fair bit of money to get doors opened for you to meet your daughter,' Greaves said quietly.

'You will be reimbursed,' Tom replied, and the cab came to a stop. Greaves paid the cabbie and asked him to wait.

Greaves and Tom walked up a driveway to the front door of a double-storeyed brick building. From the outside it did not appear to be a place that could be called a poorhouse, but rather it was more like an aging English manor house.

Greaves knocked and was met by a plump woman wearing an apron. He removed his hat and spoke to the woman. 'I am Mr Greaves and the gentleman with me is Mr Duffy. We have an appointment with Doctor Mills.'

The woman looked them over and ushered them into the dimly lit foyer of the institution. Tom could hear his footsteps echo as they were led down a corridor to a room with a glass partition on the upper half of the door engraved with the word *Doctor*. She knocked and a voice bade them to enter.

Tom stepped through to see a young man behind a desk wearing a white lab coat, a stethoscope around his neck. He stood when Tom and Greaves entered the room.

'So you are Mr Tom Duffy,' the doctor said, extending his hand to Tom. 'It is a pleasure to meet you. I was able to make some enquiries about you and learned that you had a distinguished service record in France.'

'I just did my job,' Tom replied modestly.

'A DCM and bar as well as an MM – that is more than just doing your job, Mr Duffy,' he said. 'Mr Greaves contacted me last week and explained your situation. I suspect that you have learned of the fate of Miss Joubert. I would like to express my sympathy for your loss.' Tom nodded, not trusting himself to speak.

'I was the medical officer who delivered your daughter, Jessica,' the doctor said. 'Miss Joubert insisted that I promise that your daughter have her real father's name registered on her birth certificate. I kept that promise, although I was not sure if you had survived the war. But here you are.'

'Can I see my daughter?' Tom asked.

388

'The matron has gone to fetch her,' the doctor replied, and just then the door opened and the matron walked in holding a small bundle in her arms. She passed the baby to Tom.

Tom looked down into the bundle and was met with a smile from the baby, who was wide awake and gazing at up him. She reached up a little hand to touch him on the nose.

Tears rolled down Tom's cheeks and splashed onto Jessica's face. She frowned in surprise before squawking her disapproval at being made wet by this stranger holding her.

'Jessie, my love,' Tom said softly. 'Your mother is alive in you.'

For Tom Duffy, the former tough soldier whose physical courage had borne him through some of the worst battles the Australian army had experienced, the little creature in his arms instantly became his whole world.

James Barrington Snr received a telephone call that he was needed urgently at his office at his bank. The caller was one of his senior managers and he said that he did not wish to elaborate over the phone the reason that required his urgent attention.

Barrington had his chauffeur drive him to his bank through leafy avenues and past splendid mansions to rival his own. His manager had sounded nervous, which was not like the man. Barrington wondered what was going on.

He arrived at the bank and pushed past his staff to go straight to his office. When he flung open the door he was met by the sight of a well-dressed woman in her seventies sitting calmly at his desk, a teacup balanced in her hand. Barrington's manager was standing by a window looking uncertain.

James Barrington removed his hat and placed it on the hat stand.

'Who is this woman and why is she sitting at my desk?' he demanded.

'This is Mrs Kate Tracy from Australia,' the manager said quietly. 'And she is now the owner of your bank.'

Stunned, Barrington stared at Kate, who smiled back at him as she placed the cup and saucer on the great polished desk. Kate rose and walked across the room to him. He could see that she had once been a beautiful young woman, and time had not aged the beauty of her face with wrinkles and blotches.

'Mr Barrington, it is a pleasure to meet with you,' Kate said, extending her gloved hand.

Without thinking, Barrington accepted the hand. 'I'm sorry, Mrs Tracy, but I do not know you.'

'Well, you know me now, and I must apologise for the circumstances under which we have met,' she said, smiling and withdrawing her hand. 'As your manager has just informed you, I have bought your bank and you will soon receive the papers to confirm the purchase. I must apologise that I have done so without your knowledge. It seems that your shareholders were open to my rather generous offer. After all, that is the way of American business, is it not?'

Reeling in confusion, James Barrington was trying to take in everything that was happening. 'I will fight your takeover,' he warned. 'I have spent a lifetime building on my father's achievements in banking.'

'That may not be necessary,' Kate replied, ignoring his threat. 'I have purchased banks before and find that they are always a risk. You and I have something very precious in common, Mr Barrington, and I wish to speak with you in private about it.'

Barrington turned to his manager and with a movement of his head dismissed the man from the room. Then he turned to Kate. 'I cannot comprehend why an Australian would wish to buy an American bank, Mrs Tracy. You are out of your depth over here.'

'Well, I could start by telling you that my dearly departed husband and father of my only son was an American citizen,' Kate replied, removing one of her gloves. 'So you might say that I have purchased your bank for sentimental reasons.'

'I find that hard to believe,' Barrington scoffed.

'As I said, I find the banking system risky and would give back control of your bank to you, shifting my purchase to that of a major shareholder. I am sure you would not object to the injection of money from the purchase,' Kate said, returning to the desk to sip from her cup of tea.

'That would be acceptable,' Barrington conceded, knowing he had little choice if he was to retain his principal bank. He had plans to extend and the extra capital would finance that move. 'You said that we had something in common.'

'Yes,' Kate replied. 'Our grandchildren.' Barrington thought that he had heard wrong and gaped at Kate in shock. 'Oh, I forgot to mention that my only son is Captain Matthew Duffy, who I believe you met late last year under tragic circumstances. I know the difference in surname is confusing but my son took on my maiden name when he enlisted many years ago against my wishes in the South African campaign against the Boers. He chose to retain my maiden name in honour of the men he served alongside and who died in the fighting.'

'Goddamn!' Barrington exclaimed.

'All I ask is that I am able to see my grandchildren while I am here and I will draw up papers to switch the purchase to a stakehold in your bank,' Kate said serenely, placing the cup of tea on the desk. 'And this desk will be your desk again,' she said, stroking the highly polished surface.

Barrington stood at the centre of the room, shaking his head in disbelief. 'Mrs Tracy, you have a deal,' he said, extending his hand once again. After all, his bank was his identity and he would have killed to have it back. He was smiling and Kate could see an expression of begrudging respect for her ruthless mission of blackmailing him. She accepted the gesture and returned his smile.

'I feel that you and I should be able to get along in the future, Mr Barrington,' she said.

'I underestimated your son last year,' Barrington said. 'If I had met you earlier, I would not have made the same mistake.'

'Well, I think it is time for us both to retire to your home,' Kate said. 'Your decision has made a grandmother a very happy woman, Mr Barrington.'

'I have always said that those of Irish blood are cunning and not to be trusted,' he said. 'I will ensure that I am more careful in the future.'

Within the day Kate Tracy held in her arms her reason for being on this earth. For she held in her arms the future of her blood line.

AUTHOR NOTES

During the 1950s I grew up on a soldier settler farm at a place called Warrawidgee, west of Griffith in New South Wales. At the end of a working day the settler families would gather at a crossroads where a former yank, Danny, ran a sly grog shop. As kids we would mingle with the adults: the ladies in the back of the shop swapping stories, the veterans shouting beers and talking of farming woes and, sometimes, their war experiences. I vividly remember seeing the scars of war on the men drinking, and observing the lingering effects of what they called shell-shock. They were veterans of the Boer War, the Great War and more recently World War II and Korea. The Korean veterans were the youngsters. I listened to the men swap stories of action they had seen from the veldt of Africa to the hills of Korea, and only now do I truly appreciate that I was hearing history. Now, those men are just about all gone and even our World War II veterans are becoming scarce. Soon they, too, will be a memory.

This book has been written with the thought that we must never forget the sacrifice generations of men and women have made to give us what we take for granted today. I am grateful to Professor Michael Roe's lectures in Australian history at the University of Tasmania in the late 1970s, and it is to him that I owe a lot for research methods and inspiration to write this saga.

The terrible influenza epidemic of 1919 has almost been forgotten. It has been said that if it had lasted another month or so, Western civilisation might have been set back a hundred years. Australia was able to quarantine the epidemic through far-sighted medical procedures, but the death toll was still horrendous. It could be said to be nature's extension of the Great War as the conditions in the trenches weakened men and the disease was carried by them home to kill those they had fought to protect. It was a time when two of the four horsemen of the apocalypse rode the earth.

In my research for this novel I was fortunate to have a former commanding officer of my old army reserve unit, the First Nineteenth Battalion of the Royal New South Wales Regiment, release his brilliant account of the battalion's day-to-day life on the Western Front. Peter McGuinness is the author of *Boldly and Faithfully: The Journal* and in my many years of research rarely have I found a source so detailed of those terrible days. As such, most of the experiences of Sergeant Tom Duffy and his comrades are based on the actual events of the battalion's experiences on the Western Front. This magnificent book is a day-to-day account from the battalion's actual diary and brings readers closest to the conditions of what it was like for our digger ancestors. It is a collector's item and may be purchased by contacting

Bob Pink through email at bob.pink@optusnet.com.au. Limited editions are available from the publication of this historical record.

For the coverage of the air war in Palestine, I was fortunate to be able to refer to FM Cutlack's *Australian Flying Corps Vol VIII: Official History of Australia in the War of 1914–18*, Angus & Robertson: Sydney, 1940.

All sorties described in Captain Matthew Duffy's experiences are based on the actual missions by the AFC. The incident of being forced down and then taking off again actually happened to Lieutenant Drummond and all the following missions that Captain Duffy flew are records of real sorties.

It is interesting to note that other than the charge against Beersheba by the Australian Light Horse, very little is mentioned these days of the desert war where Australians played such a critical role in defeating the Ottoman Empire. Our AFC and Light Horse continuously found themselves in action at the most critical points of battle, helping change the course of history.

All else in the story is fiction.

ACKNOWLEDGEMENTS

My thanks are extended to the team at Pan Macmillan publishers who have worked on this project directly or indirectly. They are Cate Paterson and Libby Turner, who read and commented on changes, Julia Stiles, copyeditor, Deb Parry, cover design, Roxarne Burns in accountancy, Tracey Cheetham, head of publicity and my publicist, Caitlin Neville.

As always, my many thanks to my agent, Geoffrey Radford for his continuing support.

On the subject of publicity I would like to extend my thanks to one of Australia's best broadcasters in radio, John Carroll. John has consistently brought to attention my books through the *Super Radio Network* on Sunday mornings to a great bulk of NSW listeners. In the same field I would also like to thank Kristie Hildebrand for her work on my Facebook page and those who have joined.

A thanks to Peter and Kay Lowe. Peter keeps my web-page up to date and a special thanks to an extraordinary man and fellow author, Dave Sabben MG, whose stay with us in Maclean has inspired me in my future work.

A continuing thanks to Dr Louis Trichard and his wife, Christine. Louis helps keep me alive.

As usual my thanks are extended to friends whose influence is felt in my writing life. They are Mick and Andria Prowse, Larry Gilles, John and Isabel Millington, Kevin Jones OAM and Family, Jan Dean, Bill and Tatiana Maroney, John and June Riggall. A special thanks to my wonderful Auntie Joan Payne and family in Tweed Heads for their never-ending support.

A reminder to Peter Watt readers that they should also purchase Tony Park's *Dark Heart* novel at Christmas time. Tony covers the other side of the Indian Ocean with his truly exciting novels centred around Africa, whilst I look after the eastern side of the Indian Ocean.

A special thanks to Rod and Brett Hardy who are still working to get the *Frontier* project on the screen. It takes time and patience. A special mention to the real Diane Hatfield whose name appears in the pages of this book. Diane participated in a name inclusion auction conducted by the *Mackay Flagon and Dragon Club*, raising a generous amount of money for two hospital wards for children in Mackay.

I would also like to extend my thanks for the camaraderie extended to me by the members of the Gulmarrad Rural Fire Service team of which I have recently joined. They are a wonderful band of community members who volunteer to protect against one of the major enemies of Australia in the fire season. Whilst writing in Finch Hatton, Queensland, I spent eighteen months as an emergency ambulance driver, and I would like to thank that community for the friendship I experienced living there. You are not forgotten, nor are the people of Corowa, on the Murray River.

On a sadder note I would like to mark the passing of my wonderful younger sister, Kerry McKee nee Watt this year. But life is such that born into the family has been Eliza to my niece, Shannon and her husband, Aaron Herps. My love is extended to my brother Tom and his Family at Hazelbrook and beyond.

In Tasmania my congratulations to my sister, Lindy and my brother-in-law, Jock for becoming grandparents for the first time to Frida Winsome Barclay.

Fair winds and safe sailing to my much loved brother-in-law, Tyrone McKee who has set off to sail his yacht, the *Sahara*, solo around the world with my sister's ashes and spirit travelling with him.

To Naomi, my undying love and thanks for being there in tough times and good. You are the reason I keep going.

MORE BESTSELLING FICTION AVAILABLE FROM PAN MACMILLAN

Peter Watt
Cry of the Curlew

I will tell you a story about two whitefella families who believed in the ancestor spirits. One family was called Macintosh and the other family was called Duffy . . .

Squatter Donald Macintosh little realises what chain of events he is setting in motion when he orders the violent dispersal of the Nerambura tribe on his property, Glen View. Unwitting witnesses to the barbaric exercise are bullock teamsters Patrick Duffy and his son Tom.

Meanwhile, in thriving Sydney Town, Michael Duffy and Fiona Macintosh are completely unaware of the cataclysmic events overtaking their fathers in the colony of Queensland. They have caught each other's eye during an outing to Manly Village. A storm during the ferry trip home is but a small portent of what is to follow . . . From this day forward, the Duffys and the Macintoshes are inextricably linked. Their paths cross in love, death and revenge as both families fight to tame the wild frontier of Australia's north country.

Spanning the middle years of the nineteenth century, *Cry of the Curlew* is a groundbreaking novel of Australian history. Confronting, erotic, graphic, but above all, a compelling adventure, Peter Watt is an exceptional talent.

Peter Watt
Shadow of the Osprey

On a Yankee clipper bound for Sydney Harbour the mysterious
Michael O'Flynn is watched closely by a man working
undercover for Her Majesty's government. O'Flynn has a
dangerous mission to undertake . . . and old scores to settle.

Twelve years have passed since the murderous event
which inextricably linked the destinies of two families, the
Macintoshes and the Duffys. The curse which lingers after
the violent 1862 dispersal of the Nerambura tribe has created
passions which divide them in hate and join them in forbidden
love.

Shadow of the Osprey, the sequel to the best-selling Cry of
the Curlew, is a riveting tale that reaches from the boardrooms
and backstreets of Sydney to beyond the rugged Queensland
frontier and the dangerous waters of the Coral Sea. Powerful
and brilliantly told, Shadow of the Osprey confirms the
exceptional talent of master storyteller Peter Watt.

Peter Watt
Flight of the Eagle

No-one is left untouched by the dreadful curse which haunts two families, inextricably linking them together in love, death and revenge.

Captain Patrick Duffy is a man whose loyalties are divided between the family of his father, Irish Catholic soldier of fortune Michael Duffy, and his adoring, scheming maternal grandmother, Lady Enid Macintosh. Visiting the village of his Irish forebears on a quest to uncover the secrets of the past, Patrick is bewitched by the mysterious Catherine Fitzgerald.

On the rugged Queensland frontier Native Mounted Police trooper Peter Duffy is torn between his duty, the blood of his mother's people – the Nerambura tribe – and a predestined deadly duel with Gordon James, the love of his sister Sarah.

From the battlefields of the Sudan to colonial Sydney and the Queensland outback, a dreadful curse still inextricably links the lives of the Macintoshes and Duffys. In *Flight of the Eagle*, the stunning conclusion to the trilogy featuring the bestselling *Cry of the Curlew* and *Shadow of the Osprey*, master storyteller Peter Watt is at the height of his powers.

Peter Watt
To Chase the Storm

When Major Patrick Duffy's beautiful wife Catherine leaves him
for another, returning to her native Ireland, Patrick's broken
heart propels him out of the Sydney Macintosh home and into
yet another bloody war. However the battlefields of Africa hold
more than nightmarish terrors and unspeakable conditions for
Patrick – they bring him in contact with one he thought long
dead and lost to him.

Back in Australia, the mysterious Michael O'Flynn mentors
Patrick's youngest son, Alex, and at his grandmother's request
takes him on a journey to their Queensland property, Glen
View. But will the terrible curse that has inextricably linked the
Duffys and Macintoshes for generations ensure that no true
happiness can ever come to them? So much seems to depend
on Wallarie, the last warrior of the Nerambura tribe, whose
mere name evokes a legend approaching myth.

Through the dawn of a new century in a now federated nation,
To Chase the Storm charts an explosive tale of love and loss,
from South Africa to Palestine, from Townsville to the green
hills of Ireland, and to the more sinister politics that lurk behind
them. By public demand, master storyteller Peter Watt returns
to this much-loved series following on from the bestselling *Cry
of the Curlew*, *Shadow of the Osprey* and *Flight of the Eagle*.

Peter Watt
To Touch the Clouds

They had all forgotten the curse . . . except one . . . until it touched them. I will tell you of those times when the whitefella touched the clouds and lightning came down on the earth for many years.

In 1914, the storm clouds of war are gathering. Matthew Duffy and his cousin Alexander Macintosh are sent by Colonel Patrick Duffy to conduct reconnaissance on German-controlled New Guinea. At the same time, Alexander's sister, Fenella, is making a name for herself in the burgeoning Australian film industry.

But someone close to them has an agenda of his own – someone who would betray not only his country to satisfy his greed and lust for power. As the world teeters on the brink of conflict, one family is plunged into a nightmare of murder, drugs, treachery and treason.

Peter Watt
To Ride the Wind

It is 1916, and war rages across Europe and the Middle East.
Patrick and Matthew Duffy are both fighting the enemy, Patrick
in the fields of France and Matthew in the skies above Egypt.

But there is another, secret foe. George Macintosh is passing
information to the Germans, seeking to consolidate his power
within the family company. And half a world away from the
trenches, one of their own will meet a shocking death.

Meanwhile, a young man is haunted by dreams of a sacred
cave, and seeks fiery stars that will help him take back his
people's land.

To Ride the Wind continues the story of the Duffys and
Macintoshes, following Peter Watt's much-loved characters as
they fight to survive one of the most devastating conflicts in
history – and each other.

PHOTO: DEAN MARTIN